When Beauty Is Terror,
When Love Is Despair,
Then the Songs of Blood
and Darkness Begin . . .

Barbara Hambly's "Madeleine": She lives beneath the city of her pleasure, devouring pretty boys without hearing the voices of her victims—but a student's curse is about to open Madeleine's mind—and her ears. . . .

☆

Larry Niven's "Song of the Night People": An episode from the long-awaited sequel to *Ringworld*, the classic Hugo and Nebula award-winning novel, in which even the Grass Giants have cause to fear the night. . . .

☆

Jane Yolen's "Sister Death": *"The blood has been kind to me, the blood I take nightly from the dying children. The ones who breathe haltingly, the ones who are misused, the ones whom fire, famine or war cut down. . . ."*

☆

"Wildly different . . . well-written . . . fresh approaches. . . . There isn't a loser in the whole fourteen assembled here."
—*Vampire's Crypt* (Web site magazine)

Turn—if you dare—for more praise
for *SISTERS OF THE NIGHT* . . .

PRAISE FOR
SISTERS OF THE NIGHT

"Crisp and inventive . . . Greenberg hit on a happy idea when asking fourteen writers, including Hambly, to write about 'the woman as vampire.'"

—*Kirkus Reviews*

☆

"Teeth-rattling horror . . . a rich, literary scope. . . . Hambly and Greenberg have done an excellent job of selecting stories that represent a variety of genres, from traditional fantasy to hard science fiction."

—*Middlesex News*

☆

"The stories are well written and well conceived. . . . It's impossible to choose a favorite. . . . Highly recommended."

—*KLIATT*

☆

"An entertaining collection . . . the effects are hard and hitting and long on substance."

—*Baryon* magazine

☆

SISTERS OF THE NIGHT

EDITED BY BARBARA HAMBLY
AND MARTIN H. GREENBERG

ASPECT®

WARNER BOOKS

A Time Warner Company

WARNER BOOKS EDITION

Copyright © 1995 by Barbara Hambly and Martin H. Greenberg
All rights reserved.

Cover design by Don Puckey/Carol Russo
Cover illustration by John Jude Palencar

"Empty" copyright © 1995 by M. John Harrison
"The Bloodbeast" copyright © 1995 by Diana L. Paxson
"Madeleine" copyright © 1995 by Barbara Hambly
"Mama" copyright © 1995 bySteve Rasnic Tem and Melanie Tem
"Survival Skills" copyright © 1995 by Deborah Wheeler
"Tumbling Down the Nighttime" copyright © 1995
          by Dean Wesley Smith
"La Dame" copyright © 1995 by Tanith Lee
"Sometimes Salvation" copyright © 1995 by Patricia Cadigan
"In the Blood" copyright © 1995 by Michael Kurland
"Victims" copyright © 1995 by Kristine Kathryn Rusch
"Marid and the Trail of Blood" copyright © 1995
          by George Alec Effinger
"Food Chain" copyright © 1995 by Nina Kiriki Hoffman
"Song of the Night People" copyright © 1995 by Larry Niven
"Sister Death" copyright © 1995 by Jane Yolen

Warner Books, Inc.
1271 Avenue of the Americas
New York, NY 10020

Visit our Web site at
http://warnerbooks.com

 A Time Warner Company

Originally published in trade paperback by Warner Books.
Printed in the United States of America
First Mass Market Printing: October 1998

10 9 8 7 6 5 4 3 2 1

Sisters of the
Night

CONTENTS

INTRODUCTION

My best friend in high school was the oldest of eight girls. (There were boys in the family too, but for a variety of reasons having mostly to do with age, they barely impinged upon my consciousness.) In the long years since, I have watched these ladies pursue careers as mothers, auto mechanics, real estate agents, editors, and musicians; blondes and brunettes, brown eyes, blue, or hazel, round chins, square chins, heart-shaped faces and rectangular, bones and curves.

They all look completely different until you put them in the same room, and then you wonder why you never noticed that they all look alike.

Which is, I suppose, one of the things about sisters.

What, exactly, *is* a vampire?

Legend varies widely—contemporary fiction, more widely still. The main points agreed upon seem to be that they are creatures who live on human blood, which prolongs their lives indefinitely; that they cannot abide the daylight, although there is a certain amount of disagreement about the effect the sun's light has on them; that they use sexuality and desire as a lure, to summon and incapacitate their victims.

This last is a powerful image, and to some,

an all-pervasive metaphor when applied to the woman as vampire: loving that absorbs and destroys the lover; the moth going willingly to the flame. The immortal beloved who lives on the blood of a thousand mortal men.

When asked to edit this anthology, I wondered whether the stories sent to me by men would differ in some distinctive fashion from the stories written by women; whether there would be some kind of shear line of perception based on gender.

Instead, of course, I discovered that any story turned in by anybody was wildly different from everything else. Even stories with ostensibly similar themes ended up in strange territory indeed— witness the three stories in the anthology that deal with the vampire as mother.

To the timeless feminine cultural archetypes of Maiden and Mother, Lover and Crone, have been added PTA Member, Bimbo, Alien, and things that cannot even be seen or defined: trolls, angels, the smell of blood behind your shoulder in the dark.

Yet when you look at them again, they're all about the same thing. All completely different until you put them together in the same room: the Sisters of the Night.

—Barbara Hambly

SISTERS OF THE NIGHT

Empty

❧

M. JOHN HARRISON

Not everyone looks in a mirror one day and sees they've grown old. But we all get some reminder.

You slip off the curb and break your ankle. Or you suffer something you think is angina, a pain in the heart on a wet Monday morning. Or someone you depended on leaves you. ("Our marriage always stifled me.") Your whole life lurches, and that's when you get your glimpse of the doorway between the two big rooms of existence. Suddenly your confidence has gone. You were middle-aged: now you're old.

I can always tell when this has happened to someone I know. They get well, remarry, beat the clock: but their eyes take on a wounded, flabby look. They've stopped trusting other people, perhaps. Certainly they've stopped trusting themselves. Most of all they've stopped trusting life. Young people can shrug things off, shave their heads, queue in the rain for hours for tickets, crash a motorcycle, juggle with a gun. But the rest of us are just standing there in rows, with a nice touch of gray in the hair, watching the cars rush past and wondering if we'll ever dare cross the road again.

Some people go longer than others before that pain in the heart knocks them down. I lasted a long time; and in the end none of those ordinary things happened to me. The shock I got was in some ways easier to understand.

In some ways it was harder.

My name is Jacob Wishart. I find other people for a living. Kids especially. They go off course, they bolt and get lost. Perhaps that was never their real intention, perhaps it was just language, a confused emotional invitation, "Follow me." So I follow them into the bash cities in Birmingham, Leeds, and London, tell them my favorite band is Pearl Jam, which is not entirely a lie, then entice them back to their middle-class parents. Cruel, I know: but by the time I get to them they're sick of living in a cardboard box anyway. And yet sometimes you think these kids have eyes like old glass beads. If they're looking at anything, it isn't you. They hear music in their heads all the time: you forgot it long ago. Worse than that, you can't get over the feeling that they would eat you if they refocused, if they woke up long enough. No: that they have already eaten you. But this is to jump the gun. And to be honest I never found a runaway that didn't really want to go back.

Most of my clients are private, although I get the occasional case from the social services. My office is in King's Cross, but I don't keep paper there. To tell the truth I throw away anything that bores me. I once began a CV, "My name is Jacob Wishart and I don't own much. Live alone, travel light, never sign your own name." They didn't give me the post. I dress twenty, pass for thirty, but the day Ann Mc-Grath phoned me from Manchester, I was forty-seven years old.

"Annie!" I said. "Hiya!"

We talked for a moment about the weather, the job. Then she said, "I've got work for you if you want it. I need someone to charm a runaway. She won't open up for us."

"You've already got her back?" I said.

There was a silence.

"Yes," she admitted.

"I find the kids," I pointed out. "Someone else can counsel them. Life's too short."

"It's not like that."

"So what is it like, Annie?"

When she didn't answer, I said, "How long was she away?"

Another pause.

"Two days."

"Two *days*? Don't waste my time."

"She can't tell us what happened to her."

"They keep it to themselves, Annie. They want to forget it."

"I won't be happy until I know."

"Annie, you already know. You know what the luckier ones do. They take the train into Manchester. They dance. They get lost looking for crack. The real street kids steal their money the first night. They try begging and it makes them feel sick. They spend the rest of the weekend in the bus station and the rest of their lives trying to guess if they caught AIDS from someone's dreadlocks—"

"Jake, will you listen for once?"

"I always listen."

She put the phone down. I heard it go down, click.

"Annie?"

I rang her back.

"I'm sorry," I said. "What happened to her?"

"She got lost on the moors between Manchester and Sheffield, Jake."

"So?"

"So it's the back end of nothing up there. Just a lot of empty hills. She spent two nights wandering about without even a coat. When we asked her what happened, she says, 'A lady looked after me.' Do you understand, Jake? No crack, no dreadlocks. Just, 'A lady looked after me.' It's not that she won't tell. It's that she can't. She doesn't seem to *know* what happened to her."

I thought about it.

"Who would be paying me for this?" I said.

"Oh, so now you're interested."

"Who would be paying?"

"The department."

"Try again, Annie. Remember me? I'm Jake."

"All right," she said tiredly. "I'm paying for it."

"You really do want to know, don't you?"

I drove up two days later with my real office, a fifty-megabyte Dell laptop, beside me on the front seat of the car. I took the M1, then swung west from Sheffield along Woodhead Road to get some feel for the scene. It was late March, the weather by turns squally and bright; very cold. The moors unfolded suddenly in front of me—long black slopes dotted with sheep, a chain of reservoirs like molten tin, the big quarries glittering with icy rock against dirty blue clouds. I thought about the girl stumbling around on her own, able to make out the city lights one minute, the next staring into darkness. Snow had fallen while she was missing. You could see the remains of it salted across the upper curves of the moor. Further down it had already cleared.

I shivered and turned the heater up. The roads were empty. By midday I had checked into the Britannia Hotel. From there I phoned Ann McGrath.

"You were right," I admitted. "It's the last place God made."

"Never doubt me," she said.

She gave me an address in Hyde, a burnt-out industrial sub-
urb which had somehow spawned middle-class suburbs of its
own.

"Talk to the girl," she said. "But don't upset the parents."

"Are we sure she was really up there?"

"Yes. Don't upset the parents, Jake."

In the event I didn't see them. Not then.

Their house was about five years old. The stonework
looked raw and new, but the "Georgian" window frames were
already peeling in the Pennine weather. Like many of the
other houses on the estate, it was for sale. There was a strip of
bare lawn at the front, and at the back, double-glazed patio
doors from which you had a view north and east to Harrop
Edge. As I knocked on the door a bitterly cold wind was
blowing down off the moor. The girl herself let me in and
showed me to the dining room. There, the afternoon light lay
obliquely across a reproduction refectory table, where it discovered kitchen scissors, a white vase half full of water, and
two or three bunches of orange lilies recently unwrapped
from florist's paper. As we talked, the girl busied herself with
the flowers. The first thing she said to me after she let me in
was, "These moors used to be a sea."

She waved her arm toward Harrop Edge, as if she could
still make out the brackish Carboniferous shallows lapping
there.

"Did you know that? Of course you'll say you did."

"Adults know everything," I said. "I thought you understood that."

We laughed.

"The lilies are nice," I said.

"They are, aren't they?"

She was perhaps sixteen years old, eager to talk one moment, a bit detached the next. Of her parents she said apolo-
getically, "They take too much care of me." She found her

first night on the moor easy to explain, her subsequent disorientation more difficult. This had so shocked her mother and
father she was reduced to denying it, insisting instead, "I got
a bit muddy, that's all. They shouldn't have been so upset. I
got a bit tired, wandering about all night." She assured me
several times, "I wasn't drunk. You couldn't have been drunk
on what I had." I didn't think she was lying.

There had been an end-of-term party at Ashton Technical
College on the Friday; an anarchic affair which lasted all afternoon. Suddenly some of her friends, growing bored, had
decided to drive down Longdendale to the big quarry above
Crowden. "They had this idea of watching the sunset from the
top," she told me, with a kind of musing pride, as if she were
bringing them out to show me. "They're all mad." Entering
the pass and looking back, they had glimpsed Altdorfer
clouds, the sun already smearing itself the color of carnations
behind the church-topped hill at Mottram. Further west, orange light flared off an office block miles away in Stockport.
"It was lovely," she said. "It really was." She had enjoyed the
drive, too. "I felt safe." The big sides of the moor had closed
in over her: a stoat had looped across the road on a tight curve
in the twilight. "We were all laughing and singing. We had the
stereo on as loud as it would go." Between the trees she had
glimpsed the gray water of the Etherow reservoirs racing
along beside them.

"It was almost dark when they parked the car," she told me,
"but they still thought we would have time to walk up to the
quarry and back. It's steep, but it's not far. There are so many
little paths up there, all going in different directions."

She thought about this.

"Somehow I got separated," she said. "They didn't notice
and they drove back without me."

"Nice friends," I said.

"It wasn't their fault. It's very steep up there in the dark. I'd really been enjoying it until then."

"This woman who found you the next morning—you remember her."

"Not really. I was so tired. I'd been walking about all night. Up there it's all lumps of grass and mud. At first I could see the road but I could never get down to it. Later, just as I was completely lost, I seemed to be with someone." She looked at me as if I could help her understand this. "At first I thought it was Mum," she appealed. "The way someone you know is with you in a dream. But it couldn't have been, could it? And anyway this woman was too young."

"After you had got down to the village," I asked, "what happened?"

"We talked," was all she would say.

"What about?"

"Miss McGrath asked me all this."

"Annie," I said.

"Annie asked me all this. I've told her all this before."

She moved her hands in her lap. Something she remembered caused her to smile down at them. "It was the most beautiful morning," she said. "I was really tired, but I had a feeling of being *inside* it. We talked about that." She had walked round the old moorside village of Tintwhistle with the woman whose face she was not yet ready to recall, and that was what they had talked about. "How sometimes you're so happy everything seems to take you into itself." A Burmese cat, she remembered, had run up to them along a stone wall, purring to be let into its house. "No one was awake yet. The valley was full of mist. Then, as we were looking, the sun came up and it all poured away." The whole valley had emptied itself like a jug of milk, westward toward Manchester. "She didn't know the names of any of the hills you can see from there: so I told her. Then we went into a little grave-yard."

After a time I managed to ask, "Which of you suggested going into the graveyard?"

She didn't remember.

"It could be important," I said.

"I can't remember now. She said she had once lived near the Danube. She was beautiful. She was too tall to be my mother, and too sad. Anyway, Mum was down here all the time."

"For God's sake!" I heard myself shout. "You were with her all that day and most of the next! Where did she take you?" The girl shrugged and winced. I knew she couldn't an-swer: I knew I ought to stop trying to make her. "Did she show you anything in the graveyard? What did she say? Tell me again what she said!"

Suddenly I remembered the weather.

"Two inches of snow fell up there and then melted again. Where on earth did you go during that?"

"I didn't see any snow," she said. "It was beautiful and sunny. It was warm."

She looked stubbornly away from me, blinking.

I let a minute go by, then asked as lightly as I could, "And it was this woman who told you the moors are a sea?"

She surprised me by laughing suddenly.

"The river that came out here was bigger than the Danube," she said. "You can say you knew that but you can't prove it!" She sniffed. She pushed her hair out of her eyes and deftly wiped them with the back of her wrist. "Every pebble ever washed down that river to the sea is embedded somewhere in these moors. I understood that when I was up there. Even when I was in black mud to my knees, I could feel the cur-rents and the tides."

She thought for a moment.

She said, "Everything is so old."

Then she said, "The moors *are* the sea."

I tried for half an hour to get further, then gave up and left. "The moors are the sea." This image of a fixed landscape as being comprised of movement—the flux of suspended sand, the quartz pebbles sucked along by plaited streams of water— was the very last thing I had come for. As I was going she said, "Wait a minute," and ran back into the house. After a moment she returned, with some of the orange lilies wrapped in green tissue paper. "I know you liked these," she said gravely. "And I've got far too many."

I was so surprised I took them.

"Thank you."

There was still plenty of daylight, so I put the flowers carefully on the backseat of the car and went to look at the graveyard.

I couldn't think where else to start.

Wishart. My mother often pronounced it "wish hard." "Wish hard, Wishart!" she would encourage me, when I was little. Wish hard for what? To stay four years old, and have her attention forever, and not end up in the ground the way she did when I was eleven?

Effectively there were two graveyards at Tintwhistle, one a little higher than the other on the steep hillside above the A628, with thirteen stone steps to connect them. It was like deep winter up there that afternoon. I had no idea what I had come for, but I knew I wasn't tempted to look for it in the upper cemetery. The graves were old and unkempt, dead leaves frozen onto the narrow gravel paths between them. In more than one place a good-sized young tree had broken the stones, or pushed them aside. The flower vases were full of ice. There was a bitter rime on everything, and a rusty iron angel on a plinth to watch over all of it. At least below the steps the living were still making an effort. Someone was keeping the bramble suckers cut back, and I could have had my choice of mixed bouquets in cellophane and yellow ribbon. I left the car blocking the lane outside and wandered from stone to stone, blowing into my hands, reading off the epitaphs as if all that marble were a database whose organizational principle I didn't yet understand.

"Passed into the Higher Life." "Faithful Unto Death." (A line of music was inscribed underneath, with the words "Come unto me all ye that labor.") "Fell asleep aged 63 years." And finally:

"They died that we might live in peace."

I could hear the heavy traffic grinding past down on the Woodhead Road, the empty bleat of the sheep on the moors above. Light began to go out of the air. It wasn't the approach of evening: just that sudden flattening or graying of the light you sometimes see in the late afternoon. When I looked up again, there was a woman in the upper graveyard, toiling between the stones in silence, just like me.

Later, when Ann McGrath asked me, "So what was she doing?" I would answer, "Moving something from one grave to another."

But at the time who could be certain? Thirty yards away in that illusive light I wasn't entirely sure I could see her anyway. Bundled up in a peach-colored raincoat and a headscarf, she looked old. Yet when she turned round I saw that she was younger than me, with a sallow Italianate face too broad and heavy in the bones, distorted further by some birth defect which dragged the mouth down in a permanent sneer. Her eyes were dark and beautiful. They winced away from the rest of her face. They repudiated it, moment to moment. I don't believe she saw me there. At the same time I'm convinced she was perfectly aware of me. Can you understand that? Slowly, she turned away again and went back to the graves. One hip was higher than the other, and she walked with an odd, painful roll.

"She must have been doing something."

"She was taking flowers off one grave and putting them on another. That's what I thought. But there weren't any flowers up there. Okay?"

"Don't shout, Jake."

What happened next—why I did what I did—is hard to explain. There was never any reason to mistake this woman for the one the girl had seen. She wasn't tall. She wasn't beautiful. Her gait was so distinctive the girl couldn't have failed to mention it. But when she left the graveyard I turned up my coat collar and followed her: back down the hill, across the Etherow and into Hadfield, where she waited for five or ten minutes at the unmanned rail halt for a stopping train to Manchester Piccadilly. I got on the train behind her and put two or three rows of seats between us.

It was an odd journey. The wide shallow cuttings streamed past us. She stared at a magazine. I stared at her. Every time the train approached a station she got up impatiently and waited for it to stop, only to change her mind as soon as the doors opened. Back in her seat, riffling energetically through the pages of the magazine, she shook her head as if somebody had said something she didn't want to hear. Up and down, up and down: but then when her station turned up at last she seemed to vanish without preamble, as if all that had been designed to confuse or hypnotize me. I woke up and rushed the open doors. There she was, waiting calmly on the platform for me. We looked each other full in the face. Across her upper lip was a distinct black mustache; her enlarged pores seemed to exude some clumsy power—pheromonal, speechless, very direct. Her raincoat had fallen open. Under it she was wearing a red velvet evening dress, gathered into pleats and pipes and volutes at the shoulders and round the big, awkward-looking breasts. I was still in the train. I waited a moment for something to happen, I didn't know what. I felt my mouth open to speak, but something made me turn my head as quickly as I could and stare away from her until I heard the doors wheeze shut between us. I stared up at the station signboard in astonishment.

Hyde.

The train had begun to move again.

At the other end it was getting dark; lights were coming on in the shops and cafes around Piccadilly. I went back to my hotel room and sat on the bed. When I next looked at my watch, it was half past seven. I felt too tired and too puzzled to go and fetch my car from Tintwhistle. And anyway it was time to make my report to Annie McGrath.

Annie, a tall girl who had sweated out the Thatcher years in AIDS counseling in West London, still wore 501s and a black leather jacket to work. In those old days we had had something going, but I caught her too many times staring out onto the traffic on the Fulham Palace Road at lunchtime, stooped over her own folded arms, her kind, damp, slightly protuberant eyes full of some sense of inadequacy and professional frustration I didn't want to share. How either of us ended up in that sort of work I don't know. She was too easily hurt and I was too impatient. When I stared out of the window, it was to try and catch sight of the hot German saloon cars heading across the overpass for a weekend in the country. I wanted one of my own. "At least if we'd gone into the media," I once said to her, "we'd still be together, living in north London with the rest of our generation, stuffing down the lamb passanda at the Anglo-Asian on Stoke Newington Church Street and saying, 'There's someone over there I know, but I'm not sure he'll remember me. Nick Hornby, you know, he wrote *Fever Pitch* . . .' "

Now, a decade or more later, we found ourselves in a wine bar in an alley just off St. Anne's Square. For some reason they had called it Ganders Go South. You went down a flight of steps, past the bouncer, and inside was a small dance floor, really just a space cleared among the tables in front of the jazz band on its pokey dais in the corner. Ann liked Ganders Go South because they would still serve you garlic mushrooms there at half past eleven at night. Sometimes she didn't get finished until then. We sat down near the bar. Ann ordered the vegetarian lasagne, but I didn't feel like eating, so I had a couple of San Miguel beers instead.

"I went to Hyde," I said.

"So tell me."

I gave her a version of my interview with the girl, concentrating on the end-of-term party, the drive up to the moor, the girl becoming separated from her friends.

"They were having so much fun they drove home without her."

"I already know how she got lost," Ann said. "I want to know how she was found."

I told her. I said, "If you can make anything of that you're welcome to it."

I went to the toilet.

"You should have been more persistent," Ann said when I came back.

"Look," I warned her, "I'm not a policeman. This is enough of a nightmare already. This woman, whoever she was, enticed the girl into Tintwhistle graveyard. Then they wandered about in the sunshine all day, while the world you and I live in got two inches of snow. How do you want to explain that?"

"I can't."

"Can the police?"

"Oh come on, Jake."

"I might talk to them," I said.

She laughed.

"They won't talk to you," she warned me.

"Why?"

"Have you seen yourself today?"

"These are my work clothes."

She looked round the bar. "I wonder why they let you in here at all, Jake," she said. Then she added, "Do you know what's wrong with men like you? You force the rest of us to live in the real world so you don't have to. It's quite clever what you do."

I kept things light. I said, "That sounds like the politics of envy to me."

"I wash my hands of you, Jake."

People were drifting in from the square with its dark book-shops and trembling rainy light. A couple had begun to dance. The girl was only a secretary, approaching thirty but still pretty in a nervous way, and she was only going to take the man home and fuck him until he passed out, if he didn't pass out before. It couldn't lead to anything but emptiness, misunderstood intentions, and a bad head, and it had happened before in the history of the world. But I suddenly felt fiercely protective of her. I loved the delight on her face, the way her arms laced round his neck, the way she kept on dancing when the music stopped, her delicate, attractive greed.

I heard myself say to Annie, "Do you want to come back to the hotel with me?"

"No."

"The police, then. Give me a name."

"I know a detective sergeant at Hyde," she said. "His name is Booth. You could talk to him. He always gets missing children because he was a minor player in the old Hindley and Brady investigation. Remember Hindley and Brady, Jake? All those kids tortured in a council house in Hattersley, then dumped on the moors?—"

I remembered them.

"Brady played 'The Little Drummer Boy' while Myra Hindley forced a ten-year-old girl to suck him off. They taped it all, and took bad black-and-white photos."

"I remember, Annie."

Later, unable to sleep, I booted up the Dell and plodded aimlessly through my database. Children's names and ages: nothing but children's names and ages. I wouldn't find the girl in there, I knew. I would have trouble finding her in herself. Her adult calm, her care with me and all the others, the sense that she knew—somehow without knowing that she knew—something I would never know, could only leave me puzzled, unassuaged.

When I woke up on Sunday morning I found that the flowers the girl had given me had dropped pollen onto the black plastic casing of the computer. It was light and gritty, a burnt orange colour.

Still unwilling to believe she had spent her missing days on the moor, I wasted three hours touting a Polaroid of the girl around central Manchester, asking people if they'd seen her. Bouncers, dealers, sixteen-year-old Indie clubbers trudging home in the cold with eyes like the bottoms of rivers, old women who lived in doorways off Piccadilly: the girl smiled out of the picture at them, and they all said how pretty she was. Everyone I spoke to wanted to help, but no one could say they had seen her. She looked too much like all the others. At noon I packed it in and caught a bus to Hyde, where I met Detective Sergeant Booth outside the Onward Street police station in the rain. "Cheerio, then," he was saying to someone as he came out. He was eating from a paper bag printed with the words FRESH BAKERY TAKEAWAY in red block letters.

Booth and I were much of an age, but thinning hair and a kind of sad disaffection with the realities of his trade made me think he was a lot older. He must have concluded the same, because he gave me a straight, kindly look and called me "lad." I was obscurely comforted. He had, he added, three children, including a teenage daughter, of his own.

"Good fun, kiddies," he maintained. "But they'll wear you out if you let 'em."

"I've been careful not to have any."

He waited politely in case I wanted to develop the argument. Then he said, "Ay. Well. Sensible enough. Look, about this girl you're interested in. There's not a deal more I can add to what Annie already knows." He studied his watch. "Have you got a minute?"

I said I had.

"Then I'll show you why."

We got into his car, an old red Vauxhall Astra which smelled faintly of his wife's running shoes, and he drove up through all the decaying mill towns onto the moor. Stalybridge, Mossley, Greenfield: I soon felt lost. "Aren't we going to Tintwhistle?" I asked, but he didn't answer. Every house looked like every other house. They could have been killing children at every curve of the A635 where it coiled up through the Chew Valley, beneath thousand-foot slopes chaotic with the spoil from old quarries, and out onto the watershed. Booth stopped at the boundary of his jurisdiction, where decent men like him toggle endlessly and amiably between the emotional states "Yorkshire" and "Lancashire," and the peat rolls away north and south, apparently forever, like the landscape of some unimaginable nuclear disaster.

"Look over there, lad," he invited me. "That's Wessenden Head, where we dug up what was left of Lesley Ann Downey. A month, we'd been looking. We were freezing cold and piss-wet through. No one's sure how many kiddies Brady and Hindley buried in this area alone. There were more toward

Huddersfield. No one's dared dig yet over at Crowden rifle range."

He stared at me hard.

"Do you see what I'm suggesting? It's a big moor, this, and your missing lass is home and well."

"Still," I said. "*Something* happened to her."

"She's home and well, lad."

"Don't you want to know the truth?"

"I crossed her off the books in less than forty-eight hours," he said stubbornly. "She turned up alive and well."

Without warning, black rain swung in across the moor toward us from the direction of Marsden. Booth started the windshield wipers, then as an afterthought, the engine. "Ay up," he said. "We're in for it now." Water blurred the windows. It hammered on the roof. A gust of wind rocked the Astra sideways on its suspension. The world became vague and smeary, shrinking to a few clumps of bog-cotton, a bank of peat, a shallow pool pocked with raindrops and full of discarded household rubbish. Booth sat there calm and unmoved. The inside of his car seemed like an enclave of life in a lot of mud and wind.

"It took years to find some of the poor little fuckers," he remembered. "When we did, they were nowt but bones and clothes."

I couldn't argue with that. We sat without speaking for a moment. The rain turned to sleet, then passed away quickly toward Stockport, as if it had something else to do. Booth watched it go, then he said, "I'll take you to Tintwhistle to pick up your car, then." He grinned. "Dark blue F-registered Mercedes 190E, was it? We had it reported as blocking a road there."

"Ah," I said.

"Bit daft to leave a nice car like that all night unattended."

"I suppose it was," I said.

"No suppose about it, lad."

When he let me out twenty minutes later it was raining again. Tintwhistle looked sodden and dark. The graveyard was empty. When I started the Mercedes, the sound system came alive too. I had had them fit a 120-watt Alpine RDS CD tuner with a six-disc changer in the trunk. Music tumbled out of it into the wet air like blocks of concrete into a skip, John Mellencamp's *Jack & Diane*, with its mournful injunction, "Hold on to sixteen as long as you can." As if attracted by the noise, Booth, who had been about to drive off, got out of his Astra and wandered over. He listened to the music for a moment, then leaned in through the open driver's window and made turning motions with his right hand to indicate that I should drop the volume. As soon as he thought I could hear him he said, "Try and see it this way. Truth is just something that's happened. You may find it out, you may not. It's a policeman's job to keep folks safe. Home and well, lad, or bones and clothes? I know which I prefer."

He nodded briefly.

"Say hello to Annie for me," he said.

"Ay," I whispered to myself as I watched him drive off toward Hyde. "I will that, lad. Mind how you go."

I never saw him again. It was nearly dark, and there was only one place I hadn't been yet: so I went there.

I started from Ashton, just the way the girl had done. Water glittered like strips of silver paper as I dropped into Longdendale. Oak trees green with lichen seemed to hang motionless at each blind curve—dip toward me like oriental dancers, pivot away suddenly. In the driving mirror I could see last year's dead leaves panicking about in my wake. An hour later I was stumbling into Crowden Great Quarry in the dark.

Civil engineers had sliced the top off the hill in the 1800s, using high explosives which left the rock shattered to its heart, a permanently unstable frieze of hanging ribs and collapsing pillars a hundred feet high and three hundred yards long, over which gusts of wind now ruffled and boomed. The floor beneath was hummocky, furrowed, strewn with bits of rusty angle iron and fallen rocks the size of front room furniture. I entered this landscape with sore ankles and wet feet— nervous, out of breath, cold despite my felt-lined Afghan jacket. I had no idea why I had come. For twenty or thirty minutes I poked about—picking up a Coke can whitened by the weather, examining a name scratched on a stone—as if the quarry itself might be a clue. I trod in sheep shit; talked to myself for company.

I said, " 'Loz woz ere.' "

I said, "Jesus, it's fucking cold in the natural world."

I said, "Wish hard, Wishart."

As if that had been the key, the air filled itself with brightness like a glass filling itself with water.

A dawn evolves, color to color, tone to tone, changing all the time. We expect that. We welcome it. But from the outset this was the light of a sunny August morning. Night to day, winter to summer, like theater lights coming up: and when the transition was complete I stood knee-deep in bilberry and heather. Foxgloves grew on the ledges above me, ferns in the shadows, and bright green moss where water trickled down the rock. Bees zoomed across the open spaces in long flat trajectories. There were sheep cropping unconcernedly at the top of the spoil heaps; sheep bleating distantly from the valley. I could smell the strange, spicy smell of the gritstone itself. I could see the hills in the distance, sleeping like animals, brassy with sunlight, huge with the shadows of clouds, patched with little fields and hanging woods. Beyond all that I thought I could make out the Cheshire Plain, the misty hook of Frodsham Edge on a long, gray, layered horizon. Closer to, oak trees clung to the slopes, there were holly trees in the curves and braids of the old riverbed, little collapsed stone walls half hidden in the bracken. Up from Crowden, with its shining slate roofs and smoky chimneys, its bright green pocket-handkerchief campsite full of blue and orange tents, came the smell of food.

"It was beautiful and sunny," I heard the girl whisper. "We walked about all day."

Another voice added firmly, "No death."

I had time to look at the clouds white and gray in a very blue sky, at the dark, fluted combe of Torside Clough, at the vast scoops and salients on the edge of Bleaklow, where the moors were chamfered off as if someone had sandpapered them long ago. Then it all darkened to night again.

"Come back?" I shouted. "I'm sorry!"

The quarry walls hung like the volutes of a rotten curtain. Two or three pieces of wastepaper blew round my ankles. Then there seemed to be somebody standing behind me. The air was filled with a vile smell, which I thought for a moment was my own blood (so that I couldn't stop my hand flying up to my mouth to stem some silent, painless hemorrhage), and I stumbled away between the spoil heaps until I felt it was safe to look back. After a moment I saw the woman in the red velvet evening dress moving off toward the mouth of the quarry. At first she seemed to be floating. Then I heard her picking her way carefully over the broken stones in her high heels, and after that the smell faded. The worst thing was that I wanted her to come back. She had put everything equally out of reach to me, the ordinary world as far away as that endless August day. "Fuck you!" I shouted. And then quieter, "Just fuck you." I wiped my nose on the back of my hand and plunged directly down the waiting hill-side in the dark.

Back at the Brittania I tried to phone Annie McGrath: no answer.

Never any answer.

God save us from the half-abandoned breakfast room of a provincial hotel on a gray morning after dreams of some faded old sexual jealousy whose object we can barely recall. Where they play "Petite Fleur" and other ballroom favorites at 9:30 in the morning. Where the headwaiter follows newcomers helplessly around saying, "Ah, you're going to sit down there are you, sir?" then gives two people the same table. Where you suddenly hear someone say triumphantly, "The—answer—isn't—zero!" separating the words exactly to give them full value in the empty room. Where the only normal people have already had breakfast and gone. I drank half a cup of coffee and then tried to ring Booth from a pay phone in the lobby. He wasn't in his office. Annie was just leaving hers.

She said, "This is a bad time, Jake."

"I know," I said. "It's the hotel phone."

"A bad *time*."

"Look Annie, I'm coming apart here. I need to talk."

"I can spare you five minutes."

"No you can't," I said. "You can fuck off." I put the phone down.

It took her ten minutes to ring back.

"This had better be worth it, Jake. Save your tantrums for someone else."

I considered hanging up again. Instead I told her about Tintwhistle graveyard, the woman in the velvet dress, and what I thought might have happened to the girl. "Something happened to me up there, too," I tried to explain. "It wasn't the same thing. It wasn't so complete. At the time I wanted it to be, that's the horror of it." I said I knew that this didn't help, but I didn't care. "Places like that—" I said. And, "We met something up there." I said I was going back to London.

Annie was silent for a moment, then she laughed bitterly.

"I'm not paying you for this, Jake."

"I know," I said.

She cut the connection without saying good-bye. I went to my room and packed. On the way out I caught a glimpse of myself in the long mirror by the door. I was wearing a plaid work shirt, gray Levis dutifully out at the knee, old-fashioned industrial boots, unraveling fingerless gloves. My hair was going gray, and everything I valued except my German car was stuffed into a bicycle courier's shoulder bag with the Marin logo on the flap.

I asked myself aloud, "Why the fuck can't you grow up, Jacob?"

No answer.

I thought of all the hotels I'd ever been in, and Annie Mc-Grath saying, "I wash my hands of you." I washed my hands of myself. After I check out, I thought, I'll go and see the girl again. I would go and see her once more, just in case I could make head or tail of her.

It was Monday market in Hyde town center. From stalls outside the Clarendon mall, people were trying to sell one another the most broken or pointless things they could find: secondhand shoes, rusty tools, "Wooden handles, 50p." Rain lashed the suburbs, to which an easterly wind had brought the smell of sulfur dioxide from factories in Sheffield and Rotherham. Rain dripped steadily down the fronts of the houses into the flower beds. Rain beaded the mahogany-look window frames, darkened the stone beneath the eaves. What I had expected was this: that the girl would greet me at her door, smiling gravely, a pair of scissors and some flower stalks held in one hand so that with the other she could brush her hair out of her eyes in a gesture so uncomplicated I would understand everything. That we would both be survivors of an experience no one else could share. But she wasn't there. The door hung open.

"Hello?" I called.

"Just a few more questions," I called.

Then, "It's Jacob Wishart."

The hall floor had been polished that morning. In the dining room a watery light fell on brown and gold picture frames. I looked in on the kitchen, which smelled of Kenco coffee and Dettox Creamy Jel. I went up the stairs.

"Hello?"

I found her parents in the bathroom. They were about my own age, perhaps a little younger, but having children had tired them. Someone had thrown them into the bath, where they lay higgledy-piggledy, like cast-off shop dummies, the woman's arms across her husband's face. They were naked, marble-white, and covered all over with small puncture wounds, as if a table fork had been stuck into them repeatedly. Around each group of punctures the flesh was lightly bruised. There was no blood, anywhere. Their eyes were closed, and I thought they were dead. Perhaps they were: but they were still talking to each other.

"We had such hopes for her."

"We had no hopes at all for the boy."

"Oh, dear no, the boy was all computer games and daft shoes."

"No hope for him at all."

I made some sort of noise from the doorway. The woman's eyes sprang open.

"Oh dear," she said. "Wake up, Stan."

"Gah!" he said, very loudly. His eyes opened too, but he couldn't seem to turn his head to look fully at me. He waved his arms for a moment and became still. He asked his wife,

"Has he come to see the house? Because they never told us to expect him. Will he want showing round?"

"Oh aye, he'll want showing round, love."

"It's an Italian boiler," he said. "Very reliable. Gas, but electrically controlled."

"After all, why would he come if he didn't want showing round?" She gave me an embarrassed smile.

"Were we here the first time you called?"

"Would you like a cup of tea?"

All this time, they had been trying to stand up and get out of the bath, scuffling with their thin red hands at its rounded edges, trying to pull up on each other's shoulders, fingers leaving in the pale flesh slowly filling indentations, the yellowish soles of their feet skating about on the nonslip surface. The woman would crouch, get both feet under her, and begin to straighten her legs, only to fall backward into the taps, legs splayed in the air to reveal through a grayish tuft the sorelooking lips of her sex. Her husband pawed at the tiled surround. They made shallow panting sounds, like children with colds. Their knees and elbows bumped hollowly on the sides of the bath.

"Nice cup of tea," the mother repeated.

"Have you *cleaned* this bath, Linda?"

I slammed the door on them and ran. Forty-five minutes later I put the Mercedes through a stone wall somewhere between Penistone and Barnsley. At the time I had no idea that was where I was. Evidence suggests I was doing eighty-five miles an hour in a built-up area. I walked away from it. Would you call that lucky?

"Wish hard, Wishart!"

Age calms you down, they say, but it's only ever made me anxious. I'm fifty now.

A month or two after I wrote off the Mercedes, a letter arrived for me at King's Cross. It was from Annie McGrath.

Whatever had happened in Hyde, the girl's parents were still in their house every day, eating frozen food from Waitrose and doing the ironing. The FOR SALE board was still up. Perhaps that's just what happens to you when the vampire has emptied you out: Birds Eye Lean Cuisine and a slow property market, more of the same things you had all your life. You recover, you beat the clock. Nobody but me ever saw their wounds, anyway. Their daughter had gone, this time for good, or so DS Booth thought. He was still patiently covering the ground. Her parents had wanted her to do law, at the University of Liverpool. She had a place, but she never enrolled there. Through Annie, Booth sent a message: Would I keep an eye open for the girl? I knew I would, but not because he asked. The thought of her made me shudder. I don't think she's in the cardboard cities yet. I'd know. If I ever so much as sensed her there, I'd sell the database and sublease the office and never go back or follow that trade again.

The rest of Annie's letter was personal. She seemed down. She was sick of the north, she said. She was sick of the amiable way her clients accommodated themselves to a life blurred by drink, handicapped by debt, "pissed away," as she put it, "among rusty gas stoves and bits of broken furniture. And I hate the fucking rain," she added.

"Take care of yourself Jake," she advised me. "No one else will."

And then: "I wonder if we could have tried a bit harder, you and me."

Everyone says that when they're lonely. Next day they wake up and remember you're just something they used to want. After we broke up, Annie went through a lot of boyfriends. She chose probation officers, teachers she met on summer courses, people in the social services generally. They all had lives as ramshackle as hers. After a while she would push her hands through her black leather belt whenever she was talking to a man: cup them over her lower belly. "Keep Out." I don't think she was aware of doing it. One of her favorite phrases was "a haystack of last straws."

The Bloodbeast

DIANA L. PAXSON

There was a man called Torund who lived away up in Svithiod in Sweden. He was a notable man with many sons, and after his time the valley was called Torundale. But when some generations had passed the old line died out, and there was no one to inherit the home farm but a great-niece, Freydis. She was not a fair woman, but the holding was said to be a good one, and her kin arranged a marriage for her with Kalv Adilsson, a younger son who had won some repute for himself a-viking. And so they traveled to Svithiod with their housecarls and servants to take up the holding.

Kalv and Freydis lived together contentedly enough, and when they had been in Torundale for two winters a daughter was born to them whom they called Aslaug. They got along well with most of their neighbors, and folk began to look up to Kalv as a chieftain. Only with the folk who lived in the woods to the west of them, Old Gamle and his wife Ulla, did they have bad friendship. But in this they were no different from the rest of the district. Folk whispered there was Finn blood in that family, and they were said to be trollwise, versed in magic.

When Aslaug was three seasons old the winter was a particularly hard one. Spring came late, and even when they brought the god around in his cart to bless the fields, as the custom then was, the weather stayed so wet it was close to Sumarmál before they could sow. Foodstocks were low and folk faced a starving season, for all that it was spring. Kalv shared out seedcorn from his storesheds, and men praised him. Only Gamle and Ulla got nothing, for there was still a dispute about a boundary between them and Kalv. Still, the days grew longer; doors were flung open to let in the clean wind, and the people started to feel a little hope as they watched their crops grow.

One evening, as the long daylight of early summer slowly faded, Freydis sat spinning before the house-door while Aslaug played on a blanket laid out on the grass. Earlier that day it had been raining, and the sinking sun turned the last clouds into banners of fire. She heard shouting from beyond the trees and looked up as little Asti, the thrall's son, came pelting up the path.

"Strange cows in the home pasture," he gasped. "Six scrawny beasts, eating up our good grass—" He broke off as Kalv came out of the house, pulling his tunic back on. He was a tall man, all hard muscle from the work of the farm, with black hair, a man whom women's eyes followed when he came into a hall.

"Take care, husband," said Freydis, frowning, and he laughed and kissed her on the top of the head. But she saw that before he went off he took up the hunting spear that leaned against the wall. She was his wife. He had never needed to say he loved her. But if he took her advice, she supposed he must value her.

It was late, and full dark, before Kalv came home again, and Freydis could tell by his breathing that he was angered. She rose from the boxbed and touched a splinter to the coals on the hearth to light the lamp.

"Did you find out the owner of the cows?"

Kalv swore. "They were Gamle's cattle, may the trolls take them and their owner too!" Freydis held up a hand to hush him, because of the sleeping child, and poured ale. "I recognized that bell-cow of his with the twisted horn."

"What have you done with them?"

"What do you think? I drove the ugly beasts all the way through the wood to his yard and beat on the door. Gamle was off somewhere, but the old wife came out to me, moaning and muttering how their own meadows were flooded and their beasts would starve. But the hill pastures are as free to Gamle as to any man, and I told her so, and promised that if their beasts strayed onto my land again I would butcher them for the Midsummer feasting!" He drank deeply and wiped his mouth with the back of his hand.

"And what said she then?" asked Freydis. Instinctively she made a sign of warding.

"Oh she whined some more about their age and how hard it is to do all alone—as if it were not the fault of their own evil tempers that no man will stay to work there! And then she said that there were ways to take what luckier men would not freely give, and I would rue my words. But I laughed in her face and came home. And it's glad I am to be sitting, and gladder still I'll be to lie down—" He set down the empty horn. Freydis turned to him, and he began to pull out the pins that held her fair hair.

While she was nursing Aslaug they had not lain together, but though Kalv loved his daughter, Freydis knew he wanted to make a son to follow him. It would be more sensible to wait until she was eating well enough to be sure of bearing a healthy child, but when he touched her hair she began to tremble. She had always known it was not wise to want a man as she wanted this one, even when you were married to him. But Freyja's power could not be denied. When Kalv kissed her, the flicker of anxiety that had troubled her was forgotten, and she came into his arms.

Things went on well enough for a while then. The weather held, and where the fields were not too wet, the barley was beginning to grow. But the cows they kept by the farmstead began to give less milk each day until some of them were producing nothing. The beasts they had sent to the mountain pastures were doing well enough, but when they drove them back down to the farm the same thing happened, whereas the ones who had not been giving picked up amazingly once they got up into the hills.

Kalv and his folk thought that perhaps the trouble was in the grass of the home farm. And so it went until the time came for the Midsummer Meeting, when all the men of the district came together outside Sigtun to settle whatever legal cases had come up during the previous year. It was the custom at that time for the jarl to confirm new district chieftains, and he awarded to Kalv the position that Freydis's kinfolk had filled formerly, and the land-rents to support it. But when they had finished adjudging the fine for a manslaying and settled a disputed inheritance and all the other quarrels that had been pending, the talk turned inevitably to the bad year they were having. And soon enough it became clear that though the crops were bad everywhere, it was only in Kalv's neighborhood that the milk was failing.

The Torundale men were still talking about it when they rode back up their own valley. Kalv had sent word ahead that some of their neighbors would be guesting with them to celebrate his chieftainship before returning to their own farms, and Freydis prepared as well as she could. Knowing that the jarl's gold would buy more, she rolled out one of their last barrels of beer. The men saluted her, for she had gained a reputation for wisdom, if not beauty—a good thing in a chieftain's wife.

There had been some rain the day before, but that evening held fair beneath a sky that glowed with glimmering color like the inside of a shell above the jagged black bordering of the trees. In such mild weather there was no need to crowd into the hall, and the men sat out around a bonfire, retelling every lawsuit they had seen, and every fight as well, until Freydis might as well have gone with them. But her thoughts were not on politics. Kalv's kiss of greeting had been warm. She wondered if he would find a way to leave his guests and come to bed that night, or whether she would have to lie alone listening to their laughter. Her need for her husband, almost forgotten while he was away, had awakened with new and demanding power as soon as he touched her again.

After the Thing-meet had been fully rehashed, the conversation returned inevitably to their own troubles. The local cows were still dry, and as the talk went round it became clear that every farmer in the valley was having the same trouble, though none quite so badly as Kalv.

"It is trollcraft—" Old Halvor said then. As if he had invoked the world of the Invisible by saying it, men looked uneasily around them.

Freydis paused, her grip tightening on little Aslaug, who should have been in bed long since but had been too excited by her father's return to sleep. But now at last the child's fair head was nodding. Freydis shifted her weight so that the little girl lay across her shoulder. The world was full of powers, good and ill. The gods were great, but often their concerns seemed far from the simple needs of men. It was often more needful to deal with the beings who haunted field and forest.

She had learned some of the craft from her aunt, who was accounted a wise woman. She looked around her, and suddenly the lengthening shadows seemed darker than before.

"And not far to look for a cause of it," growled another man. "Have we not all heard Gamle and Ulla at their cursing?"

"But how could they do it?" asked Kalv, his face a little flushed from the beer. "I gave Ulla a good warning the last time we quarreled, and she would not dare come near my land! That's so, isn't it?" He turned to Freydis. "You haven't seen either the old man nor his hag-wife here?"

She shook her head, but there had been something—she frowned, trying to remember, as Halvor laughed.

"Do you think that one who is trollwise needs to appear in any shape you'd know? Why do you think no servant will stay with them? After their son was outlawed a dozen winters ago they had a thrall who died babbling from no cause anyone could see. Mark me, Gamle, or perhaps it is Ulla, will have sent a trollcat to do their evil here."

"What do you mean?" Kalv asked then. He reached out to Freydis and she moved into the circle of his arm. She leaned against him, holding their child, feeling safety in his strength, and the promise of something more. She had assumed he would find a woman to sleep with at the Allthing, but perhaps it was not so.

"It is a creature made from wood shavings, or the haircastings of cattle, or some such," she said softly, remembering what she had heard. "The trollwise gives it life with his own blood, and it carries his soul to steal the milk from other men's cows."

"That must be the thing they call a milk-rabbit where I was raised," said Kalv, "because it looks like a running hare as it rolls along."

"Just so," said Halvor. "And when it has drunk too much it

vomits up the extra onto the ground. Have you seen anything like that, mistress?"

"Nothing that moved," she answered slowly, "but it's true that some mornings near the barn there has been slimy stuff on the ground."

"Well you see, then—" The old man nodded and took another pull of beer.

"But we cannot be sure who the creature belongs to," Kalv objected. "Gamle, or Ulla, or someone from the next valley for all we know! I would betray the jarl's trust if I condemned anyone on such evidence, no matter what hard words she's given me."

Halvor snorted and shook his head. "Let your cattle stay dry then, but I'll be keeping a watch out when I get back to my own place, and a silver knife handy as well. If I can once wound the wretched thing we'll see who goes limping. Will that be proof enough for you?"

And Kalv laughed and agreed that it would be, and the conversation passed off onto other matters. But Freydis felt her husband's strong fingers stroking down her back, and knew what he was thinking of. And sure enough, he soon announced that it was time to put the child, who had finally fallen asleep in her mother's arms, to bed and accompanied them back into the house so that he could kiss the babe good night. But it was Freydis whom he began kissing as soon as Aslaug was safely laid down.

"Do you really think that Ulla is stealing our milk?" she asked as she unhooked the silver brooches that pinned her long apron to the straps of the hanging-skirt wrapped around her body beneath the armpits. Kalv had already stripped off swordbelt and tunic, and was getting rid of his breeches.

"Right now," he said hoarsely, "I can only think of the milk that will fill your breasts when I have got you with child. . . ." In such warm weather Freydis wore only a shift under the hanging-skirt. He jerked at the neck strings and slid the garment off her shoulders.

After that, for a time she had no coherent thoughts at all. But afterward, when she lay listening to Kalv's regular breathing, she found herself remembering what old Halvor had said and shivered despite the warmth of her husband's strong arms.

Another moon passed without trouble and the hay began to ripen. Rolf Einarsson's wife bore a boy-child and the folk from Kalv's steading all went up for the naming feast. Rolf was their nearest neighbor, his land bounded, like theirs, by the forest. The babe looked strong despite the hard season, and Freydis, watching how lustily he pulled at his mother's breast, felt her longing to bear Kalv's son like a physical pain. That summer he had labored in their bed as faithfully as in his fields, but she was not yet with child. It worried her, for she could never forget that she had no beauty to hold him, and surely his interest would flag if all she could give him was one girl.

They were just sitting down to the feast when from over by the milk-barn there came shouting. Kalv leaped up with the other men and ran to see. When they did not soon return, Rolf's wife went down to find out what had happened and Freydis followed her.

The men had formed a great ring, watching something that was rolling hither and thither like a windblown dustball. She supposed it must be the trollcat—a round gray creature the size of a baby's head, and in the afterglow of sunset, curiously hard to see. But the men were jabbing at it with farm tools and spears, and laughing.

"Now's the time for Halvor's silver knife!" said Harek, the strongest of Kalv's carls, and Rolf began to grin.

"Wife," he said, "go up and get me that piece of bar-silver

that was part of your dowry, and you"—he spoke to one of the carls—"find me a stout pole and some thongs." As soon as the things were brought he tied the silver to the wood crossways and swung the pole through the air.

"I'll swear Thor himself never had such a hammer. Let us see now if he will speed my arm!"

Rolf stepped forward, and the rest of the circle began to close in. And still the trollcat rolled back and forth with that same sickening speed, but to Freydis it seemed that a humming came from it, and as the warriors got closer the sound became more shrill.

With a shout, then, Rolf leaped, and his weapon thudded down. There was an ear-piercing squeal and the warrior went sprawling, the silver bar flying one way and the shaft another. Men ducked, and in that instant something gray streaked past them and went bouncing erratically down the hill.

"It's making for the forest!" cried Kalv.

"Old Halvor was right. It is heading for Gamle's farm. I think I wounded it," said Rolf. "Bring up the ponies and we'll follow."

"If that's so one or the other will show the hurt—" said Freydis. She found herself hoping that the witch would be Gamle. Men were too quick to believe evil of women, especially when they were old.

"Well, that will be proof enough for me," said Kalv. He called to the housecarl who had come with them.

"Bring my mare too," said Freydis. "Gamle's place is halfway to our own. Why should you have to ride twice as far to come back for me?" She would not say that if they did not catch the creature, their own farm lay closest, and Aslaug was there with only the farm servants for guard.

For a moment Kalv stood frowning, then he shrugged. "I suppose it can do no harm. Those two are old, even if they are trollwise. But stay well back, for even a toothless beast can do damage when it is desperate." He reached out to squeeze her shoulder, then turned back to the men. Freydis could feel her heart beat as she watched him. Perhaps he really did care for her.

By the time they neared Gamle's cottage, it was full dark, but the men had brought torches. Freydis tensed as they came out through the band of half-grown trees that had sprouted at the edge of the clearing. One great pine tree even stretched out its branches over the cottage. The forest was trying to reclaim this place from humankind, and it seemed to her, looking at the moldy thatch and scattered fence poles, that it did not have far to go. As the warriors trotted forward and dismounted in front of the doorway she reined in.

"Gamle, come out!" cried Kalv. "Your neighbors have come calling. Will you not offer us hospitality?"

There was no response from the house. After a moment Kalv swung his spear butt-forward and struck the door. Wood boomed hollowly. Kalv stepped back, and as the echoes faded they heard voices arguing within. Then there came a sound of scraping wood and the door was pulled ajar. Freydis could just make out the pale blur of a face within.

"What kind of neighbors are you to come calling so roughly?" It was a woman's voice, cracked with age.

"Men from whose cows someone has been stealing the milk!" said Rolf.

"I am sorry to hear it," said Ulla, "but what is that to do with me?"

"Nothing," answered Kalv, "unless you are the thief. But that's easily told. Not long ago Rolf wounded a trollcat. Do you and your man come out to us and if we see no hurt on you we'll bid you a good even and be off home."

They waited, hearing the man's voice muttering behind her, and then the door opened wider, and Gamle pushed past his wife and came limping down the steps, glaring from one to another of the men who were waiting for him.

"He *is* hurt!" exclaimed one of the housecarls. "It was him then and not the old woman at all!"

"I'm an old man!" Gamle rounded on him. "And my joints ache in the cold. I have limped this past year and more."

It was true that the old were often lame, but the weather for the past few weeks had been unusually dry and warm.

"Your step did not halt at the Thing-meet last spring, and it had been raining," said Kalv in a grim voice. "We followed the trollcat here. You are the trollman, and you will stand your trial!"

Gamle cast a quick glance at the dark doorway behind him, then straightened.

"And if I am?" He glared around the circle. "Should you not be grateful I have taken nothing worse than your milk— if I have such trollcunning? Do you not fear what worse evil my curses might bring?"

"You can drum up no magic if your tools are broken," said Rolf, "and say no spells if we gag you!" He gestured, and his men began to move forward, eager as hounds.

"You do not have me yet!" Gamle spat over his shoulder, nipping back to his doorway more nimbly than Freydis would have thought possible. If Rolf had wounded him, the blow had done him little harm. "You stand there so strong and proud, judging me!" cried Gamle from the doorway, "but no man's luck lasts. Once I was as strong as you, and my woman was fairer than that cow who brought you your land!"

Freydis recoiled. Had he seen her, or was that spite an arrow shot at random, striking her heart? Gamle was still ranting.

"But we have lived to old age, and that is more than most of you will do. As I have lost everything, you will lose what you hold most dear! You may take that as a curse or a prophecy as it pleases you, but heed my warning. If you want to prosper, leave me and mine alone!"

"If you had left *us* alone we would not be here!" Rolf rushed forward, but the old man darted backward, the door slammed shut in his face, and they heard the harsh scrape as the bar was drawn.

"Well, Rolf," said one of his men, "you always were a clumsy fisherman! Gamle's escaped your net and now what will you do?"

"Fire the place!" exclaimed Harek. "Those two trolls will come out fast enough if it is a choice between a trial and staying to be roasted like trapped hares!"

They turned to look at Kalv and after a moment he nodded. In the midst of the woods there was no lack of fuel, especially in this dry weather. Freydis could hear the men crashing about as they gathered branches, but from nearer at hand came a hollow tap-tapping. After a moment she realized that its source was inside the dwelling; someone was beating on a rune-drum, and chanting.

Whether or not they had witched their cattle, there was no doubt now that the one of the two was trollwise, and the other, if not an equal partner, surely must have known. Freydis pulled her shawl around her shoulders, though it was still warm. On the back of her neck, the fine hairs were lifting.

Now the housecarls were returning, dark shapes distorted by the branches they carried, and beginning to pile their burdens against the log walls. Gamle's house was not a big place, and for a dozen men it was no great labor. Shape and shadow sprang into sharp relief as they came into the torchlight.

"Gamle! Ulla!" cried Kalv. "We have enjoyed your singing. But it is time to make an end. Come out now, or we will burn your house about your ears." The torch crackled loudly, but from the house they heard only that thin, weird singing, and the tapping of the drum.

Rolf swore softly, went up and banged on the door. "Come out, man! We do not want to burn you!"

Perhaps he did not, thought Freydis, looking around the circle, but in the flickering light she could see a look like hunger on the faces of many of the others that made her feel a little ill. In her own husband's eyes, thank the gods, there was only irritation. Nonetheless, he was the one who finally motioned to Rolf to come away and gave the order to set the brushwood alight.

At first the wood sizzled and sputtered, and Freydis thought that perhaps Gamle's magic was strong enough to keep it from burning. But presently the small sticks began to catch, and then the bigger branches, and here and there a tongue of flame leaped up, tasting the straw thatching above it, and soon enough parts of the roof blazed up and she knew that the people inside were doomed.

By now smoke must be curling along the ridgepole. Already the fire was making too much noise for her to hear the drum. There were stories of folk who had survived such a burning by burrowing into cellars or curling up inside barrels of ale. But this was too small a place for such tricks. For a while there would be some clean air near the floor, but soon the place would become a furnace. If those inside were lucky the smoke would kill them before they fried.

There was a shout, and through the wavering air above the thatching she saw the straw quiver as if someone were trying to poke through the roof above the sleeping loft. They must be mad—to make a hole there would only draw the fire in faster, and the walls below were already aflame. Men clustered as near as they dared, squinting against the brightness. From the back of the horse Freydis could see a little better; she stiffened as a hand and then a face appeared, contorted so that it seemed scarcely to belong to humankind.

The straw heaved as the rest of the body pushed through—no, it was being lifted from below. It was Ulla. The warriors ran round the building, wondering if she meant to slide down. Freydis shook her head, frowning. If she were innocent, why hadn't she come out before they lit the fire?

Ulla's eyes gleamed red as she glared around her; she looked like one of Muspel's children rising from the flames. Her lips writhed as if she were still chanting, though they could not make out words.

Then Ulla stood. Her shape wavered in the smoke from the smoldering straw, but her weight was all on one leg. *That is why she did not come out*, Freydis understood suddenly. *We would have seen that she was limping worse than the old man. She might as well have stayed to burn with her husband—she cannot get down from there.*

But impossibly, she stretched, and jumped—she must have jumped, but it looked as if her shawl had extended into wings and she were taking flight—into the overhanging branches of the pine tree.

It took one moment too many for the men to understand. In the next instant three spears flew toward the spot where Ulla had been standing, but they pierced nothing but smoky air. The trollwife had disappeared.

The men were still cursing when the beams of the farmhouse burned through and with a roar and a shower of sparks the roof fell in.

I was wrong, thought Freydis as she followed the housecarl whom Kalv had told off to escort her away from Gamle's pyre. *Those two were not pathetic after all*. Gamle had died to save his woman, and Ulla, pushed beyond reason by extremity, had found the purity of will to move beyond petty evil to real power. Kalv was still combing the woods with Rolf and most of the other men. Freydis had known better than to tell them it was useless, but she had little hope that they would find Ulla now.

As she rode she still saw the contorted features of the troll-wife against the darkness. The old woman's curses rang in her ears. It had been horrible, but that was not why she was shivering. From her old aunt Freydis herself had some knowledge of herbs and rune-spells, simple magics for healing and protection. But if all else failed, would she have cursed Kalv's enemies? Would she have sent out a trollcat to get food for her man or her child?

In the days that followed, Freydis gathered spear-leek and hung it over the doorways and under the eaves of the hall. She filled an old jug with bent nails and pins and buried it beneath the threshold, and painted bindrunes on Aslaug's truckle-bed. Kalv did not scoff at her precautions, but he did laugh at her attempts to protect him, and would go no farther than to wear a silver Thor's hammer around his neck on a thong. The farm folk, however, were more cooperative, and for a time the smell of garlic hung about the place like a fog.

But a week passed, and then another. The cows began to give milk once more and men joked that if it had been the trollwife herself they had seen escaping, and not just her spirit, she must have died in the forest. "Like a rat in a hole—" said Kalv, but Freydis did not think so. The figure she had seen erupting through the house roof had pulsed with power.

The days were busy, for in the northlands every hour of light was precious, and a whole summer scarcely long enough to store up the food that would get them through another year. But the nights were another matter. Though she might fall into bed too weary to move, Freydis found it hard to sleep, and when she did close her eyes she was haunted by evil dreams. In sleep her soul wandered.

She found herself drawn to the marshlands along the river, a trackless tangle of alder and bramble and reeds and black water beneath a haze of stinging flies. But something had made a pathway through the morass and hollowed out a nest-place among the reeds. It was a flesh-eater, for the place was littered with small bones, and something more as well, for what remained of the hides was rolled together. And each night that she spied thus, the ball of blood-caked hair and rotting skin was larger. She thought the creature that had gathered them must be a night hunter, for she never saw it. But though her dream-fetch had no physical senses, each night the stench of evil about the place grew more foul.

One morning they found one of the calves lying stiff and cold in the pasture, and though there was no wound beyond a gash such as the beast might have gotten on a stone, when they went to butcher it, no blood flowed from the body. That night they guarded the pasture, but nothing happened. The next day, though, a thrall came over from Rolf's place to tell them that one of his master's calves had been killed the same way.

There were seven farms in the dale. Each night a beast was killed at one of them, always a young animal. But the evil did not strike the same place two nights running, nor was there any pattern to its attacks. Freydis did her best to ward barn and byre, but you could not hang the cows with garlic, for they would eat it, and they rubbed off the runes she painted on their hides. One of the housecarls was sent down to Sigtun, seeking for someone with the magic to fight the evil, but though the word of their need had gone out through the land, no help appeared.

They lost another calf, and two lambs, but there were no tracks to show what beast had killed them, only a flattening in the grass, and sometimes a few smears of bloody slime. These nights Kalv was too weary for lovemaking, and Freydis too tired for any more dreams. But in an odd way, when he lay sleeping exhausted in her arms, Freydis felt more sure of him than she ever had before.

The wind was beginning to blow chill with a foretaste of winter when the Einarsson thrall came once more, his face white and grim. And this time it was not a cattle-slaying that he came to report, but the death of Rolf's little son.

"Not three moons old," the man repeated, shaking his head, "and as lusty a child as you might look for. Dead in his cradle, the poor lad, with only one little wound to let the blood out. . . ."

Freydis's eyes sought her own child, who was piling up pebbles and knocking them down again, her bright hair blazing in the sun.

"Like the cattle," echoed Kalv, who had come up just in time to hear the last of it. "We thought ourselves badly off when we had a milk-rabbit to deal with. But it is a bloodbeast that comes against us now!" His face was grim.

Freydis reached out to him. In the past moons he had grown gaunt with strain. How long had it been since they had been able to sleep out the night undisturbed? And this was in the summer, when the days were long. What would it be like when winter came and light left the world?

"There are still cows left for the creature to kill," said Freydis slowly. "That poor babe was scarcely a meal for it. I think it is killing now for pleasure. . . . It will come for our children next, and then for women and men. But I will not let it have Aslaug!"

"I will send you down to your kinfolk in Birka," said Kalv. "The risk is too great for you and Aslaug to bide here. . . ." Three families from Torundale had already packed up their gear and abandoned their farmsteads.

Freydis thought about the stout walls of her half brother's house on the island, and about her sister-in-law, who had jeered that Kalv had only married her for her land. And then she looked around her at the hangings of the boxbed which she had embroidered with such care, the skin of the bear Kalv had killed last winter and tanned with the fur on to use for a rug so that Aslaug could play on the floor. Outside it was the same—every beast and building something they had gained together and cared for.

"I will not abandon you, my husband," she said, then added quickly, "or my home. Honor will keep the housecarls with you, but if I ran away I think that the rest of the farm folk would go."

Kalv looked at her oddly for a moment. "Your wisdom never fails, does it? But wisdom may not be enough for what faces us here." She blinked, and he reached out to squeeze her shoulder. "Never mind, wife, only take care, and guard the child."

Freydis hardly needed that warning. She hung her little daughter about with charms and tried to confine her to the safety of the hall, but Aslaug was reaching the age where her curiosity was growing as quickly as her body. It was hard to always watch her, for summer was ending, and every hand was needed to get in the hay and the slow-ripening barley. The cattle were brought down from the shieling to the home pastures, and the women got busy making cheese and butter before the milk should fail. But they worked looking over their shoulders fearfully, and even Freydis's presence was not enough to keep several of the thralls from running away.

It was just past sunset, and Freydis was squeezing the last of the whey through the cloth when the girl who was watching Aslaug burst through the door.

"Mistress, the babe is gone! She was sleeping on the blanket under the birch tree, and I never left her—"

"Were you sleeping too?" Freydis asked sharply, wiping her hands and heading for the door.

"I was not, I swear to you—it was magic! That creature—"

But Freydis was no longer listening. No doubt the girl was lying, even if she believed her own words. She paused, looking from the empty blanket across the farmyard. Where would an enterprising three-year-old, waking from a nap to find her watcher dozing, be most likely to go?

In the failing light she made out a few marks in the dust that might have been footprints, half obscured by the marks where Aslaug had dragged her doll behind her. The trail headed under the fence around the pasture—she might be making for the stream. Freydis slid between the bars and started across the grass.

She broke into a run as the cows who were grazing at the far side of the field threw up their heads and began to move as if they had scented something disturbing. Now she could hear Aslaug's laughter. It came from the hollow by the alders; she glimpsed her daughter's bright head, and then, beyond her, a thing like a pile of rotting hides. Even from here Freydis could smell it, as if all the death in the world had been rolled up in one appalling bundle. The bloodbeast was moving slowly, stalking its prey.

She wasted no breath in calling. Hitching up her skirts, she slid down the bank and grabbed for the child.

"It wants to play, but it's stinky!" exclaimed Aslaug, wrinkling her nose and holding up her arms to be lifted.

"Yes, my darling—" Freydis kept her eyes on her enemy, torn between horror and pity. The thing was rocking back and forth, changing shape every time it moved. "Go back to the hall now, as fast as you can run. Gerd is waiting for you with a honeycake there!" She gave the child a shove and stepped between her and the bloodbeast, which was now almost her own height, growing more grotesquely human in form with every twitch.

"Ulla Guthormsdaughter—" Her voice shook only a little. "I name you, and you must hear me—" A tremor went through the creature before her, but she could tell that it was listening. "If you were in want you should have asked us for help, not sent the trollcat, but I forgive you that, and you have taken a bloodprice in cattle for the death of your man. It is right to hold to life while the gods will it, but you are neither dead nor living. Give it up, Ulla, and find peace. There is nothing for you here . . ."

She waited, and the thing twitched and shifted once more. Now it certainly had a woman's form. And though it did not have a mouth to speak with, it seemed to her that words were coming from the figure, and she could not tell if she heard them with her mind or her ears.

"Blood . . ." That thought came clearly. *"Blood is life. . . . I will drink yours!"*

The human mind was gone, thought Freydis numbly. The only thought left to this creature was bloodhunger. Her gorge rose at the stench as it lurched toward her. From the corners of her eyes she saw movement—Harek and another of the housecarls were running toward her with poised spears. The first spear flew and sliced rotting hide, but the bloodbeast twitched it aside. The second pierced, but the creature took no more notice than if it had been a fly.

"Iron will not harm it—" Freydis shouted. "It wants blood—bring a cow!"

The creature stretched out one reeking arm. Had Aslaug reached the safety of the hall? How slowly it seemed to move, and how slow her own response as Freydis fumbled to undo the silver brooches that held her hanging skirt and apron. As she pulled them free the beads strung across her breast between them went flying, the scissors and other housewife's tools scattered across the grass. But now she had a firm grip on the brooches, with the strong pins projecting outward. The arm came down and she jabbed upward. The bloodbeast recoiled. Freydis kicked away the tangle of skirt and apron and stood in her shift, facing it.

"You don't like that, do you?" she said softly. The only answer was a wave of hatred as appalling in its own way as the smell. From behind her she heard scuffling and the bawling of a cow. The bloodbeast swayed toward her again and she took a step back, jabbing with the brooch pins when it came too near. But she knew it would take more than pins to do the creature any real harm.

Now Freydis could see the cow, plunging and dragging on the ropes. The thralls who held it were white with terror, but Kalv was running toward them, sword drawn. "Cut the cow's throat!" she cried, and leaped away as the long blade flashed and the hot blood smell filled the air. The heifer fell, thrashing, and the bloodbeast turned toward it.

Kalv's other hand closed on her wrist. "Run, all of you—back to the hall!" He dragged her after him up the slope. Behind them, the cow ceased its shudders at last as the bloodbeast bent to feed.

In the next few hours Freydis began to understand how Gamle and Ulla must have felt when they heard the wood being stacked against their housewalls. The trollwife would not use fire, but nonetheless Torundstead was besieged. Except for Gerd and little Asti, the thralls had all fled, and all but two of the housecarls. But there was no time to curse them. Kalv was not wealthy, but he still had some of the jarl's silver coin besides Freydis's brooches and some other ornaments. The air rang with the sound of hammering as Kalv beat them into points for arrows or spears and scratched the runes Freydis showed him onto the blades.

At all times a man was posted at each of the doors, but the night stayed still and calm. It seemed to Freydis she could hear each breath; even the crackling of the hearthfire sounded loud to senses tuned painfully to the silence.

"If the creature does not come here tonight, we will go after it tomorrow," said Kalv. "We must get what rest we can. Thorfinn, take the first watch, and wake me at midnight." He gave orders to the others in terse, unemotional tones.

But when he climbed into the boxbed beside her, Freydis could feel his tension. He drew her hard against him, taut as a strung bow. Before his men he had showed nothing, but she could feel the passion in him and did not know if it was fury or fear. If he had been Aslaug she would have tried to comfort him, but she could not tell what he needed from her now. At last she turned her head a little and kissed him, just where the dark hair grew so strongly at his temples. And at that some of the strain gusted out of him in a long sigh.

"Freydis . . ." he whispered harshly. "Why would you not leave here when I asked it? The heart froze in my breast when I saw that thing reach for you. Why didn't you run?"

"I had to buy time for Aslaug to get away."

"Aslaug!" Kalv raised himself above her, hard hands gripping her shoulders, his face a dim blur in the light that came through the bedcurtains. "Is she all you care for? I would mourn if we lost her, but you could give me other children. But to do that, you must live!"

"Any woman could give you children," she whispered.

"Not with your brave spirit," her husband sank down on one elbow and stroked the hair back from her brow, "not with your wisdom and kindness." She shivered as his hand moved over the soft skin of her neck and slid beneath her shift. "We will leave here tomorrow. Some lord will take me on—I will even serve your brother if need be."

"And give up the farm?" He could not mean it. This land

had transformed him from a penniless younger son into a man of substance, from a housecarl to a chieftain with followers of his own.

"I want you alive, Freydis, my seed in your womb—"

Kalv kissed her, and the life within her surged to answer the question in his roving hands. There was no sense in this joining, not when they needed rest so badly, when at any time the attack might come. But the need of the flesh to make life in the face of destruction could not be denied. And in his extremity, when the words of love come easily to a man, Freydis heard them and for the first time since he had married her, believed they might be true.

Afterward, when they lay twined in mingled satiation and exhaustion, Freydis dreamed. Once more her spirit moved across the land, and once more she found the thing like a nest where she had seen the blood drinker taking shape before. It was gone now, but she was surprised to realize that there was something in its place—cautiously she moved closer, and saw lying there an emaciated body that had once been a woman. Gaping tears in her wrists showed where her life had bled away, but though there were a few smears of blood on the reeds, there was no bloodtrail, and nothing like the volume of blood Freydis should have seen. It was as if all the blood had gone somewhere—or into something—else. Closer still she moved, and the last of the moonlight showed her the face of Ulla, set in a malevolent smile. Appalled, she stared down at it, and in that moment the features twisted and became her own. Gasping, Freydis fled back to her body and woke whimpering in Kalv's arms.

"What is it?"

"Ulla!" she exclaimed, sitting upright. "I know where her body is! She sends the troll-thing out to drink blood to feed it. Destroy her human body before dawn, and the bloodbeast will die!" Swiftly she began to tell him what she had seen. "The place is just upriver from the otter falls where the alders grow. Sink the body in the swamp with a stake through its heart and withies to hold down hands and feet, and it will not walk again." She clutched at him, unable to tell him the end of her dream.

"I will give her a good earth-fastening, never fear!" he said grimly. He swung his feet over the side of the boxbed and stood up, calling to the other men.

Before they left, Kalv turned to her once more. "I do not like to leave you, but I trust your sense. Promise me you will not leave the hall."

Don't go— her heart cried. *Stay with me and we'll flee in the morning. . . .* He had even offered to do it. But not now, when she herself had showed him how to defeat their enemy. She would feel safe only when it was destroyed. She bit her lip and kept silent, even when they slammed the door shut behind them.

The men had been gone for perhaps an hour, and Freydis was dozing off once more, when the thrall, Asti, touched her arm.

"Something is out there—I hear a sound like something being dragged along the ground."

Freydis could not hear it, but she could track it by the sense of evil that came in waves like a stench as the thing moved around the hall.

"Hungry . . ." the thoughts came clearly. *"Give me hot blood, life blood, let me feed!"*

She got to her feet, the rough silver blade Kalv had hammered out of one of her brooches in her hand. In the other boxbed Gerd sat up, Aslaug still asleep by her side.

"Mistress, what is happening?" whispered the girl. "I am afraid."

I am afraid too, thought Freydis. *We were so sure these walls would keep us safe, but what if we were wrong?*

As if in response to her words, the door creaked as something large and heavy pressed against it. A moment passed and the house shook as the thing drove against the door more forcefully. Freydis looked in alarm at the hinges and saw white wood where they were beginning to splinter. If the door went, the bar would be no barrier, and it looked to her as if a few more blows would bring it down.

She plucked a torch from its bracket on the wall. For a moment she paused, looking down at her daughter. Then she kissed the sleeping child and moved swiftly toward the other door, the small one, at the end of the hall. Wyrd was at work here. She had been a fool to think she could evade this confrontation.

"What are you doing?" cried Gerd.

"Tell Kalv that I tried to keep my promise, but at least this way he may still have a child."

And then she slipped through into the darkness, the torch flickering wildly above her and the silver knife in her hand. Quietly she moved around the hall, swallowing bile as she slipped in the bloodbeast's trail of stinking slime.

The moon was long set, and the sky was lightening with the featureless pallor of early dawn. Before the door to the hall she saw a monstrous shape: it heaved, and stressed wood screamed.

Freydis cast the torch onto the woodpile and ran forward. "Ulla!" She caught her breath and tried again. "Ulla, here is sweeter meat for you!" Biting her lip, she slashed the silver blade across the fleshy underside of her arm. "Cannot you smell it? The red blood is flowing, hot blood for you to drink, sister. Come to me, come to me!"

And the bloodbeast turned. Torchlight flared and flickered, throwing its monstrous shape into silhouette and shining on the crimson life-fluid that was flowing down Freydis's white arm. For a moment the creature hesitated, but the scent of her blood was irresistible.

Light flared as the woodpile caught. Freydis began to move slowly away from the hall. The bloodbeast came after her. How long could she evade it? Until dawn? Until the men came back to aid her? The pressure of the creature's hunger overwhelmed all other awareness, and worse still was that dreadful sense of *familiarity*. She had called Ulla sister, and it was true. The temptation to release the darkness she had discovered within herself in order to fight it tore at her soul. Only the pain in her arm reminded her that she was Kalv's wife and Aslaug's mother, and she would die rather than win by becoming the thing she feared.

In the firelight she could see all too clearly every wound the warriors had made in the bloodbeast's mismatched hide, but in the middle of what might be a head, there was a sucking gash that pulsed more quickly the closer it came.

Its mouth . . . she thought numbly. *It is getting ready to feed.* . . . She was past the barns now, but the bloodbeast was moving more quickly. She began to run. The blood drinker lurched after her, and from it she sensed now a dreadful glee. Her spirit quailed, and in that moment she tripped over a stone. As she went down the bloodbeast, like a monstrous shadow, followed her.

You shall not have me! Her senses swam at the touch of rotten flesh as the blood drinker began to gather her into its embrace, but she thrust at it in the ultimate repudiation, jabbing the silver knife into its sucking maw.

Then the sweet, sick stench of old blood engulfed her spirit and she fell into darkness.

Freydis opened her eyes to a confusion of light and dark and heat and cold in which the only constant was pain. Kalv was bending over her. Beyond him she could see the remains of a pyre, burning down now to glowing brands. She stank of old blood, and the reek of burnt flesh hung in the air. But the light that hurt her eyes was the growing radiance of dawn.

"Am I dead?" she whispered. She felt numb.

"You ought to be!" he said grimly. "When we pulled that thing off you I was sure you were, and ready to kill you again for leaving me!"

She sucked in breath, remembering. "I . . . jabbed my silver knife down its gullet."

Kalv nodded. "That would have slowed it, and destroying the old hag's human body released the soul from both the flesh and the being it rode to feed."

"You found her, then!"

"Right where you told us. May she not be reborn soon!" said Harek, behind them. "When we got here, we burned what was left of the bloodbeast, just to make sure *it* does not return. Kalv, do not be angry with your lady. I have looked at the hall door, and with another few blows the creature would have had it down."

Suddenly Kalv grinned. "I see that I have married a Valkyrie—"

Freydis stared at him. He must be thinking of the terrible spirits who haunted the battlefield, not the wish-maidens of Odin's hall. She shuddered, feeling on her skin the foulness of dead blood and slime.

"You have married a hag . . ." she said harshly.

In the growing light she could see him clearly, smeared with swamp mud and gore. Kalv was not handsome now. Perhaps a beast lived within men as well—there were tales of how it got loose sometimes, in war. But a woman did not have the option of taking up the sword. She had only magic, and the shape her evil took could be more terrible.

"Come down to the stream, wife, and when we are clean again, we shall see . . ." He was still smiling. How could he look at her that way? Could he not see the memory of darkness in her eyes?

Freydis let him pull her to her feet. She supposed that after the bloodbeast, nothing could seem ugly. The horror of its foul embrace would always haunt her, and the greater horror she had felt when she knew that they were kin. But she had not given way to it. At the touch of Kalv's hand she felt life returning, as the rising sun led the world once more into day.

Madeleine

❧

BARBARA HAMBLY

T he young man's name was Philip. He was a solic-
itor's clerk somewhere in the city, thin and very
fair—Madeleine liked fair and slender young men.
On winter evenings she would watch them from the shadows
of an alleyway at one end of the street where all the firms had
their offices. The lighted windows were like illuminated pictures in the city's cindery winter dusks; clerks in frock coats
closing up the ledgers, returning deed boxes to high shelves.
She pictured the movement of the muscles under their shirts,
thought about the texture of the lips under those brave attempts at mustaches, imagined the taste, the freshness, of the
soft skin between high celluloid collar and ear. They would
come out into the gaslight of the narrow street, pulling on
their gloves, chattering with one another happily, about the
matters dear to the hearts of young men: tobacco, boating,
cards, girls.

Sometimes, Madeleine would follow one of them.

In the summer when the darkness did not fully come until

nearly nine o'clock, she would lie in her coffin and stretch out her awareness, listening across the city for their voices, fragile and light as the voices of children playing in some other part of a great garden. She could trace them, every one, if she concentrated; pick out a certain set of footsteps, the jaunty whistling of a popular waltz, through the clamoring of carriage wheels and hooves on cobbles, the yammering of costermongers trying to dispose of the day's stale wares and the whooping oompah of tavern bands; trace them sometimes each back to his own shabby rooms.

When full dark came, sweet with the gluey warmth of the city's summer, she would set forth in her glitter of lace and jet, to find the streets where they lived.

This was what she did with Philip.

She watched him for weeks, for young clerks were her hobby, her treat, rather than the staple of her nights.

He lived with a woman named Olivia, five or six years older than he, a sort of bluestocking who pursued studies in the Old Library at the university. Madeleine would see them through the lace curtains of her flat when the lights were up in the darkness, talking as they cooked supper, hands waving with the earnestness of lovers, brandishing sausages at one another on the end of forks; or else would listen to them make love, from where she stood on the flagway, or in the next street, or three blocks away, seeking out the sound through all the night sounds of the city, all the lovers, all the children playing on the night pavements, all the parents arguing over money or dreams. She knew how their breaths entwined, heard the words the woman said—surprisingly coarse for that tall, thin, old-maidish form, that narrow bespectacled face—and the soft little sound Philip would make, between a gasp and a whimper, at her touch.

It was that sound that decided Madeleine. That, and the fineness of his skin. She waited until Olivia departed on some journey of several days, then encountered Philip, as if by accident, in the street on his way back to his flat.

She took him that night, draining his blood until he collapsed, fainting, in her arms; stroking his face, his throat, his shoulders with her long glassy fingernails as he lay in the tangle of his bedsheets gazing up at her with wonder and terror in his wandering brown eyes. She treasured him so much she left him a little alive, and when she lay at dawn in her coffin in the expensive and heavily secured town house that was hers, she sleepily, satedly probed out with her mind, to hear his labored gasps as he struggled for air, picturing him lying there in extremity, unable even to call for help. She took that picture down with her into the dreamless vampire sleep and hoped vaguely that he would live until night.

He was alive when she threw back the tall windows from his balcony again. It was clear to her that no one had come to him all day. He only just managed to turn his head on the pillows when she came in, and she treasured the moment of his exquisite despair. He had known all day that she would be back with the darkness.

She savored that, as much as she savored the blood that finally drew out his life.

Two nights later Madeleine went to the cemetery of St. Joseph, to see his tomb.

It was a family tomb, like a gray granite temple. He had been the younger son of some bourgeois with aspirations to the professions. In the warm gloom of the late spring evening the smell of mortar was sharp in the air, contrasting with the waxy pungency of funeral wreaths. Madeleine had killed on her way there, a carpet-seller in his grimy shop near the bank of the river, a man no one would miss, except perhaps his wife, if he had one . . . and probably not her, much. So she felt indulgent with the world, as she moved through the darkness of tombs and ivy and ornamental trees toward the place.

A veiled woman stood on the tomb's steps. But though Madeleine walked with a vampire's soundless, weightless stride, the woman seemed to hear, and raised her head, putting back her veil with hands gloved in shabby and mended black kid. Her spectacles flashed like all-seeing eyes in the dark.

"I thought that you would come here," she said.

Madeleine laughed. Men had told her—before they died, before they knew what she was and the extent of their danger—that she had a laugh like silver bells, like the cold tinkling of glass chimes. "Oh, it's one who knows, is it?" she mocked.

Olivia stood for some moments, regarding her in the near-total darkness beneath the trees. With the sight of night-walking things, Madeleine could see this woman quite clearly; not precisely beautiful, with her long, narrow face and those enormous gray eyes behind the thick rounds of glass, but oddly compelling. Her brown hair was piled on her head beneath the veiled black hat, and her hands, though narrow, were as long as a man's. *She must have the most dreadful time finding gloves*, thought the vampire, with detached amusement. *If her feet are anything like in proportion she probably hunts all over the city for shoes*. Madeleine's own hands and feet were small, exquisite in high-buttoned shoes handmade for her by an old man on the fringes of the financial district. The money she'd taken from the carpet-seller's shop—and from Philip's desk drawer—would probably go toward paying for another pair.

"Nobody will believe you, you know," she said, coming closer, dainty as a bisque doll in her small-waisted gown, the silk taffeta of her petticoats murmuring like last fall's leaves on the grass. "They never do. What did his family put it down that he'd died of, a 'wasting sickness'?"

Then she stopped, for Olivia was not backing away from her, not hiding her face. She only stood, looking at Madeleine with a kind of calm sadness, like, Madeleine thought in irritation, some placid cow observing her over a fence.

"And that is all that he was to you?" Olivia said.

"Darling, how can you say that?" Madeleine smiled dreamily. "He was a desperately sweet boy—as I'm sure you know, my dear. I've always had a terrible weakness for sweet boys." Her smile broadened, to make her white teeth gleam. She felt warm throughout, and powerful, the blood of the carpet-seller rich and sweet in her veins for all his unprepossessing appearance. *Sometimes one dines on caviar*, she thought, *and other times, on pot roast*. Her cheeks, she knew, would be rosy with the flush of stolen life, her lips dark crimson.

Olivia's face was as white as her own had been when she'd risen from her coffin with the coming of night.

"What, are you worried he'll turn into a wicked, wicked vampire like me?"

The woman shook her head. "No. I know that is not how vampires are made."

"Oooh." Madeleine formed a little moue with her lips. "A scholar, no less."

"After a fashion." Olivia stepped forward suddenly and lifted her hand. Madeleine scented the coldness of silver on her, a great deal of silver. Under that black mourning dress with its high collar and long sleeves she must have chains of it, circling her throat and her wrists, perhaps small discs sewn into the flounces of her petticoats, the cotton of her corset cover.

Madeleine stepped back, her flowerlike nostrils flaring. "Don't try it," she said, and her voice was suddenly a snarl. "I am warning you, my dear. Just because you know what I am doesn't mean you can do anything about it. The blood I have taken, the lives I have taken, are all within me, giving me strength. All your learning, and all your study, can't prevail against that."

"No," replied Olivia. "You took their blood, and you took their lives, uncaring of who they were and what they were, only to add to your own life and strength."

Madeleine laughed again, not the sweet silver-bell laugh of the lady now, but cruel and hard and scornful. "Who and what they were? They were *ordinary*, darling. Ordinary and common and dull. Like yourself, I'm afraid; are we really going to go through a sermon on how evil I am? I expected more of you."

"Is that why you came here?" Olivia spoke without irony, without trace of anger in her clear gray eyes. "Because you expected something of me? I'm sorry to disappoint you. You took their blood, and you took their lives, and so all I can do is charge you to be aware of what you have taken. To be aware fully. Then maybe you will not be so quick to do it again."

Madeleine was angry now, irritated at the argument and impatient to leave. She considered taking this woman, here and now, for the cemetery was utterly deserted, but her native caution prevailed. First, because Olivia had come prepared, her clothing thick with hidden silver, and Madeleine was not sure she could overpower the other woman without getting badly burned. Second, because the vampires of the city lived upon the city's poor. If too many young and handsome clerks died in too rapid succession, or if family members or lovers died too—even if not upon the very grave of the earlier victim—the police would begin to inquire. There were priests, and strange old scholars at the university, who knew things that other men scorned to believe, and it did not do to bring matters too much to their attention.

And third. . . .

No, thought Madeleine, backing from Olivia until she was little more than a glitter of jet beads, like colorless fire within the smoke of her lace. *There is no third reason. This woman is only a stupid woman, praying and sniveling over a man she couldn't even keep.*

There was no third reason.

But she found no cutting remark, no perfect exit line, upon which to make her departure. So she had to content herself with saying. "Fool—a thousand times a fool," as she faded into the night.

Olivia, standing upon the steps of the granite tomb, did not move until she was gone.

Lying in her coffin at dawn. Madeleine let her mind rove through the city, tasting the final perfumes of the night. Mist rising from the river, the smell of the hay barges coming in from the country, the voices of marketwomen at their barrows. "'Ere, get 'em fresh, new from the country, cucumbers cool as ice!" Prostitutes gathering in the cafes for a final cup of coffee before going home. "Well, I'll give 'im the money, if he wants to gamble so bad, but damned if I'll let that bastard tell me what to do in me spare time." Small children waking and being got ready for school. The wheels of milk wagons rocking over pavements beneath chestnut trees, the self-satisfied purring of cats padding up stone steps for the first cream of the day. Summer was coming, a bad time for vampires in northern latitudes, but there was an enchantment in it, too; returning to her coffin long before sleep was ready to come, and lying in its darkness for hours before it was safe to rise, Madeleine walked through the city with her ears, with her mind. Frequently she chose her victims that way, only later trying to trace down their voices, their footfalls, their smells.

It gave her amusement, and a sense of keenness to her hunt.

"So I says to my wife, I says, 'How you gonna deal with a man like that?' He brings carpets in from the East, he says. . . ."

Madeleine twitched uncomfortably in her narrow coffin, as a memory from last night's predawn dozing intruded into her mind. Whose voice was that?

Yes, the carpet-seller. A loud boor, and no loss to anyone. His voice grated even yet in her memory.

"Them guys that go to Turkey all the time, buying up carpets, they gotta be a little crazy, you know? You could get yourself killed, traveling around on some cockamamie camel or donkey or whatever, carrying money 'cause they don't got no banks there. . . ."

She tried to push the voice from her mind, tried to silence her thoughts. She hadn't heard the old man's grating voice for more than a few minutes last night. In her after-sunset rambles, looking almost at random for a victim in the swarming alleys of the riverside slums, she had heard it again and remembered it from that half-dozing listening. Had heard it then and had smiled. She remembered thinking, *His wife will probably thank me. . . .*

Why did she hear him say now, "Ruchel and me, thirty years we been married, you think she remembers which tie I always wear on Sabbath? Always she's asking me, What tie you gonna wear to *shul*, Jakov, like she hasn't seen me put on the red one every goddam Sabbath. . . ."

Shut up, old man, Madeleine thought savagely, and turned her mind away, seeking the darkness of sleep, the quiet of dreams. But she was still awake when, long after sunrise, the day-duty policeman walked past the house whistling opera, and the gardener came to tend the place and make it look like it was lived in, though during the day none of the neighbors ever saw movement behind the locked doors, the drawn blinds.

When she slept, there was no quiet in her sleep.

Madeleine woke feeling somewhat refreshed, but only by careful concentration on the sounds outside could she avoid remembering what the carpet-seller's voice sounded like. For a time she lay, listening and breathing in the scents of the coming night, feeling her mind and senses stir, her blood and her hunger rise. She remembered, more than the carpet-seller, the woman Olivia, and felt a vicious desire to seek her out and kill her, though she knew that such a thing was out of the question for months, if ever.

Still, when she rose at last from her coffin, when she slipped out of the cloud of lace that was her negligee, and stroked her cold, slim, white body in the blood-orange glow of the lamplight, when she dressed carefully, in dove gray this time, all trimmed with black lace like a tabby cat, she found herself thinking she wanted a woman.

The woman she killed was tall and gawky and wore spectacles, though she was older than Olivia, and getting fat with the starchy diet of the working poor. She was a seamstress, stitching over lamplight to finish a client's order before some party tomorrow night. Madeleine was careful not to get blood on the shimmering apricot-colored silk, which she then held up to herself before the seamstress's long mirror. It was a little too big, but she took it anyway, liking the fabric. It would not take much, she told herself, to alter it to her own more fragile body.

That she had nearly thirty such dresses, taken in the confidence of alterations she had no concept of how to perform, did not cross her mind. All those were out of style by this time, anyway.

She did not even realize whose voice she heard in her mind, like the memory of an overheard conversation, as she was walking the dark streets, watching the night go by. "Poor Alicia was in labor with her for two days, no wonder the dear little thing was so sickly as a child," she seemed to hear a woman's gentle voice say. "But she was always smart as paint. Her father would never hear of her going with the other children to Sunday school to learn reading, but little Nicole, when she was four years old she slipped out of the house and ran away with her friend Lettice . . . You remember Lettice? That dear redheaded girl. . . ."

Madeleine shook her head angrily, her admiration of the ghostly shimmer of lights through river mist broken by that constant, murmuring recollection. . . .

". . . so I says to him, Morrie, I says. You want me to pay top price for a piece of carpet some Moslem heathen has had laying out in front of his shop for donkeys to walk over? Is that what you're telling me?"

Damn! thought Madeleine furiously. *Don't let that infernal carpet-seller start up again!*

She tried to turn her mind away, to think of something else, but all that would come to her was the woman's soft voice, talking about her children. Endlessly.

Madeleine usually didn't kill twice in a night, but she felt the desperate need for the intense concentration of the hunt to take her mind off those voices. She made her way to the poorest section of town and found a beggar, a wretched and whining specimen no one would miss and, because she needed excitement, let him see her, let him know her for what she was, with the seamstress's blood still on her mouth and the flames of hell gleaming in her eyes. She pursued the man through the dripping and filthy alleys, cutting him off easily when he tried to run to pubs and police stations where there were lights and people, driving him back into the garbage-smelling lanes that fronted the docks, feeling her own excitement rise with the stepped-up pounding of his heart, the frantic heat of his blood. The little man was sobbing, mumbling desperate prayers to a half-forgotten God, unable to run or even to stand anymore when she overtook him at last, and then she let him escape her, two or three times, pursuing him languidly, easily, in the dark.

When she was done she threw his body in the river and watched the tide take it out.

"I never had the chance other people got."

Madeleine woke up, broad awake, though she knew it was barely past noon.

"Ma, she always said we wasn't supposed to smoke her tobacco, so whenever any of her tobacco was missin', my brothers'd tell her it was me that took it, just me, not them or anything, and I'd be the one that got the buckle end of the belt. It was always the same. Look, I can't help it if I'm little. I can't help it if I had this twisted foot. . . ."

The swell of rage in her was like a heat about to blow the lid off the coffin.

". . . so you'd think a boy with opportunities like that, he'd go into business for his father, wouldn't you? Nice shop, good money, seat in *shul* by the eastern wall for High Holy Days. . . ."

"I wanted Elizabeth—that's my oldest—to have the best education, to have the best start in the world she can get. That's why I took in extra work, to get her proper schooling, though the nuns at St. Irene's are terribly expensive and I do have to make her extra clothing, because some of the other girls there are so unkind. Still, when I offered the Mother Superior to do the embroidery on the new altar cloth. . . ."

The heat was followed by cold, and the terrible, first sinking drop of fear. She understood whose those voices were, speaking chattily in her head.

That bitch! I'll kill her . . . I'll ram her sniveling voices down her throat!

Madeleine had never been awake in the daytime. Another time she might have savored the experience, the overpowering weight of languor that made even the movement of a hand into effort; might even have tracked the policeman by his whistling—Rossini and Verdi—back to his house, to call upon him some night on his way back from the pub. But now all she heard was the carpet-seller's diatribes on the short-comings of his suppliers, the seamstress's gentle praise of her children, the beggar's complaints about his ill health, poverty, and misuse by his next-door neighbor's dog.

She did not sleep, from noon until the coming of dark.

Thanks to her double meal of the night before, she rose at last not hungry. As a general rule Madeleine spent consider-able time in her town house preparing for the hunt, washing, curling her witch-black hair, sometimes only stroking her body, observing the trim perfection of the pink-tipped apples of her breasts, the slight, bony projections of hipbone and knee, running her hands down the small of her back to feel the tiny indentations there, one on either side of the spine, which only slender and perfect women had. Then she would stand naked before her huge armoires, holding up dress after dress, intent on matching each ensemble exactly with her mood of that night and the image she desired to portray. Would she be the gracious lady extending favors tonight? The mysterious dark beauty? The deadly serpent?

Tonight she pulled on a walking suit of black-shot red, like old blood. *She will see me in my rage*, she thought with bitter fury. *She will see the kind of danger she has tampered with. And she will rue the night she brought herself to MY attention.*

"You know, I see people passing me by every day, and you know, they could afford a couple of coins," whined a voice in her mind. "I don't ask for a lot, but I can't work—my consti-tution won't take the strain of a factory job, and I never had the education for one of the professions, though Father Ben-jamin at the church, he always said I had the brains for it. . . ."

The windows of the flat that Olivia had shared with the beautiful Philip were dark when Madeleine reached the street.

By the glow of the gaslights, she could see that the lace curtains which had hung there were gone.

The rooms were empty of everything save dust, and the faintly mealy smell of Olivia's books.

And Madeleine's rage had made her hungry.

Down in the street again she heard passing footfalls and looked around, her anger seeking the outlet of blood, the drugged satisfaction of the warming of her cold flesh. But she heard one of the women passing say to the other, in a voice that would have scratched glass, "Well, you know how he gets when he's drunk, and I wasn't gonna get a black eye just for the satisfaction of breakin' a bottle over his greasy skull."

She thought about hearing that voice, over and over in her mind, and shuddered. But her hunger did not ease, and knowing that she could not immediately slake it, it became all she could think about. All she could think about, that is, in between what Ruchel's parents did on the occasion of last Passover and how Alicia had gotten married to Nicole's father in the first place.

You took their blood, and you took their lives, Olivia had said. *And so all I can do is charge you to be aware of what you have taken.*

Bitching, stinking, ordinary CATTLE! thought Madeleine furiously. *What the hell does she know about it? What the hell does she know about* ME?

But there was fear in her heart as she moved off through the city, to find others who might know what to do; others who had made her what she was, and had taught her the hidden ways, the little tricks, the secret joys. She went quickly, as if she were being pursued, but found that she could not outrace the voices in her mind.

"You hear their voices in your mind? Of your *victims*?" Sazerac burst into a whoop of delighted laughter.

"It isn't funny!" cried Madeleine furiously, but the cool, fine-boned face, white as silk by the gaslights of his parlor, convulsed with amusement, almost to tears.

"Good Lord, Count, what if you were forced to listen to yours?" chuckled Cecile, the master vampire's new favorite—taller than Madeleine and fuller of figure, and without her serpentine, dancer's grace. In an exaggerated nasal imitation of lower-class accents, the blonde vampire continued, "Gee, are you a real *count*? Like with a *castle*? Ooo, is that an honest-to-Christ *ruby*? Oh, *Count*. . . ."

Sazerac collapsed into renewed gales of mirth.

Cecile's eyes—pale blue and cold as sapphires—danced maliciously as she looked up at Madeleine. "What, darling, are you actually spending time *thinking* about their nasty little lives?" She, like Madeleine—for Sazerac had made and initiated them both—dressed for whatever role she planned to play in her hunt, and tonight she had evidently been a temptress. Flushed pale rose with the internal warmth of her kill, her breasts rose like thick cream above a low-cut gown of amber silk, intricately beaded on the bodice, so that in the warm half-light of Sazerac's town house parlor, she resembled a florid golden dragon in her lair.

"Not any more than I can help," gritted Madeleine.

"My darling, I'm sorry I laughed." Sazerac put out a hand to cup Madeleine's cheek, but his white lips still twitched with the effort not to giggle again. "Truly. Forgive me."

"What can I do?" begged Madeleine, trying not to sound as if she were begging. Not in front of Cecile. Possibly not in front of Sazerac. "The woman has left the city. Who can I go to, to remove this . . . this charge? This curse?"

"Try a priest," purred Cecile. "That way if he doesn't lift the curse at least you can hear mass all night afterward."

Nerves rubbed beyond endurance, Madeleine spun on her in a flash of fury, but Sazerac laid a reproving hand on the arm of each woman. "My darling," he said gently to Madeleine, "you need perspective on this. It's a dreadful thing, yes, but you know it's something that will fade. It must, simply with usage."

"Oh, I don't know." Cecile laid one white, rounded arm along the back of the green-black velvet settee which she shared with the vampire count. "One's love of new sensations doesn't. Or at least it hasn't for me, and you say it has not for you. One's . . . one's *relish* for the touch of every sunset, the taste of each new kill. Those don't fade."

"This is different," said Sazerac quickly. "And if not . . ." His face made a grab at sobriety and then dissolved into laughter again. "And if not, think what a time you'll have searching the city for a mute!"

Toward morning, driven by hunger, Madeleine killed a child. After seven and a half hours of listening to the little boy's unceasing—and utterly unvarying—complaint about the disappearance of his toy horse, she regretted it. She had forgotten how infuriatingly persistent children can be.

Whether she slept or not during that day, or the days following, she was not sure. If she did, the voices persisted into her dreams, until she was ready to swear that they were all sitting in the great, heavily curtained bedroom in a circle around her coffin, each yammering on about his or her own affairs, like hideously ill-mannered guests. She woke exhausted, her nerves scraped raw, the monologues intruding into her thoughts, preventing her from listening to the world outside. She spent the dark hours pacing the streets of the city, searching, listening, trying to stretch out her crippled senses to pick up the whisper of the woman Olivia's voice, the sound of her sensible-heeled shoes clacking on the pavement, the smell of her books, her bath powder, her hair.

She searched the Old Library, the university quarter with its steep, soot-black buildings jostling one another along the riverbank among ancient churches and crumbling fountains in half-forgotten squares. There were young men there, studying late by lamplight or tupping shopgirls in their garrets. She thought about killing one of them, for hunger was driving her frantic, but every time she listened to their conversations she drew back. *Dear God, don't let me get a law student! Or one who's having trouble with his girlfriend.*

They all seemed to be having trouble with their girlfriends. Or else they belonged to doctrinaire communist groups vociferously protesting the government's latest policies, or were having philosophical crises of conscience about the meaning of their lives.

Madeleine killed rats instead, though they did little for her hunger, and went hungry to bed; she woke feeling as if she had spent the day being dragged over broken bottles and cobblestones.

She grew thin and edgy. The voices did not fade with familiarity, as Sazerac had promised. Rather they grew, rehashing the old topics over and over endlessly. Sometimes she turned, positive Jakov the carpet-seller was walking along at her heels; it was as if their reality grew with feeding. There was no satisfaction to be had in the blood of animals. By two in the morning she felt that the only way to obtain relief, for even a few hours, was to hunt, to kill, as she had hunted the beggar. She stalked a dockworker for hours and never heard him speak one word . . . not until after he was dead, and she was lying in her coffin once again, hearing his constant, muttered, foul-mouthed spew about his hatred of rich women and how he was going to beat the tar out of his nigger foreman if the asslicker ordered him around one more time.

She went two more nights without killing, listening to the voices unabated all around her. Hunger and the need for the kill clouded her mind, robbed her of whatever pleasure in life she had left. She tried killing a novelist, reflecting at least that his conversation should be interesting, and discovered that novelists' chief concerns are their royalties, and how their publishers and agents conspire to rob them, and whether their wives are cheating on them and with whom. The following week she killed a young woman of breeding and refinement and was driven nearly to the screaming point by meticulous speculations about glove length, the genealogies of acquaintances, and who should sit next to whom at dinner.

Sazerac and Cecile sought her out the night after that and warned her. "A sweet young man, or a tender girl, is all very well two, maybe three times a year," the master vampire said gravely, toying with the small cup of café noir in the blaze of gaslight at the Cafe New York. He inhaled deeply, savoring the perfumes of the ladies at the next tables, the expensive tobaccos which permeated the clothing of the fashionable gentlemen who strolled by on the flagway outside. In Madeleine's mind, the stevedore cursed at the bosses who cheated him and the pansy faggots who wouldn't even throw him a tip, the child cried shrilly, *David took my HORSE. David took my HORSE. He's going to break it. David took my HORSE.*

"But you mustn't make a habit of it, my dear Madeleine." He took her chin in his hand, gazed deep in her eyes, and there was no pity in his, only a dangerous, steely glint. "You had your fun with your little attorney's clerk. You know the rules. Too many deaths of a 'wasting sickness' will have the police wondering about the strange marks on the bodies, wondering about old legends. You have me, and Cecile, to think of as well, you know."

She whispered, "You don't understand."

The eyes did not soften one fraction with the smile that

only moved the pale lips. "What, still fretting about your silly voices? I thought you were stronger than that."

Cecile rose, her eyes already following a dusky-skinned young waiter who was pocketing his tips, taking off his apron, joking with his friends about finding a girl on his way home. "Just see," she said, "that it doesn't happen again."

But of course it did. Those with some education, some style of living, at least did not have the obsessive narrowness, the foul-mouthed resentments common to so many of the poor. One hot morning as Madeleine lay tossing wretchedly in her coffin, she heard voices outside, hushed and grim, and knew them for detectives, heard a man's quiet voice say, "Have you ever wondered, gentlemen, why so many of the old legends all speak of the same things?"

She knew, as she listened to the sounds of the endless summer twilight, that she must shift her quarters, and shift them soon. But she had not fed properly in two nights, only cats and dogs, and it was difficult for her to think. Even more difficult, with the hectic clamor going on in her head, complaining, worrying, recounting old stories of loved ones, detailing conversations with friends and the minutiae of the lives she had stolen. She tried to concentrate on a letter to her house agent, on plans for emergency quarters, but her hunger made her insane with restlessness, and the voices would give her no peace. She ended by going out to hunt, with the high summer twilight barely gone from the sky and all the world smelling of lilacs and the river, and killed a young girl sitting alone on her balcony, speculating, it turned out, about whether Thomas or Louis, or perhaps George, loved her the most, and how she was going to get Andrew to propose to her, and whether she should get the shell-pink silk made up into a dress, or the oyster taffeta.

Madeleine heard about it all.

She was lying awake, gritting her teeth in fury and

wretchedness, when she heard, beneath the cacophony of the voices, the crash of a rear window breaking, the snap of a latch. Her mind drugged and thick with lack of sleep, with the loginess of daytime, she thrust the lid of the coffin back, struggled to rise. Her limbs felt weighted, sodden, almost as if those who jangled and bickered in her head were clinging to her wrists, her negligee, her feet.

The room was pitch-black. She couldn't seem to open her eyes, couldn't keep them open. She fell, weak and muzzy with the daylight she knew had to be outside; in the depths of the house she heard men's footfalls, smelled their bodies, the sweat in their shirts and the mud on their shoes. Her mind reached out to hear their voices, to tell her what to flee, but all she heard was ". . . told Ruchel once I told her a thousand times, you can't trust those door-to-door salesmen for anything! That soap is worthless!"

Shut up, you old bastard. I'd kill you if I hadn't already. . . .

". . . and do you know what that editor said to me? He said I didn't kill enough people in that story! He said, there's paper and a pen in the next room, and here's your manuscript, and you go in there right now and write me another death scene. . . ."

"David took my HORSE. . . ."

She blundered into a door, fumbled the knob, trying desperately to open her eyes. Rooms thickly curtained, lightless; why did she feel, when she pulled the door open, that the chamber was crowded with people, people all talking as they came toward her. . . .

"But if I seat Jeffrey next to Caroline, that will put Caroline across from Mr. Fontaine, and after what Mrs. Fontaine said about Caroline's sister we can't risk that, . . ."

GET AWAY FROM ME!

"Lousy no-good women, hump any man they see; I'd beat the lot of 'em with a strap, the filthy whores. . . ."

"I never was strong enough to join the army, you see. If I had been, my whole life would have been different. But they'd never take me because I'm small. . . ."

"*GET AWAY FROM ME!*" She wasn't aware she'd screamed it aloud until she heard footfalls in the stairwell, and then she wasn't even sure. For there seemed to be footfalls all around her, dark figures. . . . Her eyes felt gummed as she stumbled, weaving like a drunken woman, seeking the hall, the back stairs, the cellar. Get away. . . . Get away. . . .

"So I said, Ruchel, I said, is it any shame to make a little money off *goyim* swine who'd just as soon burn my shop down as look at me, just because I'm a Jew?"

"David took my HORSE . . ." She could almost feel small hands clinging to the fragile stuff of her nightgown.

"But you see, if Andrew proposes to me, I'd have to accept him because if I turn him down this time he'll ask Violette, and I *can't* let him marry her, only I don't want to get married either, at least not to Andrew. . . ."

She fell against walls, stumbled, barking her knees on the sharp edges of stairs. Darkness everywhere, voices shouting behind her, less real to her than the jabbering in her head. *I charge you to be aware of what you have taken. . . .*

Their blood. And their lives.

Her hands groped at a door latch, her head lolling on her shoulders, her knees like water. For some reason the metal was warm under her hand. The cellar door . . . it had to be the cellar door.

Then she opened the door, and like a colorless moth bumping blindly from a cellar, staggered outside into the all-devouring blaze of light and heat.

The detectives and the priest buried what they found, the pile of bone and ash and rags still smoking on the threshold of the rear door. It took only a small space in the municipal potter's field. The priest, and the elderly scholar from the university who had been with them, came back later and mixed certain holy things in the earth of the grave, to give its inhabitant what rest they could.

The following night a woman came to the cemetery, veiled in black. She found the grave easily, by the voices that whispered around it in the warm night air.

"Who are you?" she asked the first voice. "What is your name?"

"My name is Jakov Bernstein," said the voice. "I sell carpets, down by the river. I have a wife, Ruchel. . . . Is she all right?"

"I will tell her," said Olivia, "that *you* are all right, now." And she told him, in the Yiddish that he best understood—for she had been a scholar of languages at the university, before her studies had led her into other and stranger paths—how to find his way across to the world where he now must go, and how to release his hold on this one.

"And what is your name?" she asked again.

"I'm Emma Normand," said a woman's voice. "I'm Elizabeth's mother, and Annette's, and little Gerard's. I've been so worried. . . ."

"They will be well," said Olivia. "As well as any can be in this world. Go now, and be in peace."

So many, she thought, listening to the voices of the shades. But they were fewer than the number of days that had passed since Philip had died. That was something.

For a long time she stood, hearing their names, hearing what they said about their concerns, their families, their lives; even the stevedore Finn, and the beggar Lucius del Valle. When she had heard them out, she gave them such instructions as she thought they would understand, and let them go. From the earth beneath her feet came no sound, no whisper from the ashes and the bones.

It was almost dawn when she left Madeleine's grave, disappearing into the luminous summer darkness, the silence like still water. As she passed out of sight beneath the trees, almost hesitantly, a bird began to sing.

Mama

STEVE AND MELANIE TEM

lizabeth's mother was dead.

Which was a shame, because right now Elizabeth wanted to kill her herself.

She guessed she didn't mean that. She guessed it wasn't Mama's fault that she'd gotten the cancer. No, that wasn't true either. Mama deserved the cancer because she'd always smoked, smoked in secret in the bathroom and in the garage but everybody knew about it—they just pretended they didn't know. That was the kind of power Mama had. Dad had pretended so well that one time he smelled cigarette smoke outside Elizabeth's room and he yelled at *her*, accused *her* of it, until he realized it was Mama who had done it and he'd looked all embarrassed, and then he'd looked angry and he'd said, "But someday it *will* be you, Elizabeth. You're just like her!" And then he'd stomped away and Elizabeth felt like she'd been slapped in the face.

That was another reason for being mad at Mama, she guessed. Everybody said she was just like her Mama. She had her Mama's face, her Mama's temper. Dad said he couldn't tell how she was going to feel about anything from one minute to the next. Dad said she was "moody" like Mama, too. That meant she got depressed like Mama.

Sometimes she wondered if maybe it had really been Mama's depression that had given her the cancer. Mama had been depressed as long as Elizabeth could remember. Sometimes she'd stayed in bed for days, just lying there like a dead person, with no interest in anything. The only reason Elizabeth knew she wasn't dead was because Dad took Mama trays sometimes, and sometimes there'd be a little bit of food missing. But lots of times that was the *only* way to tell, and that had scared Elizabeth bad. What if Mama had been dead for days and Dad just hadn't been brave enough to tell them yet? They'd never know. Parents never let kids know anything, even kids as old as fourteen.

When Mama got depressed, it was like she wanted to be dead. She was just waiting for somebody to notice and bury her. It was scary because Elizabeth knew exactly what that felt like.

It was all so dramatic. Like a soap opera. All that gave Mama lots of power. Before anybody in the family did anything they first had to figure out how it might affect Mama. There was no telling what might make her mad, or make her depressed. Everybody got exhausted trying to figure out what Mama wanted, until finally they didn't have any life left for themselves.

Some days Elizabeth wanted to be like that. To lie down, to give up. To be dead and still have everybody focusing on you. To use up their life because you didn't have any of your own left to use. Mama had been selfish. She'd deserved to die.

Which was a terrible thing to be thinking. It made Elizabeth feel awful, which made her even more furious with her mother.

Not that she hadn't thought that same thing lots of times before. She'd even said it in a couple of their fights when she'd said everything else she could think of. "I *hate* you! You're the worst mother in the whole world! I wish I didn't even *have* a mother! I wish you were dead!"

That wasn't why Mama had died. Elizabeth was fourteen, and she knew better than that. Everybody she knew hated their parents, and *their* parents didn't die. Leave it to Mama to do something that would embarrass her and make her feel bad all at the same time. Mama was *always* on her case. Nothing she ever did was good enough.

One time Mama'd started crying and said she felt the same way, like nothing *she* ever did was good enough for Elizabeth. It had made Elizabeth feel so guilty to see her mother cry, like she was supposed to *do* something and she didn't know what. So she just walked out of the room and then out of the house. She wasn't running away or anything. She just needed to get away from her mother.

I'm sorry, Mama. You were good enough. Please come back. Please don't be dead.

Elizabeth was also old enough to know that, just because she'd wished so hard and so often that she had a mother again, just because she kept having those dumb dreams that Mama came back to life, that didn't mean that Mama would come back to life. Stuff like that didn't happen except in the movies. Once your mother died and left you, she was gone forever.

But now all of a sudden Mama wasn't dead anymore. Just like all those times she'd been too depressed to get out of bed. And Dad had kept her back in the bedroom, and hid her, and fed her like he was in her power and had no other choice. Now here she was, yelling at Elizabeth for coming home late last night, and Elizabeth was really pissed, just like always, and her mother was *dead*. Dead six months.

Mama had had her way again. She'd turned everything upside down.

"You're grounded!" Mama yelled.

"You're dead!" Elizabeth yelled back, and the power of saying that took her breath away. She wanted to tell Mama she was sorry but she was too scared. She'd gone to a memorial service but she actually hadn't seen Mama's body. Had Dad been keeping her in the bedroom all that time? What was Mama trying to pull now? Just because she was her mother didn't mean that she could do anything she damn well wanted. It made Elizabeth hate her dad, just for a minute—it was too scary to hate him any longer than that—but he should have *told* them. They had a right to know, even if they were only kids. He was just so *weak* where Mama was concerned. Sometimes her dad was so weak Elizabeth thought she would die.

She stormed out of the room and on out of the house, making a show of ignoring her mother calling her name behind her. She was just going for a walk, for God's sake. She wasn't some little kid.

She went over to Stacey's house. Stacey used to be her best friend before that boyfriend of hers came along. Stacey didn't have much time for her after that.

"So do you like it better this way. . . ." Stacey pushed up the back of her hair, making it flop down in front. "Or this way?" She pulled down hard on the ends, straightening the curl out.

"Stacey, did you *hear* me? I said my mother's not dead anymore. She came back today."

Stacey looked at her out of one eye, the other one hiding behind a big fall of hair. "That's a sick joke, Liz. She was your *mother*, after all."

"Stacey, you gotta let me stay here. I'm *scared*."

"I can't." Stacey turned back to the mirror behind them,

playing with her hair. "See, I got a date tonight . . . and Mom says I can't have girlfriends over if I'm just gonna leave. . . ."

"Stacey!"

"I'm *sorry*, okay? My mom's a bitch sometimes—I can't help it."

"You're supposed to be my friend."

Stacey looked at her then, trying to look serious, and that just made Elizabeth even angrier. "Liz, *really*, this isn't real. Your mom's dead. I went to the funeral, remember? You oughta see somebody. I mean, your mom, she's been screwin' with your head for years, makin' you feel guilty about everything. I mean, you always said you couldn't please her. Now she's dead, and she's still doing it to you. Your mom, I know you loved her and everything, but she could be a real bitch sometimes. . . ."

"My Mama wasn't a bitch!" Elizabeth didn't mean to, but she slapped Stacey as hard as she could. Stacey fell back against the mirror with her hair flying everywhere, and she just started bawling, just like a baby. But it wasn't funny— Elizabeth felt like she'd just done the worst thing. She was so scared she jumped up and ran out of Stacey's house, and Stacey's mom was screaming behind her and cursing, and Elizabeth couldn't help it, but she kept wondering if her Mama would still stand up for her the same way.

It was on the way home that she finally started figuring things out. Her dad and Mama had done something weird. They'd wanted people to think Mama was dead for some stupid reason, and because she and Mark were just kids they hadn't told them anything. Typical. It made her really angry. Like they didn't care how she felt. Sure—Mama stayed inside the house. In the shadows. So now Mama was some dirty little secret in the family. Something perverted. Elizabeth was already feeling dirty because she'd tried to tell Stacey about Mama. She wasn't going to try *that* again. She'd just pretend like Dad and Mama were pretending. Maybe she'd talk to Mark about it. They'd have some kind of a plan together. That would show them.

When she got back Mama screamed at her for being late, like she'd had permission to go in the first place. What a laugh. Elizabeth didn't even argue. That way Mama would know how really mad she was at her.

Dad used to really hate it when Elizabeth and her mother fought. Sometimes he'd go back and forth between them, trying to explain to each of them what the other one had meant or what the other one was feeling. Once in a while that worked, but usually they both just ended up mad at him, too, and Elizabeth would feel a little sorry for him. "You're so much alike," he'd say, kind of helplessly.

Everybody always said that. That was not what Elizabeth wanted to hear, although secretly it made her kind of proud. She knew it wasn't what Mama wanted to hear, either, and that hurt her feelings.

Dad would tell Elizabeth, "You know, a lot of girls your age have trouble with their mothers, especially when they've been close like you and your Mama have been. You guys love each other. You'll get through it." Now, of course, they never would. Even if Mama wasn't really dead after all, things couldn't be fixed. Not after they'd lied to her and her brother. Not after they'd made their family weird.

Tears burned her eyes, and she rubbed them away hard with her knuckles. She was not going to cry anymore about her mother. She was *not*. She'd been crying practically nonstop for six months.

But she was crying when Mark came rattling up behind her on his Rollerblades, grabbed her around the waist, and spun her halfway around so that she practically fell down, and whooped, "Yo, Lizzie!"

She loathed it when he called her Lizzie, which, naturally,

was why he did it. At least he made her stop crying. "You little turd!"

"You big butthead!" he yelled, and then he giggled this silly little giggle like he always did, like everything was just one big joke to him, and the joke was always on her. He took off past her. For a twelve-year-old creep, he was pretty good on those Rollerblades. But she wouldn't tell him that in a million years.

She watched him speed around the corner and made herself not hurry up to see where he went from there. She was not going to worry about him. She was not going to take care of him. She was *not* going to be his mother. She'd figure out some way to tell him about what Dad and Mama had done, the right way so that he wouldn't freak out or anything.

Since Mama'd died, Elizabeth had felt so sorry for Dad that she couldn't stand to be around him. He went to work every day and he came home every night, and he tried really hard to take care of Mark and Elizabeth even though Elizabeth tried to show him she didn't need anybody to take care of her. The clothes got washed and the meals got cooked and as far as she knew the bills got paid, and he showed up at their school stuff and he helped Mark with his homework, but his heart didn't seem to be in it.

But now that she knew the truth about Mama, she didn't know what to feel about Dad. He'd lied to her, lied to her for months. It was just so sick, the kind of sick only adults could do. It was scary.

Once, maybe a week after Mama'd died—after Dad *said* she'd died—when Elizabeth was just starting to realize what it meant, she'd asked him, "Are you ever going to be happy again?"

She'd expected him to say something like, "Sure, honey. Of course I'll be happy again." Even though she wouldn't have believed it, even though she'd have been furious to think he could ever be happy without Mama, it still would have been a relief. But he didn't. He'd looked at her with a sad face like she didn't know a human being could have and he'd said, "I don't know, honey. I don't know anything about what happens next."

But knowing now that Mama had been alive all along, she didn't know what to think about what Dad had said that day. She *knew* he'd been terribly, terribly sad—Dad had never been able to hide his true feelings about anything—but now she had no idea what he'd been sad about. Maybe the whole sick thing had been Mama's idea. Mama had done something to him, to make him like that. She'd been doing something to him for years. That was the only explanation. He had no backbone: he was like some kind of slimy jellyfish. He had no life of his own—he'd given it all to Mama. And he was so pale, depressed, and he moved so slowly these days—now Elizabeth was afraid of losing him. Mama had come up with something terrible, and made Dad go along with it. And now it was killing him. She had to *do* something.

She went for a long walk. She thought about school. She thought about how all her friends were getting their ears double-pierced and some triple. She thought about how she was never going to get a boyfriend because she was dumb and ugly. She thought about how Stacey would never be her friend anymore. She thought about everything she could think of that wasn't Mama.

But Mama got in there anyway. Everything she thought about came back to Mama. Mama saying maybe they ought to get her a tutor for algebra—which was *just* what she needed, to have to think about stupid algebra even *more*, like she was ever going to need $x(x-y)$ in real life. Mama laughing and saying she didn't care how many holes Elizabeth got in her ears if Elizabeth paid for it with her own money, and not to worry about Dad, he'd get used to it. Mama telling her she was beautiful and smart and a nice person and interesting, and just wait, pretty soon she'd have to beat 'em off with a stick.

Missing her mother made Elizabeth's stomach hurt. She *missed her mother*. She wanted her mother to *come back*. That ought to count for something, how much she *wanted* Mama.

It didn't, though. Once somebody was dead, they were dead.

But Mama was back. It had all been a trick. She was in the house like always, making breakfast. And it was Dad who was looking pale, sick, and depressed, like he wanted to die. Like Mama had taken everything away from him. Like Mama had gotten her way again and he had taken Mama's place. But Elizabeth hadn't gotten Mama back either, because of the trick, and Mama had changed, and nothing would ever be right again.

Elizabeth kept walking and walking. Tears kept trickling down her cheeks, but she was determined not to cry anymore.

"Elizabeth! Breakfast!"

She was right back by her own house, and that was Mama calling her. Elizabeth didn't know what was going on, but her mind refused to think about it anymore, so she just gave up and went inside.

Mark was already there, sitting at the kitchen table reading the comics. He stuck his tongue out at her. She grabbed the paper out of his hands, and it tore some, but she got it. Brat.

Mark whined, "Mama, she stole the comics!" and Mama, standing at the stove just like she always did, said over her shoulder, "Now, children, let's have some peace while we eat," just like she always did, and Elizabeth thought, as hard as she could, *Mama's dead*.

Mark was so dumb, just like a little kid. If he knew something was wrong with Mama being back and everything he sure didn't act like it. He acted like everything was *normal*. But then a little kid wouldn't know something was perverted even if he saw it. It was scary. Now she was afraid something was wrong with Mark, too.

She pulled a handful of sticky, linty gumdrops out of her sweatshirt pocket and stuffed them into her mouth. Mama crossed to the sink and opened up the window, just like she always did. Elizabeth hated that. Mark hated that, Dad hated that—the whole family complained about Mama's thing for fresh air. Dead of winter, middle of the night, first thing in the morning, it didn't matter. They could all freeze to death just so Mama could get her fresh air.

Elizabeth pushed the gumdrops out of her mouth with her tongue, the gross chewed-up mess into her hand. Mama would give her hell for eating sugar before breakfast.

Mama didn't notice, though. She was busy scraping the eggs out of the cast-iron skillet. No aluminum for her. Good old-fashioned cast iron, which Elizabeth thought was disgusting because it had little grooves in it where bits of food could hide and black stuff came off on the dish towels.

Just like in her dreams. Mama cooking breakfast in the big cast-iron skillets. Mama raking the yard, ironing Dad's shirts, loading the dishwasher. Letting everybody else know what to think, how to feel, just by the way she looked at you. Doing all the stuff she always did that kept the house going and you didn't even notice until she wasn't around anymore to do it.

Except Mama was supposed to be dead. They'd lied.

Then Mama turned and looked at Elizabeth. Her eyes were as black as the skillet bottoms, and way too big. "Don't you feel good, Elizabeth? You look a little peaked. Maybe you should stay home from school today and rest? I'll take care of you, sweetheart," she said, and grinned.

Mama doesn't grin like that. Mama never calls me sweetheart.

"Hey," complained Mark. "No fair."

"Don't worry about it, *baby*," she said to him, not daring to say anything to her mother. She felt herself backing away, scared that her mother might touch her. "I'm going to school. I've got an algebra test."

Mama set a plate full of fried eggs in front of each of them. Elizabeth went to the bathroom to get rid of the gooey gumdrops in her hand. She heard Mark say, "Yuck! There's *yolk* in mine!" and it kind of gave her the creeps because he'd never, in his whole life, liked yolks and their mother knew that. If she was their réal mother. Which she shouldn't be, because their mother was dead.

When she came back into the kitchen, Mama was standing behind Mark with her hands on his shoulders. Mama's face was tight and stiff like when she was really mad, and she was pinching Mark's shoulders hard. Then she grinned, and wrapped her arms around him. Tighter, tighter, so that Elizabeth saw his face go pale, as if Mama were squeezing the life and blood right out of him. He looked kind of sick, but he was still eating his eggs.

She should have done something. Gotten Mark alone and talked to him. But she didn't know what to say. He was just a little kid, really. She was alone in this. It was all up to her.

Elizabeth didn't even look at her eggs. She just grabbed her books off the counter and practically ran out of the house, mumbling that she'd get breakfast at school, she had to study algebra. Mama was paying too much attention to Mark to even try to stop her.

The algebra test wasn't that bad, and she thought she passed it. Not that she much cared. She thought about not going home from school, and she walked around for a while, but Stacey wasn't her friend anymore—she didn't say anything or even look at her all day—and Elizabeth couldn't think of anywhere else to go. She wanted so badly to tell somebody what her parents had done—whatever they had done—but she knew it must be too dirty a secret to tell.

When she got home Mark was sick in bed. Dad was there, home early from work, taking care of him. She didn't see Mama.

"He's running a little fever, honey," Dad said, but it didn't look like a little fever. Mark was shaking all over. At first she thought maybe Mark was faking. But he kept throwing up. Even water made him throw up. His skin was the color of concrete. Dad said, too many times, "It's just the flu. Everybody gets the flu." But Elizabeth saw how worried he looked, and she didn't want to see, so she went to her room and shut the door and sat on her bed for a while, trying not to think about Mama.

She thought about whether she should tell Heather what Julie had said about her. "You should be the one who *stops* gossip," Mama would have said. But maybe if she told Heather, then Heather would be her friend and let her stay at her house.

She thought about Jeff. He was pretty much of a jerk, and she was sure he did drugs, and she didn't understand why she was so attracted to him. "He's dangerous," Mama told her. "Lots of women find dangerous men attractive. Nothing wrong with feeling that way. But you don't have to act on your feelings."

Elizabeth threw herself facedown on her bed and covered her head with her pillow. *Mama is dead.* "It's not fair," Mama said, not loud but in a way that Elizabeth knew meant she was really, really mad. "I've been cheated." *I've been cheated, too,* Elizabeth found herself thinking, and fell asleep, and dreamed that Mama was in Mark's room, taking care of him, grinning, wrapping her arms around him, hugging him, hurting him, too, making him sick.

Mark died before morning. Elizabeth woke up because Dad was moaning, and she didn't want to go see what was the matter, but she couldn't help it. Dad was on Mark's bed, crying, with Mark's body in his arms, and Mama was standing in the shadows with her hands over her face.

"Oh, honey," Mama said softly, and went over to Elizabeth, and before Elizabeth could pull away Mama kissed her lightly on the cheek with lips as dry as dead leaves, lips that smelled of earth, and insects, but most of all, of copper.

"You should've called the doctor," she accused her father, then felt terrible for talking to him like that, for putting him through even more pain.

"I know, I know. . . ." he said from his chair in the shadows. "I don't know what's the matter with me. Sometimes I *know* what I should be doing about something, and I *think* about it, but for some reason I can't seem to *do* anything." His voice sounded weak, kind of crackly, as if he were speaking to her on a long-distance connection. "I just want to sit here. I just want to sit, and do nothing."

"But, Daddy . . . you have to . . . have to take care of Mark. His body? Daddy, *please!*"

"Honey, it's okay. I . . . took care of things. They came for it while you were sleeping."

"But the funeral?"

"We'll have it later, honey. A memorial service, at least. With the neighbors, and Mark's friends. There'll be time. I'm . . . I'm going to ask them to cremate the body. I think that would be best."

"Daddy. . . ."

"Hush now, baby. Hush. . . ."

"Daddy, it was Mama's idea, wasn't it? Having Mark cremated. So people wouldn't find out what she did. . . ."

"Baby, oh honey. . . ." Dad pulled her close. "I'm *so* sorry. I should have paid more attention. We *all* loved your mom very much. But she's *dead*, honey. She's dead."

Elizabeth pulled away and looked at him. He *thought* he was telling the truth. She could see it in his eyes.

"Daddy? Daddy?"

But he was crying and couldn't answer her anymore. Elizabeth got up and started for the door, but stopped when she saw her mother standing there in the shadows. "You don't feel good, Elizabeth. It's understandable. Maybe you should stay home from school today and rest? Mama will take care of you, sweetheart," she said, and grinned with something dark staining the grin, and held her soft mothering arms out to hug her, but Elizabeth pushed past, shuddering.

She didn't go to school the next day. Or the day after that. Her Dad understood, of course. He knew she was grieving. He'd just call in sick for her and explain everything later. He'd take care of her.

But he couldn't. Sure she was grieving, but she was staying home because she had to take care of him. She tried to call Stacey to apologize but the phone was dead. She wondered if maybe her dad had disconnected it so that he wouldn't have to talk to anybody. But then she wondered if maybe Mama had something to do with it.

She could go out, tell the police or something. But she and Mark were the only ones who had seen Mama, and now it was just her. She wasn't a kid anymore, but they would think she was. Nobody listened to kids. They treated them like crazy people. They'd put her in the hospital or something and then Dad would be all alone with Mama. She couldn't leave him alone in the house. Not even for a minute.

All day long Elizabeth's mother walked back and forth in front of her father's door. Waiting. But her father never came out. Not once. He might be dying in there, but if she opened her father's door then Mama might get in there. And then she'd lose her daddy, too.

Elizabeth knew she was going to be left all alone. All alone in the house with her mother, who was dead, who had been dead for months.

Over the next couple of days people knocked at the front door, but they always went away. Elizabeth was afraid to go to the door, afraid of what Mama might do if somebody else learned about their perverted secret.

Elizabeth tried to learn as much as she could about Mama's new routine. It made her feel a little safer. Every morning Mama shuffled slowly out of her bedroom as if she had almost no strength left for the day. Sometimes she had all her clothes on but sometimes she just wore a big torn slip. After an hour or so of standing in the hall outside her dad's bedroom door, Mama started walking around the house, avoiding the windows and just walking like she'd forgotten what it was she was supposed to do. Sometimes she'd stop walking and stand there with her head kind of sideways like she was listening for something, but maybe she'd forgotten what it was she was listening for.

Sometimes Mama would fix something on the stove and then just throw it into the garbage. Sometimes Elizabeth would see Mama eating flies. Sometimes Elizabeth would see a mouse's head poke itself suddenly out of Mama's mouth before getting pulled back inside again. Sometimes Mama's chin would be covered with blood.

Elizabeth stayed out of Mama's way the best she could, and although she didn't exactly understand why, she figured she was pretty safe as long as Mama kept hanging around outside her daddy's bedroom door. It wasn't too hard staying out of Mama's way—she seemed pretty sleepy most of the time, like she'd had too much to eat or drink.

Sometimes Mama would call out her name, though. Sometimes Mama would look into Elizabeth's empty room (she'd stopped sleeping in there days ago) and say, "Elizabeth? Elizabeth, honey? Do you need a hug? Let me give you a hug, sweetheart!" And it would make Elizabeth depressed because Mama had never hugged her very much before—not like her friends' moms—and she'd always wanted her mama to hug her like those moms did. She *did* need a hug right now for sure, but not from Mama.

And after a while she started seeing Mark around the house, and then she knew her daddy had never gotten around to ordering the cremation. And she was almost glad, but not quite. Sometimes Mark would walk through the house, and eat flies, and call out to Elizabeth with sugar in his voice asking if she would give *him* a hug, too. And then he'd giggle, just like he used to, just like it was all a big joke he'd pulled on her.

Finally one night when she could hear Mama and Mark in another room moving around and bumping into furniture and chasing things, Elizabeth slipped into her father's bedroom. He was lying there on the floor in the dark very very still but she figured if she could just get him off the floor she could help him out of the house and they could stay at a neighbor's house or in a hotel somewhere until they could figure out what else to do.

But then Elizabeth saw that her daddy didn't have a face anymore, just part of a tongue sticking out with teeth marks along the edges where it had been chewed. And most of one leg was gone. But still she kept asking him if he could stand up, if he was ready to go now, but he didn't say a word. She'd let him down. Just like with Mama, she hadn't been good enough.

Elizabeth was in the house alone with Mama and Mark. They'd never let her go. Even if she walked out the back door nobody would believe her and anyway Mark and Mama would never let her go. And it was almost time for her period, maybe only a couple of days away. And Elizabeth didn't want to think about how Mama and her brother were going to act when her period came.

So that's why she's waiting in the kitchen now for Mama and Mark to come into the room and find her. Everybody always said she was just like her mother anyway. She guessed it must be true—they were always saying it and now look at Mama crawling into the room on her hands and knees and licking Elizabeth's feet, and there's Mark licking her hand and getting up, getting closer.

"I'm ready for my hug now," she says, trying to keep her voice steady as her mother and brother come closer and wrap her in their terrible long arms and squeeze her in her family's cold embrace until she isn't alone anymore.

"I'm ready," she says, smiling, thinking maybe that at last her Mama would be pleased, pleased that now she was so much like her. But the joke would be on Mama, Mama with her dirty little grown-up secret.

Because Elizabeth would be even better than Mama. Even stronger.

Survival Skills

Deborah Wheeler

Valeria woke to deep rumbling, felt rather than heard. The San Francisco quake? she wondered. Naples in the shadow of Vesuvius? Gas in her bowels? Could be. Animal-rights activists always gave her indigestion.

Boom—*boom*—boom! The rumbling resolved into a basso rhythm. Not even triple-paned glass and blackout curtains could keep out the drumbeat bursting from her neighbor's garage. She supposed it was some form of rock music, although it reminded her of a steam engine with hiccups.

Boom—boom—*BOOM*!

Where else but California, Hollywood to be precise?

As Valeria sat up, the water-bed mattress of her coffin oozed under her weight. Condensation had turned the native soil within it to mud. In the velvety darkness, she circled the living room, checking the locks on door and windows. Her nerves prickled, a sign of her hunger. She should have hunted last night, she knew, but she was trying to diet.

Through the rumbling, Valeria heard the tapping of footsteps up the stairs. Smiling, she headed for the front door. With any luck, breakfast had come to her. She remembered to flick on the lights.

The man on the doorstep carried a clipboard bristling with papers. He waved a badge in her direction, then shoved it back in the pocket of his rumpled, avocado-colored jacket. "Mrs. Romanek?"

Valeria nodded, deciding it would be imprudent for him to disappear in her vicinity. Someone else with a badge would surely come looking for him. Nobody minded his own business in this century.

"Leo Martinez, L.A. Unified Child and Welfare Attendance Counselor. That's a newfangled way of saying 'truant officer.' I'm investigating an anonymous tip that you have two children who are not currently enrolled in school. May I come in?"

This was really too bizarre, Valeria thought, a *human* asking permission to cross *her* threshold! But refusing would not change the fact that the authorities had become aware of her and her children. Records already existed of that complaint, from some snoopy neighbor no doubt, records on those damnable computer networks. She must cause them to become unsuspicious as quickly as possible.

She led the way to the living room. With the indirect lighting system she'd installed, it suggested a cavern. The central skylight had been roofed over and the cobwebs were finally thick enough to give the ceiling a pleasingly decrepit appearance. The few pieces of age-darkened furniture blended into the shadows.

Martinez brushed a layer of dust from the sofa and sat down, glancing around. "Now, then, you have two children? And how old are they?"

Valeria tried to reckon how old Kyra and Jess looked in

human terms. She'd kept them with her far longer than her own mother had done with her and her sisters. Three hundred years ago, a child wandering alone and apparently helpless was nothing more than an easy victim or an unpleasantness to be ignored, but today they could not be turned loose until they looked adult. Who knew how many vampire parents had been driven insane in this century, when "the terrible twos" might last for several decades?

She made a guess at ten and eight years old, adding, "I teach them everything they need to know."

"Home schooling, eh? You're a certified teacher?"

"Not exactly—"

"Mrs. Romanek, today's society is even more complicated than ever and we have to give our children every advantage if they're to compete successfully. The three R's are only the beginning of what a child needs. That's why we offer special classes in computers and—"

"You do not understand! My children have a rare condition, an . . . allergy to sunlight. They cannot leave the house except at night."

"Oh, that explains why this place is sealed up so tight. Must be some allergy." Martinez smiled, showing even, white teeth. He probably had no idea how threatening the expression was. "Normally we would require a doctor's certificate for an exemption, but I can offer you a better solution. Last year, we received a Baird grant for families whose parents work at night. Classes start at nine P.M." He slipped a fresh form on top of the stack in his clipboard and clicked his pen open. "Sign here, please."

Valeria scrawled something illegible on the form. She had learned over the years to avoid outright confrontation with authorities. It was far safer to quietly disappear.

* * *

After Martinez left, the children crept out of the bedroom. They wore their usual hunting clothes, torn and stained as if they'd been foraging in the alleys, which of course they had. One glance at their faces told Valeria they'd overheard the entire conversation.

"Do we have to move again?" Kyra asked. Relocating involved safeguarding their supplies of native earth, traveling at night and securing new accommodations, as well as protecting the hoard of uncanceled postage stamps which furnished Valeria's income. She still had two Penny Blacks in her cache, although it was getting more difficult to sell them to private collectors, even the Japanese, without documentation.

Reluctantly, she nodded. "We have no alternative."

"We could do what he said," Jess piped up.

"Send you to school? Impossible!"

Jess marched up to her, Kyra at his heels. "You've taught us to hunt in stranger places."

"Do you have any idea of the risk involved?" Valeria shrieked. She had not felt such roiling anxiety since she fled Victorian London. Her mate had perished when his coffin was discovered empty one night, stolen, and subsequently sold to a museum in Auckland as an Etruscan watering trough. "This is not the beaches or video arcades. One slip and the authorities will surely take notice!"

Both children immediately hushed. Once, when they had been particularly disobedient, she'd taken them to a Dracula movie. They emerged from the theater whimpering from the graphic depiction of stakes driven through the heart, crosses branded on naked skin, coffins splintered or set ablaze, flesh crumbling into dust at the touch of dawn. *"You be good,"* she'd told them, *"or the vanhelsing will get you!"*

This time Jess held his ground. "No one will notice us. We're good at blending in, you said so yourself. And besides. . . ." He paused. "It's so *boring* having to stay here when we're not out hunting. There's nothing to *do*."

Kyra's eyes brightened. "Please? We'll be good, we promise!"

In the end, Valeria gave in. After all, they had far more discipline than she'd had at their age. If they could successfully pass as humans, then a short attendance at the school might buy them all some precious time. And maybe lead to a solution to those blasted computers.

Before the children left the first night, Valeria reminded them, "Keep your fangs retracted at all times. No draining, no sipping. And absolutely no turning into bats!"

"Yes, Mama," Kyra murmured. In her new clothes, she looked like a street waif who'd been given a bath in white-wash.

Jess's mouth twitched, and Valeria glared at him, her eyes flashing red, until he squirmed and hung his head. She grasped his hand in hers, hard enough to snap the bones of a normal child, and led them to the neighborhood school. She'd surveyed it earlier when delivering the forged immunization papers to the office.

This time, a uniformed guard stood just inside the gate. It was too late to retreat without drawing attention to herself. Valeria pressed her lips together and passed him at a stately walk, not daring to respond when he nodded to her.

After the teachers led the children into the classroom, Valeria glided into the shadows. She kept turning back, wondering what was happening, what sort of catastrophe might be brewing. She'd never been inside a modern school, she had no idea what the other children might say or do, or how Kyra and Jess might react. There was so much she hadn't warned them about. Suppose another child offered them bubble gum?

Fretfully, she went to hunt, selecting several out-of-town

businessmen. She sipped shallowly so as not to render them seriously anemic and left them with a posthypnotic suggestion to contribute generously to the Wildlife Fund's "Save the Bats" campaign.

At the end of the school session, she arrived early to find a cluster of parents standing in the pooled streetlight. One of them, a wiry, pale-haired woman, spotted Valeria and marched up to her, hand outstretched.

"Hi! I'm Marge, PTA Hospitality—here's my phone number—and I'd like to personally invite you to our Planning Committee meeting this Friday, ten P.M. There are so many ways you can help improve the school—class parent, library volunteer, bake sale for the Open House—"

Valeria gave Marge her coldest, most predatory stare. Marge seemed not to notice.

"—assisting in our new science lab, running a booth for our Halloween Festival. It's our big fund-raiser. No, forget the booth, I'm drafting you for our raffle hostess." Marge slipped one hand through the crook of Valeria's elbow and drew her toward the other parents. Valeria was too surprised to resist. "Hey, Al! We've got a new recruit here. Won't she make a great Lady Dracula?"

Valeria nearly dropped her fangs, she was so horrified. How had she given herself away?

"Oh, perfect!" one of the men said. "Camp is camp, but another year of Raoul as Elvira is just too much."

Someone else said, "Do you work in the Industry?"

"Industry?" Valeria asked, desperate to change the conversation.

"You know," the man named Al said, "movies, TV, live theater. Showbiz." He looked vaguely familiar, and she realized with a shock that he was her rock-music neighbor.

She lifted her chin and said in her iciest voice, "Certainly not."

"Too bad, you have great stage presence."

The group of parents turned, like birds swerving in flight, as the children began filing out, each class behind its own teacher. Valeria could see no bruises or torn clothing, no signs of dried blood. Kyra and Jess rushed forward with the rest of their classmates, their faces alight.

As Valeria hurried away, a child in each hand, Marge's voice floated after her. "We'll see you at our next meeting!"

Valeria locked the door behind them, although she didn't bother turning on the lights. "What happened? Did either of you draw attention to yourselves?"

"Only when the other kids ate their meals," said Jess. "The teacher was upset that we didn't have any, so she gave us tickets to get ours in the cafeteria."

"We hid in the toilet until it was time to go back to class," Kyra added, her eyes big.

"*I* didn't hide in a toilet," said Jess.

Kyra punched him hard enough to send him tumbling over the arm of the sofa. Valeria reached out to prevent Jess from retaliating. "Remember your manners, both of you! Is this how the other children at school behave?"

"Yes," Kyra said sweetly.

"Well, this is one thing you are *not* to learn from them, is that clear?"

"But Mom." Kyra looked thoughtful. "What if someone bites me first?" She held out her arm, unmarked, but Valeria sensed the pressure residues from an arc of human teeth.

"Carlos," Jess said, somewhat smugly.

"And I *didn't* bite him back," Kyra sniffed.

"And then Carlos said it was because one of his teeth was loose—"

"*Loose!*" Kyra echoed dramatically.

"Yeah," Jess rattled on, growing more expansive with every phrase, "and it's gonna fall *out*—"

"And *then*," Kyra concluded triumphantly, "the *tooth fairy* is going to come and put *new teeth* under his pillow!"

If Valeria hadn't been so anxious, she would have laughed. Neither Jess nor Kyra had been allowed to hunt human children; how could they know? "I assure you that no matter what happens to Carlos's teeth," she said, "*yours* will not fall out. They will enlarge naturally as you grow. What you do about this Carlos is to stay as far away from him as possible."

Once the children had gotten the meal routine down and learned to ask to go to the bathroom from time to time, things went relatively smoothly. Every day they brought home drawings, PTA announcements, and homework assignments. Once they emerged from class with a grubby-faced boy in tow.

"This is Carlos," Jess said proudly. "He wants to come home with us."

"Absolutely not," Valeria said.

"I won't bite her no more." Carlos grinned, revealing a large gap between his top teeth.

"I'm quite sure you won't, but you nevertheless cannot come home with us." Valeria grabbed Jess and Kyra by the hand and hurried them away from the school yard and down a side street. When they were out of earshot, she demanded, "No hunting at school! And a child, too!"

"We weren't—" Jess began.

"Then what were you going to do with him? Keep him as a pet?"

"We-ell," said Kyra, brightening.

"How many times do I have to tell you not to play with your food!"

"Okay, we get the point," Jess said. "Then how about a

VCR instead? There are all these great cartoons we could tape on Saturday mornings."

Kyra piped up, "And I want six Barbies, just like Allison—"

"Barbies? Eww, gross!" Jess rolled his eyes.

"—and Dino Doodles and a skateboard and My First Telephone—"

"That's enough, both of you!" Valeria cried with such force the children flinched. They looked at her with bright, accusing eyes, and she couldn't think of a suitable follow-up. They'd never hounded her for toys before. She didn't know what half the things they'd asked for were.

When they got home, she found the slip of paper with Marge's phone number and called up to ask what other mothers did in such circumstances.

"I call that one the Great American Twinkie Ploy," Marge laughed. "My own kid never *touched* white sugar until the day he started kindergarten and then he came home crazy for every sort of processed garbage."

Valeria gave silent thanks there was one form of insanity her children had escaped.

"It's tough enough raising kids in this town on a normal schedule," Marge chattered on. "There's a bunch of us who get together Friday nights at Pizzaland. You know, the one with the play area? We order a few beers, maybe an extra large with everything on it, and swap war stories."

"I do not drink . . . beer."

"Me either. Never could stand the taste of the stuff. Don't worry, we've got other parents in A.A., too."

Pizzaland was outside Valeria's normal hunting territory and on Friday night—Saturday morning, by the time the half dozen of them were all settled in the corner table—the place was still doing a brisk business.

Valeria sat down, dizzy from the lingering reek of garlic, as

Marge made introductions all around. Valeria recognized some of the parents from the group that waited at the school gates. They worked at such places as all-night bars, a twenty-four-hour health club, the "Industry," or night shifts at Memorial Hospital.

"You know what the hardest thing is?" one of the nurses said to Valeria. "It's trying to give the kids the same sense of community as they'd get at an ordinary school."

Marge, sitting across the table, nodded. "That's why it's so important to put on family events like the Halloween Festival. Valeria here is going to be our Lady Dracula for the raffle."

"Aah, Marge has put you to work already," said Al, who was sitting on the opposite side of the table. "How about helping out in the computer lab? It took us a solid year to get the equipment donated and even now we don't have enough parent volunteers to staff it."

"Perhaps because they know nothing about computers," Valeria said haughtily.

"That's the easy part. My real job's designing security systems for computers. I can teach you more than you ever dreamed possible about them."

"You can? You will?" Valeria blinked in surprise. She had read of ways to manipulate the information computers contained, change it or even remove it entirely. If mortal hackers could break into closely guarded military systems, surely she could forge a driver's license or a credit history. Or eliminate a school attendance record.

Al grinned, his eyes crinkling. "We'll count on you for Monday."

Before Valeria could reply, Kyra and Jess came running up with the news that Carlos had invited them to play with his Nintendo set. Valeria opened her mouth to refuse.

"It's really all right, I'd love to have them," said Carlos's mother, a cashier at a twenty-four-hour grocery. "I'll pick them up after school and drop them at your place."

"Please, Mom!" Jess and Kyra said in chorus.

"We'll talk about it later," Valeria said.

It had been a long time since Valeria had walked along a hallway as noisy as the school's. Her ears quivered with a dozen jumbled rhythms, which made her neighbor's drumming seem sedate by comparison. It was almost as bad as the incessant clanging of the pipes during those three unpleasant years in the tunnels beneath the New York City subways.

The door to the computer lab stood open, and she peeked in. Rows of tables filled the room, each one the center of a cluster of squirming, chattering children. At the far end of the room, Al looked up and gestured for her to come inside.

Dodging several parents as they darted from one group to another in response to calls for help, Valeria made her way across the room. She looked over Al's shoulder at the computer screen. Every diagram was labeled, and a border running below the main display listed various codes, including one that said HELP. Could it, she wondered, truly be that simple?

Al explained to her the children's current project, constructing a bar graph from the measurements of their heights. "The thing to remember about computers is that they're powerful but very stupid. They'll do exactly what you tell them and nothing more."

"A truly human device," she murmured.

"Just make sure the kids follow the steps in order. If the computer erps at them, chances are they've made a typo. If you want to know more, we can hang around after class."

Hang around? Valeria suppressed a smile at the image of the two of them suspended by their feet from the ceiling. Despite her objections to his music, she did linger after the class had left.

"You pick this stuff up faster than anyone I've seen," Al said afterward. They went around the classroom, turning off the computers and picking up trash paper.

"It's just a set of instructions," she said, shrugging. Compared to the passport regulations for Rumanian nationals resident in post-Revolutionary France or the laws of sixteenth-century Naples, these rules were pitifully simple.

"I would like to learn more about computers," she said.

"Got the bug, huh? Well, there's a bunch of us hackers that get together Thursday nights at the high school, and you're welcome to come."

"I do not possess one of these machines myself."

"That's no problem, there's usually someone selling a system cheap in order to upgrade. I'll make sure you get what you need."

Valeria thought, *You have no idea what I need.* But then it occurred to her that she herself was no longer so sure what that was.

The computer club meetings ran past school hours, so after some deliberation, Valeria allowed the children to play at Carlos's that night. It was a risk, but their behavior had improved considerably. Jess had even come home with a "Satisfactory" mark in "Work Habits and Cooperation."

The club members were something of a novelty to Valeria. They were almost as pale as she, either painfully thin or obese, their blood reeking of sugar and caffeine. Yet there was an irreverence about them she found appealing. They cared more about whether a problem was challenging than whether solving it was strictly legal.

Before the evening was over, Valeria had purchased a used computer system, including a printer and modem. Al drove her home and helped her carry the equipment inside. He set it on the antique desk, connected the modem, and showed Valeria how to sign up for an electronic bulletin board. To her surprise, she detected the unmistakable traces of another vampire on the medical network, a trilingual pun on the word "coffin" and a coded recognition signal in medieval Slavic. She suspected she'd met him before, maybe in Naples. He ran a service for hospitals and clinics, locating rare blood types. Al didn't seem to notice anything odd about it.

A knock at the door signaled Carlos's mother, dropping off Kyra and Jess. They bounded in the front door, chattering about Carlos's new Nintendo game.

"What a dumb setup," Jess said. "Can you believe it, there's a mummy, Frankenstein monster and a werewolf, together with a real vampire. All of them up against this creepy vanhelsing. And guess who wins? The vanhelsing! Pathetic."

"Mom, I bet you could design a better game!" said Kyra.

"Sounds great to me," said Al. "You've got a real knack for the logic, and a screwball imagination. I've got some game designer friends I could put you in touch with."

For a moment, Valeria thought, *Why not?* Computers used a language like any other, and languages, like regulations, were something with which she'd gained considerable facility over the centuries. She would benefit from a second source of income and she could certainly set her own hours. But what was wrong with her, to even consider working with a human?

"Bye, kids," Al said as he walked out the door. "See you around, Val."

Jess spotted the computer, which Al had left turned on. "Wow! Wait til Carlos sees *this*!"

" 'Wait til Carlos,' nothing," said Valeria. "I've warned you about developing friendships with mortals."

"Too late now," said Kyra breezily.

"So what about this computer dude of yours?" Jess said. " *'See you, Val'!*"

Valeria glared at him. He swallowed. "I guess this is a bad time to ask for a Nintendo set, huh?"

"Very bad time."

"I think you're wrong about humans being so suspicious." Kyra ran one finger along the edge of the computer keyboard. "When we started school, I was scared of making a mistake and having someone find out. But I had it all backward. Once they get to know you, you can do any kind of wacky thing and they won't care. Chances are, they won't even notice."

"Not in this town, anyway," said Jess. "You think we're weird, Mom, you should see some of the other kids' families. Marco's parents won't let him wear leather shoes, Tom's dad works in a job that's so secret it doesn't even exist, and Heather has three daddies, two iguanas, and a linear accelerator in the garage. I'll bet I can turn into a bat in front of a hundred people and no one will think anything's strange."

"Don't you dare!" Valeria said.

"Okay, okay," Jess said, but after her initial spasm of relief had faded, Valeria thought he'd given in a bit too easily.

On Halloween night, Valeria wore her festival costume, a long stretchy black dress and wig. She set aside the false fangs in favor of the comfort of her own. Jess was going as a samurai turtle and Kyra a fairy with glitter-dusted wings. She'd promised them a night of true trick-or-treating afterward.

The night of the festival was warm, the air tinged with firecracker smoke. Orange and black crepe paper streamers festooned the gymnasium, along with balloons and cardboard figures of skeletons, goblins, and witches. At the far end, a plywood castle dripped string spiderwebs and construction-paper bats from its painted towers. Marge, dressed as

Raggedy Ann with her wig of red yarn hair askew, waved hello as they entered.

The room filled quickly with families and neighbors. Valeria's nerves tingled with the closeness of so many warm-blooded bodies. She made a slow circuit of the room, the booths where one could win a live goldfish, dunk a Barbie doll in a tub of water, or throw a whipped-cream pie at one's teacher.

"Good eve-ning," came a voice at her shoulder.

She whirled, controlling her attack reflex. It took a moment to recognize Al under the white face paint, false fangs, lipstick dribbled over his chin. Swirling the folds of his high-collared black cape, he executed a theatrical bow and reached out to take her hand. She jerked it away just as he was about to kiss it.

"Sorry," he said in his normal voice. "I didn't mean to scare you. You look really terrific in that outfit."

Suddenly, a bloodcurdling wail came from the top of the plywood castle, filling the gym as it degenerated into a mad cackle. A figure appeared next to the turret, its face a pale glimmer in the shadows. It spread its arms wide, extending batlike wings to a chorus of gasps and murmurs. A few children giggled in delight, crying, "Batman!" or "the Phantom!" but Valeria stood frozen in horror.

Too late to intervene without revealing herself, she watched Jess lean further and further until he began to fall. The audience cried out, pointing and howling with laughter. The next instant, he was gone, replaced by a flurry of tissue paper bats, swirling and swooping over the heads of the audience so that no one noticed a single real bat as it darted out the exit door.

Wild applause burst out around Valeria. All around her, people exclaimed at what a realistic stunt that had been.

Al plucked a paper bat from her hair. "I wonder where the school hired that stunt man. You could almost believe he was really going to fall. I expected some kind of wire-harness flying act, but this was great."

She stared at him, caught between fury at Jess and astonishment at how easily the mortal mind supplied a rational explanation.

"Listen," he said, "we're having a block party Saturday night. You've probably heard our band practicing, huh? We'll fire up the old barbecue—"

"I cannot come," Valeria cut him off automatically. "We have certain dietary restrictions—"

"Oh." He waved one hand. "Half the neighborhood is either vegetarian or kosher Jews or on some crazy macrobiotic diet. Don't worry, just bring your own food. And your dancing feet, okay?"

Valeria said she'd think about it. She was about to go looking for Jess when the raffle was announced. She managed to get through it, drawing the winning numbers from a large papier-mâché bowl in the shape of a human skull. A number of people came up to her afterward and complimented her on her costume, her makeup, even her fangs.

"They look so real," one woman said. "It's simply wonderful what they can do with plastic these days."

"And now," Marge's voice came floating across the loudspeaker system, "for our special award, to the most valuable new volunteer. For her outstanding contribution to the computer lab, as well as her memorable Lady Dracula impersonation—we will count on her to repeat it next year—I award this certificate, redeemable for a steak dinner for two, to Ms. Valeria Romanek!"

The crowd applauded as Valeria made her way to the loudspeaker. Jess and Kyra, who had reappeared in the audience, jumped up and down, cheering. Several parents shook her hand or patted her on the back, almost dislodging the wig.

Valeria looked out over the sea of faces and for the first

time she could remember, she did not feel afraid. Instead, she was filled with a mad bravado, a desire to equal Jess's spectacle. But what? What would these mortals think if she started feeding off them, one by one?

But, Valeria realized with a shiver, that was the one thing she could never do now. If the school community had made her into a sort of mascot, the reverse was also true. They belonged to her now, Marge and Carlos and even rock-music Al, all the children who played with her own and pestered her during computer lab.

She would have to move in a few years, before the children's slow growth became too noticeable or the romantic attentions of Al too pressing. But until then, these bumbling, inept people had ensured their own survival.

Valeria took a deep breath and stepped up to the microphone, praying for inspiration. It came in an unexpected form.

After all, this was Hollywood.

"Thank you, everyone!" Valeria bared her fangs and spread her arms wide in her most dramatic gesture. The wide sleeves of her costume swirled out like a cape. The audience fell silent, waiting. "You know, we vampires are just like ordinary people. We get up in the evening, go to work, meet our friends at the corner bar. I like a good Bloody Mary. Especially if she's still alive and kicking."

Laughter ripped through the crowd. The uniformed guard in the front row guffawed. Valeria tingled all over. She'd never felt this wild exhilaration before, better than flying. Ideas exploded in her mind like firecrackers.

"Of course," she went on, "being a vampire lends an entirely new meaning to many ordinary situations. Suppose, for example, someone says they've been *dying to meet you*? Or asks you out for a *steak dinner*? Or how about *just hanging around*?

"Speaking of which, did you hear the one about the undertaker, the spaceman and the vampire. . . ."

She went on like that for more than ten minutes, until tears ran down the faces of the people in the front row and Marge was bending over, holding her sides. The audience ate up every moment of it.

In fact, you might say they went bats.

Tumbling Down the Nighttime

DEAN WESLEY SMITH

Nightly routine:

Between one and one-fifteen, the nurse, an over-busted, overthighed woman with bottle-thick glasses, would rudely flip on the overhead light, pull back his covers, and check to see if the sheets were wet.

They usually were. A source of continued embarrassment. More so with the presence of the almost-always-young, almost-always-pretty aide.

The routine went on.

Without a smile, the nurse would say, "Ed, I'm going to change your bed now and clean you up. All right?" With the help of the aide she'd grab him under the arm and butt and roll him to one side. God, that hurt. Their rough, always-clean hands were sandpaper against his thin, aged skin.

They never asked him to help. He always groaned. What more was there for him to say? Some nights he would try to remember being young, being with Rebecca, running and playing baseball. Anything but the routine. But it very seldom took him from the reality. So he just groaned.

In answer to his groan, the nurse would say, "Ed, I've got to change your sheets. It will just take a minute. All right?"

As if he had a choice.

The routine went on.

They'd pull up the sheets from the hall side of the bed while he lay with his back to them, bare ass exposed to God and anyone who chose to walk down the hall at that moment. Then she'd take a wet cloth, always cold, and clean him. He wished some night the nurse would use a warm cloth.

She never did.

The routine went on.

The two of them would grab him again, roll him back over on the clean sheet side, pull up the rest of the old sheet, and finish putting down the new one. Then, with their sandpaper hands, they'd roll him onto his back, pull the sheet loosely over him and flip off the light on the way out, leaving him bruised, battered and exhausted from the battle.

End of routine.

He glanced at his glow-in-the-dark clock: 1:00 A.M. The nurse and the aide would be in any moment. He focused his mind on Rebecca, her dark eyes and jet-black hair. They had been lovers for years until finally she had left him, without warning or reason. But those years with her had been his best, and they were now the years he focused on when trying to escape the routine.

An intense white flash brought the room into sharp focus before he could snap his eyes shut. It surprised him and he jumped. For a brief moment he thought it might have been the nurse and the overhead fluorescent bulb had just exploded.

But instead of the nurse's voice or footsteps, a loud crash filled the room. The building groaned. His bed shook. The picture of Maggie, his dead wife, rattled on the nightstand. He could hear glass shattering from somewhere down the hall.

Then it ended.

Another new sound. He opened his eyes as shouting came from down the hall. It sounded like he was suddenly in a hospital and someone was trying to die.

The hall lights flickered, then went out. A dull engine sound came from the back of the building and the lights came back on, not quite as bright. Probably the standby generator. He wondered what could have happened to cause the power to go out.

Next he heard doors slam, a woman sob, "Oh, no," and footsteps running. It all ended with one final door slam.

Buzzers exploded in the nurse's station like horses from a starting gate as residents, disturbed by the noise, rang for the hired help. That was a sound he always tried, and failed, to put to the back of his mind. The buzzing sound was a part of nursing home routine that he heard every day. Every hour. A sound that annoyed him, grated at his nerves, and made him angry. He never understood why, since he was here to die, he couldn't do it without the metallic sound of others doing the same thing.

He quickly checked the darkened room. His roommate, Mel, still slept, snoring like he always did. Mel could sleep through anything. Everything else seemed to be in its place. The clock said 1:03. He strained to listen for any sound as the clock's ticking got louder and louder until it fought to cover the sounds of the buzzers.

Mel's snoring kept time with the clock. He always slept soundly, dreaming dreams of the war he'd fought in years earlier. His dreams continued through his waking hours and he talked of nothing else. WW II . . . the Big One. Mel yearned for the time when dying seemed glorious and purposeful instead of boring and without pride. Someday, in a dream, Mel would catch a bullet while leading his platoon and die in his sleep. For him it would then be worthwhile.

The nurse and the aide would change Mel's sheets and roll in a new roommate so Ed would have company. Then he and his new roommate would race to see who would die first.

It had happened twice before. Ed had lost the race both times.

But tonight they were racing on a new track. Over the buzzers, the ticking of the clock and Mel's battle snores, Ed could hear Mrs. Reeges, two doors down, ring for the nurse. He could tell her buzz because it sounded higher, as if something was slightly broken with it. She always rang around one in the morning. She needed her fix of pills. Sometimes she rang before the nurse attacked him. Sometimes during. Once in a while after. She stayed in her routine now and rang for the nurse, mixing her useless annoyance with that of others.

Mel continued his snoring, successfully dodging bullets, the clock kept its ticking, and a moment later, Mrs. Reeges rang again. No one answered any of the rings. No movement in the halls at all.

Mrs. Reeges rang again.

Then again.

Where the hell was the damn nurse?

Ed thought about the large woman who changed his bed five nights a week. He knew through the grapevine that she had two kids and a husband who worked swing shift at the plywood plant. She didn't much give a shit about any of the residents. To her they were just like the rough lumber her husband tossed around. The two aides who were the only other employees who worked the night shift were both students and both newly married. They cared even less. It had been lucky nothing much ever happened on graveyard shift.

Except people dying. The nurse and the aides never had any trouble with that.

Mrs. Reeges let out a yell.

"Nurse!"

Ed knew she would yell eventually. Others were starting to. Mrs. Reeges would panic and follow their lead.

"Nurse!" Her voice, weak and raspy, barely carried over the rhythmic duo of Mel and the clock.

"Nurse . . . please?"

All the yelling and buzzing was becoming damn annoying. He could imagine the nurse's station echoing, empty, its colored metal folders in stacked slots with name tags below each. Last week he had noticed that every name tag had a small white tab on the right side to ease in the tag's removal when the owner died. That's how it was around here.

Tonight no workers answered the grating sound of the buzzers. No one rushed in to change his sheets. No one would remove his tag when he died. Not even the white tab would help at the moment. Something major had happened out in the street, or against the side of the building, to make all three employees leave.

Mrs. Reeges rang again, then yelled, "Nurse!"

She had now combined the ring and the yell. She sounded desperate. His sheets felt cold and downright uncomfortable.

Damn it all. "Nurse!" he yelled. His voice sounded weak and hollow. Mel snorted in time with the clock.

Mrs. Reeges rang again. She didn't yell. Maybe she figured that he would do all the yelling. She would do the ringing and he the yelling. Now they were a team of sorts.

"Nurse!" he yelled again, this time his voice carrying more authority. He waited, breathing shallowly, to hear the answer. He could almost hear Mrs. Reeges waiting, breathing shallowly.

She rang again. He yelled with authority. They waited. He

could hear over the buzzing some movement from other residents. No help.

No amount of authority in his yell would bring help. The workers weren't coming back for a while. He was sure of that. He could feel it in the silence over the buzzing and the snoring and the ticking.

Mrs. Reeges rang. She expected him to yell. There was no point.

A minute later, she rang again and yelled, taking up his part of the team. He turned his head from the door toward the curtain over the patio door and the faint light coming from outside.

"Hello, Ed," a soft voice said and a shadowy shape stepped toward the bed. "Do you need something I can get for you?"

He jerked on the wet sheet like a fish out of water and for a moment he thought his heart was going to pound right out of his chest. The shadow outlined against the curtains moved closer to the bed as he fought to catch his breath.

"I'm sorry," a woman's voice said. "I didn't mean to startle you."

"But you sure as hell did," Ed managed to choke out, taking deep breaths. "How'd you get in here?"

She laughed softly, and Ed's stomach twisted. He knew that laugh. But it couldn't be.

"How about turning on a light so I can see who's giving me a heart attack?" He pointed to the lamp on the nightstand beside the bed. The shadow moved to the lamp and with a click lit the room with soft yellow light.

Down the hall the buzzers and the yelling for the nurses continued. Mel kept snoring and life beyond the circle of the lamplight kept on. Ed blinked a few times and then looked up into a face he hadn't seen in forty years, a face that every night he dreamed about, a face that couldn't be. "Rebecca . . . ?"

"Hi, Ed," she said, putting her hand on his arm. Her cool touch sent shivers though him. "It's good to see you again."

All he could do was stare. She was still just as young as he remembered her. Her black eyes sparkled in the lamplight and her long black hair shined. She had on a short black leather coat and Levis. And she was more beautiful than he remembered.

He wanted to run, but his body wouldn't move. He wanted to scream, but he knew it would do no good mixed with the calls and buzzers of the others. He wanted to reach out and hug her as he had done forty years ago, but fear held him back.

"Can I sit for a moment?" She pointed to his wheelchair, and he somehow managed to nod.

He watched her, trying desperately to clear his mind, as she pulled the chair over beside the bed and sat in it, again putting her cool hand on his arm. He shook his head and laughed. "I'm dreaming, aren't I? Or I'm dead and you've come to take me to heaven. That's it. I'm dead." Somehow that thought comforted him and he managed a deep breath. If he was dead, why couldn't he move? Why couldn't he climb out of bed and go down to the nurse's station and pull his white tag, so everyone would know?

She laughed and again the memories of all those wonderful nights of laughter with her flooded over him as if they had happened yesterday.

"You're not dreaming and you're still very much alive."

Ed sighed. "A guy can always hope."

She squeezed his arm and laughed at his poor joke, but this time he could tell her laugh was not sincere.

"So," he said, rolling the best he could to face her, "after all these years, why are you here? Better yet, why did you leave me in the first place?" And as he talked he noticed that there were absolutely no wrinkles at all in her face or around her eyes. She looked twenty-five years old. "And an even more important question, what's the name of your plastic surgeon?"

She smiled. "To answer your questions one at a time, first I'm here because I wanted to see an old friend and maybe see if I can help you a little."

He didn't say anything. There was no way this could be his Rebecca. She was too young. The real Rebecca would have been eighty-one, two years younger than he was. This must be her granddaughter. But why would her granddaughter pretend to be Rebecca?

"Second," she said, "I left you because I had to. If I had stayed you would have noticed that I wasn't aging and you were."

She held up her hand to stop his comment. "Remember how, that last year we were together, people were commenting on how young I looked? Remember how old Charlie the bartender even said I looked like your daughter? I never changed, did I? In all the years we were together, did I age at all?"

He fought his memory, but he knew she was right. It just hadn't seemed important at the time. It had seemed more like a bonus to him. Not important enough for her to leave him. So what if she looked younger than he did? "Go on," he said. "Not that I believe any of this, but do please tell me how you stayed so young." He swept his arm in the general direction of the room around them and then at his almost useless body. "I would love to know your secret."

She held his arm firmly and looked him directly in the eye. "I'm what you would call a vampire. I was over three hundred years old when we met. My four hundredth birthday was two months ago."

He stared into her dark eyes, wanting to believe her, and almost, for a short second, he did. Then he realized fully what she had said, and the laughter overcame him, slowly building in his stomach and finally erupting in such force that it hurt. Tears filled his eyes, and he could feel that he was wetting himself again, the familiar warm feeling mixing with the cold, damp sheets.

She sat up straight in the wheelchair, and it rolled an inch or so back from the bed, but she never let go of his arm, and the serious expression on her face never changed. After a minute or so he finally stopped laughing and worked at catching his breath.

Mel snorted and rolled over. Down the hall the buzzers and the yelling continued.

"I suppose," he said, between gulps of air, "that you are responsible for the nurse and aides leaving."

She nodded. "It was necessary. I just helped a car go out of control. It hit a power pole and plowed into the side of the building. The driver and three passengers were all drunk, but no one was seriously hurt. The nurse should be returning shortly, as soon as the police arrive, so we don't have much time."

He almost started to laugh again, but the cold sheets under his butt and her stern expression stopped him. "You're serious, aren't you?"

She nodded.

"Okay," he said, lifting himself as best he could with his arms and turning so that he could completely face her. "Assuming that I believe you are a vampire, which I don't, why would you come here to see me now after all these years? You want my thin old blood?"

She looked almost hurt at his sick joke. "Think back," she said. "Did you ever see me in the full light of a summer day?"

"You worked days," he said, but that sounded weak even to him.

"No, I usually slept days. Not that the old myth about sunlight killing us is right. It's not. But direct sunlight is very uncomfortable to me, so I have always preferred nights. All vampires do, thus come the myths. And we haven't killed for blood for centuries."

"That's good to know," he said. "Okay, Rebecca was always a night owl, I will grant you that. But that doesn't make you her. Tell me something about her that only I would know." He smiled at her, figuring he had her. But she smiled back, let go of his arm, and stood. In a flash she had unzipped her Levis and pulled them down enough to expose white lace panties. Facing the lamp she pulled the panties down to the top of her black pubic hair, and there was the birthmark.

Rebecca's birthmark.

He glanced up into her serious eyes and then back at the apple-shaped birthmark. An apple with what looked to be a bite taken out of it. A very distinctive, one-of-a-kind birthmark.

"You always used to call it the 'apple of your eye' because you liked to look at it so much." She laughed, again a sincere, deep laugh. "In fact, the last few years you called it an appetizer because it always came right before the main course."

The room was spinning, and he closed his eyes to force it to stop. The clock kept ticking and Mel kept snoring. Down the hall the buzzers were still gong strong. He must be having a nightmare. He would wake up, open his eyes, and the nightly routine would be about to start. It would only be 1:00 A.M. and the nurse would be coming to change his sheets.

He would laugh at the nightmare and tell Mel about it tomorrow morning, birthmark and all. Rebecca was a vampire who had come back to visit him. That would get old Mel laughing for sure.

He opened his eyes. The buzzing continued and the clock said fifteen minutes after one. Rebecca was again sitting in his wheelchair, her cold hand on his arm.

For the longest time he did nothing but stare into her eyes.

The clock ticked. Mel snored. Buzzers buzzed. And he looked into her eyes.

Finally he said, "It really is you, isn't it?"

She had the grace to only nod.

He nodded with her, suddenly more tired than he had felt in years. "So why come back to me now, after forty years?"

She looked away, her gaze moving in jerks around the room. Finally her gaze stopped on the picture of his wife, Maggie, that rested on his nightstand. Maggie had been dead for seven years. They had met and married three years after Rebecca had left him. It had been a good marriage, but nothing more.

"I think I would have liked her," she said, nodding at the picture.

"You can tell that from a picture? Another special power?"

She half-laughed. "No, I'm afraid not. I don't think you ever realized how much I loved you. For most of the past forty years I have kept track of you, watched your life, always from a distance."

"You did?" He stared at her while she continued to stare at the picture of Maggie.

She nodded. "I even managed to meet and talk to Maggie a number of times when you weren't around. Twice, as a matter of fact, in the grocery store line. She seemed to be a very nice person and I was happy for you. It made me very sad when she died."

He glanced at the picture of Maggie and then back at Rebecca, his first and only true love. "I loved her, but never as much as I loved you."

Rebecca turned to face him. "I know," she said. Her grip was firm on his arm, and he placed his other hand over hers.

They stayed that way, in silence, as Mel snored, buzzers called for attention, and the clock ticked the night away.

After a short time a door slammed down the hall, and the sounds of talking drifted over the commotion.

"I don't have much time," she said. "The nurse will be coming soon."

"So come back tomorrow night. We can talk about old times."

She shook her head. "I'm moving on. I have a husband and he was transferred back east to Chicago. We're leaving tomorrow."

"Is he a vampire, too?"

"No," she said softly.

"So you will one day leave him too?"

She looked away, back at Maggie's picture. "Everyone leaves someone sometimes. It's the way of the world."

He glanced at the picture of Maggie and then back at Rebecca. "I knew why Maggie left me. She even said good-bye. I always wondered why you did."

"I know. That's one of the reasons I'm here tonight."

"What's his name?"

"Craig. His name is Craig."

"And you love him?"

She nodded. "Yes, I think I do. But I also still love you." She looked him directly in the eyes and he knew, without a doubt, that she was telling the truth.

They continued to stare at each other. She was still so beautiful, so young and he was so old, so crippled. It didn't seem fair to him that it had turned out this way.

When the buzzers all shut off at once he knew the time was short. He could feel Rebecca starting to pull away. "You said you might be able to help me? What did you mean by that?"

Rebecca glanced at Maggie's picture again and then back into his eyes.

"Can you make me young again? Make me into someone like you? A vampire?"

She shook her head no. "It doesn't work that way. But I can help you out of this."

She nodded at the room, and it took him a moment staring into her serious expression to completely understand. "You could do that?"

She nodded. "If it's what you want."

He laughed a light, halfhearted laugh. "It's been what I have wanted since my legs quit working and I ended up in this damn room. Every night I hope, and even pray, that I will die so I won't have to wake up in a wet bed, or have some nurse's aide lift me onto the toilet in the morning. Getting out of here has been my strongest wish for five years."

She didn't say a word, and again, after a short moment of looking at her, he asked, "You're serious aren't you?"

She nodded.

He closed his eyes and listened to the sounds of the night. The sirens outside, the police coming to the wreck, the muffled talking from the nurse and aides drifting down the hall, Mel's snoring, and the continuous ticking of the clock.

How many nights had he wished for this very thing?

How many thousand nights had he wished he could see Rebecca again?

How many thousand nights had he wished he would just die so he could escape this old, useless body he found himself trapped in?

How many nights?

And now he had both of his wishes all wrapped up together like a sick joke.

He opened his eyes and gazed into her concerned face. "You know, you are as beautiful as ever."

She half-smiled and squeezed his arm as the nurse and aides went into the room across the hall. He would be next on their rounds.

This time her smile filled her face, and the relief was obvious. "I still love you," she said as she leaned forward and kissed his cheek.

"And I love you."

She stood and looked at him for a short moment. Then she moved toward the window.

"Wait!"

She turned, one hand on the drapes.

"Say good-bye this time."

She nodded. "Good-bye, Ed."

"Now that wasn't so hard, was it? And when the time comes, promise me you will say that to Craig."

She stared at him for what seemed like a long, long time. Then she smiled. "I promise."

"Good," he said.

"I love you." She pulled the curtains back and disappeared into the black night.

"I love you, too," he said to the swaying curtains.

A moment later the fluorescent overhead light snapped on and the nurse, an overbusted, overthighed woman with bottle-thick glasses stepped into the room. "Sorry we're late, Ed," she said. "There was an accident outside, so it's been a long night."

"No, actually," he said, still staring at the curtains, "it's been a short life."

The nurse looked at him oddly for a moment, then said, "Let's check to see if these sheets are wet."

And the routine started again.

La Dame

TANITH LEE

'The game is done! I've won! I've won!'
Quote she, and whistles thrice.

The Ancient Mariner
Coleridge.

Of the land, and what the land gave you—war, pestilence, hunger, pain—he had had enough. It was the sea he wanted. The sea he went looking for. His grandfather had been a fisherman, and he had been taken on the ships in his boyhood. He remembered enough. He had never been afraid. Not of water, still or stormy. It was the ground he had done with, full of graves and mud.

His name was Jeluc, and he had been a soldier fourteen of his twenty-eight years. He looked a soldier as he walked into the village above the sea.

Some ragged children playing with sticks called out foul names after him. And one ran up and said, "Give us a coin." "Go to hell," he answered, and the child let him alone. It was not a rich village.

The houses huddled one against another. But at the end of

the struggling, straggling street, a long stone pier went out and over the beach, out into the water. On the beach there were boats lying in the slick sand, but at the end of the pier was a ship, tied fast, dipping slightly, like a swan.

She was pale as ashes, and graceful, pointed and slender, with a single mast, the yard across it with a sail the colour of turned milk bound up. She would take a crew of three, but one man could handle her. She had a little cabin with a hollow window and door.

Birds flew scavenging round and round the beach; they sat on the house roofs between, or on the boats. But none alighted on the ship.

Jeluc knocked on the first door. No one came. He tried the second and third doors, and at the fourth a woman appeared, sour and scrawny.

"What is it?" She eyed him like the Devil. He was a stranger.

"Who owns the pale ship?"

"The ship? Is Fatty's ship."

"And where would I find Fatty?"

"From the wars, are you?" she asked. He said nothing. "I have a boy to the wars. He never came back."

Jeluc thought, Poor bitch. Your son's making flowers in the muck. But then, the thought, What would he have done here?

He said again, "Where will I find Fatty?"

"Up at the drinking-house," she said, and pointed.

He thanked her and she stared. Probably she was not often thanked.

The drinking-house was out of the village and up the hill, where sometimes you found the church. There seemed to be no church here.

It was a building of wood and bits of stone, with a sloping roof, and inside there was the smell of staleness and ale.

They all looked up, the ten or so fellows in the house, from their benches.

He stood just inside the door and said, "Who owns the pale ship?"

"I do," said the one the woman had called Fatty. He was gaunt as a rope. He said, "What's it to you?"

"You don't use her much."

"Nor I do. How do you know?"

"She has no proper smell of fish, or the birds would be at her."

"There you're wrong," said Fatty. He slurped some ale. He did have a fat mouth, perhaps that was the reason for his name. "She's respected, my lady. Even the birds respect her."

"I'll buy your ship," said Jeluc. "How much?"

All the men murmured.

Fatty said, "Not for sale."

Jeluc had expected that. He said, "I've been paid off from my regiment. I've got money here, look." And he took out some pieces of silver.

The men came round like beasts to be fed, and Jeluc wondered if they would set on him, and got ready to knock them down. But they knew him for a soldier. He was dangerous beside them, poor drunken sods.

"I'll give you this," said Jeluc to Fatty.

Fatty pulled at his big lips.

"She's worth more, my lady."

"Is that her name?" said Jeluc. "That's what men call the sea. *La Dame*. She's not worth so much, but I won't worry about that."

Fatty was sullen. He did not know what to do.

The one of the other men said to him. "You could take that to town. You could spend two whole nights with a whore, and drink the place dry."

"Or," said another, "you could buy the makings to mend your old house."

Fatty said, "I don't know. Is my ship. Was my dad's."

"Let her go," said another man. "She's not lucky for you. Nor for him."

Jeluc said, "Not lucky, eh? Shall I lower my price?"

"Some daft tale," said Fatty. "She's all right. I've kept her trim."

"He has," the others agreed.

"I could see," said Jeluc. He put the money on a table. "There it is."

Fatty gave him a long, bended look. "Take her then. She's the lady."

"I'll want provisions," he said. "I mean to sail over to the islands."

A grey little man bobbed forward. "You got more silver? My wife'll see to you. Come with me."

The grey man's wife left the sack of meal, and the dried pork and apples, and the cask of water, at the village end of the pier, and Jeluc carried them out to the ship.

Her beauty impressed him as he walked towards her. To another maybe she would only have been a vessel. But he saw her lines. She was shapely. And the mast was slender and strong.

He stored the food and water, and the extra things, the ale and rope and blankets, the pan for hot coals, in the cabin. It was bare, but for its cupboard and the wooden bunk. He lay here a moment, trying it. It felt familiar as his own skin.

The deck was clean and scrubbed, and above the tied sail was bundled on the creaking yard, whiter than the sky. He checked her over. Nothing amiss.

The feel of her, dipping and bobbing as the tide turned, gave him a wonderful sensation of escape.

He would cast off before sunset, get out on to the sea, in case the oafs of the village had any amusing plans. They were superstitious of the ship, would not use her but possibly did not like to see her go. She was their one elegant thing, like a madonna in the church, if they had had one.

Her name was on her side, written dark.

The wind rose as the leaden sun began to sink.

He let down her sail, and it spread like a swan's wing. It was after all discoloured, of course, yet from a distance it would look very white. Like a woman's arm that had freckles when you saw it close.

The darkness came, and by then the land was out of sight. All the stars swarmed up, brilliant, as the clouds melted away. A glow was on the tips of the waves, such as he remembered. Tomorrow he would set lines for fish, baiting them with scraps of pork.

He cooked his supper of meal cakes on the coals, then lit a pipe of tobacco. He watched the smoke go up against the stars, and listened to the sail, turning a little to the wind.

The sea made noises, rushes and stirrings, and sometimes far away would come some sound, a soft booming or a slender cry, such as were never heard on land. He did not know what made these voices, if it were wind or water, or some creature. Perhaps he had known in his boyhood, for it seemed he recalled them.

When he went to the cabin, leaving the ship on her course, with the rope from the tiller tied to his waist, he knew that he would sleep as he had not slept on the beds of the earth.

The sea too was full of the dead, but they were a long way down. Theirs was a clean finish among the mouths of fishes.

He thought of mermaids swimming alongside, revealing their breasts, and laughing at him that he did not get up and look at them.

He slept.

Jeluc dreamed he was walking down the stone pier out of the village. It was starlight, night, and the pale ship was tied there at the pier's end as she had been. But between him and the ship stood a tall gaunt figure. It was not Fatty or the grey man, for as Jeluc came near, he saw it wore a black robe, like a priest's, and a hood concealed all its skull face but for a broad white forehead.

As he got closer, Jeluc tried to see the being's face, but could not. Instead a white thin hand came up and plucked from him a silver coin.

It was Charon, the Ferryman of the Dead, taking his fee.

Jeluc opened his eyes.

He was in the cabin of the ship called *La Dame*, and all was still, only the music of the water and the wind, and through the window he saw the stars sprinkle by.

The rope at his waist gave its little tug, now this way, now that, as it should. All was well.

Jeluc shut his eyes.

He imagined his lids weighted by silver coins.

He heard a soft voice singing, a woman's voice. It was very high and sweet, not kind, no lullaby.

In the morning he was tired, although his sleep had gone very deep. But it had been a long walk he had had to the village.

He saw to the lines, baiting them carefully, and went over the ship, but she was as she should be. He cooked some more cakes, and ate a little of the greasy pork. The ale was flat and bitter, but he had tasted far worse.

He stood all morning by the tiller.

The weather was brisk but calm enough, and at this rate he would sight the first of the islands by the day after tomorrow.

He might be sorry at that, but then he need not linger longer. He could be off again.

In the afternoon he drowsed. And when he woke, the sun was over to the west like a bullet in a dull dark rent in the sky.

Jeluc glimpsed something. He turned, and saw three thin men with ragged dripping hair, who stood on the far side of the cabin on the afterdeck. They were quite still, colourless and dumb. Then they were gone.

Perhaps it had been some formation of the clouds, some shadow cast for a moment by the sail. Or his eyes, playing tricks.

But he said aloud to the ship, "Are you haunted, my dear? Is that your secret?"

When he checked his lines, he had caught nothing, but there was no law which said he must.

The wind dropped low and, as yesterday, the clouds dissolved when the darkness fell, and he saw the stars blaze out like diamonds, but no moon.

It seemed to him he should have seen her, the moon, but maybe some little overcast had remained, or he had made a mistake.

He concocted a stew with the pork and some garlic and apple, ate, smoked his pipe, listened to the noises of the sea.

He might be anywhere. A hundred miles from any land. He had seen no birds all day.

Jeluc went to the cabin, tied the rope, and lay down. He slept at once. He was on the ship, and at his side sat one of his old comrades, a man who had died from a cannon shot two years before. He kept his hat over the wound shyly, and said to Jeluc, "Where are you bound? The islands? Do you think you'll get there?"

"This lady'll take me there," said Jeluc.

"Oh, she'll take you somewhere."

Then the old soldier showed him the compass, and the needle had gone mad, reared up and poked down, right down, as if indicating hell.

Jeluc opened his eyes and the rope twitched at his waist, this way, that.

He got up, and walked out on to the deck.

The stars were bright as white flames, and the shadow of the mast fell hard as iron on the deck. But it was all wrong.

Jeluc looked up, and on the mast of the ship hung a wiry man, with his long grey hair all tangled round the yard and trailing down the sail, crawling on it, like the limbs of a spider.

This man Jeluc did not know, but the man grinned, and he began to pull off silver rings from his fingers and cast them at Jeluc. They fell with loud cold notes. A huge round moon, white as snow, rose behind the apparition. Its hand tugged and tugged, and Jeluc heard it curse. The finger had come off with the ring, and fell on his boot.

"What do you want with me?" said Jeluc, but the man on the mast faded, and the severed finger was only a drop of spray.

Opening his eyes again, Jeluc lay on the bunk, and he smelled a soft warm perfume. It was like flowers on a summer day. It was the aroma of a woman.

"Am I awake now?"

Jeluc got up, and stood on the bobbing floor, then he went outside. There was no moon, and only the sail moved on the yard.

One of the lines was jerking, and he went to it slowly. But when he tested it, nothing was there.

The smell of heat and plants was still faintly about him, and now he took it for the foretaste of the islands, blown out to him.

He returned to the cabin and lay wakeful, until near dawn he slept and dreamed a mermaid had come over the ship's rail.

She was pale as pale, with ash blonde hair, and he wondered if it would be feasible to make love to her, for she had a fish's tail, and no woman's parts at all that he could see.

Dawn was so pale it seemed the ship had grown darker. She had a sort of flush, her sides and deck, her smooth mast, her outspread sail.

He could not scent the islands anymore.

Rain fell, and he went into the cabin, and there examined his possessions, as once or twice he had done before a battle. His knife, his neckscarf, of silk, which a girl had given him years before, a lucky coin he had kept without believing in it, a bullet that had missed him and gone into a tree. His money, his boots, his pipe. Not much.

Then he thought that the ship was now his possession, too, *his* lady.

He went and stood in the rain and looked at her.

There was nothing on the lines.

He ate pork for supper.

The rain eased, and in the cabin, he slept.

The woman stood at the tiller.

She rested her hand on it, quietly.

She was very pale, her hair long and blonde, and her old-fashioned dress the shade of good paper.

He stood and watched her for some time, but she did not respond, although he knew she was aware of him, and that he watched.

Finally he walked up to her, and she turned her head.

She was very thin, her face all bones, and she had great glowing pale gleaming eyes, and these stared now right through him.

She took her hand off the tiller and put it on his shoulder, and he felt her touch go through him like her look, straight down his body, through his heart, belly and loins, and out at his feet.

He thought, She'll want to go into the cabin with me.

So he gave her his arm.

They walked, along the deck, and he let her pass into the cabin first.

She turned about, as she had turned her head, slowly, looking at everything, the food and the pan of coals, which did not burn now, the blankets on the bunk.

Then she moved to the bunk and lay down, on her back, calm as any woman who had done such a thing a thousand times.

Jeluc went to her at once, but he did not wait to undo his clothing. He found, surprising himself, that he lay down on top of her, straight down, letting her frail body have all his weight, his chest on her bosom, his loins on her loins, but separated by their garments, legs on her legs. And last of all, his face on her face, his lips against hers.

Rather than lust it was the sensuality of a dream he felt, for of course it was a dream. His whole body sweetly ached, and the centre of joy seemed at his lips rather than anywhere else, his lips that touched her lips, quite closed, not even moist nor very warm.

Light delicious spasms passed through him, one after another, ebbing, flowing, resonant, and ceaseless.

He did not want to change it, did not want it to end. And it did not end.

But eventually, he seemed to drift away from it, back into sleep. And this was so comfortable that, although he regretted the sensation's loss, he did not mind so much.

When he woke, he heard them laughing at him. Many men, laughing, low voices and higher ones, coarse and rough as if torn from tin throats and voice boxes of rust. "He's going the same way." "So he is too."

Going the way that they had gone. The three he had seen on the deck, the one above the sail.

It was the ship. The ship had him.

He got up slowly, for he was giddy and chilled. Wrapping one of the blankets about him, he stepped out into the daylight.

The sky was white with hammerheads of black. The sea had a dull yet oily glitter.

He checked his lines. They were empty. No fish had come to the bait, as no birds had come to the mast.

He gazed back over the ship.

She was no longer pale. No, she was rosy now. She had a dainty blush to her, as if of pleasure. Even the sail was like the petal of a rose.

An old man stood on the afterdeck and shook his head and vanished.

Jeluc thought of lying on the bunk, facedown, and his vital juices or their essence draining into the wood. He could not avoid it. Everywhere here he must touch her. He could not lie to sleep in the sea.

He raised his head. No smell of land.

By now, surely, the islands should be in view, up against those clouds there—But there was nothing. Only the water on all sides and below, and the cold sky above, and over that, the void.

During the afternoon, as he watched by the tiller for the land, Jeluc slept.

He found that he lay with his head on her lap, and she was lovely now, prettier than any woman he had ever known. Her hair was honey, and her dress like a rose. Her white skin

flushed with health and in her cheeks and lips three flames.
Her eyes were dark now, very fine. They shone on him.

She leaned down, and covered his mouth with hers.

Such bliss—

He woke.

He was lying on his back, he had rolled, and the sail tilted
over his face.

He got up, staggering, and trimmed the sail.

Jeluc attended to the ship.

The sunset came and a ghost slipped round the cabin, hiding its sneering mouth with its hand.

Jeluc tried to cook a meal, but he was clumsy and scorched
his fingers. As he sucked them, he thought of her kisses. If
kisses were what they were.

No land.

The sun set. It was a dull grim sky, with a hole of whiteness
that turned grey, yet the ship flared up.

She was red now, *La Dame*, her cabin like a live coal, her
sides like wine, her sail like blood.

Of course, he could keep awake through the night. He had
done so before. And tomorrow he would sight the land.

He paced the deck, and the stars came out, white as ice or
knives. There was no moon.

He marked the compass, saw to the sail, set fresh meat on
the lines that he knew no fish would touch.

Jeluc sang old songs of his campaigns, but hours after he
heard himself sing, over and over:

"*She the ship*

"*She the sea*

"*She the she.*"

His grandfather had told him stories of the ocean, of how it
was a woman, a female thing, and that the ships that went out
upon it were female also, for it would not stand any human
male to go about on it unless something were between him

and—her. But the sea was jealous too. She did not like women, true human women, to travel on ships. She must be reverenced, and now and then demanded sacrifice.

His grandfather had told him how, once, they had had to throw a man overboard, because he spat into the sea. It seemed he had spat a certain way, or at the wrong season. He had had, too, the temerity to learn to swim, which few sailors were fool enough to do. It had taken a long while for him to go down. They had told the widow the water washed him overboard.

Later, Jeluc believed that the ship had eyes painted on her prow, and these saw her way, but now they closed. She did not care where she went. And then too he thought she had a figurehead, like a great vessel of her kind, and this was a woman who clawed at the ship's sides, howling.

But he woke up, in time.

He kept awake all night.

In the morning the sun rose, lax and pallid as an ember, while the ship burned red as fire.

Jeluc looked over and saw her red reflection in the dark water.

There was no land on any side.

He made a breakfast of undercooked meal cakes, and ate a little. He felt her tingling through the soles of his boots.

He tested the sail and the lines, her tiller, and her compass. There was something odd with its needle.

No fish gave evidence of themselves in the water, and no birds flew overhead.

The sea rolled in vast glaucous swells.

He could not help himself. He slept.

There were birds!

He heard them calling, and looked up.

The sky, pale grey, a cinder, was full of them, against a sea of stars that were too faint for night.

And the birds, so black, were gulls. And yet, they were gulls of bone. Their beaks were shut like needles. They wheeled and soared, never alighting on the mast or yard or rails of the ship.

I'm dreaming, God help me. God wake me—

The gulls swooped over and on, and now, against the distant diluted dark, he saw the tower of a lighthouse rising. I was the land, at last, and he was saved.

But oh, the lighthouse sent out its ray, and from the opposing side there came another, the lamp flashing out. And then another, and another. They were before him and behind him, and all round. The lit points of them crossed each other on the blank sombre sparkle of the sea. A hundred lighthouses, sending their signals to hell.

Jeluc stared around him. And then he heard the deep roaring in the ocean bed, a million miles below.

And one by one, the houses of the light sank, they went into the water, their long necks like Leviathan's, and vanished in a cream of foam.

All light was gone. The birds were gone.

She came, then.

She was beautiful now. He had never, maybe, seen a beautiful woman.

Her skin was white, but her lips were red. And her hair was the red of gold. Her gown was the red of winter berries. She walked with a little gliding step.

"Lady," he said, "you don't want me."

But she smiled.

Then he looked beyond the ship, for it felt not right to him, and the sea was all lying down. It was like the tide going from the shore, or, perhaps, water from a basin. It ran away, and the ship dropped after it.

And then they were still in a pale nothingness, a sort of beach of sand that stretched in all directions. Utterly becalmed.

"But I don't want the land."

He remembered what the land had given him. Old hurts, drear pains. Comrades dead. Wars lost. Youth gone.

"Not the land," he said.

But she smiled.

And over the waste of it, that sea of salt, came a shrill high whistling, once and twice and three times. Some sound of the ocean he had never heard.

Then she had reached him. Jeluc felt her smooth hands on his neck. He said, "Woman, let me go into the water, at least." But it was no use. Her lips were soft as roses on his throat.

He saw the sun rise, and it was red as red could be. But then, like the ship in his dream, he closed his eyes. He thought, But there was no land.

There never is.

The ship stood fiery crimson on the rising sun, that lit her like a bonfire. Her sides, her deck, her cabin, her mast and sail, like fresh pure blood.

Presently the sea, which moved under her in dark silk, began to lip this blood away.

At first, it was only a reflection in the water, but next it was a stain, like heavy dye.

The sea drank from the colour of the ship, for the sea too was feminine and a devourer of men.

The sea drained *La Dame* of every drop, so gradually she turned back paler and paler into a vessel like ashes.

And when the sea had sucked everything out of her, it let her go, the ship, white as a bone, to drift away down the morning.

Sometimes Salvation

PAT CADIGAN

Ginny's dad turned her out. Yeah, that's right—it ain't an unusual story. Wish I had a dime for every little snipe turned out by dear old dad or the equivalent. Spend a couple days down here and you'll get the idea that that's all anyone's dad does is turn them out. And I don't know which ones make me feel sicker, the girls or the boys. Maybe what makes me sickest of all is that they're all down here with me.

Time was when you never saw a kid living rough and now you can't go ten feet without stepping on one. What is that shit, you may wonder, Shit? Yeah, that's right—you think about what'll make a kid rather sleep rough than stay around home—"home," make that—and you'll think *shit* isn't a strong enough word for it.

Do not, please, get me wrong. I am not St. Francis of Assisi of the street children, my heart is not gold, and I do not want to do anything to improve society or the world. What I am and what I want to do are all very simple: I am a drunk and I want to be drunk as much as possible as long as possible. Very dull compared to what some other people want, or so I hear. Mainly from the kids.

Some of the kids think what I want is too easy, or not interesting enough. I say to them, Yeah, that's right—going off with a john is a lot more interesting, lotta extra challenges in there: will I live through this, is this the one who's gonna give me AIDS. So I guess I can do without *interesting*.

With all the kids coming and going all the time, I don't always notice them right away, and some ain't around long enough for me to notice them. But Ginny I noticed first thing.

She was trying to look like any other chronic troublemaking and repeat-offending dead-end type of kid, and she was good enough that any stupid-ass citizen-zombie would have been fooled. But I know the difference between a kid that got thrown away early and been processed by the sewage-treatment plant they call the juvenile justice system, and a kid who's spent most of her life eating regular and doing homework. Plus, she slipped up when Dropkick brought her around to meet me. Not that I was looking so all-fired up to par that day, it was just that her old civilized reflexes kicked in when the Dropper said, "This is May, she's been here the longest." She actually put out her hand and said, "How do you do."

Even the Dropper stared at her, and the Dropper learned enough manners to pass in polite society himself. Well, never let it be said that I ain't house-trained when I want to be—I invited them both for a drink. Yeah, that's right, I did. And what I gave them is pretty benign shit compared to what everyone else in the world was giving them. Besides which, alcohol is a disinfectant, so it probably killed a bunch of germs and viruses in their systems.

She had just a capful, sipped a little and made a little face. As I recall, I was on the last half of that bottle, so I was stretching it some and it didn't have a whole lot of kick to it. I've mellowed out a lot since the old days when I used to do that trick with a can of Sterno and a loaf of bread.

So I watched her, sitting there under my bridge with me and old Dropkick, and I saw how she was. She was real tall for thirteen, taller than Dropkick, which actually wasn't too hard, and I could tell that she didn't like being so dirty. She kept combing her fingers through her hair and wiping her hands on her jeans, which were pretty loose on her. This girl was, like, *skeletal*, I realized after a bit and I got kind of annoyed. I heard all about anorexics like anybody else and I hate them. Because while I am not St. Francis of the street kids or anything, I ain't completely heartless either, and thinking about how the kids I know don't eat regular, I got no pity in me for someone who's starving on purpose and throwing food away. Or worse, throwing it up. I mean, I am not one to talk but I think that must be one of the few things in the world I'd name a sin if someone asked me. But nobody *did* ask me, did they.

So I looked at her pretty closely then and without too much kindness. And then I thought that if she really was one of those, she probably wouldn't be sitting there sipping Old Overbolt, even watered-down Old Overbolt, because we all know how fattening booze is, right? (I'm laughing my head off at that one.) Finally I say to her, "You hungry?" just to see what she'll say.

And she looks at me with those big brown eyes and nods just ever so slightly. And I look over at Dropkick and say, "What kind of host are you? Go get some food."

Dropkick says, "This isn't *my* place."

And I say, "You know what I mean. You brought her here, I supplied the beverage, so go get us all some hors d'oeuvres."

That got a giggle out of her, and the Dropper obediently got up and went off to see what he could scrounge and left the two of us eyeing each other.

After a long moment of silence, she says, "So how long have you lived under the bridge here in the park?"

And I laugh and say, "You're not from around here, are you, girl."

And then she looks *ashamed*, of all things. So I say, "Yeah, that's right, you're not, but that ain't no big deal. Nobody *around* here is from around *here*. You don't think anyone'd live like this in their own hometown, do you?"

She giggled again and covered her mouth quick, like she'd done something wrong.

"Chill," I say. "It wasn't that funny." The brown eyes get that trapped-animal look. "Never mind, hon, I already got it figured. Only thing I can't figure is why an honor student like you didn't have nowhere else to go."

"Nobody would believe me," she said in that dead voice they all get when they're on about it.

"You know that for a fact?" I asked her.

"Pretty much. I've got three sisters. Two of them don't believe me. The third one knows for sure I'm telling the truth but she also tends to laugh a lot at nothing and she hears voices. She's older than me, and Dad used to like *her* best." She stared at me, daring me something—maybe not to believe her, or to be not squeamish enough to hear her out. Or maybe even both.

"Your mother know?"

"My mother *helped*."

I nodded at her. "Old story around these parts. Plenty others can tell it in several variations, some of 'em even nastier than yours."

She looked a question at me and I shook my head. "Nah. My story's pretty simple. I like my booze and I don't want to be bothered. I don't want men and I don't want women and I sure don't want any kids." She got this defensive look at that one. "Come on, honey, none of you are kids anymore and you should also try not to take the world so personally anyway. I just like my booze, and it likes me. It's always there, it's always good, it don't criticize and it don't make demands. It just does what it says it's gonna do and I say when you got something like that in your life, you're coming out ahead. Think about it."

So then she looks down at the capful in her hands and up at me with this dizzy kind of expression. "Are you telling me I ought to become an alcoholic?"

"Shit, no, honey. I'm just telling you why I am. You go be whatever your heart tells you. While you still have a heart."

And that gave her a turn so that she went even paler than she already was. Yeah, that's right—I told you I am not St. Francis or anything like that, and I have seen them come and go over and over and I know what happens to them. The job that their parents start on them, the streets'll finish up, and if the streets don't do it, juvenile justice surely will.

Assuming none of them gets "saved," that is.

Yeah, that's right—"saved." They come in vans with sodas and coffee and bags full of burgers, blankets during the cold weather. They're all from God, usually, though they don't make the old mistake of trying to get the kids to pray and shit. Even the Salvation Army seems to have wised up to the old casting bread upon the waters gig—what it really is, you throw a bunch of your shit overboard and it sinks and you never see it again. You're gonna help somebody, that's what happens and you don't get your blanket back, okay? But hell, that's the nature of a gift, isn't it? And nobody asked them to come around with their stuff anyway.

But always, some budget somewhere gets cut, and the first thing that goes is the so-called street ministry (this is what

they usually call it). Because they can't think of selling their
fucking mahogany desks or their furniture or shit like that—
they keep their *things* and let the kids go wanting, which is the
way it's always been anyway. So it's not like the kids really
hurt over it or anything.

But they really piss me off when they do that and it just
makes me surer that I like booze better than anything or anyone. Like I said, it always does what it says it's gonna do, and
it don't make any stupid promises it can't keep.

One day I woke up and Ronald Reagan was president. I
thought for sure it was the DTs, and maybe it was, because the
next time I looked, it was some other guy, but things weren't
any better. I think they'd gotten a lot worse, as a matter of fact,
because there were practically no rescue squads coming
around. I'd never thought I'd actually miss Jesus people in a
van with coffee and burgers, and *I* didn't. It was the kids that
needed that stuff, and there was nobody coming around with it.

Just before Ginny showed up, though, times changed
again, and the vans came back with new faces but the same
old things going on—food, and promises of more food and
some help if the kids would come to the shelters. I don't tell
nobody to go and I don't tell nobody not to go, even if the
kids ask me. I just tell them what I told Ginny: you do what
your heart tells you to do, while you still have one. This is,
I think, the only thing you should tell anybody when they
ask you what they should do. Because really, all they're asking for is permission to do that, and if they feel like they
gotta get somebody's permission, why the hell not give it to
them?

Yeah, that's right—I had it all figured out, didn't I. Me and
the booze, we had it all mapped out. And then something happened that made it all different.

Then *she* came along.

* * *

Now when I think about it, I'm surprised someone like her didn't show up sooner. The pickings here're pretty good for that kind. Plenty other kinds came around; besides the Jesus people, of course, we had all manner of pimps—no, excuse me, there's really only one kind of pimp, and they only got one thing they sell and some might think it's all kinds of this and all kinds of that but then, there's some so stupid they think fifteen-year-old boys blow strange, ugly men because they like sex, too.

When *she* showed, I thought at first she was another Jesus person. I was on my way home from a Dumpster run with not too bad pickings—expiration dates and shit like that mean that some of us on tighter budgets eat as well as anybody. So I was passing the old truck dock on my way down the hill to my end of the park, and there she was, handing out doggy bags and cans of soda. Now I was impressed with the canned sodas, though someone was probably gonna bleed over them. Recycle money can mean one less blow job, which is pretty serious stuff. So all the kids were there, it looked like, and her being a new face, I stopped to check.

Handing out like Jesus, smiling like a pimp. Yeah, that's right, I thought, what we needed around these parts was a pimp pretending to be Jesus. That would make everything perfect. Since most of the kids never got a smile that didn't come from a pimp anyway, she must have looked like just some nice lady with plenty of food to give away.

I had a couple swallows with me—don't leave home without it, especially when you don't actually have a home. See, the way it is, I got to drink as much as would get a regular person hammered just to get sober so I can go on from there and get drunk. So sometimes I have to dose up on the fly to keep straight. I know when I need some because I get a little taste of the DTs when it's been too long. That's what I figured I was getting standing there watching her with the kids because there she was with her pimp's smile and her pretty face and her shiny hair and suddenly I saw an animal.

Big eyes with slitted pupils, nasty teeth; hungry. Sniffing them kids, tasting the air around them to get their flavors. If you saw that, you'd reach for a fucking drink, too.

A couple swallows was all it took to make stuff look normal again. Mostly normal. Still had the pimp's smile, which made me think of the nasty teeth, but I didn't see any.

Then Dropkick pushes Ginny over to this woman and Ginny is trying not to go. The woman is holding a bag in one hand and a can in the other and her pimp's smile goes from sort of curious to outright—shit, how to describe this. You'd see that look on someone's face when they fall in love at first sight, I think, or if they find a wallet in the gutter with a thousand dollars in it. That kind of look, lust and greed and pure-ass delight. *Candy, little girl? Or a burger?*

I went as far as to take a step toward them. Yeah, that's right, I wasn't thinking. Mainly I think I wanted to get a better look at her, see if there was any look of the beast left to her now that I'd had my swallows.

And then her and Ginny both turn to me and I think, shit, the DTs are bad this time. They look *wrong*. Like a matched set, but *wrong*. That's all I know. Better hurry home and get outside of a bottle. Which it so happens I have, some not-so-bad stuff that I was intending to stretch. But my rule is, first prevent delirium tremens, and worry later.

Quite a bender. I disappeared down a black hole for a while. Weird visions and crazy dreams; I ain't too wild about that part of it. Everybody I ever met in my life came to visit me under the bridge in the park, and I think some of them might actually have been there. Dropkick, for example, and Ginny.

And some little kid I couldn't remember the name of; hadn't seen her for a long time. Little eleven-year-old throwaway.

She'd been living rough for a while by the time she found her way to the old truck docks where most of the kids stayed. I was drinking hard a lot of the time she was around: the most I remembered about her was she was letting her hair go dread, like a Rastafarian, which doesn't look as weird as you might think on a pubescent white girl, at least not if you've seen half the shit I've seen, anyway.

But yeah, that's right, she came to see me in my bender visions. She was a little bit older, just the way she would have been in real life, but she was also dressed better, dressed up and no cheap shit out of some thrift shop. Overpriced denims from some store with an overcute name and a trend-color T-shirt with a little breast pocket barely big enough for an M&M. And still the dreads in her hair. Ms. Pimp came with her. The way they were both staring, I knew the little one had told Ms. Pimp about me and I tried to remember what she would have known. Maybe just that I was down here under the bridge, nobody's queen bee and nobody's mother and nothing like St. Francis.

She gave her pants a little tug to save the knees, just like a citizen, and squatted down to look at me closer. "You listened," she said. "Maybe you don't remember now, but I know you were listening then when I told you. I told you everything and you heard me and you didn't tell me I was bad, and you didn't try to tell me what I should do. All I wanted was to tell someone, just get it out."

I tried to focus on her, but somehow my vision went right past and fixed on Ms. Pimp behind her. The way I was and the position and all, she looked twenty feet tall. And she didn't squat down.

That head tilts to one side. The kid says, "Help her."

She says, "I haven't been invited." So then the little one says, "Well, *I* was, once."

Like that, I understand, and I pass out.

*   *   *

I woke up right after someone took the gym socks out of my mouth. It felt like, anyway. What sky I could see from where I was lying looked gray and blah. I didn't feel much like moving, so for a long time, I didn't. Eventually, I got a sense for how I was laying there on the ground—almost spread-eagle, with my neck bent over to my right. I think I must have looked kind of dreamy, actually, or I would have except nobody coming off a bender looks that good.

Nobody makes you do anything after a bender when you don't matter, so since there was nobody to make me move, I just laid there until I felt like doing something else.

And *then* it hurt. The top of my head caved in and went crashing through six floors of brain, a couple levels of throat bile and made a direct hit on my stomach so that the dry heaves bent me in half and I sat up without meaning to. There she was, slumped against the wall, deep asleep like she didn't have a care in the world. Except, of course, she did, lots of them, but I couldn't figure why she'd brought them to me.

I picked up a little pebble and tossed it at her. She just twitched. Took two more direct hits, one on the shoulder and the other on her forehead, before she woke for me. That last one must have stung like a hornet.

"What're you doin' here," I say to her.

Ginny yawns, covering her mouth politely, pushes her dark hair back. She's got wavy-curly hair that could go dread pretty easy. "Watching over you."

"I don't need nobody to watch over *me*," I tell her. "And if you think I want to work out a deal where we take care of each other, you're dumber'n I look, 'cause I thought it was pretty clear I ain't down here to be no mother."

Ginny gets that smile like certain drug counselors I have known. Very patronizing smile, even if none of them mean it that way, or think they do. "Don't you ever worry about what could happen to you while you're passed out?"

"No," I say, "why should I? I'm passed out, I won't feel it."

Now she gives a that's-not-funny laugh and rolls her eyes. "Suppose it's a rapist with AIDS?"

"I guess you got a point," I say after a moment, "but I don't understand why you want to make it." I got her confused now. "I mean, I *tol'* you what I wanted out of life. Why are you tryin' to worry me with rapists with AIDS when you know I don't give a good goddamn about most anything, and I'd appreciate the world returning the favor."

She pressed her knuckles together. "I think it's because when I first looked at you, I knew I could have been looking at my own future. And now that I have a chance to prevent that future, I want to go all the way and save you, too."

Save me? Did this little piece of chicken just say she wanted to *save me?* All I can do is stare at her.

"I guess it's because I'll feel like I've erased every chance of this happening to me if I can help you," she goes on. "The way she wants to help me."

Yeah, that's right: *she.* Tiny little push on that word as it comes out of her mouth lets me know she's talking about who I think she's talking about. "What's that pimp got in mind for you?" I asked her.

She gives another little laugh. "She's not a pimp. She's something entirely different. Something new."

"New? I doubt *that.* Ain't nothin' new that comes around *here.*"

"Well, yeah, okay, she's actually very old. *Very* old. But what she's doing, she's doing in a new way. A way that's never been done for us before."

"Us?" I feel like a stupid echo. Maybe that's what I've come down to under this bridge, just a stupid echo. That's okay, as long as I can still drink when I'm not doing my echo thing.

"Us women. Us females." She pushed herself up on her knees and leaned toward me, looking hard into my face. Considering the way I know I smelled, that was no cheap trick. "Don't you ever think about that? How we always have to work our way out of being some man's adjunct? That we all end up belonging to some man and have to break free of him?"

"You see any men around me here?" I said. "The only men *I* ever been in thrall to're Jack Daniels and Jim Beam, and they ain't the jealous type."

"It's *why* you drink," she insisted. "All we ever seem to do is fight to keep from being used one way or another. Or we try to dull the pain of having been used up and thrown away by using booze, drugs, things like that."

Now I'm getting it—this is not coming out of her own mouth, this is all shit the pimp put in her head. Sounds real good, sounds like what you'd think you'd want to hear. But it's also got this canned sound. Like this little Ginny, in spite of everything, she still isn't sold, she can't quite believe no matter how much she wants to, and she's even maybe still a little scared of what the fine print on this deal is gonna say when she finally reads it.

"What do you want?" I say to her finally. "What do you want to do, what do you want me to do?"

"I'll bring her to you. Tonight. You'll be here, won't you." Not a question. Off she goes, leaving me there to wonder if my brain really could be swelling up inside my skull the way it feels. My hands are shaking, too.

I really do not fucking want to see this pimp. This was another idea Ginny got put in her head for her and didn't think up by herself, and doesn't even know it. So what this pimp has in mind for me, I'm right to be scared about it.

Son of a bitch; you know, this is just why I took up drinking—so I didn't have to do shit I was afraid of.

So all I had to do was take off, right? Yeah, that's right. Obviously, you never been on a bender, if you don't know how sick you get after. I was maybe about able to crawl out from under the bridge and then collapse. I should probably have been in a hospital or a drying-out place with a hangover like this. I've shaken it out in some of those places on the morning after and what I can tell you is, you'll wish you were dead no matter where you are. But at least when you wake up under a bridge, there aren't any goddam moralizing medical types brutalizing you and calling it treatment, and then claiming you're just so screwed up that you can't stand them knocking you around.

But it's also generally a lot cleaner and better smelling than under a bridge, so there's that, too. It's all got its price, whatever you do. I had a lot of time to think about that, lying there staring at the underside of the bridge and listening to people's footsteps while they walked over. With any luck, this wouldn't be the day some cop got ambitious and decided to clean up the park by starting with me. Mostly that happened only in election years, but not being the most conscientious voter, I couldn't remember if this was one or not.

Sometime in the afternoon, when the sun had moved from one side of the bridge to the other, it comes to me that I'm a lot sicker than usual this time, sick and weak. But with the sound of people walking over the bridge and the distant traffic and sirens and junk noise a cityful of human beings tend to make, dead-of-night visitations don't look like anything more than the same old booze phantoms wearing new masks. And then you wonder for a moment, maybe, what booze phantoms really are, but you don't really know anything for sure.

Except I decided I *did* know, and I didn't like it, but there wasn't much I could do. The little one, what *was* her name? Had I ever known it while I—apparently—sat and listened to her spilling her guts. Drinking *real* hard those times. Sometimes the only way you can stand to hear any of it is while you're shitfaced.

Well, I was, once.

She was *what*. Invited; now I remember. Invited to what, though—a bottle party under a bridge? What did that entitle her to?

A drink. I offered her a drink. I offer all of them drinks, and they never turn them down. Maybe, I thought to myself, I should have been more specific about what they were drinking.

I just lay there all day, mostly because the hideous pain in my head wouldn't let me move any more than a blink, and tried to feel the spot where she must have leeched on me. Past the pain in my head, though, I just plain hurt all over; even feeling all weak and faded wasn't so unusual.

And maybe I should have known something by that. All my little friends that came and went, and some of them even stopping to say good-bye to that crazy old lush, May. Did they ever take a good-bye sip I maybe didn't know about?

And while we're at it, what kind of blood cocktail did I make?

I felt her coming. It must have been like a Friday or Saturday night because the park was still real busy and sometimes, when the wind was right, voices carried from 'way up the hill where the docks were. The kids having some kind of party, it sounded like. Maybe some new ones had come in. Weekends you can see new faces, especially when the weather's good and nobody minds sleeping outside. Although the docks are such good shelter that they're almost not outside. No trucks unload there anymore and I couldn't tell you what was in the building. Stolen shit, maybe, or drugs, or illegal guns. Or maybe just a lot of dust and an owner who didn't care except for the tax write-off. Nobody connected with the building ever bothered the kids, anyway, which was why they all stayed around there. And then at night, the chicken hawks would come around. They weren't much for noise.

And then it was like my mind flew out like a bird, out from under the bridge and up the hill to the docks. Jumble of images, kids' faces, other faces, in and out of the shadows and then turning away to the street, light streaks from the street-lamps, from cars passing with their brights on, to looking up at *her*. And her smiling down at what I know now must be my little friend who came to see me in my bender. Coming back, some kind of goon squad, except they're supposed to be on my side—

The little one stops, feeling me like I feel her. She's under the white light of a streetlamp, and it's swinging overhead like a yo-yo doing the around-the-world trick.

She stops looking around and I get this *gotta-do-it* sensation inside: the old need for a drink, *now*. Except it's not from me but from inside her. And so here they come, to have a drink from what's stashed under the bridge.

It makes my head hurt worse, but I shove away all those pictures that don't belong in my brain. I shove them down and away by making myself look at stuff, really *look*, and name what I see—what *I* see. Graffiti up above me, says *Eddie was here* and somebody else put *and sukked my kok GOOD* and a third person had added *with duck sauce*, which was good for a two-second laugh while I tried to get up.

I rolled over and managed to get up on my hands and knees. On the ground in front of me was—

—the top of the hill; looking down into the park, and just walk a little further on, the bridge would come into view, though you couldn't see what was under it until you got further down, especially in summer, when the trees were so thick—

—a fucking *flyer* for a church pancake breakfast, all-you-can-eat pancakes and sausage, Knights of Columbus would be doing the cooking. "Yeah, that's right, swords into ploughshares," I muttered; except in urban areas, where they became spatulas. Get your red-hot flapjacks, get your red-hot cross buns. I could have used some of those, I thought, trying to get my feet under me so I could stand up. I crawled closer to the wall. It curved but I thought I might be able to walk my hands up it.

The image of the bridge jumps into my head and I stagger sideways, feeling my feet go like they're dancing, but somehow, I stayed up, hands scraping on the dirty wall. Pain keeps me awake, new pain. I have to catch my breath, launch myself out of here and if I can put enough distance between me and her, maybe I'll fade like a cheap AM station—

But now the three of them were standing there, just out of the shelter of the bridge, watching me stay up. The flashlight Ginny's carrying lights up the whole inside under here. I even get a look at my own startled, dirty face, wide-eyed like *I* was some kid making a few discoveries about life lived rough.

Ginny and *her* give the little one in the middle a gentle push forward, toward me. She looks great now. Like a sleek, strong animal in her expensive denim trousers—you can't call those jeans, they've got *creases*, chrissakes—and her neat white blouse and her tapestry vest. Fashion-magazine teenager. Dread hair, yeah, but when the style changes, cut it off. It grows back, or so I hear. Or is that a myth about hair and nails growing on corpses after they're dead?

She laughed at me. "I don't know about that, but *our* hair

grows just fine, even if *we* never grow any older. Come on, my sister." She holds out a hand to me.

I look from her to Ginny. "It'd make more sense if it was you six months from now. But her I don't remember at all."

"You remember me a little bit," the girl says. "But that's okay, really. Come on, my sister. Let us help you now."

She lets me see myself standing in front of her like some kind of living rack for hanging rags on, with my arms almost straight over my head, hands shifting on the rough stone while I hold myself up on the low arch of the bridge. Vertigo strikes and I almost fall forward into her, *almost*, but I have been out here a long time and I have held myself up in some terrible states, benderized, tenderized, and deep in DTs I can't describe and can't forget. So I can hold myself up under the bridge facing this. For a little bit longer, anyway.

My head cleared and what she'd been saying finally got through. "Sister?" I said. "Not me."

She nodded, and behind her, they nodded, too. "We both have a thirst, don't we." I felt her need-a-drink along with my own, which had been running along like an engine on low idle all day long and was now starting to rev higher. "I know why you've been thirsty, what you really wanted. Now you can drink something that will really give it to you."

"Oh?" I croaked. "You bring me some vodka?"

"Better," she says, and starts to go on.

"Oh, don't say that," I interrupt, feeling her words taking shape in my own throat. "That's *so corny*. 'Dark wine.' Besides, I ain't no wino." Not unless I'm really desperate, but there was no law that I had to tell anyone that. Even if they already knew it.

She blinked at me. "You don't understand," she said. "This, too, will be your friend; it will love you and it won't be critical, and it will always do what it says it's going to. See? I remember what you told me, even if you don't remember what I told you. Come on. This is no way for a woman to live."

"Your way *is*?" I said, and laughed. I walked my hands down the wall and leaned against it with my neck bent due to the curve. My arms had been getting numb.

She nods. "For thousands of years, women have done what they've had to do to stay alive. Now we'll do what we *want* to do and flourish. We've been saved."

Where does she *get* this stuff? And finally I understand who's really doing the talking here.

"She turned you out real good. Better job than anyone else's done on you," I say, letting her see me look from *her* to the beast who did the deed. "Probably nobody else could do anything to make you say it's right to rape somebody, but she got you. I guess blood's the thickest stuff you can get, huh? Yeah, that's right."

"Women don't rape each other," she said, starting to get angry at me.

"Rapists rape anybody they wanna rape. Did you want it when she came at you with those fuckin' teeth and those beast eyes?"

"I didn't understand then," she said, but I see her wavering.

"Yeah, that's right," I say. "I guess you didn't see how it was for your own good, huh? How you was really gonna *like* it when you got going and even though it hurt like a bastard at first—am I right about that, was it painful?—even though it hurt like anything, you'd be happy afterward that you went through it, you'd want it again and again, and you'd want to do it as much as you could. So what the hell, let's turn pro, right? Isn't that right?"

And now I look right at Ginny, who was gonna get turned out tonight along with me and I see that for the moment, whatever cloud came over her starting with a doggy bag of food and a canned soda, it's lifted up now, at least temporarily, and if anyone's gonna do anything, it's got to be now.

I throw myself down and the little one makes a jump at me, but then I come up with the only thing I can think of to back her off and I hope it works.

For once. I was right. The Knights of Columbus pancake breakfast, with a line drawing of the Sacred Heart of Jesus and its happy come-one-come-all-break-bread-together sentiments driving it—*that* gets her. Sometimes all salvation is is somebody who cares about feeding the hungry, not feeding on them. Exact opposite of a pimp. Or a rapist.

It sends her backing away from me, confused and scared that a dirty piece of paper I picked up off the ground has some power she can't handle and can't understand.

"May," Ginny says, stepping toward me, and she's looking at the other two and then at me and there are so many hard questions there.

"I already told you," I say, wishing it didn't hurt so much to kneel, wishing my head would just explode if that's what it was going to do, "you do what your heart tells you, for as long as you have a heart. How long did you want to keep it?"

The flashlight beam turns away from me, and the darkness feels suddenly so good and cool on my throbbing, burning head. And I must be on the verge of passing out or something, because I'm lost in the cool and soothing dark for I don't know how long before I hear Ginny say, "I won't stop you if you leave now."

And sometime after that, she comes and takes the paper out of my hands. I have been holding it up like St. George's shield or maybe like I was a Knight of Columbus myself. Ginny helps me sit down and she stays by me for a while.

I didn't understand why until I stopped shaking. First I knew of it.

* * *

Now you want to hear the happy talk part about how I realized the error of my ways, that there was some even bigger evils out there and I decided to clean up, dry out, and join the holy war against them. And Ginny went with me; we found a safe place to stay and I learned I wanted to be a mommy after all and she learned to trust me. And pretty soon we had enough to buy a used van and a coffee urn and a bunch of old blankets.

This is because you're a fool. You can't help it. In your world, the cavalry always shows up on time. Out here in the rough lane, the cavalry deserted as soon as it was out of sight of the fort and it ain't coming back. And if Mommy and Daddy were in the cavalry when that happened, it means they're not coming back either. So get used to it.

I didn't want to think about what had happened, so I went back to drinking as soon as I could manage it. That same night, as a matter of fact. Dropkick came down to see what was going on because he'd seen the three of them trooping down this way. He owed me a favor, so I made him scrounge me a flask. It went down raw, but it went down and stayed down. I gave Ginny some, but only a little. It takes a lot more for me and I wasn't in a sharing mood especially.

She didn't like it but Dropkick took it off her hands for her. Then she just sat and watched me. The Dropper set up the flashlight with the paper so that it was like a lamp and we were lit up for as long as the battery held out. I know she didn't understand, but I wasn't in an explaining mood, either. I was in a drinking mood.

I tried to get her to leave with Dropkick but she wouldn't go. So I knew I'd have to talk to her about it just to get her out of my hair, which, for all the neglect, wasn't going dread. Maybe dreads were a young woman's game and hell, I was practically thirty.

So she barely got the word *Why* out of her mouth before I said, "Only if you never ask me again." And she nodded and I said, "Really. Never again. Because I drink instead of do this shit, and that's the way I like it."

And she goes, "But they offered—"

"Yeah, yeah, yeah, that's right, isn't it. They offered. And I guess, you being a good educated girl, very smart and all, you see what they like to call parallels between their habits and mine. But I will remind you that there are some important differences, one of the big ones being that my choice of beverage doesn't have to be inside some other person before I can drink it. And the other being that I'm this way because I want to be.

"Yeah, that's right, I'm sure they told you that they chose their way to be, too. You believe that? Maybe it's true. But now they got no choice. There's no clinic they go to to kick the habit and get straight again. There's no meetings to help you stay quit. They're fuckin' *animals* now. I saw her, she's a beast. I'm a drunk and no good, but I'm still human. Sometimes that's all the salvation you get."

Ginny shook her head like someone had hit her and she was dazed. "Are you saying that you're gonna quit this someday, dry out, or whatever? Get straight?"

"Could if I wanted to. Don't really want to." I shrugged. "Listen, that creature that turns you out, that's a beast. Your heart tell you to be one, too?"

"I don't see how you can be here like this and say stuff like that," she said.

"Me, either," I said. "Mostly, I don't. Mostly, I drink. And I'd appreciate being left to it."

She stood up and then paused. "One for the road?"

I held up the flask to see what was left. "Okay, a little one. Make sure it's a little one or I might take a notion to suck it back out of you."

She laughed a little nervously and took a very small polite sip, not bothering to wipe the neck first. "Thanks, May. I don't know what I'm going to do now."

"That's good," I said.

Yeah, that's right; sometimes that's salvation, too. Think about it.

In the Blood

MICHAEL KURLAND

don't remember much that happened before I was twelve years old. That was, after all, a long time ago. I remember summers of piercing heat and bright skies, and grapevines growing on steep hillsides. I remember ice-crusted windows in the winter and fields of mud in the spring. I remember a dark brown wool blanket that protected me from all harm when I cuddled under it; and being driven to school in an open trap by Horst, our manservant, who seemed older than time to me then; and wearing short pants even on the coldest days, when I thought my knees would freeze up and fall off if I didn't keep moving my legs. I remember Saturdays in the kitchens, helping Estmann the pastry cook produce beautiful puff pastries for the evening's dinner and taking my reward in giant thick gobs of vanilla- and chocolate-flavored whipped cream. And I remember Mother, beautiful Mother, in elegant ball gowns, dancing until dawn with men in bright uniforms while I watched hiding behind a vase big enough to hold a full-grown man on the staircase landing. And I remember Mother creeping into my room late at night to tuck the covers up around me and lovingly suck the blood from my neck.

My name then was Almeric, which is a noble name, and mother's was Rosalys, which has something to do with flowers. I had a nursemaid who took care of me. Her name was Lizbet, and she was a chubby, good-hearted person who taught me French and kept me out of trouble, mostly. She also answered all my questions, both in French and in my native German. At some point I realized that she made up what she didn't know. And much of what she did know, wasn't so. Her world was populated with hobgoblins and ghouls and vampires, as well as with fairy princesses and handsome princes. It was particularly full of handsome princes who were riding around searching for beautiful young nursemaids to marry. One time I asked Lizbet, with the inexorable cruel logic of the young, "Why would any prince want to marry you? You don't know how to be a princess. Why wouldn't he just take you back to his palace and ravish you whenever he felt like it and make you clean pots the rest of the time?"

Lizbet called me a cruel, heartless boy, and reported the conversation to Mother. Mother scolded me but I could see that she was more amused than annoyed. She wanted to know what I thought "ravish" meant, and I told her that it meant something like "kiss," but I wasn't sure just what. It happened in all the books Lizbet read; thick Gothic novels full of ghosts and murderers and gloomy castles, and other wonderful things. I read them as soon as Lizbet put them down. I read anything that wasn't nailed down or locked up. As a result I had a wide knowledge of things that I didn't have the slightest understanding of.

My father's name was Casimir, which was the name of kings. He was a tall, dark, silent figure who was notable in my life mostly for his absence. I can remember him being with us no more than three or four times in those days, and then for less than a month each time. His presence was not known in the village. I was instructed to never mention it, and he kept to his study when tradesmen or visitors called upon my mother. I knew, without being sure how I knew, that most of the young men who paid court to my mother thought she was a widow, and she did nothing to discourage this illusion.

Occasionally, when I worked up my courage, I asked Mother about my father. I don't remember at this remove what I was afraid of. Mother didn't get angry, and she replied to my questions with full, if vague, answers. Perhaps it was the vagueness that made me apprehensive, afraid that one day she would answer me more directly and I wouldn't like what I heard.

"What is father like?" I asked her one day.

She paused to consider her answer. "He is a great and wise man," she told me, "and very—strong. Men who think themselves important and powerful tremble when he walks into the room."

"Do you tremble?" I asked.

She smiled and nodded. "Oh, yes," she said. "I tremble."

It was shortly after my twelfth birthday that Mother suddenly announced that we were moving. She gave no reason, and it didn't occur to me that she might need one. The ways of adults are mysterious, and the ways of Mother were mysterious even to other adults. The only explanation Mother would give me was that in times of stress, people often take their fears out on strangers. The villagers had indeed become frightened of something over the past few months, and had taken to locking their doors at night and putting up their shutters. But when I asked the shopkeepers about it they looked at me strangely and changed the subject. I told my mother that they couldn't consider us strangers, as we had lived there for as long as I could remember.

"That is so," she told me. "But not for as long as they can

remember. You are regarded as a stranger here for at least three generations."

Mother had pulled me out of the village school several days before, saying that she was preparing me to go to boarding school. This had thoroughly alarmed me, but when we were alone she hugged me and told me that it wasn't so, that she wasn't planning to let me out of her sight anytime soon. "Always remember you are my blood," she said, "and I love you—" She paused to consider. "I love you more than oranges." A powerful oath indeed, as Mother truly loved the fleshy oranges that were shipped to us from Spain in heavy oak barrels.

We spent those days preparing, and then we left in the middle of the night. A dray carrying most of our possessions had gone two days ahead of us, also leaving in the dead of night. Mother placed a large envelope on the hall table for the butler, with a letter dismissing the staff and enough money in gold coins to give each servant two months' wages in lieu of notice. We went in the carriage, surrounded by trunks and boxes. Horst drove, and I noticed that the carriage's axles and springs had been heavily greased and the horses hooves had been muffled with rags. Our carriage lanterns were not lit, and we took the old road that ran behind the manor house and up the side of the mountain. It wasn't much of a mountain, as mountains go, but Horst still had to climb down from his seat several times and lead the horses. Twice Mother and I got out and walked to ease the burden on the horses.

Near the top of the mountain—we were perhaps two leagues from the manor house—we paused to rest the horses before beginning the steep descent into the valley below. I turned to get one last look at the house, or at the dark space in the night where I knew the house to be. But it wasn't dark.

"Look Mother," I said. "Little lights all around our house."

She turned to look. "Torches," she said. "I hope the servants get out all right."

"Get out of what?" I asked.

"The house," Mother said.

Just then the ground-floor windows along the side facing us lit up from the inside, casting a bright glow as though a hundred candelabra had been lighted all at once. And then I could see flames coming through one window, and then another.

"We'd better go," Mother said to Horst.

"Yes, Baroness," Horst agreed. "It is a pity."

"Yes," Mother agreed. "Some of the paintings. . . . But it's a pity we've seen before, eh Carl?"

We got back into the carriage and the horses started slowly down the steep path. I was silent for a long time, thinking. "Mama," I asked, "why are they burning down the house?"

"They are angry," she told me.

"At us? What did we do?"

"Nothing, but they do not know that. There were rumors about us—about me—and in times of trouble rumors become facts."

"What sort of rumors?"

Mother smiled. "They say I change form and go out at night killing sheep and children."

"Mama! How can anyone think such things?"

"It is happening," Mother said. "Sheep are dying and small children are being taken from their bedrooms through locked and shuttered windows. Also oxen and rabbits. And occasionally young foolhardy men who venture out at night to catch the marauder."

"Who could be doing such things?"

"Those who don't say it's me," Mother said, "say it's a wolf."

"But wolves don't attack people," I said. "Not unless they're threatened."

"That is so," Mother agreed. "But some claim to have seen a wolf."

"Then. . . ."

"A werewolf," mother told me. "A shape-changer. An ancient nemesis rapidly dying out because of their lack of judgment. But we will speak no more of this."

I have noticed that changes in one's life are not gradual, but come tumbling all at once when one least expects them. One week I was a contented twelve-year-old boy going to the village school, basking in the reflected importance of my mother, who occupied the manor house and was thus the most important person for leagues around. And the next we were fleeing in the night, suspected of hideous crimes, and the manor house itself was in flames.

I fell asleep and had exciting and uncomfortable dreams. Sometime later, as the coach took a particularly heavy jounce, I woke up to find myself cradled in Mother's arms. She was staring out the window at the rising moon. I looked at her slender, intelligent face gleaming pale white in the moonlight and marveled at my fortune at having this wonderful woman as my mother. Another question came to me. "Baroness?"

Mother reached down and smoothed my hair. "Yes, my son?" she said.

"What sort of baroness are you? Does that mean Father is a baron? And why did you call Horst 'Carl'?"

"This is a time of change," Mother told me. "We go to a new place and start a new life. And to mark that change, we will all take new names. Horst is now Carl. As of tonight I am the Baroness Idelia von Hochbergen. You, if you approve, are Peter von Hochbergen."

I mentally savored the name and decided that it had a good feel. "And Father?" I asked.

"Father will not be spoken of by any name," Mother said.

We travelled by zig and by zag, with many stops, to Paris.

First we stayed for two months on Corfu, an island at the mouth of the Adriatic across from the heel of the boot of Italy. We lived in a whitewashed house surrounded by fig and olive trees in sight of the sea. Mother saw many visitors who came to pay homage to the visiting baroness, and I didn't go to school. From there we moved to Trieste, a city of narrow, twisting streets which then belonged to the Austrian Empire, although almost everyone who lived there spoke Italian. We stayed in a long, narrow, three-story house on one of the windy streets with a carriage house in back, and we had nine servants. The bare minimum, Mother said, for civilized living.

Visitors came to see us here, too, and I was introduced to some of them. Most were local dignitaries greeting the newly arrived elegant young baroness, but some seemed to know Mother from an earlier time. These were the ones I was introduced to, and they treated me with great respect and said things that made me realize that my world was a far more complicated place than I had imagined.

A tall man dressed in black, with a prominent nose, skin like white parchment, and deep-set eyes like a hawk, shook my hand gravely when Mother called me into the library to meet him. Count Sigismund was his name.

"So this is the boy," he said. "Has the Power begun to grow in him yet? Does he know the Words? Does he know the Way?"

"Not any of it yet," Mother said. "There is time."

"Yes," the man agreed. "Much time." He bent over until his nose was but inches away from my own. "My hidden name is Hasha Pit-Letzer," he told me. "And I am of the Inner Circle. I respect your father and I cherish your mother, and I pledge my aid in times of trial. I hope you shall never have to call my pledge."

"Sigismund!" Mother said. "That's very kind."

"No more than you have done for me and mine," Count Sigismund Hasha Pit-Letzer said. "I leave now. We must not gather. I feel the need approaching, and I would as soon be in the countryside."

My mother nodded. "The first rule," she said. "Take care."

"And you." He kissed my mother on the cheek, shook hands formally with me, and left.

Now had I questions indeed. "Mother—" I began.

"Come upstairs," Mother said.

We went up to Mother's sitting room, and she settled down on the chaise lounge and took her shoes off. "There are some things you must know," she told me. "And you will learn them over the next few years."

I stood by the window, so full of suppressed excitement that I could hardly keep still. "Years?" I raised my arms in supplication. "Mama, I can't wait years. There are things I have wondered for as long as I can remember, and I have not asked. But now I see that they concern me, don't they, Mama? And I want to know."

Mother smiled and shook her head. "Some I will tell you now," she said. "And some you would not understand, and you would be frightened and perhaps horrified without cause, because you did not understand. I could make up a fiction, but I will be honest with you and tell you nothing but truth." She held her hand out to me, and I took it. "I love you more than oranges. But you must let me decide what truth to tell you when."

I took a deep breath and let it out at a slow, measured rate, remembering that Mother had taught me thus so long ago, to cool the blood she had said, and allow reasons to replace emotion. "What would you tell me?" I asked.

"What questions have you?"

"Tell me," I said, "why the villagers burned down our house. Tell me why you bite my neck. Tell me about the hidden names, and the Inner Circle, and the Power, and the Words, and how we are different from other people."

"I will tell you some of what you ask," she said. "But remember, this knowledge is not to be shared."

"I know that, Mother," I said, annoyed that she should tell me anything so obvious.

"It is not enough to know it," she told me. "You must feel it with every atom that is you. It must be a part of you. When being tortured, when making love, when trying to impress some maiden into lowering her last defenses, these are things you must not even think of saying."

"I understand," I said, more soberly.

"No you don't," she told me, "but you will."

At the side of the chaise lounge there was an ancient Chinese rug, about six feet long by four feet wide, of an intricate pattern in which I imagined I could see dragons flying and armies attacking walled cities, and other wondrous things. I sat carefully on the rug so as to disturb neither the dragons nor the armies, and looked up at Mother.

"We, you and I, are of a race apart from mortal men," she told me. "Not that we are not mortal, but for us the sands of time trickle slowly down the glass and do not rush in an ever-increasing torrent to the final grain as they do with our neighbors. For this reason, and others, men fear our sort and loathe us, and destroy without pity any of us they identify."

For a time I could say nothing. The idea—the fact—of what I had just heard was repugnant to me, and I hardly dared allow Mother to go on. Why should anyone feel so about me, or my beautiful mother, or my silent, intelligent, powerful father?

"What are we, then?" I asked. I felt a curious sort of fear as I waited for Mother's response, as though I knew that there were words that could hurt me just by their utterance.

Mother took the shawl from around her shoulders and used it to cover her legs. "We are known by many names. Lamia is a common one, as is succuba. But the first confuses us with witches and the second with demons, neither of which are we. We call ourselves the *strix*, which is Latin for a sort of owl. But the most common name that others have for us," she said, staring at me with a strange intensity, "is vampire."

The word hung in the air. I felt curiously light-headed, and my heart thumped inside my chest, and were I not sitting down I would assuredly have fallen over.

"Vampire," I repeated. The stories I had heard of vampires from Lizbet's thick books, from the whispered fears of the townspeople, assaulted my consciousness like physical blows. Vampires were the undead who sucked the blood out of children in their beds in locked and shuttered rooms. Vampires appeared in the guise of beautiful women to lure young men to their doom, and then resumed their true shape as horrible demons and ate their victims. Vampires could change themselves into huge birds or bats and fly off in the night. When vampires roamed the dark no man or woman was safe until they could be found in daylight, and an oak stake must be driven through their hearts where they slept the sleep of the undead in their coffins.

"I don't want to be a vampire," I said, when again I could speak.

Mother stared at me sadly, as though she had shared every image that had raced through my brain. "The stories are exaggerated," she told me. "Distorted, as though held up to a twisted mirror. We are not that."

"Then why do they say—what they say?" I asked.

Mother sat up and rubbed her left leg, massaging the muscle lying under a small scar in her calf. Hardly noticeable, it pained her when the weather changed, but she seldom spoke of it and I do not know how she got it. "The horrible thing about distorting mirrors," she said softly, "is that you can still recognize yourself in them."

"But I don't do those things that vampires are said to do," I said. "And you don't either, Mother. Do you?"

She smiled. "Change my shape and fly off into the night? Sleep in a coffin? Go about the countryside murdering small children? No, I do not."

There was a knock on the door, and Anna Maria, a ruddy-faced girl of fifteen who was the downstairs maid, poked her head in. "Milady has a caller," she said. "Count Brekenski. Carl put him in the library."

"Very well," Mother said, glancing over at the clock on her dresser. "Thank you, Anna Maria. Come all the way into the room when you want to tell me something, don't just poke your head through the door."

"Yes, Milady," Anna Maria said, bobbing her head and retreating to the other side of the door.

Mother turned to me. "He is a Polish nobleman and befriending him might be useful," she said. "Go so that I may change into something more elaborate."

I stood up. "I'm sorry, Mother. I didn't mean to keep you. . . ."

Mother laughed. "Don't be silly, my precious orange. You are more important to me than any five noblemen, or ten, or fifteen. Besides, if I don't keep him waiting, he'll think I'm not important. Go now, and we'll talk again."

A month or so later Mother took me for a ride in the trap, just the two of us, pulled by a dependable mare named Phoebe. We traveled the post road that curved along the cliffs above the Adriatic until we came to a delightful place with wildflowers growing along a stream that suddenly dropped off into the ocean. There we stopped for lunch, spreading the food on a flat-topped boulder that served as an admirable sideboard. When Mother finished eating she wiped her hands and called me from the side of the cliff where I was watching the waves below.

"There are some things you must know," she told me, "and it is time. Most things that mark us different will come to you of themselves, as they are laws of nature. But you must also learn the law of the *strix*."

She sat on a camp stool, beckoned me to her, and took my hand. "In case of need. In case I am not about to help you, these things must you know."

"Where would you be?" I asked.

"One never knows from day to day," she said, brushing her hair away from her face. "That was a danger sign. It means keep away."

"What does?"

Mother repeated the gesture. "It's a sort of secret language using the body instead of the mouth." She moved her hands in a certain way. "Do what I do, and I'll tell you what you said."

For the rest of the afternoon, until we left for home, I practiced moving my hands and arms *thus* and twisting my head and shoulders *thus* and my upper body *thus,* each subtle move conveying a remarkable amount of information to anyone who understood the language. Thereafter I took lessons from Mother once or twice a week and practiced daily before a looking glass. In a short time we were conversing secretly in public. It was a simple language, but amazingly expressive. Mother, who had a wicked wit, would comment on the appearance or speech of those around us, and I would often break up laughing for no reason that anyone else would see. This taught me self-control.

We arrived in Paris in May of 1816, bringing with us those of our household staff from Trieste who were willing to move with us. A large house had been prepared for us on Rue Bateleur, a short distance from the beautiful, wide Avenue des

Champs-Élysées, and staffed with enough servants to get our household going. Horst, or Carl as he was now, had gone ahead and seen to everything. Louis XVIII was king of France, Napoleon had been banished to St. Helena, and the Parisians were doing their best to make it seem as though they had always wanted it that way.

Mother hired a tutor to give me lessons in history and geography, and to improve my French. I spoke German and Hungarian fluently, could carry on a decent conversation in Polish, and had picked up a speaking acquaintance with Italian during the six months we stayed in Trieste. I thought I spoke French already also, but it turns out I was mistaken. Lizbet was from Alsace, not Paris, and the Parisians didn't recognize her accent as French. When I spoke the French of Lizbet, they refused to understand me.

My world differed from that of my young companions in ways they could not comprehend. I was learning slowly and seemingly by chance what it was to be that which I did not want to admit. Carl, my mother's faithful servitor, prowled the streets at night once or twice a month. And when he came home at dawn he was sluggish and stupefied, and sometimes there was a hint of blood about his lips.

Mother slept most of the day and was up most of the night. Sunlight, she said, hurt her eyes. It had always been thus, but I had never thought it worth noting until she told me of our heritage. No one among our growing circle of acquaintances in Paris thought it unusual that the Baroness Idelia von Hochbergen would seldom make appointments during the day. In the second year of the second reign of Louis XVIII, the king's subjects worked hard at not thinking of anything as being unusual. The emigré nobility of Europe, many of them made homeless or stateless by the predations of Bonaparte, had settled in Paris. They worked hard at being blithe, and succeeded for the most part at merely being bizarre.

Over the next few years I learned many things. I perfected my French. I learned to dance and to fence and to play the violin tolerably badly. I learned philosophy from Herr Doktor Professor Breughel, by which he meant all of human knowledge except dancing, fencing, and music. Herr Doktor Professor Breughel traveled Europe, studying and teaching. He possessed nothing except nine crates of books, a beard which went below the middle button on his vest, and, of course, all of human knowledge. When I was fifteen I asked him about vampires.

He leaned back in his wooden chair, folded his hands over his substantial stomach, and glared at me. "So!" he said. "Why vampires?"

"Just a question," I said. "Something I heard—I wondered what was true."

"What is believed or suspected, you mean," he corrected me. "For the truth, you would have to ask a vampire. This, I understand, is not a wise course."

"Then there are such things?"

Herr Doktor Professor Breughel shrugged. "What is truth? There are certainly legends. Ancient legends, although whether that would tend to make them more true, I cannot say. And then there are stories that are more than legend, but how much more? And what do they mean? Like most truth, they are capable of many different explanations."

"What legends?" I asked.

"In Poland and Hungary they tell of undead creatures that suck the blood from the living. Among the Greeks they tell of Lamia: beautiful women, kin to the succuba, who lure men to their deaths. In France they speak of a type of ghoul who murders small children and performs unspeakable acts upon their bodies. All of these are equated with the vampire."

"What do you think?"

The professor stared thoughtfully into space. "In this age of enlightenment it is difficult to believe any of it," he said. "And yet. . . ."

He paused for what seemed like an hour.

"And yet there are corpses—I have seen them—found in unlikely places, their bodies drained of blood, and sometimes partly eaten away."

"What do you think of this?" I asked.

He shrugged. "I think the eating was done by foxes or rats. But the blood—" He sat up. "Enough! What were we speaking of before this? Ah, yes; the doctrines of Mencius. . . ."

I never continued that conversation with Mother. Although as time passed she hid less and less from me, those things I did not want to know I refused to observe. As a horse wearing blinders will not be frightened by things out of its direct view, so I refused to allow myself to be aware of the meaning of peripheral events, like Carl with blood on his lips, or mother's dalliance with handsome young men who subsequently disappeared. Perhaps it wasn't blood, I told myself, but raspberry jelly. Perhaps mother's young men, disappointed in love, had merely fled to North America.

I began to look in myself for sign of abnormality; a desire to kill small children or suck blood, or sleep in a coffin, but none of these symptoms manifested themselves. I matured physically over the next few years until, when I was sixteen, I could easily have passed for twenty; except that I was able to grow neither mustache nor beard. Mathematics, the handling of an épée, ballroom dancing, the arts of love, and the supercilious manners of a young lord; all these I mastered. Face hair only eluded me.

Two weeks after my seventeenth birthday Mother called me into her chambers. As I entered the sitting room the setting sun cast its rays through the window behind her, illuminating her slender body through the filmy garment she wore. I stared at the perfection of form that was my mother and thought that she looked far too young to have me as a son. Were she not my mother I would surely have felt carnal desire, but instead I felt a curious mixture of fear and awe. She had not aged, as far as I could tell, in my lifetime.

Mother saw me looking and stepped aside, out of the sun's rays, and gathered her robe about her. "You are approaching manhood rapidly," she said, casting herself into one of the easy chairs that quartered the fireplace. "Have you given any thought to what you would like to do?"

I sat gingerly in the opposite chair. "Yes," I said. "But I have reached no conclusion. Herr Doktor Professor Breughel suggests that I enroll at the Sorbonne or the university at Heidelberg or Padua. Several of my friends have joined the army, but I confess that has small appeal for me."

"You were not destined for regimentation," Mother said. She paused for a long time, until the silence grew almost tangible between us. "The time is approaching when you will feel certain urges," she said, "which for other people would be unnatural. You must know that for you they are natural and right."

"Of what are we speaking?" I asked.

"You will know," Mother said.

It was shortly after this that I left for Padua. The city still had its medieval wall around it, but the university was a hotbed of progressive thinking. I studied art and architecture, and talked politics, and was happy. I fell in love. Her name was Madeleine Bianchi and she was the youngest daughter of a family of acrobats. Her brother Marcello objected to our seeing each other at first, but Marcello and I arm wrestled one evening and got drunk together, and he decided I was all right. He couldn't understand how I beat him in arm wrestling, since he had arms the size of young trees, and I was wiry to the point of being skinny. I was also amazed at the extent of my physical strength. I never did anything to develop it, having a strong dislike for any sort of exercise except fencing.

In May of 1824 I left Padua to travel north with the Bianchis. I did not attempt to join their act, but I made myself useful. I had not been home for two years, so I looked forward to surprising mother when we reached Paris.

It was late at night when we arrived at a field outside Paris after almost two months on the road. While the others bedded down I left the wagon and made my way to the Rue Bateleur. As it was well after midnight I decided not to wake the porter, but climbed the wall and entered the house through my old bedroom window. The room was as I had left it, except that everything was in its proper place, a result I had never been able to achieve.

The servants were, of course, long asleep, but mother was often awake until dawn. I left my room and went down the hall to mother's chambers. The door to her sitting room was partly open, and the light of a candle spilled into the hall. Someone groaned from within. And then again.

I stood frozen at the door for some time, unable to enter or leave. My mind conjured up grotesque, horrible images of what was taking place inside that partly open door. Finally, as if drawn by some power greater than myself, I crept silently through the door. The sitting room was empty; the flickering candlelight came from the bedroom beyond. The groans, also coming from the bedroom, did not stop but rather rose in intensity and frequency as I listened.

The bedroom door stood wide open. I went to it like a thief and, concealing myself against the wall, peered cautiously through the door. In the light of a candle on the dresser I saw a dress and an army officer's uniform and various articles of underwear strewn about the floor, as though removed in haste. I saw my mother on her back in the bed, her naked legs and arms wrapped around the body of the muscular young man who was on top of her. An ecstatic flush colored her face. It was the young man who was groaning, his groans coming closer together now, until he reached a climax and, with one last cry, fell like a stunned ox and rolled off mother.

I was frozen in place, hating myself for continuing to look and yet unable to turn away. I saw mother as she rolled over and rose to her knees. I saw her lean over the handsome young warrior and smile, fitting her body to his until she had pinned one arm and one leg. I saw her sink her teeth into the man's throat. For a minute the man did not move, and then his eyes flew open and a look of terror crossed his face. He screamed and tried to struggle up, but mother held him down as though he were a small child, her teeth still fastened at his throat. In another minute he stopped struggling and lay still.

She stayed at his throat for another few moments, and then released him and lay at his side. She smiled contentedly, her lips painted red with the blood of her victim.

I wanted to run screaming from that place, but I was unable to move. Slowly mother turned her head and her eyes focused on me. Perhaps it was the beating of my heart she heard. "Peter," she said. "I didn't know you were home."

I stepped forward. "Is he dead?"

Languidly she reached for a robe at the foot of her bed and slipped into it. "I should hope so," she said. "A dull, stupid, arrogant man, fit only for one thing, and not very good at that. He kept telling me how lucky I was that he had deigned to bed me. He was right, but not in the way he thought." Mother pushed at the body, and it rolled to the floor. "I'll have Carl dispose of it," she said.

Many emotions beat at my mind but I walled them off, not daring to allow them in. I do not know what I would have done or tried to do if I had heeded my emotion. Instead, shak-

ing with chills as though I were in the grip of some fatal ill-
ness from the effort of not feeling, I turned and left the room.
I walked along the hallway and down the stairs and out the
front door. I walked across Paris and out into the countryside.
For the better part of two weeks I walked, falling down by the
side of the road in a stupor when I was too tired to go on, and
then rising the next day and continuing on. In what direction
I walked I do not remember. Once three men with cudgels set
upon me to rob me. It were better they had stayed at home. I
fell on them with a savagery I did not know I possessed, and
I believe I killed two of them and left the third senseless in a
ditch.

When I came to myself I was in the little town of Clomer-
ité some distance to the west of Paris. I worked as a day la-
borer, renting myself out to various farmers as they needed
me. I stayed in the home of a local widow, who cooked my
meals for a modest fee. As I was so obviously not a peasant,
the consensus was that I must be on the run from the gen-
darmes, which gave me an undue popularity among the
locals.

It was here that my heritage caught up with me. Slowly
over the next year the feeling emerged; the morbid need for
blood. I had not returned to my beloved Madeleine for fear
that this would happen, and now, horribly, my fear was justi-
fied. The unnatural craving slowly grew in me until I could
think of nothing else. I took to prowling the town at night,
hoping to waylay some secret lover making his way home before the dawn. But when I found a victim, I could not strike.
These people had done me no harm; I could not simply kill
one of them to satisfy my unnatural lust.

But then one night I saw a man creep from a house carrying a small iron chest. I peered through a window in the house
and saw a couple lying dead within: one strangled, the other
stabbed to death. In a flash I was on the miscreant and had

him by the neck. "You murdered them for money," I said softly.

Caught in the grip of superstitious fear, he could but nod. "Who are you?" he squeaked.

"Nemesis," I told him, and in a second my teeth were at his throat. When my craving had been satisfied I took his body and the chest and heaved them back inside the murder house. Let the authorities make of that what they would. I had never felt so good.

What at first had been horrible to me soon became natural and then enjoyable. My blood lust came on me only about once every two months, and in that time it was easy to find someone who deserved death.

I moved to Nice and took a job as tutor to the two rather unintelligent children of a duke. Then, after two years, I returned to Paris.

The house was shut up. The Baroness Idelia von Hockbergen had moved away and nobody knew where. I went to find her man of business, and he shook hands with me gravely. "The baroness has returned to her ancestral estates," he told me. "When you returned I was to give you this and tell you that she loved you and you are always welcome wherever she goes." He handed me a thick envelope.

Ancestral estates? I retreated to a nearby cafe and opened the envelope. There was a letter within:

My lovely orange,

Time passes and I must move on. People are already starting to remark on how youthful I look. Forgive me as I forgive you. We shall meet again. You shall not want for money. Take care.

Mother

Along with the letter were some legal documents that told me how to access the money Mother had left for me. There was sufficient so that I would not want.

I moved from Paris to London. Having a facility for language, I picked up English easily, and soon took a position as an assistant in an import-export firm, with the intention of learning the business. I adjusted well to my new life. My need for the company of women did not lessen, but I avoided deep relationships, satisfying myself with casual affairs with women of easy virtue. Once a month or so the urge would come on me and I would do what I had to do. The guilt I suffered became less and less as time passed. I never came to like what I was forced by my nature to do, but I came to enjoy doing it. The thrill of the chase more than made up for the danger, and I feasted on no one who did not deserve to die.

But that which set me apart made me feel like an exile in the midst of life. I suffered from loneliness. I could find no others like me. Mother had said there were few of us, but not how few. For a while I used the recognition signal of the *strix* so often in public places that it was becoming an involuntary tic, but no one ever responded. Aside from sharing my dreadful secret, others of my kind could give me solace through the years as those mortals whom I befriended grew old and died—although I could never stay in one place long enough for that to happen. As Mother had, I must move on before my contemporaries noted my failure to age. I thought of creating my own partner; of gently sucking the blood from the neck of some lovely woman until, over time, the miraculous transformation took place. But I would not do it to someone against her will, and how do you suggest such a thing? I thirsted for the companionship of someone of my own kind.

I had been in London for about eight years, and was considering moving on, when I went one evening to a very exclusive bordello in the company of a brace of acquaintances who considered themselves to be dashing young men-about-town. Madam Lilith's it was called. The madam, I was told, was as young and beautiful as any of her girls, but you didn't choose her; she, if she wished, chose you.

The building, right around the corner from Blakeney Square, was a four-story Georgian structure with a wide front door straddled by a pair of ornate gaslights. A page boy answered the door pull, and my two companions led the way into the parlor. A score of beautiful women in various stages of dishabille lounged about the room. In one corner a thin, totally bald man with a very pale face played the piano. A young coquette who was in conversation with a colonel of the artillery as we came in excused herself and walked over to greet us. Her costume was less revealing than those of her sisters, but one could not call it chaste. Her body spoke of youth and innocence, her face was veiled in some silky fabric. "It is Madam herself!" one of my companions whispered to me.

Madam pushed aside the veil and stretched her arms out to me. "So marvelous to see you again. You are but little changed, and that for the good."

"You know her?" my companion asked.

I took her hand. She looked younger than I remembered. For a second I was unable to speak, but then I regained my composure. "This lady taught me all I know," I said. "And I know now that I have much more to learn."

Mother kissed me on the lips. "My precious orange," she said.

Victims

KRISTINE KATHRYN RUSCH

i

Her name had shown up twice before, in '68 when Nichols had run for governor of California, and in '72 when he made his unsuccessful bid for the presidency. No one had investigated her. Women's issues were different in those days, and women were not viewed as the voting bloc they are now. Besides, we couldn't make anything on Nichols stick.

We decided to investigate her before we talked with Senator Lurry. The task of interrogating her came to me.

I used Senator Lurry's outer office because it looked properly intimidating—mahogany trim, marble inlay floors. The desks were wide, oak and handmade. A coffeemaker, constantly in use, sat on top of one of the green metal filing cabinets, but the rich scent of French Roast couldn't overlay the mausoleum stench of an ancient building that has stood in humidity for a generation too long.

I arrived a half hour early, then adjusted my tie and peered at my reflection in the shiny glass on top of the secretary's desk. The cowlick had refused to be tamed again. I licked my hand and patted the spot, wishing for the fifteenth time that I could use boyishness to my advantage. From the neck down I was perfect: broad shoulders tapering into narrow hips, legs firm and muscular. My face was the major problem. Oval-shaped with wide eyes and pouty lips, it made me look like a twelve-year-old in his father's body, which was the reason I worked behind the scenes for Senator Lurry instead of out front as most of the Cattons had in the past.

I didn't dare look naive in front of a woman named Veronique.

Especially a woman with a history like hers.

Downstairs a door slammed shut. I jumped. High heels clicked on the marble floor, the sound echoing in the empty building. I had often worked late, but never alone. Near midnight on those evenings, the place had a hum to it that I always associated with an election or a smear campaign. Never with an interview.

She had insisted on the time. "A woman in my profession," she had said, her voice husky through the phone lines, "looks best after dark."

I tugged on my black suit jacket. I wasn't really alone. Morse sat in the senator's office, watching through the fake mirror in case the lady decided to ply her trade on me.

The footsteps grew closer. I rearranged the papers on the desktop, toyed with sitting down, and then decided to remain standing. I still hadn't learned all the tricks to power and intimidation.

The door opened and she slipped in. She was heartbreakingly thin, with perfect legs that tapered from a model's body. She wore spike heels, fishnets, and a leather miniskirt that revealed each curve around her hips. Her black Irish lace blouse set off her porcelain skin. Her lips were dark red, her cheekbones high and her eyes an amazing shade of brown. No wonder she ran the most exclusive escort service in D.C. No man would be able to say no to her.

I stepped from behind the desk, resisting the urge to wipe my hands on my pants legs. I approached her, palm extended. "Reese Catton."

She placed her fingers lightly in mine. Her skin was cool, not cold as I had expected. "Veronique de la Mer."

Her voice was husky and warm. A tingle ran up my spine. Ever since vampires and vampirism had come out of the closet five years ago, the news and the tabloid press had been full of articles on the sensual effect of the predator-victim relationship. It didn't seem to matter that all but a few psychopathic vampires had long ago given up killing human prey—choosing instead to use a handful of willing people to provide blood, much as a blood bank did for a hospital ("the supermarket approach to bloodsucking," the *New York Times* had called it)—the fear, loathing, and sexual tension caused by the human-vampire relationship filled the popular imagination.

Just as she filled mine.

Dry facts weren't giving me control. I took a deep breath and slid into the leather chair behind the desk.

"I hope you understand why we contacted you," I said.

"Oh, yes." Her voice was soft. "It's about Governor Nichols."

She had an edge when she spoke his name, a frisson of anger just beneath the surface. I swallowed, feeling calmer. "I hope you don't mind if I tape this conversation."

"I expected you to," she said, and folded her hands demurely in her lap. I pressed the button underneath the desk, activating the room's taping system, and wondered for a moment if vampires' voices taped. But I knew they did. We had gotten tape on one just a few weeks ago. They didn't reflect or film—but that was because of the silvering in the mirrors, the play of light and shadow.

"I understand," I said, leaning forward and placing my arms on the desk, "that you've never spoken with anyone about Governor Nichols."

She smiled, revealing straight, white teeth. "Oh, I've spoken with people," she said. "Only no one believed me."

I froze. Her last sentence had thrown me. We were planning, with her cooperation, to smear the former governor by linking him to a vampire as her cow. Our preliminary surveys of 150 voters showed that such a thing would work as effectively as gay bashing had in the eighties. "What do you mean?"

"On July 4, 1966, your friend, the former governor of California, raped me." She never took her gaze off mine. She spoke calmly, but the ends to the words were clipped, as if she had to spit them out.

I let out the air I had been holding. She was lying. We couldn't bring this to the media. They would skin her alive. "Why didn't you press charges?"

A half smile, curving those delicate lips into her firm cheekbones. "I tried. It was 1966. I was told that a woman who ran an escort service shouldn't complain when she got famous business."

"Who told you that?"

"The detective in charge," she said. "An unfortunately deceased man named Petrie. His superior officers backed up his prejudice. I haven't spoken of the incident since. I figure it would be even tougher to convince people now that they know I belong to a completely different race."

"Why didn't you go after him?"

Her eyes seemed to tilt downward with an expression of deep sadness, as if she were disappointed in me for asking the question. "Come now, Mr. Catton. What did you expect me to do? Fly into his house on bat wings and rip out his throat?"

"Something like that," I mumbled. My cheeks grew warm. I guess I had expected that. Old fictional images died hard. Studies had shown that vampires lacked the ability to shape-shift and mesmerize, although they did have centuries-long life spans and the appearance of eternal youth.

"Mr. Catton, I have used my political contacts for the better part of two decades to keep the former governor of California out of the presidency. But times are changing, and the country doesn't seem to care what kind of man he is as long as he presents a positive media image. Grandfatherly always seems to work in this country. Well, as you know, any connection with me would ruin Nichols's grandfatherly image." She stood and smoothed her skirt. "The problem you face is that I am unwilling to be linked to that slime romantically or parasitically. We will denounce him as a man capable of extreme violence or you will not have my cooperation."

"Forgive me," I said from my chair, "but I don't think Middle America would care that you got raped."

She took a step backward as if I had slapped her myself. "I suppose you're right," she said. "Middle America would simply figure that a woman like me deserved it."

ii

I was shaking by the time I got home. Alison had gone to bed, leaving a single light on near the fireplace. Embers glowed, light reflecting across the shiny hardwood floor. This place always filled me with a kind of pride—the way the couches framed the oriental rugs, the fresh flowers on the Duncan Phyfe end tables, the lemon-scented neatness of the condo itself. Even though I had been raised a Catton, my mother kept a messy, "lived-in" house in Connecticut that hid my father's wealth. I preferred an immaculate, House Beautiful style.

Except tonight. Tonight I wanted to kick off my shoes,

scrunch the rugs, and huddle near the television set. But I pulled off my shoes and hung them on the shoe rack in the closet beside the door, walked stocking-footed across the slippery floor and sat at the dining room table, staring at the fruit basket, perfectly arranged, with bananas on the side, oranges at the base, and apples on top.

Veronique had gotten to me.

I had never been naive, not even when I had come to Washington as a page for Senator Lurry fifteen years ago. Any pretensions I may have had remaining toward Truth, Justice, and the American Way were then bled out of me in George Washington's Poli Sci Department and at Harvard Law. Politics in this country had become the battle of the image. Whoever controlled the media controlled the campaign.

Veronique and her escort service hadn't been necessary in '68 and '72. Nichols had done a good job of destroying his own campaign. Then he disappeared behind the scenes, became a scion of the Republican party, helped Reagan and Bush achieve office, and maintained his own series of perks. The media had forgotten all about the bumbling "youth" candidate who had challenged Nixon in the '72 primaries and saw only the trim, natty grandfather who had helped the Republicans become a power in the eighties. A viceless, happily married man who spoke of family values and allowed Pat Robertson to fund his campaign.

The kind of man Senator Lurry—whose presidential ambitions had died the night of his daughter's suicide in '80—despised. Lurry had vowed to clear the way for the Democratic challenger, whether that might be Clinton, Gore, or a wild card no one had ever heard of. We had demolished Quayle before he even announced, but Nichols was proving to be as Teflon as Reagan had been.

The rape charge wouldn't stand. I had been right. Middle

America wouldn't tolerate it. They would bring down the messenger.

I sighed and placed my forehead on my arms. We had contacted Veronique because the call girls had not so inexplicably shut up, the records had disappeared on the reported spousal abuse in the mid-seventies, and the college plagiarism charge hadn't caused a ripple in the polls. An affair with a vampire, we figured, still had taint, even though it was nearly thirty years old.

Although it would be a gamble. If word of the smear got out, Lurry would lose his position as champion of the nontraditional. Vampires, gays, and minorities formed a large percentage of his constituency.

If Lurry got caught, he would, of course, blame his assistants.

He would blame me.

iii

"What'd he do?" Lurry asked. "Force her to bite him at gunpoint?"

He was a big man who barely fit in the desk chair that had been specially designed for him ten years previously. He had long jowls that spoke of too many meals and the red, bulbous nose of a hard-core alcoholic. His voice boomed, even in the small office. It always amazed me that he could tarnish the image of anyone.

I shot a glance at Stuckey, his press secretary. She had a small, heart-shaped face, almond eyes, and café-au-lait skin. Her mixed heritage was as much a part of her job as was her way with words.

"She didn't go into the details of the rape," I said.

Stuckey leaned back in her chair, her long, slender fingers playing with the ruby on her left hand. "We would need proof of some kind. Police report, photographs—"

"Photographs are impossible." I picked the lint off my black pin-striped pants leg. "And she said that the police refused to believe her."

"If they were called to the site, someone had to write it up," Stuckey said. "It's probably buried in some back file in a basement somewhere. I'll bet Nichols didn't think to cover his tracks on this one."

"I don't see any reason why he had to. Reese was right. Middle America isn't going to give a damn that some blood-sucking parasite got slapped around thirty years ago."

Stuckey jutted out her narrow chin. Forty years ago, someone might have said the same about her. I hated it when she got that look. "Be careful, Senator," she said. "The Republicans would love to hear you talking like that."

"For God's sake," he said, leaning forward. His exquisitely tailored suit strained at its buttons. "It's the truth."

"There's another truth," Stuckey said. "She has been an influential member of Washington Society since the thirties. She contributes to all sorts of charities, and it could be said that her escort business provides a necessary service for this community. There is no overt evidence of prostitution, and any employee who provides sexual services on a regular basis drops off the payroll of the service and appears on the payroll of the client. Would she make an articulate spokesperson, Catton?"

I nodded. Something about Lurry's reaction was bothering me. "She would, except that we can't film her."

"That doesn't matter," Stuckey said. "Neither can they. I say let's see what we've got and then make a decision. We might be able to use the woman after all."

"No," Lurry said. He folded his hands over his chest.

Stuckey raised one eyebrow. She opened her mouth to speak as I put a finger on her arm.

"What's your connection with her, Senator?" I asked.

His expression didn't change, but his gaze seemed to go

flat. It was a look I recognized from his press conferences: the Lurry Method of Avoiding the Truth. "She runs an escort service for the Washington elite, Reese. There's no telling what kind of dirt we might inadvertently dig up."

I suppressed a sigh. Lurry had always been a wild man; the wildness had gotten worse since his daughter's death. During my college years, the staff had worked hard at covering his destructive tracks all over this city. I had worked hard when I came on board the second time to hold on to other staff members, particularly the women, who hated his roving hands and not-so-subtle innuendo. The others trusted me, because they knew I was a family man, a man who would never treat others the way Lurry did.

But this was something that had fallen through the cracks.

Stuckey had come to the same conclusion. She hated working for Lurry, hated that the man behind the excellent political record was a petty tyrant, sexist, and a bigot. "It might be your last chance to get Nichols," she said.

Lurry spun the swivel on his chair so that he looked out the window instead of staring at us. He was silent for a long time. Finally he said, "I don't care. We can't afford the risk. We'll have to find some other way."

"I doubt there is another way," Stuckey said. She left the room. I followed more slowly. As I closed the door, I saw Lurry reach into his liquor cabinet. It was too early to drink, even for him.

iv

Despite Lurry's refusal to pursue the investigation, Stuckey continued. So did I. I was too intrigued to let it go. Maybe after we had the evidence, Lurry would allow us to run to the media. It had happened before.

Stuckey put one of our best detectives on the case, a secret infiltrator who had no visible connections to us. The detective would make it look to the police like an investigation of Veronique de la Mer instead of an investigation of Nichols.

That would keep the information out of the press until we were ready to put it there ourselves.

Stuckey and I were supposed to meet with the senator after the detective's report came in, but I had some questions of my own to answer.

Veronique's escort service had headquarters near the Hill. I parked a block away, and waited until no one was looking before I entered the building. The elevator took me to the sixth-floor offices. As I stepped through the double glass doors, a level of tension left me.

The offices were tasteful. The colors were out-of-date: the muted grays and pinks of the mideighties, but the garish purples and neon greens of the early nineties would have looked out of place here. Flowers in Waterford crystal vases stood on runners that crossed antique tables. All of the furniture was antique, mixing periods to great effect: the tables were Early American, the couches late Victorian, the lighting and the crystal were modern. The decor gave the feel of a place that had been in business for a long, long time. The carpet absorbed my footfalls, and I was alone in the waiting room. I assumed that was on purpose. It made the clients feel as if discretion was part of the service.

A woman entered through a sliding glass door. She wore a white silk dress that flowed around her voluptuous body. Her long black hair flowed down her back, as untamed as the dress. "Do you have an appointment, sir?"

Her voice was as well modulated as the rest of her. A shiver ran down my spine. "No," I said, a little more harshly than I expected. "I am from Senator Lurry's office. I would like to see Veronique."

The woman nodded once. "Come with me," she said, and without waiting went back through the glass doors.

The hallway was long and narrow and smelled faintly of lilacs. Closed doors along each side gave this area a forbidding feeling that the front didn't have. Privacy above all else.

How odd. Veronique mastered privacy in her business, yet she was willing to give it all away to bring down Nichols.

She really had to hate him.

The woman opened the double mahogany doors at the end of the hallway, then stepped aside so that I could enter. I stepped into another waiting room, although this one was more flamboyant than the one I had left. The colors were red, black and deep browns, and all of the furniture was late Edwardian: heavy with thick upholstery. The room had a masculine feel, as if it were designed by a man for a woman.

The door closed behind me. I sat on the edge of the couch, feeling sixteen again, and at the interview for my page position. I tugged on the knees of my trousers. They were tight across the groin.

A door opened, and then Veronique was in the room. She wore her hair piled on top of her head, revealing a slender, well-formed neck. This time she wore a suit. The jacket was open, and the shell was cut low across her breasts, revealing cleavage and a bit of nipple. She sat on the edge of her desk and crossed her legs. "I didn't expect to see you here, Mr. Catton."

I swallowed. I was a happily married man. Alison and I had a good sex life. I didn't need anything else. "I'm here on business."

She smiled. "Most people are."

"No," I said. "For Senator Lurry."

"Ah." She got off the desk and retreated behind it, tugging her coat across her chest. "You want to know details. How can a human male rape a woman of superior strength? It's really quite easy, Mr. Catton. It simply takes planning. He must learn where I sleep, for that's when I am most vulnerable, and learn how to tie me up, how to immobilize my mouth. Determination, Mr. Catton—"

"That's not why I'm here," I said. I couldn't stand the calm tone she was using with me. "I've been thinking about this. We're investigating your claim now, but it doesn't completely make sense to me. Assume that I believe you, what's in this for you? You have other, more subtle ways to bring down Nichols. Why choose a haphazard method that may not work?"

She smiled and leaned back, letting the coat pull open again. The shell was thin, and it stretched across her chest, outlining her breasts in detail. Her nipples were hard points against the material.

I forced myself to look into her eyes.

"You're very smart, Mr. Catton," she said.

I licked my lips. She made me nervous, here, in her lair. "I try to be."

"Then perhaps you will understand that I am tired of being hidden. My people have been out of the closet, to use your quaint phrase, for five years now, and we are still fighting myths and prejudices. We live long lives, and have experiences that encompass entire generations. We understand policy and its ramifications better than you do. But our limitations, Mr. Catton, became obvious once the camera was invented. We cannot run for office. We could not even try until a few years ago."

I tugged again at my pants legs. It was good they couldn't run, good that television cameras couldn't pick them up. With their charisma, they would win, every time. "People are too afraid of you to elect you."

"Yes," she said. "I know. But things change over time. We have seen that with African Americans and with women. We have decided that it is better to fight in an open forum than behind the scenes."

"To put you up against Nichols's media machine is to sacrifice you to the prejudices of the American people. You'll lose."

"Perhaps," she said. "But I'll damage Nichols, and I'll start the awareness that vampires are not the all-evil, all-powerful beings the movies have made them out to be."

I ran a hand along the crushed velvet upholstery. "I don't understand how choosing to become a victim will help you politically."

She shrugged and smiled, just a little. "Then, Mr. Catton, you're not as smart as I thought."

v

I immediately hurried home. Fortunately Alison was there. Much to her surprise, I dragged her to bed, and we made love like newlyweds in their sexual prime. We had just finished when the doorbell rang.

She brushed the hair from her forehead. "You go on," she said, pushing me a little. "I need to shower. I'm already late for a Woman in Business meeting."

I slid on a pair of jeans, walked barefoot to the door, and looked through the peephole. Stuckey was there, her face pale beneath the makeup. She clutched a stack of folders to her chest. Her briefcase rested on the floor beside her.

I pulled the door open.

"We need to talk," she said, and came in without an invitation. Her shoes left little prints on the hardwood floor. She set everything on the dining room table, pushing the basket of fruit aside to make room.

I sat down beside her, opened the files, and barely looked up when Alison kissed me good-bye. The files were dusty, the old police reports more detailed than I had expected, as if someone had been planning a case. A client had found Veronique, naked, blood-covered, and half dead in her waiting room. She had been tied with silver wire, a garlic bulb shoved in her mouth, and slashed from groin to sternum with a knife. The reports were filed by four separate officers and a pathologist. Veronique had been conscious enough to demand her private doctor, and instead of being treated by the hospital staff, she had been treated by a man now known as the vampire's equivalent of doctor to the stars.

The files included photos of the crime scene and Veronique's account, both on tape and in writing, of the rape itself. The investigation ended as soon as the nature of Veronique's profession became known.

Stuckey watched me as I read Veronique's account. Nichols had not been alone. Four other politicians of his generation had been there to take care of Veronique properly. Three of the four were dead—one in a single-engine plane crash over the Appalachians, one in an unsolved murder in Mexico, and one of an undiagnosed variety of pernicious anemia which the doctor associated with leukemia but which was now known to be caused by bad reaction to secretions in vampire saliva.

The fourth was alive: Senator Jason Lurry, then a first-term congressman from the great state of Texas.

I brought my head up. Stuckey was watching me, elbow on the table, chin resting on her palm. "She set us up," I said.

Stuckey rolled her eyes. "Veronique is not the problem," she said. "It's Lurry. He lied to us and to his constituents from the beginning. Did you read why he participated?"

I shook my head. I had stopped when I saw his name.

"Because she was withholding favors from them. *Political* favors. She was refusing to use her sexual influence to aid their careers."

I let my breath out slowly. "Raping her was certainly not the way to get her to help."

"No," Stuckey said, "but it sent a message throughout the community. A lot of people knew what she was. They must have figured these men had a lot of muscle behind them to get her as badly as they did."

I rubbed the bridge of my nose. A headache was building behind my eyes. It all made sense now. Lurry and Nichols had ceased being friends in '67. Something must have come between them then, something to do with Veronique. They managed to succeed without her, but not to the heights they had wanted. And whenever they had come close to achieving those heights, something had successfully damaged their careers—like Lurry's daughter's suicide.

"What I don't understand is why she's doing this now," I said. "I talked to her. I said going public would make her a victim, and why would anyone want to be a victim? She laughed at me and called me naive."

Stuckey blinked at me and then grinned. "You're not naive," she said. "You're just privileged. Reese Catton, son of politicians, product of private schools and Ivy League law schools. Even your name has the sound of wealth."

I squirmed, suddenly cold without my shirt. "What the hell does that mean?"

"It means you're one of the lucky few who've never been victimized." She leaned forward, a flush rising beneath her dusky skin. "Reese, honey, victims are victims when they remain quiet. They gain power when they speak out."

The headache had moved to my temples. "She had power. It looks like she controlled their careers from the inside."

"But that's a revenge cycle," Stuckey said, "and no more empowering than punching a man who mugged you. You need to read more about ways to help the powerless. Look what empathy did for Bobby Kennedy."

"Yeah," I said, standing. "It got him assassinated."

vi

This time we met in neutral territory, at the Lincoln Memorial. I waited on the steps after dark, in the shadow of Honest Abe himself.

Honest Abe, who had suspended civil rights and freed the slaves as a matter of political expediency. Honest Abe, who really wanted to send all the blacks back to Africa.

I heard her before I saw her. Heels clicking against the sidewalk, a purse clutched to her arm. She wasn't wearing hooker clothes or a business suit. This time she wore jeans and a mohair sweater. The outfit suited her more than the others had.

"You set me up," I said, before I could see her face in the streetlight.

"No." She climbed the stairs and sat beside me on the top. She smelled faintly of lilacs. "I have just learned that it is easier to convince people when they discover the information for themselves. You wouldn't have believed me if I attacked your precious senator. You believe me now."

I did that. If nothing else, I believed Veronique's version of those events back in 1966. "What do you want from me?"

"We need a spokesman. You are our best choice. You are young, moving into that youthful handsomeness that this country associates with its romantic leaders. But the problem is you have no dreams, no ideals. We will give those to you." She ran a hand through her hair. There was nothing seductive about her this night. "You see, what your histories have forgotten is that the symbiosis went beyond the physical. Your people provided the energy, the power, and the drive. Ours the sense of community and continuity. Over the centuries, we failed to keep our end. We stagnated, and you rebelled—a rebellion that culminated with the invention of the camera and became codified with the publication of Stoker's horrible political tract. But we have learned our lesson. We would like to forge a new voice in the political history of the Western world. We would like a new alliance, and we need your help."

I leaned back, resting my elbows on the cool concrete stairs. I should have been used to power games; I had initiated enough myself. But I had been off balance in this one from the beginning. "Why me? Why not someone like Stuckey?"

"Because," she said, "you have no personal axes to grind, no commitment to anything except yourself, your lovely wife, and your home. We don't want someone with other ties that might interfere with our cause."

Words were carved into the walls above me. Great words, spoken by a man considered by many to be one of our best leaders. Who knew why he ran for office. Power madness? A belief he could make a difference? Ego? All three or none of the above?

I shook my head. "I'm sorry," I said. "I don't know anything about you people. For all I know, you could be trying to take over the country."

She smiled, her teeth flashing in the streetlights. "Isn't that what every special interest group hopes to do?"

"Not every special interest group has the power of persuasion that you people have."

She touched my hand. Her fingers were cold. "I should make myself clear. I'm not asking you to run for president. I want you to resign as Lurry's aide, then help me make a public case against them."

Her fingers were long and slender, the nails tapered. "Forgive me," I said, keeping my voice soft. "But I was right that first night. Middle America won't care that you were raped."

"Make them care. That would be your job."

I moved my arm out of her grasp. "There are better people

for that. Image brokers, people who make their living changing public opinion."

"But none are as unimpeachable as you." She leaned back beside me. "Think of it. You worked for Senator Lurry. You discovered the information yourself. It so appalled you that you are jeopardizing your own political career to speak out against him."

I tilted my head back so that I couldn't see her. Abe's carved legs, spread slightly apart, towered above me. She would do this, with or without me. And she would fail, but the die would be cast. Conversations would start; people would talk; ideas would get aired as they had at the beginning of each intellectual and perceptual revolution.

The balance of power was shifting beneath me. I could cling to the old or leap to the new. Or I could attempt to straddle the middle, and watch the world as I knew it crumble beneath my feet.

I had planned to resign anyway.

I needed a new job.

"Let me bring Stuckey along and I'll do it," I said.

"You may have anyone you want on your team." Veronique stood and wiped off the back of her jeans. "Come to me after you've publicly announced your resignation. We'll finalize our agreement then."

She walked down the steps, heels clicking until the darkness swallowed her. I didn't know how I ever thought she wanted to be a victim. She had more power than all the rest of us combined—the power of her convictions. I envied that. It was something I had never seen in Washington.

Maybe the world was shifting more than I thought.

Marîd and the Trail of Blood

George Alec Effinger

There is a saying: "The Budayeen hides from the light." You can interpret that any way you like, but I'm dissolute enough to know *exactly* what it means. There's a certain time of day that always makes me feel as if my blackened soul were just then under the special scrutiny of Allah in Paradise.

It happens in the gray winter mornings just at dawn, when I've spent the entire night drinking in some awful hellhole. When I finally decide it's time to go home and I step outside, instead of the cloaking forgiveness of darkness, there is bright, merciless sun shining on my aching head.

It makes me feel filthy and a little sick, as if I'd been wallowing in a dismal gutter all night. I know I can get pretty goddamn wiped out, but I don't believe I've ever sunk to wallowing; at least, I don't remember it if I did. And all the merchants setting up their stalls in the *souks,* all the men and women rising for morning prayers, they all glare at me with that special expression: they know exactly where I've been.

They know I'm drunk and irredeemable. They give freely of contempt that they've been saving for a long time for someone as depraved and worthless as me.

This is not even to mention the disapproving expression on Youssef's face last Tuesday, when he opened the great wooden front door at home. Or my slave, Kmuzu. Both of them knew enough not to say a word out loud, but I got the full treatment from their attitudes, particularly when Kmuzu started slamming down the breakfast things half an hour later. As if I could stand to eat. All I wanted to do was collapse and sleep, but no one in the household would allow it. It was part of my punishment.

So that's how this adventure began. I reluctantly ate a little breakfast, ignored the large quantity of orders, receipts, ledgers, and other correspondence on my desk, and sat back in a padded leather chair wishing my mortal headache would go away.

Now, when I first had my brain wired, I was given a few experimental features. I can chip in a device that makes my body burn alcohol faster than the normal ounce an hour; last night had been a contest between me and my hardware. The liquor won. I could also chip in a pain-blocking daddy, but it wouldn't make me any more sober. For now, in the real world, I was as sick as a plague-stricken wharf rat.

I watched a holoshow about a sub-Saharan reforestation program, with the sound turned off. Before it was over, I lied to myself that I felt just a tiny bit better. I even pretended to act friendly toward Kmuzu. I forgave him, and I forgave myself for what I'd done the night before. I promised both of us that I'd never do it again.

I laughed; Kmuzu didn't. He turned his back and walked out of the room without saying a word.

It was obvious to me that it wasn't a good day to spend around the house. I decided to go back to the Budayeen and open my nightclub at noon, a little early for the day shift. Even if I had to sit there by myself for a couple of hours, it would be better company than I had at home.

About 12:15, Pualani, the beautiful real girl, came in. She was early for work, but she had always been one of the most dependable of the five dancers on the day shift. I said hello, and before she went to the dressing room she sat down beside me at the bar. "You hear what happened to Crazy Vi, who works by Big Al's Old Chicago?"

"No," I said. I can't keep up with what goes on with every girl, deb, and sex-change in the Budayeen.

"She turned up dead yesterday. They say they found her body all drained of blood, and she had two small puncture marks on her neck. It looks like some kind of vampire jumped on her or something." Pualani shuddered.

I closed my eyes and rubbed my throbbing temples. "There are no such things as vampires," I said. "There are no afrits, no djinn, no werewolves, no succubi, and no trolls. There has to be some other explanation for Vi." I recognized the woman's name, but I couldn't picture her face.

"Like what?"

"I don't know, a murderer with an elaborate scheme to throw suspicion on a supernatural suspect, maybe."

"I don't think so," Pualani said. "I mean, everything just fits."

"Uh-huh," I said.

Pualani went into the back to change into her working outfit. I reached over the bar and filled a tall glass with ice, then poured myself a carbonated soft drink.

Chiriga, my partner, arrived not long after. She owned half the club and acted as daytime barmaid. I was glad to see her, because it meant that I didn't have to watch the place anymore. I rested my head on my arms and let the hangover headache do its throbbing worst.

Nothing felt fatal until someone shook my shoulder. I tried to ignore it, but it wouldn't go away. I sat up and saw Yasmin, one of the dancers. She was brushing her glistening black hair. "You hear about Vi?" she said.

"Uh-huh."

"You know I *warned* Vi about staying out of that alley. She used to go home that way every night. That's what she gets for working at the Old Chicago and going home that way. I must've told her a dozen times."

I took a deep breath and let it out. "Yasmin, the poor girl didn't deserve to die just because she walked home through an alley."

Yasmin cocked her head to one side and looked a time. "Yeah, I know, but still. You hear they think it was Sheba who killed her?"

That was news to me. "Sheba?" I asked. "She worked here maybe eight or nine months ago? *That* Sheba?"

Yasmin nodded. "She's over by Fatima and Nassir's these days, and she *belongs* there."

Chiri wiped the bar beside me and tossed a coaster in front of Yasmin. "Why do you think it was Sheba who killed Crazy Vi?" Chiri asked.

"Cause," Yasmin said in a loud whisper. "Vi was killed by a vampire, right? And you never see Sheba in the daytime. Never. Have you? Think about it. Let me have some peppermint schnapps, Chiri."

I glanced at Chiri, but she only shrugged. I turned back to Yasmin. "First everybody's sure Vi was killed by a vampire, and now you're sure that the vampire is Sheba."

Yasmin raised both hands and tried to look innocent. "I'm not making any of this up," she said. She scooped up her peppermint schnapps and went to sit beside Pualani. No customers had come in yet.

"Well," I said to Chiri, "what do you think?"

Chiri's expression didn't change. "I don't think anything. Do I have to?" Chiri's the only person in the Budayeen with any sense. And that includes me.

The afternoon passed slowly. The other three dancers, Lily, Kitty, and Baby, came in when they felt like it. We made a little money, sold a few drinks, the girls hustled some champagne cocktails. I listened to the same damn Sikh propaganda songs on the holo system and watched my employees parade their talents.

It was getting on toward dinnertime when Lily and Yasmin got into an argument with two poor European marks. I strolled over toward their table, not because I care anything for marks—I generally don't—but because a bad enough argument might send the two guys out into the Street and into somebody else's club.

"Marîd, listen—" Lily said.

I held up a hand, interrupting her. "Are you two gentlemen enjoying yourselves?" I asked.

They had puzzled looks on their faces, but they nodded. Some people are born marks, others achieve markdom, and some people have markdom thrust upon them.

"What's the problem?" I said in a warning voice. "I can hear you all the way across the bar."

"We were talking about Vi," Lily said. "We were warning Lazaro and Karoly to stay out of that alley."

"We were going to suggest a nice, safe place where we could go," Yasmin said. She tried to look innocent again. Yasmin hasn't been innocent since her baby teeth fell out.

"Look, you two," I said, meaning my two fun-loving hustlers, "let me clear this up right now. I'll call the morgue and find out what they know about Crazy Vi."

"You're gonna call the morgue?" Lily said. She was suddenly very interested.

"Get back to work," I said. I went back to my seat at the

bar. I unclipped the phone from my belt and murmured the commcode of the Budayeen's morgue. The medical examiner there, Dr. Besharati, had helped me with a couple of other matters over the years. He was normal enough for a guy who worked surrounded by dead bodies all day. He liked to tootle a jazz trumpet in between autopsies. That was *his* kick.

I got one of his assistants. The coroner was busy putting brains into jars or something. "Yeah? Medical examiner's office."

"I wanted to get some information about one of the, ah, deceased currently in your custody."

"You a family member?"

I blinked. "Sure," I said.

"Okay, then. What you want?"

"Young woman, killed last night in an alley in the Budayeen. Her name was Vi."

"Yeah?" He wasn't making it any easier for me.

"We were just wondering if you have determined the cause of death yet."

There was a long pause while the assistant went off to investigate. When he returned he said, "Well, we ain't got to her yet, but she died on account she was murdered. Slashed throat, heavy loss of blood. That'll do it every time."

I grimaced. I could only hope they'd be a little gentler with Vi's real family. "Could you tell me, were there any puncture wounds on the throat?"

"Told you we ain't got to her yet. Don't know. Call again tomorrow maybe. We ought to have her on the slab by then. Do you need to come watch?"

I just hung up after leaving my commcode. I was sure that Lily would have happily viewed the autopsy, but even if I couldn't quite remember who Vi was, she probably deserved better treatment than that.

The two European marks got up and left the club about a half hour later. Yasmin came and leaned against the bar near me. She was brushing her hair again. "What jerks," she said.

They're all jerks, is the general opinion.

"I called about Vi," I said. "No vampire. She was just murdered in the alley."

"Huh," Lily said dubiously. "Like she could bite herself in her own neck."

I spread my hands. "They haven't confirmed the business about the puncture wounds. You're just exaggerating all of this way out of proportion."

Yasmin looked at me knowingly. "You'll see," she said. She turned to Lily, who nodded her agreement. Dealing with my employees is sometimes very hard on my nerves. I thought about having my first drink of the day, but I didn't. I went out to get something to eat instead.

Now, Chiriga's is about halfway between the eastern gate of the Budayeen and the western end—the cemetery. There are plenty of places to eat along the Street, and on this particular occasion I decided to head toward Kiyoshi's. I hadn't walked far before I saw the Lamb Lady.

"Oh boy," I muttered. Safiyya the Lamb Lady is a regular feature of the Budayeen, one of our favorite odd characters. She's harmless, but she can talk at you so long you're sure you'll never get away. She lives on money people give her and she sleeps wherever anybody will let her. I've let her stay in my club a few times. She's completely honest, just addled a bit. That's why I was surprised to see her wearing a lot of expensive-looking jewelry. She had on eight or ten silver rings, two silver necklaces, silver earrings, and silver bracelets and bangles from her wrists halfway to her elbows.

"Where'd you get all that, Safiyya?" I asked.

"Watch out for the lamb," she said in a hoarse voice. She

used to have a lamb that followed her around the Budayeen, but it was accidentally killed. Now Safiyya has an imaginary lamb. I'd almost bumped into it.

"Sorry," I said.

"Isn't this nice stuff?" she said. She jingled her bracelets. "I found it all in the trash."

"In the trash?" The silver she was wearing must have been worth four or five hundred kiam. "Where?"

"Oh, it's all gone now," Safiyya said. "I took it. I'll show you, though, if you want to see." I followed her because I was curious. She led me to the back of a whitewashed, two-story apartment building, where four trash cans had been upended. Garbage was strewn all over the narrow passageway between buildings, but we didn't find any more jewelry.

When Safiyya started showing off all this silver, she would make herself a target for robbery, or worse. I decided to mention this to one of my connections in the police department; they'd keep an eye on Safiyya. With Crazy Vi's unsolved murder the night before, I guessed there'd be a stronger police presence in the Budayeen tonight. I'd hate to see the Lamb Lady become the killer's second victim.

However, the rest of the day passed quietly. Nothing happened to Safiyya, and nothing happened to me. I went home, trimmed my beard, took a long shower, and sat down at my desk to get some of my paperwork done. After a while, Kmuzu interrupted me.

"The master of the house wishes you to meet with him in an hour, *yaa Sidi*," he said.

I nodded. The master of the house was my great-grandfather, Friedlander Bey, who controlled much of the illicit activities in the city. He was a very powerful man, so powerful that he also found it profitable to control the rise and fall of certain nearby nations. It was like a hobby with him.

Forty-five minutes later I was dressed the way Papa liked me to dress, standing at the door to his office. It was guarded by Habib and Labib, Papa's huge, silent bodyguards. I wasn't going in until they felt like letting me go in.

Tariq, Friedlander Bey's secretary and valet, came out and noticed me. "I hope you haven't been waiting long," he said.

I shrugged. "I've just been watching these two guys. You know, they don't move at all. They don't even breathe. How do they manage that?"

Tariq did the smart thing and ignored me. He ushered me into Papa's inner office. Friedlander Bey reclined on a lacquered divan. He indicated that I should seat myself across from him. Between us was a table loaded down with trays of food and fruit, juices and silver coffee things. We chatted informally while we drank the customary cups of coffee. Then, suddenly, Papa was all business.

"You are spending too much time in the Budayeen," he said.

"But O Shaykh, you gave me the nightclub—"

He raised a hand. I shut up. "There are more important matters. Representatives from the Empire of Parthia will be arriving tomorrow. They wish our support in their expansion into Kush."

"I didn't even know they—"

"I do not believe we will give them what they desire. Indeed, I think it is time that Parthia be, shall we say, disunited."

What could I do but agree? We discussed these weighty affairs for some time. At last, Papa relaxed. He took an apple and a small paring knife. "You called the medical examiner today, my darling," he said.

I was astonished. "Yes, O Shaykh."

"You are interested in the death of the young dancer. It is of no importance."

Maybe it's because I used to be a poor street kid myself, but the lives and deaths of the people of the Budayeen matter more to me.

Friedlander Bey went on. "Your employees believe in vampires." He was amused. "Lieutenant Giragosian of the police does not." Here his amusement ended. "You will not pursue this further. It is a waste of time, and it is unseemly for you to concern yourself with what is, after all, chiefly a Christian myth."

Crazy Vi's body in the morgue was no myth. And in the Maghreb, the far western part of North Africa where I'd grown up, there are still stories of the Gôla. She is a female djinn, very big and strong, sometimes with goat's feet and covered with hair like an unshorn sheep. Her trick is that she speaks sweetly and gently to people, and then kills them and drinks their blood. The Gôla is usually described as having those familiar long, fierce canine teeth and eyes like blazing fire. Still, I wasn't about to mention any of this to my benefactor.

"You and I will share luncheon tomorrow with the Parthians," Papa said. "Forget about the murdered woman, your nightclub, and the Budayeen for a while."

"As you wish, O Shaykh," I said. Yeah, sure, I thought.

I returned to my suite and relaxed with a detective novel by Lutfy Gad, my favorite Palestinian mystery writer. He'd been dead for decades, so there were no new Gad books, but the old ones were so good I could enjoy them again and again. This one was called *The Deep Cradle*, and if I remembered correctly, it was the one in which Gad's dark and dangerous detective, al-Qaddani, ended up in Breulandy with almost every bone in his body broken.

It's amazing, sometimes, how resilient those paperback detectives are. I wish I knew how they did it.

The phone on my belt rang. That meant the call was probably from one of my disreputable friends and associates;

otherwise, the desk phone would have rung. I unclipped it and murmured, *"Marhaba."*

"Marîd? It's Yasmin, and guess what?"

She actually waited for me to guess. I didn't bother.

"You know that boys' club of yours?" she said. I have a small army of kids who look out for me in the Budayeen, watch me and make sure I'm not being followed by the cops or anything. I throw them a few kiam now and then.

"What about them?" I asked.

"One of 'em's dead and it looks like Sheba all over again. Kid's throat is torn open and before you say anything, I *saw* the goddamn puncture marks this time, like from fangs. So you're wrong."

It bothered me that her notion about Sheba was more important to her than the death of that poor boy. "Who was it?" I asked. "Anybody you know?"

"Yeah, stupid. *Sheba,* like I been telling you."

I took in a deep breath and let it out slowly. "No, not her. The boy. Who was it?"

I could almost hear her shrug. "They have *names,* Marîd? I mean, how would I know?"

I closed my eyes. "Call the police, Yasmin."

"Chiri already did."

"All right. I've got to go now."

"Something else, Marîd. Lily and me and this girl you don't know, Natka, and Sheba were all going to have supper after work tonight. At Martyrs-of-Democracy. Anyway, Sheba comes in real late with this lame excuse about having this admiral or something buy her one bottle of champagne after another even though the night shift had come in. What's an admiral doing in the Budayeen in the first place? And I know Sheba's no day-shift girl. So she's all out of breath and she seems really nervous, not just to me, you can ask Lily about it. And you know what? When we ordered the food, she asked me please not to get the pork strings in garlic sauce. That's what I *always* order. So I asked her why, and she said her stomach was bothering her, like maybe she was pregnant or had the flu or something, and the smell of the garlic would make her sick. *Garlic,* Marîd, get it?"

I opened my eyes. "Maybe it wasn't the garlic, sweetheart. Maybe she just remembered that none of you good Muslim women ought to be eating pork, in strings or anyhow."

There was a pause while Yasmin figured if I was kidding her or not. She let it go. "How much more proof do you need, Marîd?" she asked angrily. "You're really being a jackass about this." I heard her slam the phone down. I put mine back on my belt and shook my head.

Behind me, I heard Kmuzu say, "If I may say so, *yaa Sidi,* I have noticed a tendency on your part to hesitate to get involved in such matters until you yourself are personally threatened. In the meantime, innocent lives can be lost. If you think back, I'm sure you'll recall other—"

"The voice of my conscience," I said wearily, turning to face him. "Thank you so much. Are you telling me I should take this vampire stuff seriously? Especially after Papa specifically told me to ignore it?" You see, Kmuzu wasn't merely my slave; he'd been a "gift" from Friedlander Bey, someone to spy on me and report back to Papa.

He shrugged. "The people of the Budayeen have no one to turn to but you."

"So if I pursued this, you'd help me?"

Kmuzu spread his hands. "Oh no. The master of the house has made his feelings clear. Nevertheless, you could telephone Lieutenant Giragosian and learn what he knows."

I did just that. I called the copshop. "Lieutenant Giragosian's office," a man said.

"I'd like to speak to the lieutenant, please. This is Marîd Audran."

"Audran, son of a bitch. The lieutenant isn't, uh, available right now."

"Who's this, then?"

"This is his executive assistant, Sergeant Catavina." Jeez, the laziest, most easily bought cop in the city. How his star had risen.

"Look, Catavina," I said, "there've been two murders in the Budayeen in the last couple of days. One was a dancer, a real girl named Vi, and the other was a boy. Both had their throats torn out. Know anything about them?"

A pause. "Sure we do." He was playing it cagey. Dumb cagey.

"Look, pal, you want me to have Friedlander Bey send over a couple of guys to question you personal?"

"Take it easy, Audran." There was a gratifying hint of anxiety in Catavina's voice. "What are you looking for?"

"First, what's the ID on the boy?"

"Kid named Mahdi il-Mallah. Eleven years old."

I knew him. He was one of my friends. I felt a familiar coldness in my gut. "What about puncture wounds on the neck?"

"How'd you know? Yeah, that's in the report. Now, I got to tell the lieutenant you called. What you want me to tell him when he asks me what you're up to?"

I sighed. I wasn't happy about this. "Tell him I'm going to catch his vampire for him."

"Vampire! Audran, what are you, crazy?"

I hung up instead of replying.

Kmuzu's expression was difficult to read. I didn't know if he approved or not. I don't know why I cared. "One piece of advice, *yaa Sidi,* if you'll permit me: it would be a mistake to begin your investigation of this woman Sheba tonight."

"Uh-huh. Why do you say that?"

He shrugged again. "If I had to hunt a vampire, I'd do it during the daylight."

Good point. The next day I arose at dawn, made my ritual ablutions and prayed, then set out to begin serious investigations. If Kmuzu wasn't planning to offer any direct assistance—meaning that he wouldn't even drive me over to the Budayeen—then I'd have to rely on Bill the cabdriver. Now, if you know Bill, you know how amusing the concept of relying on him is. He's as dependable as a two-legged footstool.

I phoned him from the bathroom, because I didn't want Kmuzu to overhear me. I told Bill to pick me up just outside the high walls that surrounded Friedlander Bey's estate. Bill didn't remember who I was for a while, but that's usual. Bill's about as aware as a sleeping skink. He chose that for himself years ago, buying an expensive bodmod that constantly braised his brain in a very frightening high-tech hallucinogen. It would have driven most people to suicide within a handful of days; in Bill's case, I understand it sort of settled him down.

On the way from Papa's mansion to the eastern gate of the Budayeen, Bill and I had a disjointed conversation about the imminent war with the state of Gadsden. I eventually figured out that he was having some kind of flashback. Before he came to the city he'd lived in America, in the part now called Sovereign Deseret. His skink brain let him believe he was still there.

It was all right because he found the Budayeen easily enough. I gave him enough money so that he'd wait for me and drive me home, after I finished the morning's legwork. I started up the Street, in the direction of the cemetery. I didn't know yet what I wanted to do first. What did I have to go on? Two homicide victims, that's all, with nothing tangible connecting them except in the similarity of method. I had, on one hand, my employees' overheated warning that a vampire was loose around here, and on the other hand, my absolute disbelief in the supernatural.

There was nothing to do but call Chiri. I knew I'd be waking her up. I heard her pick up her phone and say, "Uh. Yeah?"

"Chiri, it's Marîd. I'm not waking you up, am I?"

"No." Her voice was real damn cold.

"Sorry. Listen, do you know where Sheba lives?"

"No, and I don't care, either."

"Then who do we know who could give me the address? I think I need to just drop by and ask Sheba a couple of things."

There was a pause: Chiri was being angry. "Yasmin would know. Or Lily."

"Yasmin or Lily. I probably should've called them first."

Another pause. "Probably."

I grimaced. "Sorry, Chiri. Go back to sleep. I'll see you later." She didn't say anything before she slammed the phone down.

I called Yasmin next, but I didn't get an answer. That didn't surprise me. I remembered from the days when Yasmin and I lived together that she was one of the best little sleepers that Allah ever invented. She could sleep through any major catastrophe except a missed meal. I gave up after listening to the phone ring a dozen and a half times, and then I called Lily. She was just as unhappy to be roused as Chiri, but her tone changed when she found out it was me. Lily has been waiting for me to call for a long time. She's a gorgeous sex-change, and she was well aware that I've never had much success with real women.

She was less happy when I told her I just wanted another girl's address and commcode. I heard ice through the ether again, but she finally gave me the information. It turned out that Sheba didn't live too far from my club.

"And one other thing," Lily said. "We checked by the Red Light Lounge. Sheba couldn't have been late to supper on account of some guy buying her drinks. She doesn't work daytimes, she's *never* worked daytimes—just like we said. So she lied. You just don't see her around when the sun is up."

"I'll keep that in mind," I said.

"So what you want to get next to *that* for? If you're spending too much time all by yourself, honey, I'll help you out."

I didn't need this now. "Yasmin would scratch your eyes out, Lily. I've only been protecting you."

"Huh, Yasmin don't remember how to spell your name, Marîd." She slammed the phone down, too. I decided it wouldn't be a good idea to set foot in my own business today. I'd probably be slashed to ribbons.

I found Sheba's apartment building and went up to the second floor. It was an old place with a thin, worn carpet runner on the stairs. The paint on the walls hung down in grimy, blowzy strips. Sheba's front door was painted a dark reddish brown, the color of a bloodstain on clothing. I knocked. There was no response. Well, Sheba was a Budayeen hustler, she was probably asleep. I knocked louder and called her name. Finally I unclipped my phone again and murmured her commcode into it; I could hear the ringing from within the apartment.

It took me perhaps a minute and a half to get past her lock. The first thing I learned was that Sheba wasn't home. The second was that it appeared she hadn't been around for a while—several envelopes had been pushed beneath her door. One had been closed only with a rubber band. I opened it; it contained a hundred kiam in ten-kiam bills, and a note from some admirer. Clothes, jewelry, stuffed animals, all sorts of things were strewn across the floor of the apartment's large room.

There was a mattress with a single sheet lying tipped up against a wall. The room's only window was standing open, water-stained yellow curtains blowing in on a warm breeze. Below the window was another heap of clothing and personal articles. I brushed the curtains aside and looked out. Below me was a narrow alley leading crookedly in the direction of Ninth Street.

A light was on in the bathroom; when I looked in there, it was as much a mess as the other room. It seemed to me that Sheba had been in a hell of a hurry, had grabbed up a few things, and had gotten out of the apartment as fast as she could. I couldn't guess why.

I looked more closely at what she'd left behind. Near the bathroom was a pile of cellophane and cardboard scraps that Sheba had kicked together. I sorted through the stuff and saw quickly that it was mostly packaging material ripped from several personality modules. I was familiar enough with the blazebrain field to know that some of the moddies Sheba had collected were not your regular commercial releases.

Sheba fancied black market titles, and very dangerous ones, too. She liked illegal underground moddies that fed her feelings of superiority and power; while she was wearing them she'd become these programmed people, and her behavior could range from the merely vicious to the downright sinister and deadly. She could almost certainly become capable of murder.

I recalled that months ago, when she worked for me at Chiri's, she was almost always chipped in to some moddy or other. That wasn't unusual among the dancers, though. I was sure that Sheba wasn't using these hard-core moddies back then, at least not at work. Something had happened in the meantime, something that had drastically changed her, and not for the better.

I put some of the wrappers in my pocket and went back to the window. A niggling thought had been bothering me, and I looked outside again. My attention was drawn to the four trash cans below. They weren't just any trash cans. Safiyya the Lamb Lady had brought me here. She had found all her silver jewelry in Sheba's alley.

I took another look around Sheba's shabby apartment. There were dead flowers shoved into one corner, several books thrown together on the floor, and shattered glass everywhere. I found another double handful of abandoned jewelry, a heap of pendants and necklaces, cheap stuff. Most were decorated with familiar symbols, all jumbled together—there were a couple of Christian crosses; Islamic crescents and items with Qur'ânic inscriptions; a Star of David; an ankh; Buddhist, Hindu, and other Asiatic religious tokens; occult designs; Native American figures; and others I wasn't able to identify. These were the only things I saw that might have had some connection to the vampire mythology, but I still discounted them—the things might just have been left behind like the rest of the jewelry. I couldn't be sure there was any particular significance to them.

Nothing else set off a bell in my highly perceptive crime-solving mind. The moddies were the best clue, and so my next stop was Laila's modshop on Fourth Street. I was surprised that Laila herself wasn't in when I got there, but I was relieved, too. Laila is almost impossible to deal with. Instead, there was a young woman standing behind the counter.

She smiled at me. She didn't seem crazy at all. She was either wearing a moddy that force-fed her a pleasant personality, or something was definitely not right here. This was not a shop where you met people under the control of their own unaugmented selves.

"Can I help you?" she asked me in English. I don't speak much English, but I have an electronic add-on that takes care of that for me. I kept the language daddy chipped in almost all the time, because there are a lot of important English-speaking people in the city.

I took the wrappers from my pocket. "Sell any of these lately?"

She shuffled the cellophane around on the counter for a few seconds. "Nope," she said brightly. I was positive now that I wasn't dealing with her real personality. She was just too goddamn perky.

"How do you know?" I asked.

She shrugged. "This shop and its owner are much too concerned about upholding local ordinances to sell illegal bootleg moddies."

I almost choked. "Yeah you're right," was all I said.

"Anything else I can help you with?" She was deeply concerned, I could tell. That was some moddy Laila had found for her.

"I'll just browse a bit." I went toward the bins of moddies based on characters from old books and holoshows. For some dumb reasons, I couldn't come up with the name of the villain I was looking for. "You know what a vampire is?"

"Sure," she said. "We had to watch that movie in a class in high school." She made a scornful expression. "Twentieth-century Literature."

"What was the vampire's name again?"

"Lestat. They made us watch that movie and another classic. *Airport*, it was. None of us could figure out what they had to do with the real world. I like modern literature better."

I'll bet she did. Lestat wasn't who I was searching for. I browsed through the bins for half an hour before I came across a set of vampire-character moddies. The package had been torn open. I took it to the counter and showed it to the young woman. "Know anything about this?" I asked.

She was upset. "We don't break sets open," she said. "We wouldn't have done that." The Dracula moddy was missing, leaving the Jonathan Harker, Lucy Westenra, Dr. Van Helsing, and Renfield moddies. I gave a little involuntary shudder. I didn't want to meet the person who'd be eager to chip in Renfield.

"Do you suppose someone could have shoplifted the missing moddy?" I asked.

I almost wished I hadn't said it. The young woman paled. I could see how abhorrent the entire idea was to her. "Perhaps," she murmured. The word she used was "perhaps," not "maybe." That had to be the software talking.

"Forget it," I said, coming to a decision. "I'll buy the rest of the package."

"Even though part of it's been stolen? You know I'm not authorized to offer you a discount."

It took me a little while longer to persuade her to sell me the things, and I was already chipping in Dr. Van Helsing, that fearless old vampire hunter, as I left the shop and headed back toward the eastern gate.

The first thing Audran noticed was that he was somewhat taller and a good deal older. There was a painful twinge in his left shoulder, but he decided it wouldn't hinder him too much. He also felt very Dutch; he—Van Helsing—was from Amsterdam, after all.

Audran's own consciousness lurked in a tiny, hidden-away area submerged beneath the overlay of Van Helsing. There he wondered what "feeling Dutch" meant. It was probably just some programmer's laziness. That person had known that Van Helsing was Dutch, but had not bothered to include specific *dutchnesses. It was a weakness that Audran despised in poorly written commercial moddies.*

It did not take long for Audran's muscles and nerves to compensate for the differences between his own physical body and the one the moddy's manufacturer imagined. As long as the moddy was chipped in, Audran would move, feel, and respond as Van Helsing. There was also an annoying nervous flutter in his right eyelid, and Audran sincerely hoped it would go away as soon as he popped the moddy out.

Van Helsing was still heading east, on the sidewalk; Audran preferred walking in the middle of the street. As he approached the arched gate of the Budayeen, Van Helsing considered the things they had found in Sheba's apartment. Now, with his special knowledge, the evidence took on new significance.

How could Audran be expected to appreciate the absolute horror of what he'd discovered in the abandoned apartment? How could Audran know that the dead flowers, roses, were shunned by all vampires; that the broken glass came from shattered mirrors around the room; that the sacred symbols were powerful weapons against the Un-Dead?

More compelling yet were the books and papers left with seeming carelessness on the floor. They had looked harmless enough to Audran, but Van Helsing knew that within their pages were terrible, evil passages describing rituals through which a living human being could become a vampire, and others that gave instructions for inviting demons to invade and possess one's immortal soul.

Through Audran's inaction, the situation had become dire and deadly; more than human lives were at stake now. An unholy monster was loose among the unsuspecting people of the Budayeen. Once again, it was left to Dr. Van Helsing to restore peace and sanctity, if he could.

Cursing Audran for a fool, Van Helsing quickened his pace.

Audran should've guessed the truth when the young boy had been attacked. Dracula's victim, Lucy, had preyed largely on children. Van Helsing felt an uncomfortable stirring of his emotions. Although he'd never admit the fact to anyone, he was aware of his barely sublimated lust toward female vampires. And now he'd been called upon to battle a new one. He shook his head; at the ultimate moment, he knew, he would be strong enough. He passed through the arch and onto the beautiful Boulevard il-Jameel.

Bill the cabdriver was still waiting for him. He tapped Van Helsing on the shoulder. "Ready to go?" he asked.

"God in hemel!" Van Helsing exclaimed.

"That's easy for you to say," Bill said. "Get in."

Van Helsing and Audran glanced at the taxi. Together they reached up and popped the moddy out.

"The guy's a total loon," I muttered as I slid into the cab's backseat.

"Got a complaint about me, pal?" Bill asked.

"No," I said, "I'm talking about this Van Helsing jerk. He sees deadly gruesome creatures everywhere he looks."

Bill shrugged. "Well, hell, so do I, but I just steer around 'em." I thought that was a pretty sensible attitude.

Bill delivered me to the front gate of Friedlander Bey's estate. I hurried inside and up to my suite just in time for Kmuzu to remind me about the important luncheon meeting scheduled with Papa and the political representatives of some damn place. I showered again, feeling just a little sullied after letting that repressed Van Helsing character occupy my mind and body. I put on my best *gallebeya* and *keffiya*, going so far as to belt a gorgeous jeweled ceremonial dagger in front at the waist. I looked good, and I knew Papa would be pleased.

The luncheon itself was fine, just fine. I don't even remember what we ate, but there was tons of it and the delegation from Parthia was appropriately impressed. More important, though, was that they were appropriately intimidated. I sat in my chair and looked thoughtful, while Friedlander Bey explained to them the facts of life here in the early years of the twenty-third century of the Christian Era.

What it all amounted to was that the Parthians pretended to be grateful after being denied the help they'd come for. They even tried to bribe Papa further by guaranteeing him exclusive influence with the victorious side in the brand-new Silesian revolt. Since no one at that moment could predict which party would end up in power, and since Papa had little interest in nations beyond the Islamic realm, and since everyone in the room including Habib and Labib knew that the Parthians couldn't deliver on their promise in the first place, we acted as if they hadn't said a word. It was an embarrassing blunder on their part, but Friedlander Bey handled it all with grace and assurance. He just waved to have the coffee and kataifi brought in. Papa's extremely fond of kataifi, a Greek dessert something like baklava, except it looks like shredded wheat. It may be his only worldly weakness.

With all the formal greetings and salutations and invitations and flatteries and thank-yous and blessings and leave-takings, it was about five o'clock before I was able to return to my rooms. I started to tell Kmuzu what had gone on, but naturally he already knew all about it. He even had a little advice for me concerning the people of Kush, who no doubt would soon strike back against the weakened Parthians.

"Fine," I said impatiently. "Thank you, Kmuzu, I don't know what I'd do without you. If you'll just excuse me—"

"The family of the young murdered boy said they were sorry you couldn't come to the funeral. They know how fond of you he'd been. I explained that you'd been detained by the master of the house."

I regretted missing the service. I wished I could've at least been at the cemetery to offer my condolences.

"I think I'll just relax now," I said. "I'm going to rest for a while, and then I'm going to see how my nightclub is doing without me. That *is* all right, isn't it? I mean, I'm allowed to go down there this evening, aren't I?"

Kmuzu gave me a blank stare for a second or two. "I have been advised otherwise, *yaa Sidi,*" he said.

"Oh. Too bad. Then—"

I was looking at his back. "You have two visitors waiting to speak with you, a man and a boy. They've been here since two o'clock."

"In the anteroom? All this time?" I didn't want to see anyone else, but I couldn't just tell these people to go home and come back tomorrow. "All right, I'll—" Kmuzu wasn't paying any attention. He was already going toward my office. I followed, trying not to let all this power go to my head.

When I saw who was waiting for me, I was startled. It was Bill the cabdriver and a boy from the Budayeen. Bill was standing up with his back to the room, his hands stretched up as high against the wall as he could reach. Don't ask me why. The kid's name was Musa Ali, and his dirty face was streaked with tears. He was sitting quietly in a chair. I felt sorry for him, having to spend all those hours alone with Bill. I wouldn't have done it.

When I came in, they both began speaking at once. They talked fast and furiously. I couldn't make any sense out of it. I signaled to Bill to shut up, and then I let Musa Ali explain things. "My sister," he said, his eyes wide with fear, "she's taken her."

I looked at Bill. "The vampire," he said. Suddenly he was very calm and matter-of-fact. His hands were still raised high, but I didn't hold that against him. You took what you could get with Bill.

Between the two of them, I got an idea of the story. Not the truth, necessarily, but the story. Apparently, just at noon, Sheba, in her vampire form, had stolen another child, Musa Ali's six-year-old sister. Bill had tried to interfere, and a tremendous fight had erupted. On one side was this burly full-grown man, and on the other was a short nightclub dancer burdened with a struggling child in her arms. Bill was covered with dark bruises and bloody cuts and scratches, so I didn't really have to ask which way the conflict had gone.

"She turned into a bunch of mist," Bill said, shrugging. He sounded apologetic. "I couldn't fight a bunch of mist, could I? She just floated away on the breeze. Reminded me of that time this guy from Tunis tried to cheat me out of my fare, and just then I heard this music from Heaven that was too high-pitched for normal humans to hear, see, so I turned around as fast as I could, but he was trying to get out of the cab, so then—"

I stopped listening to Bill. "Mist?" I asked Musa Ali.

"Uh-huh," the boy said.

So now I was tracking down a fog lady. A murderous vampire fog lady. Suddenly I *really* wanted another piece of kataifi. . . .

It was getting late. I returned quickly to my apartment, to change clothes again and pick up a few items I thought might be useful. One of those things was the Van Helsing moddy— after all, the excitable Dutch fanatic knew more about hunting vampires than I ever would. I just had to try to maintain a little rational control, to offset Van Helsing's own serious hang-ups.

I avoided Kmuzu and hurried back to Bill and Musa Ali, still waiting in my office. With some difficulty, we managed to slip out of the house without any direct interference from

Friedlander Bey's staff, and I gave Bill the order to drive us back to the Budayeen. "First I take you over there," Bill complained, "then I bring you back, then I go home, then I come back here, now we go over there again. Maybe I'll be lucky and we'll all get killed tonight. I don't do this driving thing because I *enjoy* it, you know."

Bill can trap you that way, by fooling you into asking the next obvious question. That always leads into an even more bizarre rant, and I've promised myself not to get suckered in anymore. I didn't ask him what he wanted me to ask.

"Are you taking me home?" Musa Ali asked. "I can't go home until I find my sister."

He was a brave kid. "You go home," I said. "*We'll* find your sister."

"Okay," he said. He was brave, but he wasn't a fool.

"We're going to the cemetery, Bill," said. "It's the only logical place to look for Sheba."

"They won't let me into the cemetery, pal," he said.

"Who won't?"

"The dead people. They won't let me into the cemetery because I'm American."

"They don't have dead people in America?" I asked. I had already forgotten my promise to myself.

"Oh, sure, they do," Bill said. "But the dead people here in the city still hold it against Americans that they have the wrong unlucky number. It's not thirteen, see, like Americans believe, because—" I stopped listening. I reached up and chipped the Van Helsing moddy in instead.

There was another moment of disorientation, but it passed quickly. "Stakes!" Van Helsing said loudly. "We need sharp wooden stakes! How could Audran have forgotten them? We have to stop and find some!"

"Don't worry about stakes," Bill said calmly. "Got 'em in the trunk. I got some in case I ever get a tent." Van Helsing was wise enough not to pursue it any further.

Because Van Helsing wasn't as familiar with the city as Audran, he didn't notice immediately that Bill, for all his many years of experience, was getting pretty damn lost. The probable explanation was that his invisible evil temptresses were leading him astray. Both Van Helsing and Audran would have understood that. Instead, though, the vampire hunter stared out the taxi's window, watching the neighborhoods slide by.

Time passed, and the sun dropped silently toward the horizon. It was almost dark when Bill finally drove past the Budayeen's eastern gate. He jammed on the brakes, and Van Helsing and he jumped out of the car. More time was spent as Bill searched for the trunk key. At last they armed themselves with the stakes; they couldn't find a hammer, but Bill carried an old, dead battery that could be used for pounding purposes.

"We'll need something to cut off Sheba's head, too," Van Helsing said in a worried voice. "We'll need to get a large cleaver. And garlic to stuff into her mouth."

Bill nodded. "There's an all-night convenience store on our way."

Van Helsing still seemed apprehensive. "Sheba will be at her full powers soon."

"Well," Bill said, smiling broadly, "so am I." That didn't do very much to reassure his companion.

There are sixteen blocks between the eastern gate and the cemetery, the length of the Street, the width of the Budayeen. They hurried as fast as they could, but Bill had never been very agile, and Van Helsing was not a young man anymore. They pushed through the crowds of local folk and foreign tourists with growing desperation, but by the time they ar-

rived at their goal, the sun had set. It was night. They would have to face the full fury of the vampire's power.

"Have no fear," Van Helsing said. "This isn't the first time I've challenged the Un-Dead on their own territory. You have nothing to worry about."

"That's easy for you to say," Bill said. "You don't have to worry about the ground opening up in horrible fissures right in front of you."

Van Helsing paused. "Bill," he said at last, "the ground isn't opening up."

Bill put a finger alongside his nose. "No, you're right," he confided, "but that doesn't mean I'm not going to worry about it."

Van Helsing looked up to Heaven, where God was watching. "Come on," he told Bill. "We mustn't be too late to save the little girl."

They arrived at the cemetery. No one else was nearby. Van Helsing saw the flowers and other offerings on the ground near where Mahdi il-Mallah had been laid to rest. The boy's parents couldn't afford an above-ground tomb, so he'd been interred in a small, ovenlike vault built into one of the cemetery's red brick walls.

"Oh my God," Bill cried. He motioned toward the back of the graveyard.

Van Helsing turned and looked where Bill was pointing. He saw Sheba, dressed in a long, filthy black shift. Her hair was wildly disheveled and matted with leaves and twigs. There were streaks of dirt on her face and bare arms. She stared at Van Helsing and snarled. Even from that distance, the Dutchman could see the great, long canine teeth, the mark of the vampire.

"It's her," Van Helsing said in a quiet voice.

"You mean, 'It's she,' " Bill said.

"Or what remains of her earthly body, now inhabited by something of unspeakable foulness. Take warning: remember that she has the strength of a dozen or more normal people." Beneath Van Helsing's overwhelming presence, Audran realized that the vampire moddy was constructed with an endocrine controller, letting a flood of adrenaline loose in Sheba's bloodstream. Whoever was correct—Audran or Van Helsing, believer in natural law or in evil magic—it made no difference. The ultimate effect was the same.

"You know," Bill said thoughtfully, "she wouldn't be half-bad looking if she'd just fix herself up a little."

Van Helsing did not deign to reply. He moved toward Sheba, feeling terror, determination, and an odd longing mixed together. Sheba stood before a large whitewashed tomb, its marble front panel removed and cast aside. This was where she'd taken up residence after leaving behind her human dwelling place. There was a vile stench emanating from the tomb. Nevertheless, Van Helsing summoned his courage and stepped nearer.

He heard small rustling noises, and behind Sheba he saw movement. It had to be Musa Ali's sister, still alive, but bound and made captive by this loathsome creature. "Thanks be to all the angels that we are yet in time," he said.

Sheba did not cry out or utter any verbal challenges; it was as if she'd lost the power of speech. Instead, she made harsh, guttural, animal noises deep in her throat.

"Unbind the child and let her go free," Van Helsing demanded.

Once again Sheba bared her perilous fangs and hissed at them, not like a snake, but like a great feral cat. Then she rushed forward more swiftly than even Van Helsing had anticipated and leaped on him, reaching for his unprotected throat with her clawed fingers and savaging him with her demon teeth.

Bill hurried to Van Helsing's defense. "Not again," he said. "Not another one."

"What?" Van Helsing asked.

"Another what-you-call, an abomination. Yeah. Blood-thirsty, too. Bad luck always comes in threes, you know. So the third one is going to be a real showstopper."

Bill attacked first, clouting the hideous thing with all the strength he had. The blow had little effect. Bill lurched backward, shaking his injured hand. His enemy was very tall, lowering over him in a confident slouch. Despite his mental and physical handicaps, Bill was a better boxer than his opponent; he had a quicker punch, and his bob-and-weave was deft by comparison. Again and again Bill struck, but for all the pain he was causing himself, and for the complete lack of results he was achieving against his foe, Bill might as well have been beating up the brick wall.

Meanwhile, Van Helsing had as much as he could handle with Sheba. She fought like a cornered beast, ripping and tearing and biting at him. He ordered her again to release the young girl. Then he tried to reason with Sheba. Finally, he resorted to threats. Nothing worked. She was no longer human, no longer susceptible to his powers of persuasion.

He was covered with his own blood when he finally managed to throw Sheba to the ground. He'd put a foot behind one of hers, then shoved her shoulder heavily. She toppled backward, shrieking in incoherent rage. Van Helsing wasted no time congratulating himself. He reached for one of the sharpened stakes and a loose brick.

Sheba glared up at him, her lips drawn back in an animal growl. She was completely in the power of the vampire now, no longer human in any respect, yet there was also a frightened pleading in her eyes—or so Van Helsing chose to believe. Audran saw it, too.

"She's as moddy-driven as Van Helsing," Audran thought. "He's a self-righteous, demented maniac, as murderous as she is. Maybe she deserves some compassion." With an exhausting effort of will, Audran and Van Helsing reached up and popped the moddy out.

"Jeez," I muttered, dropping the plastic moddy to the ground. It was a great relief again to be rid of Van Helsing's monomania. Meanwhile, I had little time to think. I was still trying to control the enraged Sheba, who struggled and bucked in my grasp.

Bill had evidently vanquished his enemy. "That's right, pal," he said, reaching for one of the fire-hardened stakes. "You hold her and I'll ostracize her."

The first thing I did, while I ignored Bill, was to pop out Sheba's vampire moddy. The transformation was immediate and dramatic. The knowledge of what she'd done while under its influence flooded in, horrifying her. "I just couldn't take it out," she gasped between loud sobs. "Other moddies I can take or leave alone, but this one was different. I never had anything to say about it. I couldn't control myself. Once I chipped it in, that was it; I became a vampire forever."

"Some irresponsible programmer wrote that into the moddy," I said. I tried to speak in a soothing voice. I no longer feared or hated Sheba; I felt only immense sadness. She just collapsed in tears as if she hadn't heard me.

"Hey," Bill said proudly. "You notice that I took care of my guy all right."

"Bill," I explained wearily, "you were savagely going ten rounds with a date palm."

He stared at me. "A date palm? Well, hell, who knows what afrit was inside it when it hit me. Maybe we should get somebody up here to exorcise that tree."

"It didn't hit you, Bill. I saw the whole thing from the beginning."

Bill scratched uneasily with one foot in the black soil. "Anyway, I think I killed it. Now I'm sorry, if it's only a date palm."

I gave him a reassuring smile, although I didn't really feel like it. "Don't worry, Bill. I'm sure it's only stunned."

He brightened considerably. "That's easy for *you* to say," he said.

I smashed both the Dracula and Van Helsing moddies with the brick. Who can say how much good that did, because the next homicidal blazebrain still had plenty of murderous moddies to choose from, at Laila's store or any of the other modshops in the Budayeen. I let out a deep breath in a sigh. I'd worry about those killers when the time came.

I helped Sheba to her feet. She was still hysterical, but now she clung to me for comfort. Her violent sobbing was subsiding. I saw that her vampire's elongated canine teeth were fake, a bodily modification that Sheba had paid for at one of the Budayeen storefront surgical clinics. I reached up slowly and gently and pulled the fangs free.

I knew Sheba had an addictive personality—there was a lot of that going around the Budayeen these days—and although she wouldn't wear the vampire moddy again, she was more than likely going to become something just as dangerous to herself and to other people in the near future.

Still, I thought, I could hope that the sudden awareness of what she'd done would get her to seek help. There was nothing more that I could do for her now. The rest was up to Sheba herself.

Just as my own future would be shaped in part by the moddies I bought and wore. Hell, I'd just come very close to killing a seriously troubled young woman while I was under the influence of the Van Helsing moddy. I was certainly in no position to judge her.

That gave me an awful lot to think about, but I could put that off until later, or tomorrow, or some other time. Right then I turned my attention to Musa Ali's little sister. I untied her and satisfied myself that although she was exhausted and terrified, she was otherwise unharmed. Bill bent down and picked her up in his arms. He always got along well with children.

As the Budayeen characters began to arrive at the cemetery, drawn by the shouting and racket of our small war with the Un-Dead, I took Sheba's arm and led her out of the graveyard, back down the Street to her long-unused apartment. As of that moment, all she had was hope.

Food Chain

NINA KIRIKI HOFFMAN

Cissy told me Saturday night that she needed a new mother, so Sunday morning I started the coffeemaker, then woke the others a little before they normally got up. We gathered in Dark House's roomy kitchen.

"What is it this time, Alice?" Francesca said, sprawling at the big round table, her dark eyes heavy lidded and her thick black hair in snarls. I undimmed the overhead light, making it bright enough to read recipes. The kitchen was at the back of the house and didn't get any sunlight until evening. Francesca winced and covered her eyes. She was a chef at the three-star restaurant around the corner from Dark House, and she worked every night except Saturday, when she prowled in search of adventure. Sunday was the worst morning of her week.

Dora got spinach and bacon out of the refrigerator. She always woke up faster than the rest of us, even in summer when she wasn't teaching grade school. She switched on a burner and set a skillet on it. "C'mon," she said, shaking Micki's shoulder. "Wash." She pointed at the spinach by the sink. Micki sat for a moment with her broad shoulders hunched and her eyes closed, probably hoping the job would go away if she ignored it. Then she stood and ambled over to the sink.

Bettina put a full kettle of water on for tea and brought the assortment of things-hot-water-instantly-created to the table so the rest of us could pick through the packets. "What's up?" she said. Her English accent was crisp. Her voice reminded me of BBC radio news. I liked listening to her. "You should be in bed, Alice. It's your morning after."

I did feel tired. I got myself a big glass of orange juice and two chocolate-glazed doughnuts. "We need another mother," I said.

"That's ridiculous," said Zelda. I sipped orange juice and looked at her over the rim of my glass. She had just gotten a new haircut, one quite popular when I was a girl, but in those days crew cuts were only seen on boys. Her blonde stubble glistened as she tilted her head back, the better to stare down her nose at me.

"Coffee?" Gail asked, smothering a yawn with the back of her hand. She was wearing a short silky green nightgown and nothing else. It had taken me some time to accustom myself to her informality. Things were different when I was young. My parents never pranced around the house in next to nothing; if they left their bedroom, they always wore robes, and so had my husband and I when we became parents.

Zelda, Micki, and Dora said yes to coffee. Gail got down four mugs, filled them, and brought them to the table.

"Cissy told me we need another mother," I said.

"Why?" Zelda said. Her blue eyes narrowed as she stared at me. "There's seven of us. That's enough."

I put down my glass. I studied my hands, touched the fingers of the left with the fingers of my right. Skin that had once been smooth, taut with muscle and life, was papery now, pleated. When I pressed it sideways it did not spring back immediately. I felt a monumental tiredness in me. I was always tired the morning after my night with Cissy; we all were. But it had never felt so sapping before; usually it was a pleasant languor, an excuse to linger in bed and eat special foods.

"Oh, Alice," Gail said, putting down her mug and coming around the table to stoop beside me and hug me. Her warmth and her kindness and energy penetrated me as though I were gauze in the path of sunlight, and I lost my frail hold on control. Tears started down my face.

"Alice," Bettina murmured, her voice gentle.

"I'm sorry," I said. Micki came and stroked her big hand down my back, tracing the leaves of elephant clovers there. For a long while, no one else said anything. The only sounds were the sizzle and pop of bacon on the stove, and my breath catching on itself. The fragrance of brewing coffee and frying bacon reminded me of countless breakfasts stretching backward through time, some just the pleasant beginnings to indifferent days, some interrupted by news—Daddy was not coming back from the war (Mother dropped the frypan when she heard, and grease spatters from the bacon burned her legs); my sister Lucy had delivered a boy (a moment of silence, thanks to God); my own precious little daughter Johanna had not survived the night (but that had been a morning smelling of disinfectant and cigarette smoke, in a dingy hospital waiting room, because the doctors did not trust me in the room with my own child, so that I missed her last moments, missed holding her hand until God could take it from me).

I remembered how time had stretched in those moments, how during the bad ones I had thought the pain would never lessen, that I would live in an eternal Now of hurt that tears would not be able to wash away.

But in this Now, I was with those I loved, and no one was

dying. Moments moved inexorably from Now to next, and carried me away from my own sorrow. I got myself back under control, patted Gail's head, blotted my tears on a paper napkin, sipped my quiet sobs away with orange juice.

"How long have you been here, Alice?" asked Francesca, wide awake now.

"Thirty-seven years."

Dora set her spinach salad in the center of the table and handed bowls and forks around.

"How old were you when you got here?" Francesca said.

"Twenty-six."

Zelda put her hand over mine. "What happened," she said, "to the other mothers? The ones we replaced?"

"I don't know." The population of Dark House shifted; sometimes people came for a while and left; sometimes there were ten of us and our nights with Cissy were farther between; I knew that others had grown old here, but I could not remember who they had been or where they had gone. I had the feeling that there was only one Cissy, though; despite what the movies and the books said about people like Cissy, what she had wasn't a disease that turned people who came in contact with her into people like her. But then, movies and books were wrong about all sorts of things.

"I'm so afraid of leaving," I said, and hid my eyes behind my hand.

Zelda's hand was warm on mine. Her thumb stroked along the curve formed by my thumb and forefinger. "Is that what happens?" she murmured. "Do people have to leave?"

"I don't know," I said. "My memory is. . . ."

"Cissified," said Micki. She had been at Dark House for seventeen years, and everyone else for less time.

"What?" asked Bettina. She was our newest mother.

"Remember when you decided to come here?" Micki said.

"Of course—I was standing at the fence outside the

preschool where Gareth used to go, watching the children, and—no, I didn't know about you or the house then, I just had that overpowering feeling that there was nothing, nothing on Earth left for me to do, that every day would be gray and stars would never shine again. And then. . . ."

"Then," said Zelda, "I woke up. I was lying on a soft bed in a strange room I had never seen before, and little Benjamin was lying next to me. I hugged him and told him never ever to leave me again. And he said he wouldn't. Or at least that I could see him once a week."

Her gaze was fixed on a copper-bottomed pan hanging on the wall, and her voice sounded light and far away, as if she were describing a dream while she was still asleep. "How could that be? At his funeral I touched his face, I had to, because I kept thinking he wasn't really dead, he couldn't be dead, he was only two years old, such a perfect little being, and I would lie awake listening and listening for him to cry again so I could go comfort him. I touched his face and it was cold and stiff and I knew he was gone and Robert hugged me and took me away but even though I knew Benjamin was gone, I still couldn't let go of him and somehow Robert couldn't take it after awhile, and . . . and then I woke up, and there he was, my baby."

I gripped Zelda's hand. After a moment she blinked and looked at me and smiled.

Bettina looked at Micki.

"It's like that for all of us. Cissy can do something to the memories," Micki said. "I know everything I need to know about nursing, and about everyone on staff at the hospital, and I know my brother's phone number—I talk to him every week. I remember my childhood, my marriage, the birth of my child and her every word or act. I even remember her death. And then . . . there's a fuzzy period. I think I went crazy. I really think I must have. I got stuck. I stayed in the house and didn't wash or eat. I was waiting for little Annie to come back. The life was leaking out of me. My husband tried everything to rouse me out of it, but he couldn't.

"Then I woke up," Micki said. She smiled, looking inward. Her big arms curled into a cradle.

"Yes," said Dora. She had dished out salad for everybody and passed it around, but no one was tasting it. "Micki and I have been comparing memories. Cissy can manipulate them, apparently. I don't feel like a different person. I don't feel controlled. I'm here because I want to be. Still, there are some things in my head I can't seem to get to."

An image of my own hands bleeding and hurt flashed through my mind. I remembered. I remembered hammering fists against the beige hospital walls of that waiting room until I left bloody marks. I remembered my own mother trying to catch my wrists and stop me, telling me my behavior was unladylike and undignified, as if I had dropped a spoon at afternoon tea. I remembered the rage rising in me like a great smothering wave.

I blinked and the memory vanished. I was glad it was gone.

"I remember Carol and Debbie," said Micki, and as she said the names, pictures of the women came into my head. Carol had been thin and remote, and it seemed to me she came and stayed just a little while and left. Left! I remembered her packing. I remembered touching her hand in farewell, and thinking it felt cold. Debbie had been large, and friendly on the surface, but I had never found myself telling her anything important, not after I told her about the secret party to celebrate Micki's promotion to head nurse of her floor, and Debbie told Micki.

Zelda was prickly and irritable, and Francesca was lazy. There were things about each of the others that annoyed me in small ways, but I felt I could tell them anything and they would not betray me.

Micki said, "Dora and I have been trying to fish up the names of others. Alice. . . ."

"I didn't remember until you said them, Micki," I said. "Now I do, and I don't see how that helps. I'm glad they didn't stay."

"The real question is," said Micki, "how did Cissy find us? I can't remember meeting her before waking up in bed with her. If we're going to find another mother—how?"

Gail cooked Sunday nights. She was the youngest mother in Dark House and had grown up in an age that no longer demanded that its women know how to cook. Francesca had bought her a basic cookbook, and we all helped on occasion. Gail had been in the house four years and no longer lamented the loss of microwaves; Cissy said they disturbed her sleep.

That night she made some kind of Hungarian stew with a lot of spices and chunks of vegetables in a big pot. She had dropped a piece of potato on the burner and the kitchen had that after-an-accident tang in the air. The stew, besides being burnt, was a little strong for me, and I only ate a little, filling up on crusty bakery French bread instead. I was sipping heavily creamed coffee and watching the others (except for Francesca, who worked from four to nine Sunday evenings) struggle to say something nice about the food, or even to finish it, when Cissy came yawning up from the basement.

I didn't know how the others dealt with Cissy's changes. I made two places for her in my mind: Cissy-in-common, a slight, colorless girl of eleven or so, whom no one would have noticed until she smiled—something of her smile was so sweet and sad it burned like raw sugar on the tongue; and Cissy-in-private, whom I called Johanna, and whom the others called by the names of their own departed children. My relationship with Cissy-in-common was very different from my relationship with Cissy-in-private.

"Hi, kiddo," Gail said, waving a fork with a piece of potato on it.

Cissy flapped a hand in front of her face. "Phew! Paprika city!"

"You don't like paprika?" Gail asked, stricken. There were some spices and condiments we had to be careful with. I remembered, suddenly, taking Micki shopping when she first came to Dark House, nixing the garlic powder: "It gets in the milk. Not good for the baby," I had said, and Micki had accepted that without question.

"It's not my favorite," Cissy said. "It's not so bad, though." She smiled.

"So," said Zelda, laying her spoon across an edge of her bowl, "another mother, Cissy? Alice said another mother."

Cissy sat down beside me. She looked breakable. I gripped my left hand in my right. When had it happened? When had I become too old to give her what she needed?

Her small cold hand closed around my wrist and she looked up into my eyes. For a moment I saw my Johanna, her eyes like wet violets, her cheeks pink as sunrise, downy dark hair lying flat on her head no matter how I tried to tease it into curling. A rush of love, hot and red and all embracing, rose in me. I knew that what I lived for, what satisfied me most of anything on this Earth, was to care for this child, this seed of a plant not yet known, this vessel of all potentials; that the best thing I could ever do was to nurture my little one and take joy in everything she did. I knew this in my mind and in my heart and in that place deep within me that connected me to every mother who had ever lived. My breasts felt warm and full and ready; my eyelids felt too heavy to keep open.

"Alice," Cissy murmured, her small chill hand tugging at mine, pulling my right hand away from my left. "Alice."

I jerked awake again, looked down at her pale, worried face.

"I didn't—" she said. "I didn't mean—"

An arrow of heat touched my left eye and a tear spilled out of it. Sunday wasn't my night. Sunday was Zelda's night. Anyway, Cissy never spent two nights in a row with anyone. Especially not someone who didn't have anything to give her, I thought, looking down at my sagging breasts. Here in Dark House, age had crept up on me while I wasn't watching. It had shocked me when they suggested at the library that it was time for me to retire. I had always felt fine.

I glanced up at Zelda, who for once didn't look supercilious, only sad. Perhaps she had seen love and desire naked on my face in a way that I had never seen it on any of the others'. Today was the first time I had spoken with the others about what Cissy really did for each of us. I had known, the way I had known as a young woman that every woman must menstruate, but I had not let myself know; I had blanked my mind. One night a week I had with Cissy, bright as the sun, and the other nights I went to sleep alone, that was all there was to it.

"Cissy," said Dora after a moment. "We've been trying to remember how we got here, and we can't. We don't know how you recruit mothers."

Cissy patted my hand and then stopped touching me. "Do you need to know?" she asked.

"Alice told us you want somebody new."

"I will find her," said Cissy.

"What happens to those who are too old?" Bettina asked. My mother's voice rose in my memory, telling me that that was an unladylike question, though said in such a lovely tone of voice. One shouldn't speak of such things.

"Do you need to know?" Cissy said.

There was a brief silence. Micki said, "I would like to know. I'm the eldest after Alice. I imagine I'll grow old here in Dark House, as she has. I think Alice might like to know what comes next. I realize you can tell us and then take this memory away from us as you have with other memories. So why not tell us? And what happened to the people who didn't work out?"

Cissy frowned. She stared at the tabletop with furrowed brows.

"Come on, Cissy. What harm could it do?" Micki sounded like a hearty nurse telling you it was time for your shot, but it wouldn't hurt, no matter how often you'd had a hurting shot before.

"I've never told anyone."

"Aw, c'mon, kiddo," said Gail. "Not anybody? In however long you've been at this? Didn't you ever want to?"

"Is what you do so terrible?" Dora asked.

Cissy looked up, meeting each of our gazes in turn. "Everything I do is terrible," she said in a small frozen voice.

"It is not," said Zelda, in the tone one uses to reassure one's child of how special it is, even though it has just made a mistake.

"You do not know what I do," said Cissy, almost whispering, "or what I have done in the past."

I wanted to gather her into my arms and hug her into silence. I wanted to just think about her as the perfect little child who was not old enough to be responsible for its actions, whose only reason for existing was to be loved, and whom I could love in a way that made me a perfect mother. I put my hand on her shoulder. She felt cold, and her shoulder was very small.

Dora said, "We can't know, unless you tell us, Cissy. You can tell us, and then you can untell us, if you like."

Cissy put her hands over her face.

"I don't want to know," I said, surprising myself. "If it hurts you to tell us, I don't want to know."

For a moment no one said anything. Then Cissy's voice came out from between her hands. "The ones who come, the ones who do not stay, I take their memories away and give them a very strong urge to go far away from here and never to speak about it."

"What's so terrible about that?" asked Gail.

Cissy lowered her hands, wove her fingers through each other and gripped hard.

"Those of you who stay," she said, and stopped.

Bettina sipped tea. The click of her cup on her saucer was the only sound.

Cissy spoke to her hands. "You give me what I need. You give, and I take."

"You give us what we need too," Micki said after a long moment.

Cissy shook her head.

Micki cleared her throat, then said, "I would have died."

"No."

Micki, big, solid, practical Micki, said, "I would have died, Cissy."

Cissy closed her eyes and shook her head. "No," she said. "No. You can't even remember that."

"I can. I do. I would have died without you, Cissy. You gave me what I needed."

"I gave you a lie!"

Bettina gasped. Her arms came up, crossed at the wrists, to cover her breasts, as though she had suddenly realized she was nude.

"Sometimes we need lies to survive," Dora said.

Cissy looked up. Her eyes were dark. "I'm a parasite."

"We all live off life, one way or another," said Zelda. "We kill what we eat right away, and you don't."

Cissy licked her lips. Even her tongue was pale. She must, I thought, be very hungry. "Tonight, after I feed," she said, "I will go out and taste the air, searching for a particular flavor of despair. I will follow it to its source, and I will take that source away from everything she has ever known and bring her here."

And I remembered where I had been when I first saw Cissy. Lying in a bed with bars on it, with straps buckled around my wrists and ankles, and all my hair shaved off. Lying in my own urine because the orderly didn't like me; I reminded him of his mother, he had said, and I had screamed. I had still been screaming, off and on, when Cissy called to me through the bars on the window, asking if she could come in. I had screamed yes. And she came and lay on my breast and I had my Johanna back again; and I could let go of my screams.

"You took me away from my despair and gave me back a life," I said.

That night I could not sleep. I went down to the kitchen and fixed warm milk with honey, the same potion my mother had brewed for me when I was a little girl and the night seemed full of monsters. I took my mug back up to my room and sat reading in bed, pillows behind me, my wedding ring quilt lapping at my waist. My gaze wandered across the words in my book without fastening on any of them. I stared and stared, trying to drop down into the story the way I usually did, but it was no use.

I put the book away and sat thinking about being a children's librarian, how I had loved to watch the little ones discover words and pictures, as Johanna might have, if she had lived longer, how there were almost always one or two who read deeply and wanted the new and bright and best, how their ever-fresh excitement made my job new and worthwhile, even though there were others who drew on the pages or tore them or lost books. Johanna would never grow older, but other children did; with Cissy in my arms I could dream, a different dream every week, each better than the last, and all of them equally likely to come true.

I no longer had the library, though I went there and did a weekly story hour. The new librarian didn't care for it when I stayed. The children liked me better and came to me with questions.

The library no longer gave me purpose, and Cissy could no longer give me purpose. I didn't think I could stay in Dark House, seeing her every evening but not being able to spend my special time with her. I could not think of anywhere else on Earth to go. The friends of my marriage had dropped away when I went into the mental hospital, and somehow, with so many friends at home, I had not pursued relationships outside of Dark House. My mother was dead, and I had no idea whether my husband was alive.

I was staring beyond the circle of my lamp, trying without success to see the painting across the room (though I had memorized it during the daylight hours, with only a faint illumination it appeared a different picture altogether, more sinister) when the door eased open and Cissy came in, white as any angel and silent as a cloud.

Her cheeks bloomed with the transient health I had once been able to give her; her eyes sparkled. She looked more alive than most of the children I saw in the street. She came to me and climbed up on the bed, sitting nightgowned and barefoot facing me.

"Alice," she said, holding out her hand. I took it and felt the rosy warmth of her fingers.

"What is it?" I said. My throat felt tight.

"I have something to give you," she said. Her words were pregnant with joy and mystery.

My throat closed tighter still. "Cissy, I don't know what to do," I whispered.

"You don't have to know. You don't have to know anything. Close your eyes."

I closed my eyes and felt the tears gathering in my chest

and in my throat. Sadness was a swamp; the mire enclosed me and I did not know how to pull free of it.

And then I felt arms come around me, gathering me close into a warm embrace. A breast pillowed my head. I pulled my knees up close to my chest and knew that somehow, someone held me in her lap.

I opened my eyes just a little and the face I saw above mine was not my mother's, but someone's mother, the mother I had always wished I had had. Her smile was gentle, her eyes tender. "You are my special child," she whispered, "the child of all my dreams, and I love you."

She fed me the milk of contentment. There was no longer anything I wanted or could even think of wanting, and so at last I let go of all my desires.

Song of the Night People

LARRY NIVEN

This is the one entry in this anthology that requires a word of explanation. I originally asked Larry Niven to send me a short story concerning the Ringworld Vampires; a few days later he called to say, "Well, it's turning into a novel."

This open-ended novella, "Song of the Night People," is, in fact, the first four chapters of *The Ringworld Throne*. I had to break it where the action came to the first logical stopping place, but that was difficult to determine; I settled for the point at which the union is achieved among various Ringworld races to make an expedition to the Vampire nest.

As Larry pointed out, even to people who have never read the other *Ringworld* novels, it still holds up as a fantasy set in a very weird world, which is true. More, it is a strictly science-fictional view of what is generally perceived as a fantasy or horror image: the vampire that lures its prey with sex.

one

AD 2884

Cloud covered the sky like a gray stone plate. The yellow grass had a wilted look: too much rain, not enough sun. No doubt the sun was straight overhead and the Arch was still in place, but Valavirgillin hadn't seen either for twenty days now.

The cruisers rolled through an endless drizzle, through high grass, on wheels as tall as a man. Vala and Kay rode the steering bench; Barok rode above them as gunner. Barok's daughter Forn was asleep among the ropes. Vala hoped she was under the awning. Sun could penetrate cloud.

Any day now—any hour—

Sabarokaresh pointed. "Is that what you've been looking for?"

Valavirgillin stood up in her seat. She could just see where the vastness of grass turned to a vastness of stubble.

Kaywerbrimmis said, "They leave this pattern. We'll be seeing sentries or a harvesting party. Boss, I don't understand how you knew they'd be Grass Giants here. I've never been this far to starboard myself. You, you're from Center City? That's a hundred daywalks to port."

"Word came to me," she said.

He didn't ask more. A merchant's secrets. . . .

They rolled into the stubble and turned. The cruisers rolled faster now. Stubble to the right, shoulder-high grass to the left. Far ahead, birds were wheeling and diving. Big dark birds: scavengers.

Kaywerbrimmis touched his handguns for reassurance. Muzzle-loading, the barrels as long as a forearm. Big Sabarokaresh eased back into the turret. The top of the payload shell housed the cannon, and that might be needed. The other wagons were swinging left and right, covering Kay's wagon so that they could investigate in safety.

The birds wheeled away. They'd left black feathers everywhere. Twenty big birds, gorged until they could hardly fly. What might feed so many?

Bodies. Little hominids with pointy skulls, stripped of most of their meat. Hundreds! They lay, some in the stubble, some in uncut grass. They might have been children, but the children among them were even smaller.

Vala looked for clothing. In strange terrain you never knew what might be intelligent.

Sabarokaresh dropped to earth, gun in hand. Kaywerbrimmis hesitated; but nothing sudden popped out of the grass, and he followed. Foranayeedli popped a sleepy head through the window and gaped. She was a girl of sixty falans or so, and pretty.

"Must have happened since last night," Kay said presently.

The smell of corruption wasn't strong yet. If birds had arrived before Ghouls, then these victims must have been slain near dawn. Vala asked, "How did they die? If this is local Grass Giant practice, we want none of it."

"This could've been done by birds. Cracked bones, see? But cracked by big beaks, for marrow. These are Gleaners, Boss. See, this is how they dress, in feathers. They follow the harvesters. The Gleaners hunt smeerps, firedots, anything that digs. Cutting the grass exposes burrows for them."

—Feathers, right. The feathers were black and red and purple-green, not just black. "So what happened here?"

Forn said, "I know that smell."

Beneath the corruption: what? Something familiar, not itself unpleasant . . . but it made Foranayeedli uneasy.

Valavirgillin had hired Kaywerbrimmis to lead the caravan because he was local, because he seemed competent. The rest were his people. But none of the Machine People had ever been this far to starboard. Vala knew more of this place than any of them . . . if she was right about where she was.

*   *   *

"Well, where are they?"

"Watching us, maybe," Kay said.

Vala could see a long way from her perch at the bow of the cruiser. The veldt was flat, the yellow grass was chopped short. Grass Giants stood seven and eight feet tall. Where grass stood half their height, could they hide in that?

The traders pulled their cruisers into a triangle. Their midday dinner was fruits and roots from stores on the running boards. They cooked some local grass with the roots. They'd caught no fresh meat.

They took their time. Most hominids were more approachable after feeding. If Grass Giants thought like Machine People, they would let strangers eat before they made contact.

No ambassador came. The caravan rolled on.

Three cruisers rolled sluggishly across the veldt without visible means of locomotion, but making no great speed. Big square wooden platforms rode four wheels at the corners; the motor, centered aft, turned two more drive wheels. The cast-iron payload housing rode ahead of the motor, like an iron house with a fat chimney. Big leaf springs were under the bow, under the steering bench. A savage might wonder at the tower on the payload housing, but what would he think if he had never seen a cannon?

Harmless.

Shapes the color of the grass, shapes too big to be men: two big humanoids watched from the crest of a far hill.

One turned and loped away across the veldt. The other ran along the crest, toward where the cruisers would cross.

They rolled toward him. He waited in their path. He was nearly the color of the golden grass, bronze skinned, with a golden mane. Big. Armed with a great curved sword.

Kaywerbrimmis walked to meet the giant. Valavirgillin set the cruiser following him like a friendly ridebeast.

Distance put strange twists in the trade dialect. Kaywer-brimmis had tried to teach Vala some of the variations in pronunciation, new words and altered meanings. She listened now, trying to make out what Kay was saying.

"We come in peace . . . intend to trade . . . Farsight Trading . . . rishathra?"

The giant's eyes flicked back and forth while Kay talked. Back and forth between their jaw lines, Forn and Vala and Kay and Barok. The giant was amused.

His face was hairier than any Machine People's! Too many hominid types were distracted by Machine People beards, especially on the women. Pretty Forn's was just growing, just long enough to darken her jaw. Vala's was turning elegantly white just at the chin.

The giant waited out Kay's chattering, then strode past him and took a seat on the cruiser's two-pace-wide running board. He leaned against the payload shell and immediately jerked away from the hot metal. Recovered his dignity and waved the cruiser forward.

Big Barok held his post above the giant. Forn climbed up beside her father. She was tall too, but the giant made them both look stunted.

Kaywerbrimmis asked, "Your camp, that way?"

The giant's dialect was less comprehensible. "Yes. Come. You want shelter. We want warriors."

"How do you practice rishathra?" It was the first thing any trader would want to know, and any Beta male too, if these were like Grass Giants elsewhere.

The giant said, "Come quick, else learn too much of rishathra."

"What?"

"Vampires."

Forn's eyes widened. "That smell!"

Kay smiled, seeing not a threat, but an opportunity. "I am Kaywerbrimmis. Here are Valavirgillin, my patron, and Sabarokaresh and Foranayeedli. We Machine People are small in number, but great in power. We hope to persuade you to join our Empire."

"I am Paroom. Our leader you must address as Thurl."

Grass Giant sword-scythes had too little reach. Farsight Trading's guns would make short work of a Vampire attack. That should impress the Bull, and then—business.

Grass Giants, scores of them, were pulling wagons filled with grass through the gap in a wall of heaped earth.

"This isn't normal," Kaywerbrimmis said. "Grass Giants don't build walls."

Paroom heard. "We had to learn. Forty-three falans ago the Reds were fighting us. We learned walls from them."

Forty-three falans: four hundred and thirty rotations of the sky, where the sky rotated every seven and a half days. In forty falans Valavirgillin had made herself rich, had mated, had carried four children, then gambled her wealth away. These last three falans she had been traveling.

Forty-three falans was a long time.

She asked or tried to ask, "Was that when the clouds came?"

"Yes. After the old Thurl boiled a sea."

Yes! This was the place she sought.

Kaywerbrimmis shrugged it off: local superstition. "How long have you had Vampires?"

Paroom said, "Always there are some. In these last few falans, suddenly they are everywhere, more every night. This morning we found nearly two hundred Gleaners, all dead. Tonight they will hunger again. The walls and our crossbows hold them back. Here," said the sentry, "bring your wagons through the gap and prepare them to fight."

They had crossbows?

And the light was going.

It was crowded inside the walls. Grass Giant men and women were unloading their wagons, pausing frequently to eat of the grass. They looked up as the Machine People moved among them; they gaped, then returned to work. Had they ever seen self-propelled cruisers? But Vampires were a more urgent concern.

Already men in leather armor lined the wall. Others were heaping earth and stones to close the gap.

Vala could feel the Grass Giants staring at her beard.

She could count roughly a thousand of them, as many women as men. But women outnumbered the men among Grass Giants elsewhere, and she didn't see *any* children. Add a few hundred more, then, for women tending children somewhere in the buildings.

A great alien silver shape strode down the slope to meet them.

It lifted its crested helm to reveal a golden mane. The Thurl was the biggest of Grass Giant males. The armor he wore bulged at every joint; he looked like no hominid ever seen in the world.

"Thurl," Kaywerbrimmis said carefully, "Farsight Trading has come to help."

"Good. What are you, Machine People? We hear of you."

"Our Empire is mighty, but we spread through trade, not war. We hope to persuade your people to make fuel for us, and bread, and other things. Your grass can make good bread; you might like it yourselves. In return we can show you wonders, the least of which are our guns. These handguns, they'll reach farther than your crossbows. For close work we have flamers—"

"Killing-things, are they? Our good luck that you have come. Yours too, to show our need for Machine People friends. You should move your guns to the wall now."

"Thurl, the cannon are mounted on the cruisers."

The wall stood twice the height of a Machine People. But Valavirgillin remembered a local word. "Ramp. Thurl, is there a ramp that leads up the wall? Will it carry our cruisers?"

The day's colors were turning charcoal gray. It was starting to rain. Far above these clouds, the shadow of night must have nearly covered the sun.

And there wasn't any ramp, until the Thurl bellowed his orders. Then all the huge males and females broke from their labor and began moving earth.

Vala noted one woman climbing, guiding, shouting, monitoring details like a staff sergeant. Big, mature, with a voice to shatter rocks. She caught a name: *Moonwa*. Perhaps the Thurl's primary wife.

Metal payload shell and metal motor, and wide timber running boards a hand thick: a cruiser was heavy. The ramp tended to crumble. The cruisers went up one by one, with the wall brushing their right sides and ten Grass Giant males lifting and steadying on the left. How would they get the cruisers *down*?

The top was as wide as a cruiser wheelbase. The sentries guided them. "Face your weapons starboard-spin. Vampires come from there."

The wagonmasters placed their vehicles, then met to confer. Kay asked, "Whand, Anth, what do you think? Shrapnel in the cannon? They might bunch up. They often do."

Anthrantillin said, "Have the Giants gather some gravel, maybe. Save our shot. This will be handgun work, though. Spread out?"

Whandernothtee said, "That's what the Giants want."

"Me too," Kaywerbrimmis said.

Vala said, "The Grass Giants have crossbows. Why are they worried? Crossbows won't have the reach of guns, but they'll outreach Vampire scent."

The wagon masters looked at each other. Anth said, "Grass eaters."

"Oh, no. People hereabouts think Grass Giants are scary fighters," Whand said.

Nobody answered.

Pinternothtee's cruiser and Anthrantillin's rolled off in opposite directions. They were almost invisible in the rain and dark when the Grass Giant warriors stopped them.

Kaywerbrimmis said, "Barok, you on the cannon, but keep your guns handy. I'm on handguns. Forn, reloading." She was too young to be trusted to do more. "Boss, do you like the flamer?"

Vala said, "They'll never get that close. I throw pretty good, too."

"Flamer and fistbombs, then. I hope we do get to use the flamer. It'd help if we could show them another use for alcohol. Grass Giants don't need our fuel, they pull their own wagons. Vampires aren't intelligent, are they?"

"The ones near Center City aren't."

"Do they charge? One big wave?"

"I only fought Vampires once."

"That's one more than me. I hear stories. What was it like?"

"I was the only survivor," Valavirgillin said. "Kay? Just stories? Do you know enough to use towels and fuel?"

Kay's brow furrowed. "What?"

—and Vala's head whipped around at a sentry's bass call.

All was shadows now, and a sound that might be wind through taut cords, and the whisper of crossbows. The Grass Giants were being chary of their bolts. Bullets weren't replaceable either, where there was no client race to make more.

Vala couldn't see anything yet. For the Grass Giants it would be no darker, but these plains were their home. A crossbow whispered, and something pale stood up and fell over. The wind picked up . . . that wasn't wind.

Song.

"Look for white," Forn called unnecessarily. Kay fired, changed guns, fired.

It was well that the cruisers were spaced far apart. The flash of the guns was blinding. Vala thought it over, while the fire balloons in her eyes dwindled. Then she rolled under the cruiser and pulled the flamer and the net bag of fistbombs after. Let the cruiser shield her eyes from the flash.

And the cannon?

They were firing around her. Her sight was back. There, a pale hominid shape. Another. She could see twenty and more! One fell, and the rest backed away. Already most of them must be beyond crossbow range. Their song plucked at her nerves.

"Cannon," Barok commented, and she closed her eyes just as he fired.

Fire was trying to light in the stubble. There were pale bodies, six . . . eight. Thirty or forty Vampires stood in plain view, still in gun range, she thought.

Why would men with crossbows fear Vampires? Because nobody had ever seen so many Vampires together!

It was bizarre, insane. How could so many feed themselves? High Rangers Trading Group had fought no more than fifteen. Killed no more than eight.

High Rangers had died in a tower in a deserted city, forty-three falans ago. She remembered the song wafting up from the street. The Vampires pale, naked, beautiful. The terror. They'd fired from tenth-floor windows, and posted sentries down along the stairwell. One by one the sentries had disappeared, and then—

Kay said, "The wind's blowing right."

Barok said, "Cannon."

She clenched her eyelids against the flash. Barok's cannon roared, then one from further away, barely heard.

Barok's voice was faint. "They could circle."

"They're not sapient," Kay said.

To left, another distant cannon fired. To right, another.

Vampires carried no tools, wore no clothing. Reach into the lovely wealth of red or golden hair on a Vampire's corpse: you would find too much hair around a small, flat skull. They built no cities, formed no armies, invented no encircling movements.

But the warriors were buzzing among themselves, pointing, firing bolts into the dark to spin and starboard and antispin.

"Kay? They've got noses."

Barok looked down. Kay said, "What?"

"They don't have a battle plan," Valavirgillin said. "They're just avoiding the smell of fifteen hundred Grass Giants served by a primitive sewer system. It's the same smell that brought them here! When they get upwind of that, the smell won't bother them anymore. And then *we'll* be downwind from *them*."

"I'll get Whandernothtee to move his cruiser around," Barok said, and ran.

Vala bellowed after him. "Cloth and alcohol!"

He came back. "What?"

"Pour fuel into a towel, just a splash. Tie it around your face. It keeps the scent out. Tell Whand!"

Kay spoke from overhead. "I still have targets here. Boss, they're not in throwing range. *You* go tell Anth to move. Tell him about towels and fuel. Then the Grass Giants might not know either. Boss? Remember I wanted to show them some use for fuel?"

Idiot. She soaked a towel for herself and took two more with her. This could turn urgent.

In the dark, with a drop on either side, she had to watch her footing. It had stopped raining. The song of the Vampires rode the wind. She breathed alcohol fumes from the towel around her face. It made her dizzy.

She heard distantly, "Cannon." Closed her eyes, waited for the roar, walked on toward a square shadow. She called, "Anthrantillin!"

"He's busy, Vala." Taratarafasht's voice.

"He'll be very busy, Tarfa. The Vamps are circling round. Get your towels out, douse them with fuel, tie them over your mouths. Then move the truck a sixth around the arc."

"Valavirgillin, I take my orders from Anthrantillin."

Fool woman. "Get the cruiser into place or you can both tell it to the Ghouls. Get a towel on Anth too. But first give me a fuel jar for the Giants."

Pause. "Yes, Valavirgillin. Do you have enough towels?"

The fuel jar was heavy. Vala was terribly conscious of the weapons she wasn't holding. When the big shape loomed before her, she was embarrassingly relieved.

The Grass Giant didn't turn. "How goes the defense, Vaverglin?"

Valavirgillin said, "They're circling us. You'll smell them in a minute. Tie this—"

"Fowh! What stink is that?"

"Alcohol. It moves our cruisers, but it may save us. Tie this around your neck."

The guard didn't move, didn't look at her. He wouldn't insult an alien guest. So: *Vaverglin has not spoken.*

She didn't have time for games. "Point me toward the Thurl."

"Wait. Give me the cloth."

She threw it to him underhand. He snorted in disgust, but he was tying it around his neck. He pointed then, but she'd already seen the shine of the Bull's armor.

The Bull looked at the cloth in her hands even as he backed away from the stink. "But why?"

"You don't *know* about Vampires?"

"Stories come to us. Vampires die easily enough, and they don't *think*. As for the rest . . . should the cloth cover our ears?"

"Why, Thurl?"

"So that they cannot sing us to our deaths."

"Not sound. Smell!"

"Smell?"

She, Kay, *someone* should have asked when they first arrived, no matter the rush. Grass Giants weren't idiots, but . . . first somebody had to live through a Vampire attack. Even if a child survived, he would not know why the adults all went away. The Grass Giants had been unlucky.

"Vampires put out a mating scent, Thurl. Your lust rises and your brain turns off and you *go*."

"The stink of your fuel, it cures the problem? But isn't there another problem? We hear of you Machine People and your Empire of fuel. You persuade other hominid species to make alcohol for your wagons. They learn to drink it. They lose interest in work and play and life itself, anything but the fuel, and they die young."

The Thurl had a point. *Do we want crossbowmen drunk while Vampires circle the wall?* Still—"Vampire scent does all of that."

"Is fuel better? Try strong herbs?"

"When can you pick these herbs? I have fuel now, not tomorrow."

The Bull turned from her and began bellowing orders. Most of the males were on the wall now, but women began running. Bales of cloth appeared. Women climbed up the wall and along the top to the cruisers. Vala waited with what patience she could muster.

The Bull said, "Come." He entered an earthen building, the second largest.

It was fabric stretched over the top of a dirt wall, with one central pole. Here were tall heaps of dried grass, but other plants too, a thousand scents. The Bull crushed leaves under her nose. She shied back. A different leaf; she sniffed gingerly. Another. She said, "Try all of those, but try fuel too. We'll find out what works best. Why do you store these?"

The Bull laughed. "Flavoring, these, pepperleek and minch. Woman eats this, whiffle, makes her milk better. Did you think we eat only grass? Wilted or sour grass needs something for taste."

"I feel sufficiently foolish now, Thurl."

The Bull gathered armfuls of plants and strode out bellowing. She could have heard his roar in Center City, she thought. His voice and the women's, and presently the scuff of their big feet as they climbed.

Vala retrieved her fuel bottle and climbed after.

From the top she watched the big shadows, warriors motionless, women moving among them distributing impregnated towels. Vala intercepted a big, mature woman. "Moonwa?"

"Vaverglin. They kill by *smell*?"

"They do. We don't know what smell protects best. Some men already have alcohol-scented towels. Leave them those, give the Thurl's plants to the rest. We'll see."

"See who dies."

Vala walked on. The alcohol fumes were making her a little giddy. She could handle it, and for that matter her towel was nearly dry.

This morning Vala had been thinking that Forn was ready to practice rishathra, or perhaps to mate straight off. Now it seemed she'd beaten that prediction. Forn could hardly be remembering the smell of Vampires; more likely she'd recognized the scent of a lover.

That old scent of lust and death was into Valavirgillin's nose and working on her brain. And what of the Grass Giants?

The warriors were still shadows amid the moving shadows of women. But . . . they were fewer.

The Grass Giant women had noticed too. Breathy screams of rage and fear; then two, four ran down the embankment shouting for the Thurl. Another ran down . . . the wrong way. Out onto the stubbly field.

Vala moved among the remaining defenders, sloshing fuel on towels. Women, men, whoever she could find. Haste would kill. Fuel would protect. Herbs? Well, the smell of an herb might last longer.

In every direction she could see pale hominid shapes. So little detail; you had to imagine what they looked like; and with the scent ticking in your hindbrain, you saw them as beautiful beyond description.

They were closer. Why wasn't she hearing guns? She'd reached Anthrantillin's cruiser. Up onto the running board. "Hello? Anth?"

The payload shell was empty.

She used the trick lock and climbed in.

All gone. No damage, no trace of a fight; just gone.

Soak a towel. Then: the cannon.

The Vampires were bunching nicely to spin. Bunching around Anth or Forn or Himp, somewhere down there? It didn't matter. She fired and saw half of them fall.

* * *

Sometime during that night she heard a repeated whisper of sound. "Anthrantillin?"

"Gone," she said, and couldn't hear her own voice. She screamed, "Gone! It's Valavirgillin!" and barely heard that. Her bellow, his bellow reduced to whispers by the cannon's ear-shattering roar.

It was time to move the cruiser. The Vampires had pulled way back here, they'd learned not to bunch, but she might find fresh prey elsewhere. Guns weren't needed on the starboard and spin sides. Upwind from the Vampires, crossbows would reach them.

"It's Kay. Are they all gone?"

"I found the cruiser dead empty!"

"We're low on firepower. You?"

"Plenty."

"We won't have any fuel come morning."

"No. I set all mine out and told the women about it. I thought—Moonwa, the Grass Giant who was forcing towels on the warriors—teach her to use the cannon? Do we want—"

"No, Boss, no. Secrets."

"Take too long to train her anyway."

Kay's head rose into the cannoneer's chamber. He pulled out a jug of gunpowder, hefted it with a grunt. "Back to work."

"Do you need smallshot?"

"Plenty of rocks." He looked at her. Froze. He set the jug down.

She slid down. They moved together.

"Should have soaked that towel again," she said unsteadily. It was her last coherent thought for some time.

He, not Vala, *Kay* wriggled out of the door and splashed into mud in a blowing rain. Vala followed, moaning. He ripped her shirt off. She pressed herself against him, but he howled and ripped it again, and turned in her arms, and turned back with two dripping half-shirts and pushed one into her face and one into his own.

She breathed deeply of alcohol fumes. Choked. "All right."

He gave it to her. He tied the other around his own neck. "I'm going back," he said. "You'd better fight your gun alone. Under the—"

"—circumstances." They laughed shakily. "Are you safe? Alone?"

"Have to try it."

She watched him go.

She should never. Never. Never have mated with another man. Her mind, her *self* had washed away in a tide of lust. What would Tarb think of her?

Mating with Tarablilliast had never been so intense.

But now her mind was flowing back. She *was* mated.

She lifted the towel to her face. The alcohol went straight to her head, and cleared it, unless that was an illusion. She looked along the wall and saw big shadows, too few, but some. Hominid shapes in the black fields were also fewer, but very close. They were taller, more slender than her own species. They sang; they implored; they were bunched almost beneath the cruiser.

She climbed up and loaded her cannon.

two

A pale light was growing, lighter to spin. The song was over. Vala hadn't heard a crossbow twang in some time. Vampires had become hard to find.

Unnoticed, the dreadful night had ended.

If she had ever been this tired, exhaustion must have wiped the memory clean. And here was Kaywerbrimmis asking, "Do you have any smallshot left?"

"Some. We never got our gravel."

"Barok and Forn were both gone when I got back to the cruiser."

Vala rubbed her eyes. There didn't seem to be anything to say.

Whandernothtee and Sopashinthay came up leaning on each other. Whand said, "What a night."

"Chit liked the singing overmuch. We had to tie him up," said Spash. "I think I put too much fuel in his towel. He's sleeping like . . . like I would if I could just—" She hugged herself. "Just stop jittering."

Sleep. And several hundred Grass Giants males were expecting— "I couldn't handle rishathra now," Vala said. She'd put off the memory of mating with Kay. That could have consequences.

Kaywerbrimmis said, "Sleep in the cruisers. At least for tonight. Hello—" His hand on her shoulder turned her around.

Company. Nine Grass Giants and a suit of silver armor had come among them. You could see their exhaustion, and smell it. The Thurl asked, "How is it with you Machine People?"

"Half of us are missing," Valavirgillin said.

Whand said, "Thurl, we never expected so many. We thought we had the weapons for anything."

"Travelers tell that Vampires *sing* us to our doom."

Kay said, "Half of wisdom is learning what to unlearn."

"We were prepared for the wrong enemy. Vampire scent! We never guessed. But we've set the Vampires running!" the Thurl boomed. "Shall we hunt them through the grass?"

Whand threw up his arms and staggered away.

Vala and Kay and Spash looked at each other. If Grass Giant warriors could still fight . . . Whand was done, used up, but *someone* had to stand up for the Machine People.

They trailed the warriors down into the wet stubble.

Shapes stirred at the foot of the wall. Two; hominid; naked.

Crossbows and guns swung around. Arms batted them aside, voices barked. *No! Not Vampires!* A big woman and a little male were helping each other to stand.

Not Vampires, no. A Grass Giant woman and—"Barok!"

Sabarokaresh's face was slack with a terror too deep to touch surface. He looked at her as if she were the ghost, not he. Half mad, dirty, exhausted, scarred, alive.

I thought I was tired! Vala thumped his shoulder, glad to feel him solid under her hand. Where was his daughter? She didn't ask. She said, "You must have quite a tale to tell. Later?"

The Thurl spoke to the crossbowman, Paroom. Paroom led/pulled Barok and the Grass Giant woman up the slope.

The Thurl moved at a trot, away from the wall, to starboardspin. His people followed, and then the Machine People. A night of sleepless terror and wild mating had left them all without strength.

They passed Vampire corpses. None of their beauty survived into death. A Grass Giant stopped to examine a female skewered by a crossbow. Spash stopped too.

Vala remembered doing that, forty-three falans ago. *First you smell rotting flesh. Then the other scent explodes under your mind—*

The man suddenly turned away and vomited. He stayed head down, then slowly straightened, still hiding his face. Spash straightened suddenly, then wobbled toward Vala and hid her face against her shoulder.

"Spash. You haven't *done* anything, love. It feels like you want to mate with a corpse, but that's not your *mind* talking."

"Not my mind. Vala, if we can't examine them, we can't learn about them!"

"It's part of what makes them so scary." Lust and the smell of rotting meat do not belong together in one brain.

Vampires near the wall had crossbow bolts in them. Further out, they were chewed by balls or smallshot. Vala saw that Machine People had scored as many kills as a hundred times as many Grass Giants.

Two hundred paces beyond the wall, they weren't finding Vampires anymore. Dead Grass Giants lay naked or half clothed, gaunt, with sunken eyes and cheeks, and savage wounds in their necks, wrists, elbows.

That slack face . . . Vala had seen this woman run out into the dark, hours ago. Where were the wounds? Her throat seemed untouched. Left arm thrown wide, wrist unmarred; right arm across body, no blood on the rucked-up tunic. . . . Vala stepped forward and lifted her right hand.

Her armpit was torn and bloody. A Grass Giant man turned and wobbled back toward the wall, retching.

Big woman, small Vampire. Couldn't reach. Spash is right, we have to learn.

Further along, bright cloth lay near the grass border. Vala began to run, then stopped as suddenly. That was Taratarafasht's work suit.

Vala picked it up. It was clean. No blood, no ground-in dirt. Why had Tarfa been brought so far? Where was she?

The Thurl had outrun his party by a good distance. He'd almost reached uncut grass. How much did that armor weigh? He scrambled up a ten-pace-high knoll, then posed at the top, waiting while the rest straggled up.

"No sign of Vampires," he said. "They've gone to cover somewhere. Travelers say they can't stand sunlight?"

Kay said, "That tale's true."

The Thurl continued, "Grass won't hide them from the sun. I'd say they're gone."

Nobody spoke.

The Thurl boomed, "Beedj!"

"Thurl!" A male trotted up: mature, bigger than most, eager, indecently energetic.

"With me, Beedj. Trunt, you'll circle and meet us on the other side. If you're not there I'll assume you found a war to fight."

"Yes."

Beedj and the Thurl went one way, the rest of the Giants went the other. Vala dithered an instant, then followed the Thurl.

The Thurl noticed her. He slowed and let her catch up. Beedj would have waited too, but the Thurl's gesture sent him on.

The Thurl said, "Grass grows straight up. Night slides across the sun, but the sun never moves, not any more. If Vampires can't stand sunlight, they have to hide under something."

Vala asked, "Do you remember when the sun moved?"

"I was a child. A frightening time," he said; but he wasn't nearly frightened enough. Louis Wu had been among these people; but what Louis had told Valavirgillin, he didn't seem to have told them.

It's a ring, he'd said. *The Arch is the part of the ring you're not standing on. The sun has started to wobble because the ring is off center. In several falans the ring will brush the sun,* he'd said. *But I swear I will stop it, or die trying.*

Later the sun had stopped wobbling.

Beedj was still jogging, stopping here and there to examine bodies; swinging his sword to cut a swath of grass to see what it hid; eating what he cut as he resumed his patrol. He was burning more energy than the Thurl. Vala had seen no challenge between them—easy command and easy submission— but she became sure that she was watching the next Thurl.

She nerved herself to ask, "Thurl, did an unknown hominid come among you claiming to be from a place in the sky?"

The Thurl stared. "In the *sky*?"

He could hardly have forgotten, but he might hide secrets. "A male wizard, unknown hominid. Bald narrow face, bronze skin, straight black scalp hair, taller than my kind and narrower in the shoulders and hip." Fingertips lifted and stretched the corners of her eyes, "Eyes like *this*. He boiled a sea hereabouts, to end a plague of mirror-flowers."

The Thurl was nodding. "It was done by the old Thurl, with this Louis Wu's help. But how do you come to know about that?"

"Louis Wu and I traveled together, far to port of here. Without sunlight the mirror-flowers couldn't defend themselves, he said. The clouds, though, they never went away?"

"They never did. The flowers could not burn us. We seeded our grass, just as the wizard told us. Smeerps and other burrowers moved in well ahead of us. Wherever we went, we found mirror-flowers eaten at the roots. Grass doesn't grow well in this murk, so at first we had to eat mirror-flowers.

"The Reds who fed their herds from our grass in my father's time, and fought us when we objected, they followed us into new grassland. Gleaners hunted the burrowers. Water People moved back up the rivers that the mirror-flowers had taken."

"What of the Vampires?"

"It seems they did well too."

Vala grimaced.

The Thurl said, "There was a region we all avoided. Vampires need refuge from daylight, a cave system, trees, anything. When the clouds came, they feared the sun less. They traveled further from their lair. We know no more than that."

"We should ask the Ghouls."

"Do you Machine People talk to Ghouls?" The Thurl didn't quite like that idea.

"Normally, no. They keep their own company. But Ghouls know where the dead have fallen. They must know where the Vampires hunt, and where they hide during the day."

"Ghouls only act at night. I would not know how to talk to a Ghoul."

"It's done." Vala was trying to remember, but her mind wasn't working well. Tired. "It's done. A new religion pops up, or an old priest dies, and then it's a rite of ordeal for the new shaman. The Ghouls must know and accept what rites he demands for the dead."

The Bull nodded. Ghouls would carry out funeral rites for any religion, within obvious limits. "How, then?"

"You have to get their attention. Court them. Anything works, but they're coy. That's a test, too. A new priest won't be taken seriously until he's dealt with the Ghouls."

The Bull was bristling. "*Court* them?"

"My people came here as merchants, Thurl. The Ghouls have something we want: knowledge. What have we got that the Ghouls want? Not much. Ghouls own everything beneath the Arch, just ask them."

"Court them." It grated. "How?"

What had she heard? Tales told at night; not much in the way of business dealings. But she'd seen and talked to Ghouls—"Ghouls work the shadow farm under a floating city far to port. We pay them in tools, and the City Builders give them library privileges. They'll deal for information."

"But we don't know anything."

"Nearly true."

"What else have we got?" The Thurl said, "Oh, Valavirgillin, this is nasty stuff."

"What?"

The Thurl waved about him. In view were nearly a hundred Vampire corpses, all lying near the wall, and half as many Grass Giant dead scattered from the crossbow limit to the uncut grass.

Beedj was examining a smaller corpse. He saw he had her attention, and he lifted the head so that Vala could see its face. It was Himapertharee, of Anthrantillin's crew.

A shudder rippled along Vala's spine. But the Thurl was right. She said, "Ghouls must feed. More than that: if these thousand corpses were left to lie, there would be plague. All would blame the Ghouls. The Ghouls must come to clean up."

"But why will they listen to me?"

Vala shook her head. It felt stuffed with cotton.

"What then, *after* we know where the Vampires lair? Attack them ourselves?"

"The Ghouls might tell us that too—"

The Thurl broke into a run. Vala saw Beedj waving, holding—what? At that moment he shook it until it bent in the middle. He flung it, and hurled himself away from it. Where it fell, it writhed and went quiet, though Beedj was howling.

It was a Vampire.

Beedj called, "Thurl, I'm sorry. It was alive, wounded, just the bolt through its hip. I thought we might talk to it, examine it—anything—but—but the smell!"

"Calm yourself, Beedj. Was the smell sudden? You attack, it defends?"

"What, like a fart? Sometimes controlled, sometimes not? . . . Thurl, I'm not sure."

"Resume your patrol."

Beedj's sword slashed viciously at the grass. The Thurl walked on.

Vala had been thinking. She said, "You must set a delegation among the dead. A tent, a few of your men—"

"We'd find them sucked empty in the morning!"

"No, I think it's safe for tonight and tomorrow night. The Vampires have hunted this area out, and there's the smell of their own dead. Even so, arm your people and, mmm, send men and women both."

"Valavirgillin—"

"I know your custom, but if the Vampires sing, best your people mate with each other." Should she be saying this? She surely would not have spoken thus before other Grass Giants.

The Bull snarled, but— "Yes. Yes, and what the Thurl does not see did not happen. So." The Thurl beckoned at Beedj. He asked Vala, "Will Farsight Trading join us?"

"We should support you. Two species in need will speak louder than one." Farsight Trading couldn't roll away from *this* problem. No fuel. They'd poured most of it into towels.

"Three species, then. Many Gleaners died the night before last. The Gleaners will wait with us. Should we be more yet? Vampires must have hunted among the Reds."

"Worth a try."

Beedj came up. The Thurl began talking much faster than Vala could follow. Beedj tried to argue, then acquiesced.

"We should sleep during the day," Vala said.

In the cruiser. Sleep.

Something closed on her wrist. "Boss?"

She jerked awake. Her squeak was intended as a scream. She rolled away and sat up and—it was only Kaywerbrimmis.

"Boss, what have you been telling the Bull?"

She was still groggy. She needed a drink and a bath or— that rattle, was it rain? And a flash and *boom* that was certainly thunder.

She'd pulled off her filthy clothing before she slept. She slid out of the blankets, out of the payload shell, into the cool rain. Kay watched from the gun room as she danced in the rain.

Consequences. Traders didn't mate. They shared rishathra with the species they met, but mating was something else. You didn't get a business partner pregnant, and you didn't engage in sexual dominance games, and you didn't fall in love.

But in far realms, among strange hominids, you couldn't shun each other either.

She beckoned and shouted, "Wash with me. What time is it?"

"Coming on dusk. We slept a long time." Kay was pulling off his clothes in something like relief. "I thought we'd need time to arm against Vampires."

"We'll do that. How's Barok?"

"Don't know."

They drank, washed each other, dried each other, and were reassured: the mating urge could be resisted.

The rain stopped. You could see wind driving the last flurries across the stubble. Swaths of navy blue sky showed through blowing broken clouds, and a sudden narrow vertical line of blue-white dashes.

Vala gaped. She hadn't seen the Arch in four rotations.

By glowing Archlight she could see patterns in the grass stubble. An arc of pale rectangles. A tent erected within the arc. Grass Giants moved back and forth, and a handful of much smaller hominids moved with them. On the rectangles . . . sheets? They were laying out bodies.

"Did you tell them to do that?"

"No. Not a bad idea, though," Vala said.

In Anthrantillin's deserted cruiser they found Barok with a woman twice his size. He seemed abnormally subdued, but he was smiling. "Wemb, my partners Valavirgillin and Kaywerbrimmis. Folk, this is Wemb."

Kay started to say, "I would have thought—"

Barok's laugh was not quite sane. "Yes, and you would've been right, if you would have thought we slept!"

Wemb cut in. "Sleeping here, together, protects each against intent of the rest, against *yet more rishathra*! We were lucky in each other."

Groping through his exhausted mind, Barok found another thought. "Forn. You never found Foranayeedli?"

Vala said, "She's gone."

Barok's body rippled, an uncontrollable shudder. His hand closed on Vala's wrist. "I shouted down at her. 'Load!' Nothing. She was gone. I stepped out to look for her, to stop her if she followed the singing. Stepped out and my mind turned off. I was at the foot of the wall and the rain was hammering me into the ground. Someone stumbled into me. Knocked me in the mud. Wemb. We—rishathra isn't a strong enough word."

Wemb took him by the shoulder and turned him toward her. "Shared love, or even mated, but we *must* say *rishathra*, Barok. Truly we must."

"—Tore our clothes away and rished and rished, and had our minds back with not a heartbeat to spare. A half circle of those pale things was closing on us. The rain must have washed away some of the scent. I saw crossbows lying all around us. Grass Giant warriors have been stumbling down the wall all night long, dropping crossbows and anything else they're carrying—"

"We picked up crossbows," the Grass Giant woman cut in. "I saw Makee lying dead with a Vampire in his arms and a bolt through both of them, and his quiver dropped beside him. Picked up the quiver and dumped it and pushed a handful of bolts at Barok and shot the nearest Vampire. Then the next."

"At first I couldn't cock the crossbow."

"Then the next. Is that why you were screaming? We never talked till after."

"Scream and pull. For strength," Barok said. "Your cursed tools aren't built for us tiny little Machine People."

Vala asked, "You were out there all night?"

Wemb nodded. Barok said, "When the rain started to slack off I got us towels. There were heaps of towels." His grip was painful. "Kay, Vala, we saw why."

"Warriors walked past us," Wemb said. "I shot Heerst in the leg, but he just kept walking, following the singing. Vampires came up to him and tore the towel off his face and led him away. He's my son."

"If something is covering your face, they pull it off!" Barok said. "Heerst was using fuel in his towel. Rain washed it out. We looked for towels that had—Wemb?"

"Pepperleek. Minch."

"Yes, those kept their scent. They kept us alive, the towels and the rishathra. Any time it was too much for us, we rished. And crossbow bolts. The guards were dropping their swords and crossbows but not their quivers. We had to go looking. Rob the dead."

"I saw what I didn't understand," Wemb said. "I should tell the Thurl. Vampires rished with some of us, then led them away into the high grass and further. Why keep them alive? Are they still alive?"

Vala said, "The Ghouls might know."

"Ghouls keep Ghoul secrets," Wemb said.

The clouds had closed again. In the dark Barok said, "I shot the Vampire who was leading Anth away. It took two bolts. Another picked up the song, and I shot her. Anth followed a third woman, and by that time he was out of range. They led him into the grass. I never saw him again. Should I have shot *him*?"

They only looked at him.

"I can't keep vigil with you," Barok said. "I can't face rishathra now. My head is too—I don't know if I can make you see—"

They squeezed his arms and tried to assure him that they understood. They left him there.

three

The tent huddled beneath the wall, but faced outward into an arc of gray sheets.

The corpses were laid head to head, two Giants to a sheet, or four Vampires. Giants had found Anthrantillin and his crewman Himapertharee and laid them out on one sheet. Taratarafasht and Foranayeedli must be still missing. Another sheet held six tiny Gleaner dead.

The Giants had nearly finished making their patterns. Tiny hominids moved about them, not helping much, but carrying food or light loads. All wore sheets with holes for the head to poke through.

A Grass Giant could lift a Vampire with no difficulty. It took two to carry a dead Giant.

But Beedj was carrying a dead Grass Giant woman across his back. He rolled the woman off his shoulders to slump across a sheet, perfectly placed. He took her hand and spoke to her sadly. Vala changed her mind about disturbing him.

Two women finished laying out more Vampire dead. One approached. "We rubbed pepperleek along the rims of the sheets. Stop small scavengers," Moonwa said to the three Machine People. "Big scavengers we can crossbow. Ghouls won't have to fight for what's theirs."

"A polite notion," Valavirgillin said. Tables would have raised the dead out of a scavenger's reach; but where would Grass Giants find wood?

"What can I do for you?" Moonwa asked.

"We've come to keep vigil with you."

"The battle cost you too much. No Ghouls come on first night. Rest."

Vala said, "But it was my idea, after all."

"Thurl's idea," Moonwa informed her.

Vala nodded and carefully didn't smile. It was a convention, as in *Louis Wu helped the Thurl boil a sea.* She waved toward what had to be Gleaners. "Who are these?"

She called, "Perilack, Silack, Manack, Coriak—" Four small heads lifted. "These are more allies: Kaywerbrimmis, Valavirgillin, Whandernothtee."

The Gleaners smiled and bobbed their heads, but they didn't come up at once. They moved off to where Grass Giants were carefully stripping their sheets off inside out, well away from the dead and the tent, then picking up scythes and crossbows. The Gleaners stripped off their contaminated sheets, then hung slender swords behind their backs.

Beedj approached, sheetless and armed. "Towels under the tent. We rubbed minch on them," he said. "Welcome to all."

Gleaners stood armpit-high to Machine People, navel-high to Beedj and Moonwa. Their faces were hairless and pointed; their smiles were wide and toothy, a bit much. They wore tunics of cured smeerpskin with the beige fur left on, lavishly decorated with feathers. On the women, Perilack and Coriak, the feather patterns formed smallish wings. The women had to walk with some care to protect them. Manack and Silack looked much like the women. Their clothing showed greater differences; feathered, but with arms free to swing. Or fight.

Rain spattered down, just enough to send the Machine People into the tent. Vala saw grass piled thickly on the floor. Grass for bedding and to feed the Grass Giants. She stopped her companions until they had all taken off their sandals.

Already it was dark enough that Vala could barely see faces. Rishathra was best begun in the night.

But not on a battlefield.

"This is a bad business," Perilack said.

Whandernothtee asked, "How many have you lost?"

"Nearly two hundred by now."

"We were only ten. Four are gone. Sopashinthay and Chi-takumishad we left on guard above us with the cannon. Barok is recovering from a night in hell."

"Our queen's man went with the Thurl's to bring other ho-minids to bargain. If the"—the little woman's eyes flickered about her—"lords of the night do not speak, other voices will join ours tomorrow."

Legend told that the Ghouls heard any word spoken of them, unless (some said) during broad daylight. The Ghouls might be all about them even now.

The clouds had closed. It had become full dark.

One of the Gleaner men asked, "Should we only wait? Would they find that more polite?"

Manack, wasn't it? Hair thicker around the throat, as if he were an alpha male and Silack a beta. In a good many ho-minid species, one male got most of the action; but Vala didn't know that about Gleaners.

Vala said, "Manack, we're *here*. In their habitat. You may even consider that we've come to entertain the lords of the night. Will you share rishathra?" To Beedj she quickly added, "Beedj, this is for size. I expect Whand will go with Moonwa first—" Though Kay, she noticed, was deep in conversation with Perilack. Philosophies differ.

To rish' with Gleaners was no more than foreplay.

Rishathra with the Thurl's heir was something else again. It had its pleasures. He was big. He was very eager. He was very proud of his self-restraint, though it was right at the edge of his control. But mostly, he was big.

Kaywerbrimmis was having a wonderful night, or seemed to be. He was sharing some joke or secret with Moonwa, now. Good trader, that one; a generally good man. Vala kept look-ing in his direction.

They'd mated. Vala couldn't get her mind out of that mode . . . shouldn't try, really. A good mind-set for a rishathra party. Still.

Mating is a matter of order. Aeons of evolution have shaped any hominid's mating responses: approach, scents, postures and positions, visual and tactile cues.

But evolution never touches sex outside one's species, and rishathra is always an art form. Where shapes don't fit, other shapes might be found. Those who cannot participate can watch, can give ribald advice. . . .

Could stand guard, for that matter, when a trader's body or mind might need a rest.

The night was almost silent, but not all of those whispers were wind. Ghouls should be out there. It was their duty. But if for any reason word hadn't reached them of a corpse-strewn battlefield, then those sounds might be Vampires.

Vala perched on a stool three paces high and sturdy enough for a Grass Giant. The night was warm enough for nakedness, or *she* was, but loaded guns were on her back. Before her was blowing rain and little else to see. At her back any excitement had died for the moment.

"We and the Grass Giants, we love each other, but we're not mere parasites," one of the Gleaners was saying. "Wherever there once were mirror-flower forests, there are plant eaters now, prey that can feed us. We forage ahead of the Thurl's people. We probe, we guide, we make their maps."

Manack, that was. He was a bit small to accommodate even a Machine People woman, and inexperienced; but he could learn. The proper attitude was easy for some. Others never learned it.

Mating has consequences. A hominid's response to mating is not of the mind. Rishathra has no consequences, and the mind may remain in command. Embarrassment is inappropriate. Laughter is always to be shared. Rishathra is entertainment and diplomacy and friendship, and knowing that you can reach your weapons in the dark.

"We hope to make our fortunes," Kay was saying. "Those who extend the Empire are well treated. The Empire grows with our fuel supply. If we can persuade a tribe to make fuel and sell it to the Empire, the bonus would let each of us raise a family."

Moonwa said. "Those rewards are yours. Your client tribes face something else. Loss of ambition, loss of friends and mates, delusion and early death for any who learn to drink your fuel."

"Some are too weak to say, 'Enough.' Moonwa, you *must* be stronger than that."

"Of course. I can do that tonight, now. *Enough, Kaywerbrimmis!*"

Vala turned to see white grins large and small. Beedj said, "I wore one of your fuel-wetted towels last night. It made me dizzy. It threw my aim off."

Kay gracefully changed the subject. "Valavirgillin, will you return to Center City, mate and raise a family?"

"I mated," she said.

Kay suddenly had nothing to say.

He didn't know!

What had he been thinking? That he and she would become formal mates? Valavirgillin said, "I made myself rich with a gift from Louis Wu of the Ball People." How she had done that was nobody's business, and illegal. "I mated then. Tarb's parents were friends of my family, as is usual with us, Moonwa. He had little money, but he's a good father, he freed me to engage in business dealings.

"I grew restive. I remembered that Louis Wu suggested . . . no. *Asked if* my people make stuff from the sludge that remains after we distill alcohol. *Plastic,* he said. His talking thing would not translate, but I learned his word. He said it means shapeless. Plastic can take any shape the maker likes. That sludge is useless, nasty stuff. Clients might be grateful if we had a reason to haul it away for them.

"So I funded a chemical laboratory." She shrugged in the dark. "Always it cost more than anyone expected, and Tarb never let me forget it. But we got answers. There are secrets in that goo.

"One day most of my money was gone. Tarablilliast and the children are with my sire-family, and I am here, until I can feed them again. Coriak, are you ready to take guard?"

"Of course. Hold the thought, Whandernothtee. Vala, what's out there?"

"Rain. I glimpse something black and shiny, sometimes, and I hear tittering. No smell of Vampires."

"Good."

Moonwa had lapsed into Grass Giant language and was making jokes that set Beedj roaring. In the gray light of morning the Gleaners spoke together, waved at the brightening land, then more or less fell over in a pile.

"Do you think they came?" Spash asked nobody in particular, and he stepped out of the tent.

Whand said, "I don't care. Let's sleep."

"They came," Spash said.

Vala stepped out.

It was moments before she realized that one sheet was empty. Far left . . . six Gleaner dead were gone. The rest of the dead were untouched.

Beedj came forth briskly, swinging his scythe-sword. More Giants were coming down the earth wall. They conferred, then fanned out to explore, looking for evidence of what the Ghouls had done.

But Vala climbed up the wall to sleep in the payload shell.

* * *

At midday she woke ravenous with the smell of roasting meat in her nostrils. She followed the smells down to the tent.

She found Gleaners and Machine People together. The Gleaners had been hunting. The fire they had made to cook their kills Barok and Whand had used to make bread from local grass.

"We eat four, five, six meals in a day," Silack told her. "Pint says you eat once a day?"

"Yes. But a lot. Are you finding enough meat?"

"When your men came down to eat, ours went to hunt more. Eat what you see, the hunters will be back."

The flatbread was a good effort, and Vala complimented the men. Smeerp meat was good too, if a bit lean and tough. At least the Gleaners didn't have a habit found in other hominids: changing the flavor of meat by rubbing it with salt or herbs or berries.

Vala wondered about breeding smeerps in other places, but all traders knew the answer to that. One hominid's local bounty was another's plague. With no local predators to restrict their numbers, smeerps would be eating somebody's crops, breeding beyond their food source, then vectoring diseases when starvation weakened them.

Meanwhile she had eaten everything in sight.

Gleaners and Machine People alike were watching her in amusement. Silack said, "Heavy exercise last night."

"Did I miss anything?"

Kay said, "The Ghouls were active. There aren't any dead Grass Giants between the wall and the tall grass. Beedj found neat piles of bones in the grass. They didn't touch the Vampires. Saved them for tonight, I guess."

"Considerate of them." With their dead gone, the Grass Giants' mourning was over, except— "More considerate if they would take the rest of our dead. Anything else?"

Silack pointed.

It wasn't raining now. The clouds formed an infinite flat roof, way high. You could see a long way across the veldt. What Vala could see was a sizable beast-drawn wagon plodding toward Grass Giant domains.

Five great big-shouldered beasts. More than that high-sided wagon needed, though it was big.

"It will be here well before dusk. Even so, if your species can sleep in spurts, you will have time."

Vala nodded and climbed up the wall to sleep some more.

Paroom the sentry, the first Grass Giant they'd met, was riding in the guide seat beside a much smaller red-skinned man. Three more Reds rode in the enclosed space beneath.

They stopped the wagon just under the wall, near the opening. Two Reds began to tend the beasts. Two came forward with Paroom. Each carried a sword nearly as long as himself, hung from his back in a leather sheath. They wore dyed leather kilts and leather backpacks, the men and the woman both, though brighter colors adorned the woman's.

Valavirgillin, Kaywerbrimmis, Moonwa, the Thurl in full armor, Manack and Coriak waited to greet them. The group had been pruned a little.

The Thurl made introductions, speaking slowly, pronouncing names with varying accuracy.

"I am Tegger hooki-Thandarthal," the Red male said. "This is Warvia hooki-Murf Thandarthal."

"How do your people deal with rishathra?"

"We cannot," said Warvia, and did not amplify.

Paroom grinned, and Vala grinned back, picturing the male Grass Giants' disappointment. The Thurl as host spoke for all, as protocol required, but briefly. What point in enlarging upon a guest's sexual prowess for a species that couldn't do that at all? Tegger and Warvia merely nodded when he fell silent. The other Red males were not even listening. They were examining the Vampire corpses lying on one sheet, and chattering at high speed.

Tegger and Warvia looked much alike. Their skins were smooth; their faces were hairless. They wore kilts of soft leather with decorative lacing. They were as tall as Machine People, but much thinner. Big ears stood out from narrow heads. Their teeth were pointed: not filed, apparently, but grown that way. Warvia had breasts, but almost flat.

"We never hear of so many Vampires found together," Warvia said.

"You killed an army," Tegger said. "Vampires lie everywhere. Your neighbors must be glad."

"The Ghouls, have they come?"

The Thurl said, "An army of Vampires came the night before last. An army was gone when the shadow withdrew from the sun. You have seen the dead they left behind, but our own dead you do not see. The Ghouls have taken them. They were half as many or a bit more, plus a hundred of Gleaners and four of our ten Machine People. The Vampires are a terrible foe. We are glad you came."

"We have seen nothing of the terror," Tegger said. "Young hunters disappear. Our teachers lose their skill, we say, or some new hunting thing has found open territory. Paroom, if we did show disbelief, forgive us."

Paroom nodded graciously. The Thurl said, "What we knew of Vampires was half false. The Machine People Empire came in time to help us."

Vala was beginning to realize that no other Grass Giant *could* say such a thing. To disparage the tribe was to disparage the Thurl. "We must show you our defenses," he continued, "but have you eaten? Should you cook while there is still light?"

"We eat our meat uncooked. We like variety. Grass Giants eat no meat, but what of Gleaners and Machine People? May we share? Let us show you what we have."

They had five loadbeasts and the cage atop their wagon. The thing in the cage felt their gaze and roared. It was a beast as massive as a Grass Giant, and a predator, Vala realized. She asked, "What is that?"

"Hakarrch," Tegger said with visible pride. "A hunter of the Barrier Hills. Two were sent us by the Gardener People for our sport. Hunted outside its familiar terrain, the male still killed two of us before we brought it down."

It was a brag. *Mighty hunters we are. We hunt the lesser hunters, and we'll hunt your Vampires.* Vala suggested, "Perilack, shall we sample this? Not tonight, but tomorrow at our one meal."

Perilack said, "Bargain. Warvia, tonight you may kill a loadbeast. Tomorrow and after, let us play host. We will feed all until the"—shadow had bitten a piece from the sun, but the light was still bright—"eaters of the dead deign to speak. You'll want to taste smeerp meat."

"We thank you."

The fire had become the only light: not enough light to cook, but the cooking was over. The other Reds had been introduced. Both were male. Anakrin hooki-Whanhurhur was an old man, wrinkled, but still agile. Chaychind hooki-Karashk, another male, was badly scarred and had lost an arm in some old battle. They brought a gift, a sizable ceramic jug of dark fluid.

It was strong dark beer. Not bad at all. Vala saw Kay react too. *Let's see how Kay handles it.*

Kay exclaimed, "Do you make this yourselves? Do you make a lot?"

"Yes. Do you think of trade?"

"Chaychind, it might be worth moving if it's cheap enough—"

"Tales of the Machine People are not exaggerated."

Kay looked flustered. Too bad, but Vala had better step in. "Kaywerbrimmis means that if we can distill enough of this, we would have fuel for our cruisers. Our cruisers carry weapons and can carry much more. They move faster than loadbeasts, but they cannot move without fuel."

"A gift you want?" Chaychind asked, while Tegger exclaimed, "You would boil our beer for fuel?"

"Gifts for the war. Grass Giant fighters, Gleaners as spies, your fuel. Our cruisers, our cannon, our flamers. Can you contribute three hundred manweights of beer to the war against the Vampires? It would distill to thirty manweights of fuel. We carry a distilling system simple enough to be copied."

Warvia exclaimed, "That's enough to souse whole civilizations!"

But Tegger asked, "What size of manweights?"

It was the obvious question, but it implied agreement. Vala said, "Your size." A Machine People manweight would have been twenty percent higher. "I'm thinking of taking two cruisers. Leave the third here. Let the Thurl fuel the third cruiser at leisure."

"Whand and Chit can supervise that," Kay said.

"Oh?" She'd noticed that both were absent.

"They've had enough. Spash is wavering. So's Barok."

"Any foray would be murder-selves," red Warvia said, "unless we can know our enemy. Have the Ghouls spoken?"

The Thurl said, "Some bodies are gone," and shrugged.

"We're paying for our good manners," Vala said. "The bodies we guarded from vermin, the lords of the night will take last. They took your Gleaner dead because they died a day earlier." A trader must know how to project her voice on demand. The night would hear her.

* * *

Tonight Kay and Whand were on the wall with Barok, watching over them with the cannon. Spash and Chit had traded places with them.

This night looked to be less exhausting, but less joyful too. The Gleaners and Machine People and an undersized Grass Giant woman named Twuk tried to get something going. The Thurl kept his armor on. The Reds watched gleefully from beyond touching distance, and chattered in their own language, and it all sort of fell apart.

The Reds weren't unfriendly. They might be a little stiff around the Thurl himself, but around others they were relaxed and talkative. Spash and three Reds were trading stories now. The Reds had a considerable experience with hominids, despite their handicap.

Vala listened idly. The Reds were guided by their diet. They ate live meat, and they were herder-gourmets. Herding one or two life-forms was easier than trying to keep several types of meatbeast together. The Red tribes mapped their routes to cross each other's paths, to trade feasts.

They traded stories too, and met hominids in a variety of environments. They were speaking of two types of Water People, apparently not the same two Vala was familiar with.

The fourth Red, Tegger, was on watch with Chit.

The Thurl was asleep in full armor. He clearly wasn't interested in rishathra, or Ghouls either, Vala thought.

Sopashinthay lay propped against a tent pole. "I wonder what it's like inside the wall," she said.

Vala considered. "The Thurl's out here. Beedj is in there, on defense. 'What the Thurl does not see did not happen.' "

Spash came up on an elbow. "Where did you hear that?"

"From the Thurl. The Beta males are doing a lot of mating, I expect, and some fighting too. I suppose we're missing all the fun—"

"Again, in my case," Spash said.

"—but they wouldn't rish' anyway if they can mate. And I can use the rest."

"So can the Thurl. He sleeps like a near-dormant volcano," Spash said.

Chit looked at the women, and smiled, and stepped lightly out of the tent. A dense mist cloaked the night. Chit picked up a bone from dinner and threw it. Vala heard a muffled *tock*.

A great silver bulk was at her shoulder, sensed but never heard. The Thurl sniffed, while his hands cocked a crossbow, still without sound. He said, "They are not near, Vampires or Night People. Chitakumishad, did you see anything? Smell anything?"

"Nothing."

The Thurl seemed exceedingly alert for one who had been sleeping moments ago. He pulled his helm closed and stepped out. A Grass Giant guard, Tarun, followed him.

Spash said, "I had it wrong, didn't I? But why—"

Vala whispered, "Reds. They're the ancient enemy, and they're all around him. That's why he kept his armor on, and that's why he pretends to sleep. Bet on it."

In the morning there were no dead between the wall and the tall grass, save for those that lay on sheets. The Ghouls had taken Vala at her word, it seemed.

Chaychind asked of nobody in particular, "Where shall we turn the hakarrch loose?"

Coriak looked at Manack. The Gleaner female said, "Just short of the tall grass, but let me tell my companions first. Vala, will your people hunt too?"

"I think not, but I'll ask."

She spoke to the others. None were eager. Machine People did eat meat, but predator meat generally had a rank flavor. But Kay said, "We'll look timid if someone doesn't join the hunt."

"Ask some questions," she told him. "That thing looked dangerous. The more you know, the less often you get killed."

He'd never heard the proverb. He started, laughed, then said, "We want to bring it to less than *one*?"

"Yes."

She slept through the hunt. At midday she woke to share in the meal. Kaywerbrimmis bore claw marks across his forearm, the fool. Hakarrch meat had a flavor of cat. The dead were fewer, but the stench of them hovered about the tent, and the dreadful night was coming.

The Ghouls would take her at her word, she thought. *The bodies we guarded from vermin, the lords of the night will take last.* Tonight.

four

When shadow had nearly covered the sun, Vala found the Gleaners and Reds around a barbecue fire. The Gleaners were eating; they offered to share. The Reds had eaten their kills as they were made.

A fine rain began to sizzle on the coals. The negotiators retreated into the tent: Valavirgillin, Chitakumishad, and Sopashinthay for the Machine People, three of the Reds, the four Gleaners. Anakrin hooki-Whanhurhur and the Thurl and a woman Vala didn't know were already inside.

The grass had been replaced with fresh.

The thurl spoke, his powerful voice cutting through all conversation. "Folk, meet my negotiator Waast, who has a tale to tell."

Waast stood gracefully for so large a woman. "Paroom and I went to spin-port two days ago, on foot," she said. "Paroom returned with these Reds sent by Ginjerofer. I followed on foot with a guard of Red warriors, to speak to the Water People.

The Water People cannot join us here, but they may speak of our warriors to the Night People."

"They'll have the same trouble we did," Coriak said.

(Something was tickling at Vala's attention.)

Waast sat. To the Reds she said, "You cannot practice rishathra. But mating?"

"It is not my time," Warvia said primly. Anakrin and Chaychind were grinning. Tegger seemed angry.

(The wind.)

Many hominid species were monogamous, exclusive of rishathra, of course. Tegger and Warvia must be mates. And the Thurl was saying, "I must wear my armor. We know not what might visit us."

Too bad. They might have gotten some entertainment going.

(Music?)

Spash asked, "Do you hear music? That isn't Vampire music."

The sound was still soft, but growing louder, almost painfully near the upper end of her hearing range. Vala felt the hair stir on her neck and down her spine. She was hearing a wind instrument, and strings, and a thuttering percussion instrument. No voices.

The Thurl lowered his helm and stepped out. A crossbow was in his hand, pointed at the sky. Chit and Silack stayed at either side of the door, their weapons readied. Others in the tent were arming themselves.

Silack walked backward into the tent. The smell came with him. Carrion and wet fur.

Two big hominid shapes followed, and then the much bigger Thurl. "We have guests," he boomed.

In the tent it was almost totally dark. Vala could make out the gleam of the Ghouls' eyes and teeth, and two black silhouettes against a scarcely brighter glow, Archlight seeping through clouds. But her eyes were adjusting, picking out detail:

There were two, a man and a woman. Hair covered them almost everywhere. It was black and straight and slick with the rain. Their mouths were overly wide grins showing big spade teeth. They wore pouches on straps, and were otherwise naked. Their big blunt hands were empty. They were not eating. Vala was terribly relieved, even as she resisted the impulse to shy back.

Likely enough, none but Valavirgillin had ever seen one of these. Some were reacting badly. Chit remained in the door, on guard, facing away. Spash was on her feet, not cringing, but it seemed the limit of her self-control. Silack of the Gleaners, Tegger and Chaychind of the Reds all backed away with wide eyes and open mouths.

She had to do something. She stood and bowed. "Welcome. I am Valavirgillin of the Machine People. We've waited to beg your help. These are Anakrin and Warvia of the Reds, Perilack and Manack of the Gleaners, Chitakumishad and Sopashinthay of the Machine People"—picking them out as and when she thought they had recovered their aplomb.

The Ghoul male didn't wait. "We know your various kinds. I am—" something breathy. His mouth wouldn't close completely. Otherwise he was fluent in the trade dialect, his accent more like Kay's than Vala's. "But call me Harpster, for the instrument I play. My mate is—" something breathy and whistling, not unlike the music that was still playing outside. "Grieving Tube. How do you practice rishathra?"

Tegger had been cowering. Now he was beside his mate, instantly. "We cannot," he said.

The Ghoul woman laughed. Harpster said, "We know. Be at ease."

The Thurl spoke directly to Grieving Tube. "These are

under my protection. My armor may come off, if you can speak for our safety. After that, you need only have care for my size." And Waast only smiled at Harpster, but Vala could admire her for the nerve that took.

The Gleaners were in a line, all four standing tall. "Our kind does practice rishathra," Coriak said.

She could have been safe at home. Somewhere she would have found food for her mate and children, and as for her love of adventure, a person could set that aside for a time . . . too late now. "Rishathra binds our Empire," Valavirgillin told the lords of the night.

Harpster said, "Truth was that rishathra bound the City Builders' Empire. Fuel binds yours. We do practice rishathra, but not tonight, I think, because we can guess how it would disturb the Reds to watch—"

"We are not fragile," Warvia said.

"—and for another reason," Harpster said. "Do you have a request to make of us?"

They all tried to speak at once. "Vampires—"

"You see the terror—"

"The deaths—"

The Thurl had a voice to cut through all that. "Vampires have devastated all species in a territory ten daywalks across. Help us to end their menace."

"Two or three daywalks, no more," Harpster said. "Vampires need to reach shelter after a raid. Still, a large territory, housing more than a ten of hominid species—"

"But they feed us well," Grieving Tube said gently, her voice pitched a little higher than her companion's. "The problem you face is that we have no problem. What is good for any of you is good also for the People of the Night. The Vampires feed us as surely as the lust for alcohol among your client species, Valavirgillin. But if you can conquer the Vampires, that serves us too."

Did they realize how much they had revealed in a few breaths of speech? But too many were speaking at once, and Vala held silence.

"For your understanding," Grieving Tube said, "consider. Manack, what if your queen had a quarrel with the Thurl's people? You might persuade us not to touch any dead who lie near the Thurl's walls. Soon he must surrender."

Manack said, "But we and the Grass Giants— We would never—"

"Of course not. But Warvia, you and the old Thurl were at war fifty falans ago. Suppose your leader Ginjerofer had begged us to tear apart any Grass Giants who came to kill their cattle?"

Warvia said, "Very well, we understand."

"Do you? We must not side with any hominid against any other. You all depend on us. Without the People of the Night, your corpses lie where they fall, diseases form and spread, your water becomes polluted," the Ghoul woman sang in her high-pitched breathy voice.

She had made this speech before. "We forbid cremation, but suppose we did not? What if every species had the fuel to burn their dead? Clouds still lid this sky forty-three falans after a sea was boiled. What if that were the smoke of the burned dead, a stench growing richer every falan? Do you know how many hominids of every species die in a falan? We do.

"We cannot choose sides."

Chaychind hooki-Karashk had been flushing a darker red. "How can you speak of siding with Vampires? Animals!"

"They don't think," said Harpster, "and you do. But can you always say that so surely? We know of a ten of hominids just at the edge of thinking, just along this arc of the Arch. Some use fire if they find it, or form packs when prey is large and formidable. One strips branches into spears. One lives in water; they cannot use fire, but they flake rocks for knives. How do you judge? Where do you draw the line?"

"Vampires don't use tools or fire!"

"Not fire, but tools. Under this endless rain Vampires have learned to wear clothing stripped from their prey. When they are dry, they discard it."

The Ghoul woman said, "You see why we should not rish' with you, if we must refuse your other desires," Grieving Tube did not see, chose not to see, the mixed emotions that statement generated.

Well, she must try something. Vala said, "Your help would be of immense value, if you had reason to give it. Already you have told us the reach of Vampire depredations, and that they must return to their lair, that they have one single lair. What else could you tell us?"

Harpster shrugged, and Vala winced. His shoulders were terribly loose, like unconnected bones rolling freely under his skin. She continued stubbornly, "I have heard a rumor, a story, a fable. The Machine People hear it where Vampires are known. You must understand that to primitives—that is, to most of our client species far from Center City—there seems to be no sensible explanation of where all these Vampires come from so suddenly."

"They have a high breeding rate," Harpster said.

Grieving Tube said, "Yes, and clusters of them split from the main body, find other refuges. Ten daywalks was not too large a guess."

The others, even Chaychind, were letting her talk. Vala said, "But a less sensible explanation spreads too. The victim of a Vampire will rise from the dead to become a Vampire himself."

"That," said Harpster, "is purest nonsense!" And of course it was.

"Of course it is, but it explains how the plague spreads so rapidly. See it from the viewpoint of a" —careful, now— "Hanging Person widow and mother." Hanging People were everywhere. Vala set one hand on the beam overhead, and lifted her feet to hang, and said, "What is to be done, lest my poor dead Vaynya become my enemy in the night? Ghouls forbid us to burn the dead. But sometimes they permit it—"

"Never!" said Grieving Tube.

Vala said, "Starboard-spin from here by twelve daywalks, there are memories of a plague—"

"Long ago and far away," Harpster said. "We designed the crematorium ourselves, taught them how to use it, then moved away. Years later we returned. The plague was beaten. The Digging People still cremated, but we persuaded them to leave their dead again. It was easily done. Firewood was scarce."

"You see the danger," Vala said. "I don't believe locals have started burning Vampire victims yet—"

"No. We would see plumes of smoke."

"—but if one client species begins, the rest might follow."

Grieving Tube said sadly, "Then of course we'd have to do a deal of killing."

Valavirgillin throttled a shudder. She bowed low, and answered, "Why not begin now, with Vampires?"

Grieving Tube mulled it. "Not so easy, that. They, too, command the night—"

And Vala's eyes closed for an instant. *Now it's a problem, a challenge, and lesser species must see you solve it. Now we have you.*

The Ghouls had cleared the grass away from a sizable section of tent floor. They were drawing in the dark, tweetling at each other in their own high-pitched language. They argued over some feature none other could see, and settled that, and Harpster stood up.

"When the shadow withdraws you may examine these maps," Harpster said. "For now let me only describe what you would see. Here, spin by port by two and a half daywalks, the ancient structure of an industrial center floats two tens of man-heights above the ground."

"We know of a floating city," Vala said.

"Of course, near your Center City, a collection of free buildings linked. Floaters are rare enough these days. We think this one made artifacts for the City Builders. Later it was abandoned.

"Vampires have lived beneath the Floater for many generations, for hundreds of falans. The perpetual shadow is perfect for Vampires. Locals moved out of their reach long ago. Peaceful travelers and migrations were warned to avoid it. Warriors must look to themselves in that regard.

"This range of mountains to antispin of the Shadow Nest stands between there and here. It formed a barrier for the mirror-flowers. Hominids on the far side came to call it the Barrier of Flame, for the fire they could sometimes see playing along the crest.

"The flowers would ultimately have crossed the crest and burned out the Shadow Nest in their usual fashion. The Vampires wouldn't be safe from *horizontal* beams of light. But then the clouds came."

Heads nodded in the dark. Harpster said, "The Vampires' range expanded by a daywalk. Grieving Tube is right, the damage is worse than that. Their population has grown, and hunger drives families of Vampires into other domains."

Valavirgillin asked, "Can you blow away the clouds?"

Both Ghouls hooted laughter. Grieving Tube said, "You want us to *move clouds*?"

"We beg."

"Why do you think we could do such a thing as move clouds?"

Over the rising sounds of throttled laughter Valavirgillin said, "Louis Wu did that."

Harpster said, "Omnivore Tinker. Not odd as hominids go, but from off the Arch, from the stars. He had tools to prove what he said he was, but we do not know that he made clouds."

The Thurl spoke. "He did! He and the old Thurl boiled a sea to make these clouds above us—"

"Then go to him."

"Louis Wu is gone. The old Thurl is gone."

"We cannot move clouds. Our embarrassment is great," Harpster laughed. "What can we do that you cannot do yourselves?"

The Thurl said, "We will use your maps, much thanks to you. I will lead an army of whatever species will fight. We will destroy this nest of Vampires."

"Thurl, *you* cannot go," Grieving Tube said.

Harpster questioned. Grieving Tube began to explain, but the Thurl would not wait. "I am protector to my people! When we fight, I fight at the head—"

"In armor," the Ghoul woman pointed out.

"Of course!"

"You must not wear armor. Your armor keeps your smell. You, all who fight, you must wear nothing. Bathe whenever you find water. Wash every surface of your cruisers and wagons. Don't you see that the Vampires must not smell you?"

Vala thought, *Oh.*

"The bottleneck is the fuel," Chitakumishad was saying. "The Reds make a beer, it can be turned into fuel—"

"Go to your war by way of the Red pastures. We can send the design for your stills to the Reds by a secret means, tomorrow. Let them make fuel there while you make fuel here from your own still and rotting grass. You will confront the Shadow Nest no more than a falan from now."

Chit nodded, his own mind busy with plans. "Fuel to take two cruisers there and back—"

"You must cross the Barrier of Flame. I think your cruisers can do that. There are passes."

"Takes more fuel."

"Fuel to explore, or for towels or flamethrowers, would come out of that. What of it? Only in victory will you need fuel to depart, and then your third cruiser can meet you, or you may leave one behind.

"Travel in pairs," Harpster said. "Grieving Tube and I will travel together. Thurl, we know your customs, but from time to time your herds do split. Do it that way. Tegger, you and Warvia believe you can resist the Vampires. It may be so, but what of these others? Let them mate when they must, and not rish' with bloodsuckers. Anakrin, Chaychind, you should go home—"

And the arguments began. No hominid here would uncritically accept a Ghoul's plan for their war. But Vala remained silent and knew how much she had won.

They're with us. They really are. And they'll bathe. . . .

Sister Death

JANE YOLEN

You have to understand, it is not the blood. It was
never the blood. I swear that on my own child's
heart, though I came at last to bear the taste of it,
sweetly salted, as warm as milk from the breast.

The first blood I had was from a young man named Abel,
but I did not kill him. His own brother had already done that,
striking him down in the middle of a quarrel over sheep and
me. The brother preferred the sheep. How like a man.

Then the brother called me a whore. His vocabulary was re-
markably basic, though it might have been the shock of his
own brutality. The name itself did not offend me. It was my
profession, after all. He threw me down on my face in the
bloody dirt and treated me like one of his beloved ewes. I
thought it was the dirt I was eating.

It was blood.

Then he beat me on the head and back with the same stick
he had used on his brother, till I knew only night. *Belilah.*
Like my name.

How long I lay there, unmoving, I was never to know. But when I came to, the bastard was standing over me with the authorities, descrying my crime, and I was taken as a murderess. The only witnesses to my innocence—though how can one call a whore innocent—were a murderer and a flock of sheep. Was it any wonder I was condemned to die?

Oh how I ranted in that prison. I cursed the name of G-d, saying: "Let the day be darkness wherein I was born and let G-d not inquire about it for little does He care. A woman is nothing in His sight and a man is all, be he a murderer or a thief." Then I vowed not to die at all but to live to destroy the man who would destroy me. I cried and I vowed and then I called on the demonkin to save me. I remembered the taste of blood in my mouth and offered that up to any who would have me.

One must be careful of such prayers.

The night before I was to be executed, Lord Beelzebub himself entered my prison. How did I know him? He insinuated himself through the keyhole as mist, reforming at the foot of my pallet. There were two stubby black horns on his forehead. His feet were like pigs' trotters. He carried around a tail as sinuous as a serpent. His tongue, like an adder's, was black and forked.

"You do not want a man, Lillake," he said, using the pretty pet name my mother called me. "A demon can satisfy you in ways even you cannot imagine."

"I am done with lovemaking," I answered, wondering that he could think me desirable. After a month in the prison I was covered with sores. "Except for giving one a moment's pleasure, it brings nothing but grief."

The mist shaped itself grandly. "This," he said pointing, "is more than a moment's worth. You will be well repaid."

"You can put that," I gestured back, "into another keyhole. Mine is locked forever."

One does not lightly ignore a great lord's proposal, nor make light of his offerings. It was one of the first things I had learned. But I was already expecting to die in the morning. And horribly. So, where would I spend his coin?

"Lillake, hear me," Lord Beelzebub said, his voice no longer cozening but black as a burnt cauldron. *Shema* was the word he used. I had not known that demons could speak the Lord G-d's holy tongue.

I looked up, then, amazed, and saw through the disguise. This was no demon at all but the Lord G-d Himself testing me, though why He should desire a woman—and a whore at that—I could not guess.

"I know you, *Adonai*," I said. "But G-d or demon, my answer is the same. Women and children are nothing in your sight. You are a bringer of death, a maker of carrion."

His black aspect melted then, the trotters disappeared, the horns became tendrils of white hair. He looked chastened and sad and held out His hand.

I disdained it, turning over on my straw bed and putting my face to the wall.

"It is no easy thing being at the Beginning and at the End," He said. "And so you shall see, my daughter. I shall let you live, and forever. You will see the man, Cain, die. Not once but often. It will bring you no pleasure. You will be Death's sister, chaste till the finish of all time, your mouth filled with the blood of the living."

So saying, He was gone, fading like the last star of night fading into dawn.

Of course I was still in prison. So much for the promises of G-d.

* * *

At length I rose from the mattress. I could not sleep. Believing I had but hours before dying, I did not wish to waste a moment of the time left, though each moment was painful. I walked to the single window where only a sliver of moon was visible. I put my hands between the bars and clutched at the air as though I could hold it in my hands. And then, as if the air itself had fallen in love with me, it gathered me up through the bars, lifted me through the prison wall, and deposited me onto the bosom of the dawn and I was somehow, inexplicably, free.

Free.

As I have been these five thousand years.

Oh, the years have been kind to me. I have not aged. I have neither gained nor lost weight nor grayed nor felt the pain of advancing years. The blood has been kind to me, the blood I nightly take from the dying children, the true innocents, the Lord G-d's own. Yet for all the children I have sucked rather than suckled, there has been only one I have taken for mine.

I go to them all, you understand. There is no distinction. I take the ones who breathe haltingly, the ones who are misused, the ones whose bodies are ill shaped in the womb, the ones whom fire or famine or war cut down. I take them and suck them dry and send them, dessicated little souls, to the Lord G-d's realm. But as clear-eyed as I had been when I cast out *Adonai* in my prison, so clear-eyed would a child need to be to accept me as I am and thus become my own. So for these five thousand years there has been no one for me in my lonely occupation but my mute companion, the Angel of Death.

If I could still love, he is the one I would desire. His wings are the color of sun and air as mine are fog and fire. Each of the vanes in those wings are hymnals of ivory. He carries the keys to Heaven in his pocket of light. Yet he is neither man nor woman, neither demon nor god. I call the Angel "he" for as I am Sister Death, he is surely my brother.

We travel far on our daily hunt.
We are not always kind.

But the child, my child, I will tell you of her now. It is not a pretty tale.

As always we travel, the Angel and I, wingtips apart over a landscape of doom. War is our backyard, famine our feast. Most fear the wind of our wings and even, in their hurt, pray for life. Only a few, a very few, truly pray for death. But we answer all their prayers with the same coin.

This particular time we were tracking across the landscape of the Pale, where grass grew green and strong right up to the iron railings that bore the boxcars along. In the fields along the way, the peasants swung their silver scythes in rhythm to the trains. They did not hear the counterpoint of cries from the cars or, if they did, they showed their contempt by stopping and waving gaily as the death trains rolled past.

They did not see my brother Death and me riding the screams but inches overhead. But they would see us in their own time.

In the cars below, jammed together like cattle, the people vomited and pissed on themselves, on their neighbors, and prayed. Their prayers were like vomit, too, being raw and stinking and unstoppable.

My companion looked at me, tears in his eyes. I loved him for his pity. Still crying, he plucked the dead to him like faded flowers, looking like a bridegroom waiting at the feast.

And I, no bride, flew through the slats, to suck dry a child held overhead for air. He needed none. A girl crushed by the door, I took her as well. A teenager, his head split open by a soldier's gun, died unnoticed against a wall. He was on the cusp of change but would never now be a man. His blood was bitter in my mouth but I drank it all.

What are Jews that nations swat them like flies? That the

Angel of Death picks their faded blooms? That I drink the blood, now bitter, now sweet, of their children?

The train came at last to a railway yard that was ringed about with barbs. BIRKENAU, read the station sign. It creaked back and forth in the wind. BIRKENAU.

When the train slowed, then stopped, and the doors pushed open from the outside, the living got out. The dead were already gathered up to their G-d.

My companion followed the men and boys, but I—I flew right, above the weeping women and their weeping children, as I have done all these years.

There was another Angel of Death that day, standing in the midst of the madness. He hardly moved, only his finger seemed alive, an organism in itself, choosing the dead, choosing the living.

"Please, Herr General," a boy cried out. "I am strong enough to work."

But the finger moved, and having writ, moved on. To the right, boy. To the arms of Lilith, Belilah, Lillake.

"Will we get out?" a child whispered to its mother.

"We will get out," she whispered back.

But I had been here many times before. "You will only get out of here through the chimney," I said.

Neither mother nor child nor General himself heard.

There were warning signs at the camp. BEWARE, they said, TENSION WIRE, they said.

There were other signs, too. Pits filled with charred bones. Prisoners whose faces were imprinted with the bony mask of death.

JEDEM DAS SEINE. Each one gets what he deserves.

In the showers, the naked mothers held their naked children to them. They were too tired to scream, too tired to cry. They had no tears left.

Only one child, a seven-year-old, stood alone. Her face was angry. She was not resigned. She raised her fist and looked at the heavens and then, a little lower, at me.

Surprised, I looked back.

The showers began their rain of poison. Coughing, praying, calling on G-d to save them, the women died with their children in their arms.

The child alone did not cough, did not pray, did not call on G-d. She held out her two little hands to me. *To me.*

"Imma," she said. "Mother."

I trembled, flew down, and took her in my arms. Then we flew through the walls as if they were air.

So I beg you, as you love life, as you master Death, let my brother be the sole harvester. I have served my five thousand years; not once did I complain. But give me a mother's span with my child, and I will serve you again till the end of time. This child alone chose me in all those years. You could not be so cruel a god as to part us now.

BARBARA HAMBLY is the author of the vampire novels *Those Who Hunt the Night* and its sequel, *Traveling with the Dead*. She has written dozens of other novels as well, from fantasy to historical mysteries to Star Trek adventures.

⎯⎯◆⎯⎯

MARTIN H. GREENBERG is one of the most respected anthologists in the fields of science fiction, fantasy, and mystery. He has edited hundreds of volumes of stories on a variety of topics.

IF YOU ENJOYED
SISTERS OF THE NIGHT,
LOOK FOR
THE QUEEN OF DARKNESS
BY MIGUEL CONNER

In his unique first novel, Miguel Conner explores a new future when vampires no longer hide in the shadows of human civilization. After they instigate global nuclear war to blot out the sun, vampires dominate the planet. Herded into farms where they struggle to maintain their dignity and culture, the humans have become the main food staple for their undead masters. This is the story of Byron, a loner vampire whose assignment is to investigate a budding human rebellion. But, while studying the humans' cult religion, Byron becomes close to a beautiful shaman who tells him the shocking truth about his origins and his nature. . . .

**THE QUEEN OF DARKNESS
(0-446-60506-9), $5.99 U.S., $6.99 CAN**

"This is a peculiar blend of horror and SF. . . . A very strange and often fascinating first novel."
—Don D'Ammassa, *Science Fiction Chronicle*

"This riveting first fantasy explores our future on an earth that has been turned upside down. . . . Conner creates a[n] inexplicably touching hero as both man and monster."
—*Publisher's Weekly*

Available at bookstores everywhere
from
WARNER ASPECT